just

REBECCA

between

DRAKE

us

 ST. MARTIN'S GRIFFIN 📖 NEW YORK

JUST BETWEEN US. Copyright © 2017 by Rebecca Drake. All rights reserved. Printed in the United States of America. For information, address St. Martin's Press, 175 Fifth Avenue, New York, N.Y. 10010.

www.stmartins.com

The Library of Congress Cataloging-in-Publication Data is available upon request.

ISBN 978-1-250-16720-0 (hardcover)
ISBN 978-1-4668-7771-9 (e-book)

Our books may be purchased in bulk for promotional, educational, or business use. Please contact your local bookseller or the Macmillan Corporate and Premium Sales Department at 1-800-221-7945, extension 5442, or by e-mail at MacmillanSpecial Markets@macmillan.com.

First Edition: January 2018

10 9 8 7 6 5 4 3 2 1

For Margaret Sophia,
with all my love and gratitude

"I can no other answer make but thanks
And thanks, and ever thanks."

—William Shakespeare

We have been friends together,
In sunshine and in shade.

—Caroline Norton

And whatsoever else shall hap tonight,
Give it an understanding, but no tongue.

—William Shakespeare

JUST BETWEEN US

Prologue

Funerals for murder victims are distinguished from other services by the curiosity seekers. Those who come even though they have no real relationship with the victim, but have been fooled by the publicity surrounding the death into thinking that they had a personal connection.

We watched them, these sobbing and wild-eyed men and women, and endured the long service in stiff pews, part of the much smaller crowd of the truly bereaved. We were very aware, in the way the others weren't, of two guests who didn't pass by the casket, men standing at the back of the chapel in forgettable suits, watching us with gimlet eyes.

They waited until we stood, stiff-legged, and followed the coffin, which rose and fell on the shoulders of the pallbearers like a small ship at sea. They waited until we'd stepped into the cold chill of that morning, blinking in the hard light, wind whipping the corners of our coats as we grabbed the hands of our children and loaded into our cars. They waited as we queued up to follow the body to its final resting place, high on a hill on the outskirts of town. And then they got into their nondescript sedan and joined our procession slowly wending its way through slush-covered streets toward the gravesite.

chapter one

Sometimes I play the what-if game and wonder, what if we hadn't moved to Sewickley when I got pregnant, and what if I hadn't gone into labor in early August, and what if Lucy hadn't slipped, wet and wailing, into this world a full three weeks early? If my oldest child had been born on her due date or after, then she wouldn't have been eligible for school a full year earlier than expected, and I wouldn't have met the women who became my closest friends, and what happened to us might never have happened at all.

So much in life hinges on chance—this date or that time, the myriad small, statistical variations which social scientists like to measure.

What if I hadn't been the one handing Heather her cup of coffee that crisp fall morning at Crazy Mocha? And what if the sleeve of her knit shirt hadn't slid back just a little as she reached to take it, and what if I hadn't happened to look down and see what the sleeves had been meant to hide, and what if I hadn't asked, "How did you get such a nasty bruise?"

A throwaway question at first.

I distributed the other cups to Julie and Sarah, barely paying attention but turning in time to see Heather startle, a tiny movement, before jerking down her sleeve to cover that large purple-yellow mark. "It's nothing," she said. "I must have bumped it on something."

It's only when I look back that I see this moment as the beginning, how everything started, though of course I didn't understand the significance then.

We were in our favorite spot in the coffee shop on a Friday
morning, a tradition started by Julie long before I moved to Sewickley, tucked in the back corner of a shop that itself was tucked
in a back corner on Walnut Street. Our kids had been seen safely
off to school, and the only child with us that morning was Sarah's three-year-old, Josh, who dozed in a stroller by his mother's
side.

If I close my eyes, I can still see the four of us in our respective
armchairs. Julie, red-haired and energetic, couldn't sit still, her
leg jiggling or toe tapping, always moving. Sarah, her counter-
point, small and still, dark head bent over her coffee, reminding
me of a woodland creature in the way she pulled her legs under
her, fitting her whole body in the seat. Too tall to do that, I
slouched in mine, legs stretched out in front of me, hiding behind
my mousy-blond hair. And then there was Heather, with her fine
long legs hanging over the side of her chair, head back and golden
mane hanging down, her thin neck exposed, looking both effortlessly graceful and vulnerable.

Sometimes I'd notice the glances we got from other mothers,
desperate for adult conversation as they pushed strollers with
one hand while clutching coffee cups with the other. I'd been one
of those women once, coming here with Lucy and Matthew in a
double stroller, envying the conversations going on around me.
That was more than five years ago, when we'd first moved to
town, before I met Julie and became part of the shop's regular
clientele.

What if Michael and I hadn't been expecting a child? Our Realtor might have suggested a different, less family-friendly neighborhood. Or what if the male half of the elderly couple who
owned the house we visited that day in Sewickley hadn't had a
stroke and his wife hadn't decided that they should move to an
assisted-living facility? If his stroke had been in December, rather
than March, their home might have sold to someone else, and we

might easily have bought a house in another neighborhood. This is the way of fate—all of these pieces that must slot into place, one leading to the other, a progression toward a conclusion that seems inevitable only after the fact.

Years before, I'd spent those first lonely visits to the coffee shop trying to entertain my children and wondering about the lives of the baristas and their patrons. Later I barely noticed them; my friends and I always had things to talk about—children, jobs, the school and other parents we knew, husbands, homes. That nasty bruise.

If I'd seen that injury on another mother from the elementary school, we would have all been talking about it, but Heather was one of us and she was sitting right there, blowing nonchalantly on her latte. I glanced at Julie and Sarah, but they were busy discussing whether it was okay to let their boys play football, even though the sons in question were barely nine and heavily involved in soccer.

I felt a familiar twinge—just a tiny twist—of jealousy. Not because I envied their conversation, but because before I moved to Sewickley it was Julie and Sarah, Sarah and Julie. They were friends first and that always irritated me, just a little.

Of course, it was stupid, because I shared that bond, too, soon enough. It's just that I sometimes wished that I'd been Julie's friend first. She was effervescent, one of those people who seem to be friends with everybody and everybody wants to know. Very social, gabby, an extrovert and a great organizer. It was no wonder that she became a real-estate agent—she was such a natural salesperson. Of course, I liked Sarah, too, but she was a little harder, a bit prickly at times, and mostly it was just that I envied the history they had that predated me. It was childish, this feeling, like being back in school and feeling upset because your prospective BFF has already been taken.

Julie and I first met at the preschool drop-off, hovering nervously around the entrance with the other parents as our little four-year-olds trooped inside with their teachers.

The rule at Awaken Academy was that no parents should

enter the building in the mornings, in order to minimize long, weepy separations. Of course, those still happened, but I guess they thought it was better if the children associated the tears with what happened outside, rather than what happened in the class-room. These good-byes at the door were so hard; sometimes the parents wept along with their children. Lucy was one of those kids who didn't want to let go, clutching my hand long after the teachers had called for the students to line up.

She'd invariably whine "No, Mommy! No go!" while clinging to me like a tree monkey. I'd have to slowly peel away her tiny grip, all the while feeling like a monster for sending her on into the unknown. Of course I'd toured the school and knew exactly what was inside—miniature tables and chairs, play kitchens and carpenter benches, pots of finger paint and child-safe easels, and shelves filled with brightly colored toys and picture books. A wonderful place, very clean and bright, but the daily lineup seemed so rigid and regimented that I had to remind myself every morning that once Lucy got inside the classroom she was fine.

As I stood there one morning, watching my daughter throw me the big-eyed, pitiful looks of an abandoned animal, a smartly dressed, redheaded woman said, "For all we know they've got a sweatshop going on in there." She smiled at me and at the father of another child standing near us. "Little kids tethered to sewing machines and assembly lines."

The man looked confused and slightly nervous, but I burst out laughing, surprised. The woman's smile widened and she laughed, too, adding, "Do you think they're making clothes for Baby Gap or the Neiman Marcus kids' collection?"

"Oh, don't be elitist," a short woman to her right said. "It's probably Walmart or Toys 'R' Us and our kids are the ones add-ing the enormous boobs to Beach Blanket Barbie even as we speak."

The first woman winked at me and stuck out her hand. "I'm Julie Phelps, a.k.a. the mom of the little boy who refuses to share with anybody."

"Sarah Walker." The shorter woman thrust her hand past Julie to give mine a vigorous shake, her dark curls bouncing, "She means Owen, who is not nearly as bad as my son, Sam, who enjoys crashing trucks into everybody—warn your daughter."

And that's how we met. I sometimes wondered why Julie chose to ask me to join them. I thought maybe it was because the preschool was small, and the other available mothers all seemed nearly identical, with their flat-ironed hair and preppy suburban clothes, chatting about tennis or golf games. There were only a few mothers who stood out among this set—one, a glamorous banker who wore silk shirts with dark, pinstriped suits and liked to make snarky remarks, which she'd invariably follow with a braying laugh and "Of course, I'm just joking!" Another was a tiny, miserable-looking woman whose name I never did get, but who had an equally tiny, miserable-looking little boy with a perpetually runny nose named Jonathan. I only know this because his name accompanied every high-pitched shriek she leveled at him: "Jonathan, be careful!" "Jonathan, say thank you!" "Jonathan, don't run!" I have to say that her nasal voice turned me off that name for life.

Sarah stood out, too, but in a good way, beautiful and biracial in a sea of pasty white women, and with a penchant for wearing brightly colored scarves and jewelry that another mother had dubbed "ethnic," even though Sarah bought them at T.J.Maxx.

In hindsight, it's easy to see that I also stood out among this crowd. Tall and introverted, I didn't chat with the other mothers, had zero interest in or aptitude for country-club life or team sports, and brought books to read to avoid appearing to be all alone in that sea of conversation. I'd stand off to one side holding my book aloft, my free arm folded protectively across my middle.

My nervousness must have seemed like aloofness, perhaps even disdain, at any rate interesting enough to merit Julie's attention. If she'd known how desperate and lonely I felt, would she have been so welcoming? If she'd known my real history, not the abbreviated version I shared? That we'd moved to Pittsburgh because of Michael's job transfer. As far as Julie knew, I was from the eastern part of Pennsylvania, like Michael, who grew up in comfortable Bucks County. What if I'd told her that I'd spent my childhood in hardscrabble Braddock, no more than thirty miles, but an entire lifestyle, away? What if she'd known we depended on food stamps after the mills had closed, and lived in an aluminum-siding house whose Easter-egg pastel yellow exterior had faded to dingy gray, the walls so thin that in the winter my mother filled cracks with tin foil and old newspapers to try to keep out the cold? Perhaps I'm underestimating Julie; if she'd found out about my past she might have considered it exotic.

While she was friendly with everyone, I'd learn that Julie hand-selected friends who were different. Before I moved to Sewickley, there'd been Brenda, a computer-science professor who was also tall and bookish, her similarities to me something that both Julie and Sarah liked to exclaim about. As in, "That's just what Brenda would have said!"

After our first meeting, I saw Julie and Sarah again at pick-up and again the next morning at drop-off and at every drop-off thereafter, but it was always Julie who came to stand near me and started each conversation. I was hesitant to impose, and Sarah, while friendly, seemed perfectly content to hang out only with Julie. Until one Friday morning when it started to rain while we chatted in the parking lot, and Julie said, "Shall we get coffee?"

I thought at first that she was only talking to Sarah, but then she looked at me and I realized she meant both of us. I'm embarrassed by how thrilled I was to be included—like I was back in high school and being accepted by the cool girls.

As we walked through the door of Crazy Mocha that first time, I was aware of people turning to look at the three of us laughing and chatting. It was exciting, all of that attention. I wasn't used to it. I worked from home as an IT consultant, so I didn't have to dress up, wearing jeans and casual shirts, comfortable albeit boring clothing that would hide the "curves" I needed to lose. Michael always wanted me to show off my body, which he loves in a frankly admiring way that makes me love him.

Julie always claimed to admire my curves, too. Like Michael, she was good at focusing on the positive. Sarah would have called my self-assessment "self-pity."

Sarah didn't have patience for whining—she was very can-do. "If you don't feel good about your body, change it," she said once in an effort to convince Julie and me to join the Mommy Yoga class at the YMCA for which she'd impulsively registered. "Too much Halloween candy," she'd said, patting her stomach, which I thought looked better than mine. "I told myself, stop complaining and do something about it—that's my pre–New Year's resolution!"

Julie was obsessive about fitness, a runner and healthy-diet devotee, so she certainly didn't need to add any more exercise, but she enthusiastically signed up for yoga, because it would be "so fun" for the three of us to take a class together. Of course I signed up as well—peer pressure, sure, but it was also another excuse to hang out.

I regretted it almost immediately. Downward-Facing Dog, the Crane, the Big Toe—all of these wacky names for poses that reminded me of that old game, Twister. It turned out that I was terrible at yoga, because I was very inflexible. So inflexible that the instructor—a skinny twentysomething who looked glamorous in Lycra and called herself Shanti even though she was clearly not from the Indian subcontinent—kept commenting on it. "You're very tight, Alison, very tense—we need to do more Shavasanas with you."

Julie was tight like me, too, but this was temporary hamstring tightening from her running, and Sarah, mommy belly notwithstanding, turned out to be a rubber band. "Beautiful!" Shanti would exclaim, clapping her hennaed hands together. "Class, pay attention to Sarah's form!"

"The only asana I can really relate to is the Cow," I said after the third class, when we were walking out to the parking lot. "I certainly feel like a cow when I'm doing it." I saw Sarah exchange a look with Julie; it was just a slight glance, but I knew they'd been talking with each other about me. I flushed, suddenly more self-conscious than I'd been in the class, and I remembered my grandmother's advice: "Never have an odd number of children, because someone will always be left out." My mother had obviously listened; it had been just Sean and me growing up, and I'd taken it to heart, too, giving Lucy a younger brother before I stopped. Watching Julie and Sarah's secret communication in the parking lot that day, I realized that Nana's advice could also apply to friends.

I think after that I was subconsciously on the lookout for a fourth to join our group. If you believe in the law of attraction you might say that I made Heather part of our circle every time I wished that I wasn't the third wheel, though of course Julie was the one to actually find her.

The first Friday that Heather showed up at the coffee shop with Julie, I felt that little twinge again, insecurity rearing its Hydra head. Here was this tall, gazelle-like woman who was drop-dead gorgeous and clearly as comfortable in her own, flawless skin as I was uncomfortable in mine. But there was something vulnerable about her, too—I could see it in the way she looked at us with shy, yet eager, eyes. It turned out that her little boy was in preschool with Sarah's middle child, Olivia, but none of us had ever seen her at the preschool drop-off.

"I like to sleep in," Heather said. "So I let the nanny take Daniel." The nanny. The first time she said that it was Sarah and me exchanging surreptitious glances, because we used babysitters, not nannies. There were plenty of families in Sewickley who had "help," and we knew we were in a different income bracket than Julie, a million-dollar producer in real estate married to Brian, a VP of business development for a big medical-device firm. It turned out that Heather was a SAHM (stay-at-home mom), just like Sarah, but with a much bigger household income—she was married to a surgeon.

"Viktor Lysenko?" Julie asked that first morning. "As in Dr. Viktor Lysenko?" She sounded surprised and more bubbly than usual, although Julie's excitement meter always ran at a higher level than the rest of ours.

"That's him," Heather said, her casualness in sharp contrast to Julie's enthusiasm. Seeing my and Sarah's blank faces, Julie said, "Viktor Lysenko is a preeminent plastic surgeon, he specializes in craniofacial and reconstructive surgery. There was an article about him in the *Post-Gazette* last month; didn't you see it? He volunteers worldwide, too, performing operations free for people in poor countries."

"Wow," Sarah said, "he sounds like a saint."

There was only the faintest hint of snideness, but I remember that Heather flushed at Sarah's comment. "He's just Viktor to me," she said in a light tone, before deftly changing the subject.

Was he the one who'd left that large mark above her wrist? That had been my first thought when she'd jerked her sleeve down to hide it, my pulse uncomfortably quickening. I'd known her for almost two years and I'd never seen anything, never suspected, but after I tried to remember the shape of that large, purple splotch—hadn't those been finger marks on her skin?

What if I hadn't noticed that bruise? And what if another one of those familiar white envelopes hadn't been waiting for me just the day before, giving me that same awful jolt I always felt when one showed up in my mailbox? I tried not to read them, but sometimes I'd tear one open, rapidly skimming the crabbed handwriting. They always ended the same way: "I never meant to hurt you. Please forgive me."

If that hadn't been fresh in my mind, would I have been so concerned when I saw that bruise on Heather? Would I have been so quick to call Julie after?

chapter two

Heather! Abused? "I can't even begin to imagine that," I said to Alison, and quite firmly, too. She could be hypersensitive and I thought she was inflating Heather's reaction. "Perhaps she was just embarrassed that she had a blemish on that beautiful skin—I'd want to cover it up, too. Why would you assume someone's hurting her? You shouldn't think the worst of people."

If I focused on the bad and the ugly, I'd never get anything done. I'd certainly never sell another house. Look for the good in everything and you're sure to find it—I read that somewhere a long time ago and I liked it enough to scribble it down. I carry it around on a little laminated note card that I keep in my purse. It's helpful just to hold it tight when I'm dealing with a difficult client or a hard-to-sell property. Like the man I helped recently who said, "Every place you've shown me is a dump!" This after hours of driving within a twenty-mile radius to show him properties in his price range.

He used to live in a large, beautifully maintained, four-story Victorian, and that has spoiled him for anything else. He's getting divorced and doesn't seem to realize that this has seriously cut into what he can now afford. I guess all he pictured was freedom on the other side of signing that final legal document and starting fresh in some high-ceilinged, ultramodern bachelor pad. Stainless steel, stone, and a twentysomething bimbo reclining naked on a leather sectional. No can do when his ex-wife is keeping the house and he doesn't have any equity. After alimony and child support, he can only bring a limited down payment to this purchase.

I know what will happen; I've seen it before. He'll end up choosing a small apartment or townhome in a barely middle-class neighborhood with dirty white walls, stained carpeting that's just a grade above industrial, and a kitchen last updated circa 1990. He'll have plenty of time to contemplate the demise of his marriage as he eats his microwave dinners alone at the laminate kitchen counter.

This is the life he chose, so he's got to make the best of it—we all have to live with the consequences of our actions. I've had to live with having dismissed Alison's concerns about Heather out of hand. I was upset with her for even suggesting that Viktor Lysenko could ever hurt his wife. "He's a really caring doctor," I said. "If he was hurting Heather, wouldn't she have confided in us?" I forced it right out of my mind because that's what I always do to stay positive. You've got to be careful about what you allow space for in your thoughts—garbage in, garbage out.

Besides, Viktor *was* a nice guy. I'd met him soon after meeting Heather and I instantly liked him. "You must be Julie," he'd said when Heather introduced us, a hint of a Ukrainian accent and a wide smile that I found impossible not to respond to. He was quite tall, a good three or four inches above his tall, willowy wife, and had cropped light brown hair, magnetic blue eyes, and a fit build that spoke of good genes and careful dieting. He was casually elegant—the sort of man who looked like he was made of money even when he dressed down in jeans and a sweater. Maybe he seemed a little stiff at times—he wasn't the best conversationalist—but the guy was a doctor. Those science types are supposed to be nerdy, and he could be forgiven for not being particularly good at small talk. So what if he was "anal," as Alison said, about how he expected things to run in his house. I'm a type-A, hyper-organized person, too, and it's not as if Viktor expected Heather to do everything on her own. Plus, the guy was a renowned surgeon; I'm sure he was used to giving orders and having them followed, and it's hard to turn that off at home. But he didn't seem arrogant to me. He didn't go around trumpeting his accomplishments, although of course he didn't have to because everyone knew who he was.

He obviously wasn't a Pittsburgh native, but he'd been quickly embraced as one, a star at Children's Hospital, his smiling face regularly appearing in the SEEN column in the local paper, usually with Heather at his side. They were an attractive couple, that's for sure, the sort of people that I thought of back then as golden. The truth is that I was proud to call myself Viktor Lysenko's friend.

Brian and I have made it into that SEEN column a few times ourselves, although I'm not sure we appreciated it as much as Viktor. He was an immigrant; his family had arrived in Pittsburgh from Ukraine when he was ten years old, his parents working day and night to give their son a better life. He'd made the best of their sacrifices and gone on to an Ivy League university and a top medical school. My husband and I liked to think of ourselves as self-made, too, although we were born into solidly middle-class families and we're both Pittsburgh natives. Brian travels constantly for his job, but no matter how many different states or countries he's been to, he's never lost his Pittsburghese. It will slip out, especially when he's talking to locals. "Yinz guys going to see the Stillers play on Sunday?" he'll say, reverting back to the speech of his childhood. I do it, too, catching myself telling the cleaning lady that all she needs to do is "red up" the living room or warning clients in the winter that they need to be careful because it's "slippy" outside.

It always filled me with pride to think of how far I'd come from the split-level in Glenshaw where my parents raised me and my younger sister. Brian and I worked hard to move up from our own tiny starter home, and I can see now that I might have idealized Sewickley and people like Heather and Viktor. Back then, I took people at face value and it wasn't hard to believe the best of Viktor—this good-looking, supremely successful guy who seemed friendly.

I didn't think again about what Alison said until the incident about a month later at the Chens' party, but it must have stayed in my mind, because that bruise on Heather's arm was the first thing I thought of afterward.

The Chens are amazing people. I mean, Walter Chen is a renowned architect and his wife, Vivian, an expert in stem-cell research. I'd been honored to represent one of the houses Walter designed for his own family. I sold it for above asking, too, which is probably why Brian and I even made the guest list for the party at their house in the city. Our kids had attended the same summer camps, but the Chen children were older, not that we'd have seen much of them even if they had been the same age. Vivian Chen called herself a tiger mom without any irony and I'd heard that she had her fourth child in order to complete her own string quartet. While that might not be true, Vivian certainly made her kids perform at every party she and Walter hosted, and the party that night was no exception.

The sound of stringed instruments echoed off the marble that tiled seemingly every inch of the Chens' five-thousand-square-foot mansion in Shadyside. Crystal chandeliers sparkled off the sheen and their lights, in turn, sparkled off the stemware on trays borne by waiters discreetly moving through the crowd of elegantly dressed guests.

I guess I'm lowbrow, because I find violins, even heartfelt rather than these mechanical-sounding ones, screechy and grating. I discreetly left the crowd gathered in the Chens' enormous living room as the children sawed their way through Mozart's String Quartet No. 16 in E-flat Major, a title I remember only because Vivian Chen had it printed on programs with her children's names and ages. I wandered in search of a bathroom, turning down a hallway whose gold-papered walls were hung with multiple family photos and framed accolades. Just as I found a beautiful jewel box of a powder room, I heard a male voice say, "Stop!"

Thinking it was directed at me, I actually stopped and turned around. But I was alone in the hall. I heard muffled voices before the man's voice rose again: "You're not going anywhere!" Curious, I followed the voices until the hall opened up to a family room, and I saw a couple standing with their backs to me, framed by an enormous Palladian window overlooking the Chens' sizable property. The man had the woman from behind, holding her upper arms tightly against her body as she wriggled fruitlessly like a bug caught on its back. It was Heather and Viktor.

Startled, I stepped back, trying to retreat up the hall as if I were the one who had something to be ashamed of, but they must have caught my reflection in the window, because Viktor immediately let go of Heather and they both turned toward me.

"Julie! How are you?" Viktor's voice was back to the one I knew, the friendly, reasonable tone so unlike the snarl I'd heard moments before that I thought I must have imagined it. He was smiling, too, coming toward me with his arms opened wide and Heather right behind him.

I let him embrace me, trying not to shrink from his touch, but when Heather hugged me, I held on for a second, murmuring, "Are you okay?"

"I'm fine," she said in her normal voice, light and undisturbed, her gaze meeting mine for a moment before moving to her husband's handsome face. They were themselves, the same normal, lovely couple that I was used to, and I doubted what I had seen even as I found myself subconsciously searching her visible skin for bruises like the one Alison had told me about. Viktor's grip must have left marks on her arms, but Heather was a wearing a tea-length plum satin gown with a high neckline and three-quarter-length sleeves, so I could only envision the imprint from Viktor's hands.

I wanted to talk to her about it afterward, but there was never a moment. For the rest of the party she was by Viktor's side, and during the long week that followed I thought about calling her or texting, but what would I say? "Did your husband hurt you"? I mean, it seemed so rude. I'd clearly walked in on a private moment, and who knew what had really been happening. It could have been something sexual between them for all I knew.

I didn't text Alison either, though I thought about it. What good would it do to feed her imagination? I'd gotten a glimpse of a couple's private life, but what could I really conclude from that twenty seconds? Heather had said she was fine—so I should believe her, right? A part of me needed to believe her.

Except it preyed on my mind all that following week, the tight grip of those fine-boned surgeon's hands, the way she'd struggled in his grasp. I kept replaying the glimpse I'd gotten of his scowling face as they were wrestling, the sound of his angry voice. And then the way he'd suddenly changed—the creepily carefree, friendly smile that he'd turned on me.

By the time we met at the coffee shop that Friday, I'd decided to take Heather aside to talk, but I got delayed by a business call and she was already sitting next to Sarah as Alison talked about a carjacking at the local mall that had been top of the news that morning.

"At least they caught the guy, but he could have killed her—it's terrifying when you think about it," Alison was saying, and I glanced at Heather, wanting to see her reaction, but she only nodded in agreement, making me question myself again. How could I bring up what I'd seen at the party after that conversation? Would she think I was comparing her husband's behavior to that of a common criminal? Worse, if I'd misunderstood what I saw, wouldn't she be offended? I didn't want to risk our friendship, but I really wanted to talk about it with somebody. Later that afternoon I broke and pulled out my phone.

"Sarah? I need to tell you something."

chapter three

If I'd thought anything about Heather and Viktor's marriage, it was that they were less likely than the rest of us to experience marital tension because they had a much higher income than most of us. I'm not saying that money buys happiness, of course not, but what it can do is alleviate certain stresses. You can farm out the cleaning, cooking, and even child care. Of course, if I'd stayed at the law firm, we could have had all those things, but I didn't trust anyone else to take proper care of my kids. Eric's teaching salary wasn't a lot for a family of five to live on, but we pinched pennies and never hired anyone to do a job we could do ourselves, or sometimes we put off things like updating our kitchen or replacing our aging minivan. What could people like Heather and Viktor, who had more than enough money to pay for all of their living expenses, possibly have to feel stressed about?

"Who knows what was going on at the party," I said to Julie. "It was late and everybody was drinking. You said yourself you walked in on them. If they seem fine, they probably are."

"But what about what Alison saw—" Julie started.

"It was a small bruise, for God's sake," I interrupted her. "It's a big leap to conclude that Heather must be a battered spouse. For an IT consultant, Alison has an overactive imagination."

I know that sounds harsh, but there was just something about Alison's personality that could sometimes rub me the wrong way. What irritated me about her? This is where I am ashamed of myself, because it was nothing more than her needing attention.

Alison wanted company, following us around with a big-eyed eagerness that reminded me of my father's golden retriever.

Cookie sat at my father's feet every night as he read the paper in his leather wingback chair. He went straight there every evening when he came home from his law office, sinking back like a turtle pulling into its shell, only leaving his paper when my mother called everyone to the supper table. I wanted his attention, desperately wanted him to notice me, but I'd be damned if I'd wait, like that big dog at his feet, staying for the occasional moments when he'd lean down and rub one of her long, silky ears. The poor creature was content with these scraps of affection. It's one reason I've always been a cat person.

It wasn't Alison's fault that she reminded me of Cookie, with her shaggy blond hair and soft retriever eyes. She had that same eager look. Sometimes I imagined that I could see a tail wagging when Julie laughed at something Alison said. I know that Julie laughed sometimes just to please Alison, because that's the way Julie was—lightness and laughter, a person without a mean bone in her fit body.

I don't mean to sound so short-tempered about Alison, because I truly enjoyed her friendship, too; she was nice and generous and very smart, far smarter than her puppy-dog behavior initially led me to believe. Truthfully, I think part of what annoyed me about Alison was that she thought she and Julie had more in common because they'd both chosen to keep their careers while raising their kids and I hadn't.

It's not that I was ashamed of being a SAHM. I was proud of it. I loved being home with my kids and I placed great value on my time with them—but I felt defensive about having to justify my choice.

That's why I was initially happy when Heather joined us. It made me feel like I didn't have to apologize for choosing my kids over my career. Although if people asked Heather what she did, sometimes she'd say, "Nothing," which I really disliked. Being a mother is not nothing—not at all. Granted, it's not like being a model, which was Heather's past life, or even a lawyer, IT consultant, or real estate agent. You can't put "Mom" on your résumé—but it's not *nothing*.

But maybe that's the way Viktor treated it? Treated her? I'd never seen any signs of that, but I could certainly find out. Daniel and Sam had been given roles in the school's fall play and I was one of the parent volunteers. "I have to drop off Daniel's costume," I said to Julie. "I'll see if I notice anything."

Heather's house was much larger than the rest of ours. It sat high on the hill in an area called Sewickley Heights, which I sometimes referred to as Puck Palisades because of the Penguins players who owned grand homes there.

There were large stone pillars on either side of the drive up to Heather's house, and the mansion itself was also stone, an imposing, Victorian-looking structure that, combined with the circular driveway, reminded me of British period dramas. I always half expected to see a butler come out to greet me. Instead, it was Heather who opened the large, arched wooden door, giving me a languid wave as I stepped out of the car and reached in to the backseat to fetch Daniel's costume.

"Thanks for bringing it." Heather greeted me with a quick peck against the cheek. She looked amazing, but then she always did, even in an old pair of jeans and a slouchy sweater over a T-shirt. An outfit like that would make me look frumpy and even shorter, but on her it was the epitome of casual chic. "Come on in and have something to drink," she said, leading the way through the front hall and into the massive eat-in kitchen with its high-end white cabinets and huge unbroken slabs of Carrara marble. While I draped Daniel's costume over a chair back, Heather opened the door of the enormous side-by-side stainless-steel refrigerator and practically disappeared inside it. "Which would you prefer," she said, lifting something off the door.

"Anything white," I answered, before I saw that what she held was not a bottle of wine but of sparkling, flavored water.

"I've got plain, too, if you'd prefer it?"

"No, no this is fine," I said, although I've got to admit that I was a bit disappointed. It would have been much easier to have this conversation if both of us had a pleasant buzz.

She poured two glasses and sat down across from me at the kitchen island. "Thanks again for making Daniel's costume— you're so clever. I'm not crafty like that—Daniel should have you for a mother."

"No, no, you're a wonderful mom—he gets so much from you."

We went on like this for two minutes. It's the standard female friends drill—no, you're wonderful; no, you!—that can drive people outside the circle a bit crazy.

When she mentioned that Viktor was working late, I took the opening. "Those long hours must be super stressful," I said.

"Mmm," she said, which was decidedly noncommittal.

"I get annoyed when Eric's job cuts into our home life. For instance, when he has to spend the weekend grading. We argue about it sometimes."

"That's too bad," she said, but then one of the cleaners came into the kitchen and that was the end of the conversation. At Heather's suggestion, we carried our glasses out of the kitchen and into her formal living room. I thought how nice it must be to have someone to do the dirty work for you, to not have to spend countless hours fighting a losing battle against the perpetual untidiness of a house with children.

"Do you trust them?" I whispered to Heather, both of us turning at the noise as one of the women pushed a vacuum down the hall and into the dining room. Even though I knew she couldn't hear me, I still whispered, uncomfortable with the classism clearly on display. There were the two of us sitting with our drinks, doing nothing, the very definition of the idle rich, while behind us a small bevy of worker bees combed through the house putting things in order.

"No," Heather said. "I think they like to listen in on my conversations."

"Really?" I laughed. "I meant do you trust them with your things? I didn't even think of eavesdropping."

It occurred to me at that moment that there were always people in this house—the cleaners, the nanny, the lawn crew— and if what Alison suspected was true, then wouldn't these people have seen something? Wouldn't they have reported it, even if anonymously? This wasn't our parents' generation, after all, with its polite silences and stiff upper lips, when people didn't talk about what went on behind closed doors. We lived in an era of public spectacle, reality TV and confessions. See something, say something—wouldn't that apply to marital terrorism as well?

That should have been the end of it. I'd concluded that there was nothing whatsoever going on with Viktor and Heather, and I texted Julie this, giving her the green light to forget about what she'd seen and to tell Alison to forget it, too. I'd been in Heather's house, I'd seen how many people were around; if something was going on we'd know about it. "Alison needs to stop letting her imagination run away with her," I told Julie. I was utterly confident when I said that; I never apologized to Alison, but I should have.

It was over a month after Julie had seen Heather and Viktor at the Chens' party, and almost three weeks since I'd stopped by her house, when something happened that changed my mind. A weekday morning, a Tuesday I think, the kids off school for some teacher in-service day.

"I don't know why the schools have so many of these," Julie complained as she watched her kids racing around the playground. "We never got this many days off."

"Yes, and we walked uphill to school both ways," I said with mock solemnity.

"In the snow," Alison added with a laugh.

"I'm serious," Julie said, but belied that by laughing, too.

We'd met at the War Memorial Park, which despite its somber name had a bright and cheerful playground. I was almost giddy with pleasure at the chance for some adult company and conversation. The three of us sat at a picnic table near the swings, relaxing under the sun, unusually warm for fall, while keeping an eye on the kids. Julie glanced at her watch, asking, "Where's Heather?" We'd arranged to meet at ten A.M., which really meant ten*ish*, but it was almost eleven and there was still no sign of her. Usually, if one of us got delayed we'd text the others, but no one had heard from Heather.

A few minutes later, Daniel dashed past us to join the other kids, and we turned to see Heather crossing the lawn from the parking lot, carrying one of those cardboard take-out trays with coffee cups. "Stopped at Starbucks for us," she said, passing out cups.

"You're a godsend!" Julie exclaimed as she took hers, immediately removing the lid to blow on it.

"Starbucks?" Alison said. "How come?"

As in how come she hadn't stopped at Crazy Mocha, our coffee shop, which was also closest to the park? "Went to one with a drive-thru," Heather said, taking a seat at the table. She leaned back, turning her face up to the sun and closing her eyes. From the playground, Daniel's voice cried, "Mommy, come swing me!"

"In a minute," Heather called without looking. She lifted her head enough to take a sip of coffee. "It's so beautiful out."

"We'd almost given up on you two," I said. "Busy morning?"

"Oh, I just forgot the time," Heather said in her usual languid way. This was the way she always was, relaxed and seemingly without a care—that's what I want to emphasize, that she never seemed under any particular stress and that's why I never guessed that anything was wrong.

Before Heather could reply, Daniel interrupted, crying, "Mommy! Mommy! Come swing me! Come now, Mommy!"

"Okay, hold on," Heather said, sighing as she sat up and gave us all an apologetic smile before heading over to help her son. I heard the crunch of another car and looked toward the parking lot. When I turned back to the playground, Heather was going hand-over-hand across the monkey bars while Daniel laughed and clapped with glee at his mother's antics.

"What the hell?" I swore under my breath, but Alison heard it all the same. I'm sure she was surprised; I try not to use profanity, especially around the kids. I felt her look at me, but I was staring at Heather. Hanging from the bars made her coat and shirt ride up, exposing her midriff.

My envy of her firm, finely toned abdomen had been followed by shock as she turned and I saw a long swath of fiery red, raised skin—a large welt that was fresh from the looks of it. Julie must have seen it at the same time, because she blurted out, "What on earth happened to you?"

Heather seemed startled, but then she let go of the bars and dropped to the ground, immediately tugging down her coat. I swallowed hard against the sudden bile in my throat as Heather came back at a rapid clip across the grass to pick up her coffee as if there were nothing wrong.

"That's a painful-looking welt," I managed to say to Heather. "How did you do that?"

"I'm fine," she said, waving a hand as if it were nothing of consequence. "I bumped into a door."

"*Bumped?*" Julie said. "I'd call that more like a slam."

Alison's lips were compressed in a thin line and she shot "I told you so" eyes at Julie and me. Questions raced through my head: Was that mark really from a door? And if so, had someone thrown her against it? Had Viktor? I couldn't ask the questions; they stuck in my mouth, thick and unpleasant. I suddenly understood how Julie felt at the Chens' party.

I felt the same nasty shock seeing that mark on Heather's alabaster skin, my stomach turning over with the queasiness of having seen something I shouldn't, of having trespassed, unwittingly, into someone else's private life.

chapter four

HEATHER

I haven't told my friends, but I think they might suspect. It's hard to make too many excuses without my absence raising questions.

We haven't seen you in so long! Julie wailed in a text when I begged off, for the second week running, from our Friday morning coffee. A flurry of texts from Alison and Sarah followed, all expressing concern. It's very sweet, although frustrating, too, adding stress on top of the stress that I'm already feeling. They would ask questions if they saw me—they would notice what I don't want them to notice—and I just can't handle that on top of everything else. I think I might explode.

But I can't. I have to get through each day and put on that happy face before Viktor gets home in the evening. He likes me to be happy; he says if I would only smile more it would relieve the stress from his day. I know that he thinks he's given me everything and I should be grateful. I am grateful. Or I try to be. I read books like *365 Days of Happiness* and *Gratitude Your Attitude,* the kind found in the self-help sections of bookstores and libraries. All advise me to perform tasks like list the things I'm thankful for in my life.

Today I'm grateful that Viktor will be home late. He will not see the casserole that I've burned because I was out back smoking and lost track of time. No one knows I smoke, not even my friends. Everyone's so anti-smoking and judgey these days. You can't light up anywhere without some stranger getting in your face to ask you to please, please blow the lung cancer elsewhere. I can just see Sarah's judgmental glare if she knew. Actually, smoking is one of the few things that I have in common with Viktor's mother. She and all of her European friends smoke, although she doesn't make any attempt to hide it from her son, like I do. Whenever we visit her, Viktor complains, grabbing her cigarettes and throwing them out. Dramatic gestures that she likes because they make her feel loved. I wish I could be like her and just smoke in the open.

It would probably be comical to watch me sneak out of the kitchen door and along the flagstone patio to the corner of the house, where I stand on tiptoe to reach a little crevice between the stone and the graying white fascia for the pack and lighter I've hidden there. I favor Marlboros, which is ironic given their hypermasculine ad campaigns, but my lighter is girly, a purple Bic from a Sheetz gas station. One a day, that is all I allow myself now. It's not like the days when I modeled and we all lived on cigarettes and booze in between cadging free dinners paid for by older, reptilian men. Yes, I gave up all that *glamour* for the provincial life of the suburbs.

"Mommy, something smells funny!" It's Daniel at the back door, and I stub out the cigarette as fast as a wink and squirrel my pack away. At first I think he's referring to the cigarette smoke, but then I smell it, too—dinner burning. I race into the kitchen, which is more than twice the size of my mother's, and open the convection oven to find the top layer of cheese on my casserole dark brown and smoking.

Sometimes I feel as if I'm playing the role of traditional housewife—I'm cooking casseroles, for heaven's sake. If I just added crushed potato chips to this dish I could be my own mother back in the late seventies, bustling about her avocado kitchen with her shag haircut and polyester dress, consulting *Redbook* for recipes to appease the insatiable appetite of my mutton-chopped and leisure-suited father. Certainly Viktor reminds me of him sometimes, coming home every night with the same sense of expectation and entitlement.

"What's for dinner?" he asks, no matter what hour he comes

home. Once I actually said, "I don't know, I'll ask the elves." I had a brief moment to enjoy the confused look on his face before he got upset.

"He has a very stressful job." These are the excuses and justifications I hear from his mother and mine. "Viktor will always work long hours and his schedule will always be changing; being a doctor's wife means having to understand that."

That's what I am, you see. I'm no longer a person in my own right, I'm a doctor's wife. A surgeon's wife, to be precise. I serve on a hospital's charitable board, along with a host of other people, many of whom seem to spend a lot of time struggling desperately to avoid getting older. Everyone is on a diet all the time and they discuss the latest antiaging creams and regimens with a seriousness that might suggest they were cures for cancer.

All the other wives on the board are torn between envy of the plastic surgeons' spouses and gratitude that they're not one of us. On the one hand, they imagine that we can get the "work" everyone has had done or wants to have done at a big discount. On the other hand, they wonder if we ever make love without imagining our husbands mentally re-sculpting us. As one Texas transplant put it, "D'yall scream any time your husbands pick up a Sharpie?"

"Not that you have to worry," one of the older women says to me. "Not with your height and skin." She gives my upper arm a tiny squeeze like I'm a peach at the market. "Did anyone ever tell you that you could be a model?"

"No, never."

Of course I'm aware of my looks. What can I say? I won the gene lottery. But people assume that looking good comes with other luck, and that's not true at all. I've never been lucky in love, for instance, though I've been hopeful each and every time.

Viktor and I met at a party in Miami. He was attending a conference and I was down from New York doing the winter circuit, and we happened to meet at the hotel bar. He was in a crowd of doctors loudly and animatedly discussing a complete facial transplant—a horror story, when you think about it—but I felt his eyes on me as I excused my way past them to order a drink at the long teak bar. I wore a sky-blue sheath dress that was a gift from a designer whose show I'd walked that spring, and Viktor said that he thought the dress matched my eyes perfectly. Such a sweet, sweet thing to say—I remember being impressed that he noticed the color of my eyes. That was before I knew how detail-oriented he was and how much appearances mattered to him.

"We need to set up an appointment with an orthodontist," he said the other morning after Daniel gave him his best five-year-old gap-toothed smile. By "we" Viktor means "you." He does this all the time; I'm not sure he's aware of it. "We need to get more groceries," or "We need to tell the cleaners to do a better job with the vacuuming—there are lines in the carpet."

Well, "we" don't want to talk to the cleaners, who are resentful that one of us is just a more expensively dressed version of them, an American success story, who married her way out of an Appalachian backwater into a better social class. And "we" don't think that five-year-olds need to worry about their teeth, not yet—not for some time. I'd ignore these demands, but he's meticulous and will be sure to remember and ask about them. It's an unspoken agreement: He will work his obscenely long hours and barely see his wife and child, and I will make his life as smooth as possible and tolerate his moods.

"You should be happy," my mother says to me when I talk to her. I can picture her in that kitchen that has been "freshened" so it's no longer avocado, all the appliances swapped for "biscuit" or "almond." She is always in her kitchen, standing with the cordless phone as if she can't move anywhere else in the house, a holdover from the days when the cord limited her reach. "What I wouldn't give for what you have—that security." My mother is whispering because my father will hear her from the next room. He's been made redundant again, and this time there will be no other job for him. "You've got to take the bad with the good," my mother says. "That's what it means—for better and for worse. You promised."

Another thing I'm grateful for: sleeping pills. With any luck, by the time Viktor gets home tonight I'll already be fast asleep.

chapter five

ALISON

I choked on my coffee when Julie called what we'd seen a "potential domestic problem."

"Are you referring to Heather being abused by her husband?" I said once I'd stopped coughing.

"Don't use that word," Julie hissed, glancing around the coffee shop to see if anyone else had heard. "I just saw Terry Holloway come in—that woman lives for gossip."

"Who?" I asked, turning in my seat.

"Don't look," Sarah warned, and I turned back, catching only a brief glimpse of a skinny woman with a snotty expression who seemed to be arguing with a barista.

"We don't know that's what it is," Julie said in a low voice. "For all we know Heather was telling the truth and it was an accident."

We were sitting in our corner of Crazy Mocha on a rainy Saturday afternoon, a day that we knew Heather had a long-standing spa appointment and wouldn't see us. We were child-free, our kids in the care of their fathers or, in the case of our oldest three, at a birthday party for one of their classmates.

"That was no accident," I said, looking to Sarah for support, but she appeared to be waffling. "C'mon, you both saw that welt. Are you actually going to tell me that you're not worried about her?"

"I know, but they've always seemed like such a happy couple," Julie said, a slight whine in her voice. I think part of

31

her was annoyed with me for spoiling the image she had of the
gorgeous couple leading a fairy-tale life in their mansion on the
hill. Understanding that humans are flawed and often disap-
pointing was something of a birthright for me.

"They might be happy some of the time, but he still beats her,"
I said, trying to be gentle, although I know my tone couldn't hide
my impatience.

Julie flinched at the word "beats," and her hands tightened on
her coffee cup. Sarah said, "We don't know that—it could have
been an accident like Heather said." I gave her an incredulous
look, and her gaze shifted away from mine.

"Maybe you're seeing abuse because you're expecting to see
it," Julie said, voice dropping to a whisper on "abuse." "Like
you're creating the reality you want to see."

"What does that mean?" I said, no longer bothering to hide
my irritation. "That this is all in my head?" How could she and
Sarah get what we'd seen at the park out of their heads? I certainly hadn't managed it.

Seeing that huge welt on Heather's torso had unsettled me, un-
earthing old fears and insecurities, taking me into the past.

I hadn't wanted to move back to my hometown. Michael does
IT in financial services, and when his company transferred him
from Philly to Pittsburgh, I'd been afraid of the dark memories
that would come flying at me, like bats at twilight, every time I
passed something familiar. It was one of the reasons I'd insisted
we keep away from the east of the city. We moved north instead,
trading the Monongahela River for the Ohio, and except for the
occasional trip to Kennywood Park, I stayed far away from the
neighborhood that I'd once called home.

Despite my trepidation about being back, I'd been charmed by
Sewickley. The first time we drove through town, Michael and I
had seen a row of unlocked bicycles outside the library. We'd already been awed by the lovely houses and quaint shopping district, delighted that it was a walkable community with good
schools, but it was those unlocked bicycles, the sense of security
they conveyed, that had confirmed for us that this was the place

we wanted to settle and raise a family I remember resting my hand on my very pregnant belly and thinking this small town was a safe place to raise our child.

Now that sense of security had fled. It didn't help that Michael had raised the possibility of being transferred back to Philly, when I'd assumed we'd be here forever. Or that the year was turning, the days shorter and the leaves dying, the plants in my backyard garden withering. I could feel bad things coming. One night after dinner, I was washing dishes and staring out at the darkness when Michael's hands landed on my shoulders, startling me.

"Wow, you're jumpy," he said, holding his hands up. "What's up?"

"Nothing," I said automatically, and then a minute later, as his hands came to rest on my shoulders again, kneading gently, I repeated, "Nothing, I'm fine."

But I wasn't. I had trouble sleeping, lying there in the dark long after Michael was softly snoring beside me. I'd stare up at the fine cracks in the old plaster ceiling while a past I had stored as far away as I could unspooled in my brain until I'd finally fall into a restless sleep filled with haunting dreams.

"You're a whore." A face contorted with rage. "You're nothing but a whore." A rough hand grabbed my arm and I looked down to watch the formation of a purple mark that looked exactly like the bruise I'd seen on Heather's wrist.

Shifting in my seat at the coffee shop, I tried to remember why I'd insisted on having this meeting when it was clear that neither Sarah nor Julie was willing to see the truth.

"If Heather says nothing is wrong then what can we do but believe her?" Julie said, stirring sweetener into her coffee. She took a sip and made a prune face. "Oh, yuck, that's far too sweet." She dropped the cup and picked up the three empty packets of artificial sugar discarded on the table, genuinely surprised, as if she hadn't been the person who'd just stirred them into her coffee. At least I wasn't the only one distracted.

"Even if there is something going on we can't do anything

unless she's willing to talk," Sarah said, giving me an apologetic smile over the top of her coffee cup before taking a sip. I didn't say anything, feeling defeated. Sarah must have taken my silence for a rebuke, because she put down her cup with a decisive click. "Look, all we can do is offer our support and make sure she knows she can turn to us."

It seemed completely inadequate.

A group text came from Heather the next day. Would we like to bring the kids to her house Thursday afternoon after school for a playdate? "Daniel gets bored with no one but me to talk to," she'd told me more than once, although I wondered if she was really the one who got bored. She never hid the fact that she found much of parenting tedious. I texted back, **Sounds great; thanks!** Feeling fake because it was so cheery, as if everything were perfectly fine.

Thursday was sunny, one of those perfect fall days when the sky is such a vivid color of blue that it seems almost unreal, and the trees are still heavy with leaves of flaming red and deep gold. There weren't going to be too many afternoons left like this before winter descended, and for one brief moment I thought of turning back and taking Lucy and Matthew to the park instead so nothing could spoil this beautiful day.

I pulled in right ahead of Julie and Sarah, who'd carpooled, which I found strange because technically I lived closer to Julie. Had Sarah asked for a ride or had they wanted time to talk without me? As I was unstrapping Matthew from his car seat, Heather came around the side of the house and hugged Lucy, who'd raced to throw herself at Heather with her usual enthusiasm.

"Daniel's around back, go find him," Heather said, and Lucy took off running. I handed Heather a bag with some cookies I'd brought, giving her a surreptitious once-over. If she had any bruises they were hidden.

"I'm glad you could make it," she said with a big smile, including Julie and Sarah, who were both struggling to unpack kids and all the things that came with them from Julie's car.

Did Heather seem nervous? I caught myself wondering. What if Julie was right and I *was* conjuring up things to fit my own vision of what was happening? What if I was wrong and there *were* simple explanations for all we'd seen?

"Isn't it a beautiful day?" Julie exclaimed, her enthusiasm contagious as always, no matter where my mood started. She was carrying Aubrey on her hip while leaning forward to scrape something off Owen's face with her free hand. Sarah had a tight hold of Josh while she lectured his older siblings to "remember your manners and say please and thank you. Sam, stop kicking your sister!"

I was a little surprised when Heather didn't take us inside and instead led us around the side of the house. We were all bundled in jackets or sweaters except for Owen. "What am I supposed to do?" Julie said, as he ran past us in a T-shirt, his flip-flops smacking on the gravel. "It was either let him wear what he wants or don't get here at all."

Sarah didn't say anything, but I could feel her judgment of Julie's parenting. Sarah was a big believer in clear boundaries with one's children. "Who's the parent?" was a favorite expression of hers.

The sun was deceptive; it was a lot chillier outside than it looked. I zipped up Matthew's jacket and wondered if Julie would eventually fetch Owen's sweater and shoes from the car.

"They're running around enough not to feel the cold," she said, watching our kids dashing about the backyard, their cheerful cries and chatter echoing through the trees as if they were a small flock of birds. "Backyard" was an understatement. The property was vast, with a play structure almost as big as the one at the park, plus a full tennis court back behind that and plenty of wide-open green space.

"I've got coffee," Heather said, "I'll bring it right out." She headed across the lawn to the stone courtyard at the back of the house and in through a back door. Again, I was surprised that she didn't invite us inside to sit and talk, like we usually did.

Sarah raised her eyebrows at Julie and me. "Isn't it a little cold for a picnic?" Julie just shrugged and pulled the zipper of her jacket up before cheerfully heading for the wrought-iron patio set on the courtyard. I admired her ability to move forward, both literally and figuratively, because it wasn't one of my strengths— I have a tendency to dwell on the negative.

"I hope the coffee's hot," Sarah said in a low voice as we brushed leaves off the table's matching ironwork chairs. "We're going to need it."

Heather came back out the door carrying a silver tray with a porcelain coffeepot and cups. "Oh! I forgot the cream and sugar—I'll get them," she said as she set it on the table. And before any of us could protest or offer to help, she darted back into the house.

"Does she seem nervous to you?" Sarah asked as Julie began pouring coffee. So I wasn't the only one who'd noticed. I felt a small surge of pleasure at having my observation supported. Before Julie or I could respond, Heather came back out with a small white porcelain creamer and a glass bowl heaped with sugar cubes.

"I couldn't find the matching sugar bowl," she said. "I have no idea what happened to it." She chattered away, asking who wanted cream or sugar and adding it to each of our cups as if this were all perfectly normal. The cold metal from the chair seeped through my jeans and I tried to hide a shiver. We all followed Heather's lead and acted as if it were just another summer day and not late October.

"Did you sell the Tillman house yet?" Heather asked Julie, referring to a home that had been the bane of Julie's existence for more than six months. The owners, an older couple whose home was desperately in need of updates, were stubborn and wouldn't accept the lower offers they'd gotten despite having already retired to Arizona.

"I can't wait until their contract is up," she said. "Let them try to tempt another real-estate agent with the promise of a big commission that they're never going to see. Good riddance!"

"Their son is just like the father," Sarah said. "He's the soccer coach for the peewee team and everyone's just waiting for him to step down so another parent can step up and replace him."

"Speaking of stepping up, did you decide about the PTA fund-raiser, Heather?" Julie looked at her expectantly.

"What fund-raiser?" I said, warming my hands on the mug of coffee.

"The parent-child fashion show. I think it was Shelly Schwartz-man who proposed the idea and I immediately thought of Heather. I mean, how great would it be to have our own real-life model modeling?"

"That was another life, I haven't modeled in years," Heather said, shaking her head with a small smile.

"But you were a model and I can guarantee you that none of the other mothers participating can say that. And we're not being sexist," Julie said as an aside to Sarah. "Fathers are welcome to participate, too, but we don't have any takers so far."

"You should do it, Heather," I said, trying to be supportive of Julie's idea. "You could teach everybody how to walk the runway."

Before Heather could comment, Sarah's son, Sam, hit Daniel because he'd slammed into Sam and his plastic truck, which he'd been busy running up the slide as Daniel was coming down. Both kids began wailing, and Sarah yelled her son's name before running toward them.

"Oh, shit." Heather dropped her cup on the table and sprinted after Sarah. The wailing increased for a moment as the other kids stopped to stare.

"Daniel's got a boo-boo," Matthew said, looking from me to the two older children, who were being both admonished and comforted by their mothers. He'd found his way to my side, as he did any time something upsetting happened. I put my own coffee down and hoisted him into my lap, relishing the way his small body curled into mine. "He's okay," I crooned, rocking him a little as he fiddled with the zipper on my coat. He didn't like conflict, my little boy, whimpering any time he heard arguing or saw fights between other children.

"Better hope he grows out of it or he's going to get eaten alive in school," Michael had commented recently, but without any rancor.

"Oh no," Julie moaned, startling me. I turned to look at her, but she'd stood up and was staring at the children. "He's bleeding," she said.

I slid Matthew off my lap and stood, shading my eyes to see Heather cupping a hand under Daniel's mouth before lifting him into her arms and hustling back toward the house.

Sarah was yelling at a crying Sam, and as Julie rushed to help Heather, I hustled over to try to calm Sarah down. She seemed oblivious to the fact that the remaining children, including her youngest, Josh, were standing stock-still, looking from Daniel to Sam and then to us, trying to decide on their own reactions by gauging their mothers'.

Matthew trailed after me, whimpering and calling, "Mommy, come back," while Sarah interrogated her wailing son as if he were a hostile witness: "I asked you a question. Did you hit Daniel with your truck?"

"It was just a little disagreement," I said, trying to placate, only to have Sarah wheel on me.

"I'll thank you to stay out of it, Alison," she said in her most snippy, lawyerly tone. "This really isn't any of your business."

Before I could respond that she'd made it my business, I heard Julie exclaim "What happened?" in an agitated voice.

Both Sarah and I turned to see her standing inside Heather's back door. If Heather responded, we couldn't hear it. Julie looked back at us, mouth opened in an O of surprise.

I headed toward the house, hearing Sarah behind me say hurriedly to Sam, "No hitting, you know that." She caught up with me as I approached the back door.

Julie had stepped fully inside, but she hadn't gotten far. Heather's huge, usually immaculate kitchen was trashed, cabinet doors ajar, plates and glasses smashed across the tile floor. The dish washer stood open and most of the plates inside it were broken, too, and someone had overturned the cutlery bin.

Daniel was wailing somewhere off in the distance. Without saying a word, Julie stepped over the mess and began quietly picking up forks and knives from the shards of ceramic and glass, arranging them carefully on the marble island as if that small act could restore order to the space.

Sarah swore under her breath. "Who did this?" Her question came out as whisper. We were all tiptoeing in the space, because there was no way to deny that this was something absolutely awful and ugly.

I whirled on her. "Who the fuck do you think did it?" I snapped. "Daniel?"

She blinked at me, too stunned by my response to reply. I took a broom and dustpan from a tall cabinet and began sweeping up glass and pottery shards. After a moment, Sarah began cleaning out the rest of the dishwasher, putting unbroken plates in the cupboards and gently closing the doors. A block of knives on a counter had been knocked over, the wicked-looking steel blades spilling onto the marble. I set it upright, being careful not to cut myself.

We worked in silence for several minutes, and I don't know what they were thinking, but I was feeling that all-too-familiar, sick twist in the gut that I'd felt ever since I saw the bruise on Heather's arm.

We'd gotten the kitchen back into some kind of order when Heather came back, still carrying Daniel, who was tearstained but calm, and holding an ice pack against his swollen lip. Heather's shirt had bloodstains on it, and even knowing they were Daniel's, I still flinched when I saw them.

"You didn't have to clean up," she said, her voice a mixture of embarrassment and defensiveness. We stood there, all of us, and stared at her. Heather avoided our gaze, focusing on her son, whom she held awkwardly against her hip, smoothing his hair from his face. At last, Julie cleared her throat.

"What happened?" she said in a hushed voice, fiddling with the lineup of forks and knives.

"Nothing," Heather said. Still holding Daniel, she took the broom from me and stuck it back in the cabinet. "Look, I appreciate your help, but I've got it from here. Let's go back outside." She stepped toward the door, but Sarah blocked her path.

"Nothing?" she said, her lawyer voice back. "This isn't nothing, Heather. Are you okay?"

"Of course I am," Heather said. She must have seen the skeptical looks on our faces, because she sighed and brushed her hair back with one of her elegant hands, a gesture of stress or impatience—I couldn't tell which. She reached for the ice pack Daniel held against his split lip and said, "Let me see, sweetie."

"No!" Daniel swung his head away.

"Just for a second," Heather said in a soothing voice. "Let Mommy see for a second." She moved the ice pack away, and we could see that Daniel's upper lip had puffed up, giving him a cute, pouting expression. "No more bleeding—want to go back out to play?" Heather didn't wait for an answer, already moving around Sarah and putting Daniel down next to the back door.

"That's it? Aren't you even going to explain how your kitchen got trashed?" Sarah demanded.

Before Heather could say anything, it was Daniel who spoke. "Daddy says Mommy is clumsy." He laughed, looking up at the adults with an expectant, chilling smile.

chapter six

SARAH

Heather didn't react to Daniel—no correction or contradiction. Alison and I exchanged glances, but it was Julie who said, "I don't think your mom's clumsy at all—remember, she was a model and models are very graceful."

Julie always brought up Heather's modeling. She thought Heather having been a model was very important even though as far as I could tell Heather had never done any significant work. She wasn't a supermodel, after all, or one of those lingerie angels. She'd never graced the cover of *Sports Illustrated* or any other magazine as far as I knew. She'd done a bit of modeling in the United States and apparently some modeling in Europe, too, but she didn't like to talk about her life before Sewickley, so we knew very little.

Still, it wasn't just about fame for Julie; she was like this with all her friends. She always told people I was a lawyer before mentioning that I'd left the law to stay home with my kids. I certainly felt like a lawyer that afternoon, standing among all that debris while trying not to sound as if I were cross-examining Heather.

I waited until she'd sent Daniel back outside with the kids before pressing her. "What the hell happened in here?"

She crossed her arms over her chest, looking from me to Alison and Julie. "We had an argument; things got a little heated."

"So you and Viktor threw all these dishes at each other?" Julie asked, sweeping her arms to indicate the last of the rubble still strewn across the floor.

41

Before Heather could answer, Alison spoke hard and fast: "Viktor did this, didn't he?"

"He's been under a lot of stress," Heather said after a minute, which wasn't an answer to the question, but answered it anyway.

"Of course, honey, but we're all under a lot of stress," Julie said gently. "This is more than stress."

"Yeah," I said. "It's an anger-management problem."

There was color high on Heather's cheekbones, but her voice barely betrayed the emotion and embarrassment she had to be feeling. "It was just a silly argument," she said. "I didn't want you to see the mess."

"Like the bruise on your wrist?" Alison's voice was low and hard. She looked as upset as I'd ever seen her. "Did he hit you?"

"No, of course not!" Heather said, but her gaze darted away and I don't think any of us believed her. I wondered what fresh bruises her clothes were hiding. Viktor had obviously been careful not to leave any marks on her face.

Julie gathered the silverware noisily together and started loading it back in the dishwasher, her movements hurried and jerky. "We'll help you get this cleaned up, it's no problem."

"Thank you, really, but I'd rather you didn't," Heather said, sounding strained. "Please, let's just go back outside."

"Whatever you want," Julie said, shoving the last of the silverware into the dishwasher before straightening up and glancing out the kitchen window. "Alison, I think Matthew might need you."

"Oh!" Alison bolted out the back door, clearly panicked that she'd forgotten about her kids, and I followed after her, anxious that Sam might have hit another child while I was inside.

The sun had shifted and the day felt even colder. Back on the courtyard the coffee had gone cold and new leaves had blown onto the table. Julie plucked one out of her coffee cup as Heather gently shook the pot. "There's more in here," she announced before emptying the cold dregs from her own cup into a boxwood hedge that edged the patio. We all followed suit, Alison's toss landing short so a trail of milky coffee trickled across the stone, seeping into the cracks.

"Oh, sorry," she said, springing up to dab ineffectually at it with a napkin.

"It's fine," Heather said. "No big deal." She refilled our cups with a smile and Julie smiled, too, slipping easily back into the pretense that everything was okay. No one commented that the coffee from the pot was barely warmer than what we'd tossed out. Heather and Julie resumed their conversation about the fashion show as if nothing had interrupted it. I couldn't do it, not now, not after this. I'd never been good at pretending, and I knew Alison wasn't either. She'd sat back down at the table to brood over her coffee, lost in thought and absentmindedly biting her nails. I felt a sudden impatience—we needed to stop sitting there and do something.

"There's help," I blurted, and the others looked at me, Julie's expression wary and Alison's relieved. Heather's face betrayed nothing at all. She simply stared at me, her face the beautiful blank canvas of a plaster Madonna. It was disconcerting. I cleared my throat, gripping my coffee cup. "There are places to get help," I said. "You don't have to put up with this."

"Put up with what?" Heather said after a long, uncomfortable silence, her eyes fixed on mine. I wished that Julie or Alison would step in and back me up, but then Heather laughed. I was so startled my cup slipped from my hands and coffee splashed over the table. It dripped through the open wrought iron and I pushed back from the table to avoid it, my chair scraping noisily against the stone. "I'm not being abused," Heather said, still laughing, a high, brittle sound. "This is absurd."

"I know it's hard," Alison said then, and I shot her a grateful look. "But we're here for you—we want to help you."

"I don't need your help," Heather said quickly. "Look, this is just a misunderstanding. We had a stupid argument and some dishes were thrown. That's all."

There were spots of color on her perfect cheekbones, and as

she picked up her own coffee cup, I saw that her hands were trembling. She noticed it, too, and set the cup down before folding her arms.

"What if he'd cut you? Or Daniel?" Alison spoke in the same low voice she'd used before.

"He wouldn't do that," Heather said. But we'd all stood in that kitchen surrounded by broken glass and none of us was convinced. "Daniel was at school," she added in an insistent tone. "He didn't see it."

"Well, that's one bright spot," Julie said in a weak voice.

"What about your nanny?" I said. "Did she see it?"

"She's not working for us anymore," Heather said, and I felt a chill that had nothing to do with the weather. Alison looked at me and I could tell we were both thinking the same thing: Viktor didn't want any witnesses.

Before anyone could comment, Julie's son, Owen, came running toward us, clutching the front of his pants in a gesture that all of the mothers understood even before he said, "I gotta go to the bathroom!"

"I'll take him," Heather said, standing up, clearly glad for the interruption.

"Don't be silly, I'll do it." Julie got to her feet and hustled Owen into the house. Heather didn't sit back down, using the excuse of checking on Daniel to leave the table.

When Julie came out of the house with Owen, she said she'd forgotten she had an appointment later that afternoon. I got up at once, eager to leave. Alison followed suit.

"You don't have to go so soon," Heather said, but it was a halfhearted protest at best. It was clear she wanted us to go and I wondered why she hadn't simply canceled this afternoon.

We took turns saying good-bye to her on the driveway, each giving her a careful embrace, cradling her close.

"If you ever need to talk," Alison murmured when it was her turn.

"Yes, we're your friends," Julie said, adding, "Thank you for the coffee," as if trying to normalize everything. I waited to say anything to her until we'd loaded the kids into the car, and until Alison had pulled out ahead of us, and until we'd waved, parade-float smiles in place, at Heather standing in the drive, her slender arms wrapped around her midsection.

"I feel terrible leaving her there," I said in a low voice, conscious of the kids. "Viktor is a monster."

"We don't know that," Julie whispered, eyes darting to the kid mirror to see if they were listening in the backseat. "They had an argument. Granted, it looked like a really bad argument, but all couples argue."

"C'mon, he trashed their kitchen—that's more than an argument and you know it."

"Shh. Careful about certain little someones with big ears. Look, I know it seems . . . excessive, but we weren't there and we don't know what really happened. Maybe they were both throwing dishes."

"If that were true, then wouldn't she just tell us that? And have you forgotten the welt?"

Julie had no answer to that. Noticing her hands clutching the steering wheel, I realized how stressed she was about it. Julie liked things light and happy. She was the one who always tried to defuse tension in our group. One reason she was such a successful salesperson was that she didn't internalize negative feedback about the properties she listed, focusing only on what worked and plowing ahead to highlight it. Clients loved her bubbly personality and I did, too, but this wasn't the first time I'd felt frustrated by her attitude.

"I know you admire Viktor—"

"Of course I admire him—he's a very well-respected doctor."

"But how well do you know him? How well do any of us know him?"

We knew one another's husbands only as the accompanying spouse for the occasional cocktail party or kids' sporting event. We'd gone to dinner once or twice as a group, but eight people required a pretty large table, so I hadn't had much of a chance to talk with Viktor. One time, Julie and I decided to separate the couples in order to spark more lively discussion, and that had been the longest conversation I'd ever had with him.

Sitting there in Julie's passenger seat, I tried to recall my impressions of Viktor. He was a tall man, much taller than me, of course, but he also towered at least two inches above Eric. He was good-looking in a way that could make people feel slightly nervous when he turned his blue eyes in their direction. I'd been nervous before first meeting him, having heard he was a plastic surgeon and feeling self-conscious about my body and afraid that I'd see a negative assessment in his eyes. I needn't have worried. He was friendly, with old-school manners, always holding doors for women and offering a hand to his wife when she had to take steps or climb out of the car. Granted, it was a bit paternalistic, but I'd never seen any hint of bullying behavior.

What had we talked about at that dinner? Something innocuous—was it about cooking? A cooking show? I remembered being surprised that he had any time to watch TV, much less to cook, given the busy schedule he somehow maintained, albeit with all the help that having a doctor's salary afforded him. "Heather doesn't care for cooking," he'd said in his easygoing way. "I've tried to explain that kids need more to eat than PB&J." He'd laughed when he said it, but had there been an edge to it? Or was I only imagining that now I'd seen the rage he was capable of?

"Did you know Viktor was married before?" Julie said in a musing voice. I turned to look at her, my mouth literally dropping open.

"No, I didn't know that. How on earth do you know and I don't?"

She shrugged. "Heather told me. I guess I just assumed she told you and Alison, too."

"Divorce?"

"I assume, but I didn't want to pry." Which was just so typical of Julie. Alison or I would definitely have asked questions.

"What if he abused his first wife?" I said, flashing to all the cases I'd seen in court, bruised women and men desperate to escape, filing restraining orders against battering exes.

Julie took her eyes off the road to look at me and whispered, "I was just wondering the same thing."

As soon as we got home, I set the kids up in front of the TV so I could Google Viktor Lysenko. My kids usually weren't allowed to watch TV on weekdays, and they plopped happily on the couch to stare glassy-eyed at some Disney princess, while I poured myself a glass of chardonnay and sat down in front of the desktop in the small alcove that we'd turned into a home office. Our house was only a three-bedroom and space was at a premium—we'd bought what we could afford to get into the school district. I'd carved out this little work space in the only place available and Eric and I vied to use it, although it didn't really afford any privacy. The minute I sat down, Hansel, our large orange Persian cat, jumped up into my lap.

It had been a stressful afternoon and I needed to take the edge off. I sipped the wine, trying not to gulp it down, while searching online, occasionally reaching down to absently stroke Hansel's soft fur. There was nothing marriage-related except Viktor's wedding announcement to Heather. Instead, what jumped out at me was how much more information was included about Viktor than Heather: Her bio was two sentences about being related to some people in West Virginia and having modeled, while his was a veritable Who's Who, listing his connections to various hospitals and organizations, and his embrace of Pittsburgh when he came from the Ukraine as a youngster. And their wedding had taken place in Pittsburgh, not the bride's hometown. Had that been at Viktor's insistence? It smacked of someone who needed to be in control.

I grabbed a pad of paper to jot down what I'd found, but when I looked for my favorite pen—a black Montblanc that had been a law school graduation gift—I couldn't find it. Eric had probably taken it to grade papers; I wished he'd remember to put things back where they belonged. Josh called from the other room, needing me, and I didn't have time to get back to the search until later that evening. Once I'd done laundry, made dinner, and bathed the kids, I finally had a moment free to call Alison. Of course, techie that she was, she managed to find more information online than I had.

"There's a wedding announcement for Viktor and a woman named Janice Franz. I found another reference to her and there's a Janice Franz who lives in Penn Hills."

Just east of Pittsburgh, only fifty minutes away. It hadn't occurred to me that she'd be so close by. "What if we called her and asked about Viktor?"

"I think we should talk to her in person," Alison said. "We don't know what happened with their marriage and how she feels about Heather."

Alison patched Julie in to our call so we were all on the phone together. Not surprisingly, Julie didn't jump at the chance to question Viktor's first wife in person. "How on earth are you planning to bring that up? 'Excuse me, did your ex-husband ever hurt you?'"

"Something like that."

"Count me out. What if she's still friendly with him and calls Viktor?"

I said, "We could ask her to be discreet."

"What about Heather?" Julie said. "What are you going to say if it gets back to her?"

"That we're concerned about her," Alison said. "That we think she's being abused and isn't facing reality."

"She asked us to stay out of it," Julie said.

"Are you saying you're comfortable doing nothing?" I said. "What, you just want to sit by while your friend is the victim of domestic violence?"

"Allegedly," Julie said. "She's allegedly a victim—we don't know that for sure."

"Yes, you're right," Alison said in an acid voice. "And he allegedly destroyed their kitchen, and allegedly squeezed her wrist hard enough to bruise, and allegedly grabbed her at the Chens' house and allegedly threw her into a door."

There was silence for a moment so long that I thought we'd lost the connection. Finally, I said, "Hello? Julie?"

Julie let out a sigh, like a balloon deflating. "Okay, okay, I'll go with you. But I don't want Heather to find out."

I thought that was more than we could promise, but before I had a chance to respond, Alison said quickly, "Don't worry—she won't."

chapter seven

JULIE

It wasn't until we turned in to Janice Franz's neighborhood the following Saturday that we thought about how it would look for three complete strangers to show up on her doorstep.

"I think it should just be Julie," Sarah said, pulling her minivan over to the side of the road and putting her blinkers on so we could plan. Alison rode shotgun and I'd taken the backseat.

"Me?" I spluttered, dribbling the coffee I'd brought down my chin. "I didn't even want to come on this trip!"

"She might feel threatened," Alison said, passing back a tissue. "But you're so friendly that you'll melt any possible hostility." Sarah nodded and I wondered if they'd talked ahead of time, waiting to spring this on me. Why had I agreed to be part of this plan?

"You'll have to be careful about how you bring up the abuse," Alison said. "Even if she seems eager to talk about Viktor's behavior, I'd still be careful about using the actual word."

"I'm no good at this sort of thing!" I protested. "I don't want to have this conversation at all."

"Oh, you'll be great." Sarah waved a hand dismissively. "Everybody loves you. As soon as you mention Viktor you can gauge her reaction. If she can't stand him, then you can probably bring up domestic violence right away."

"That still wouldn't be proof that he's hurting Heather," I said.

"Yes, but if he battered his first wife, then maybe we can use that to help Heather," Alison said. "And maybe if she knows that

51

Viktor did this to another woman, and how bad it got, that would be enough to convince her to leave him."

This seemed like wishful thinking to me. Heather had denied being abused; I didn't see her leaving any time soon. As Sarah pulled back onto the road, I started to sweat, nervous about what I would say.

Sarah drove slowly, searching the house numbers along the steep street. Penn Hills has lots of small brick homes—ranches and Cape Cods—some on slightly bigger lots than others, but most of them modest, middle-class houses. I thought of Viktor and Heather's neo-Gothic stone estate in Sewickley Heights. Apparently Viktor's ex hadn't done well in the divorce.

The destination turned out to be a tiny ranch with lace curtains in the front window and a wooden sign declaring GOD BLESS THIS HOME hanging from the front door. "His ex lives here?" Sarah said with surprise, as Alison double-checked the address. We circled the block once, before Sarah pulled up out front. I hoped Janice wasn't peeking out from behind those curtains, wondering about the strange van parked outside her house. I got out and turned up the short concrete walk. As I rang the bell, I could feel Alison and Sarah watching from the car. Other than its faint chiming, there was no other noise from inside the house. The neighborhood was quiet, except for the distant sounds of traffic on the main road and some far-off neighbor's leaf blower. I waited a few minutes and rang the bell again. It felt like an eternity before the door finally opened.

A short, squat older woman with a soft cloud of graying hair stood there with an inquiring look. Dozens of little white hairs clung to her navy-blue sweater, and a powerful aroma of cat made me take a step back. I was so surprised by her age that I just blinked for a second, unable to speak. "Yes?" she said, beating me to the punch. "Did you want something?"

"Yes, hi, maybe I'm at the wrong house. I'm looking for Janice Franz?"

"I'm Janice Franz."

"Oh, um, you are? I mean, you're not who I was expecting."

"Are you selling something, miss? I'm sorry, but I already gave to the Boy Scouts and the United Way—" She tried to close the door and I stuck my foot out to block her.

"I'm not with any organization, I'm a Realtor, but—"

"I'm not interested in selling at this time."

"No, no, it's not that—I'm sorry, this is awkward, but I was expecting someone young—that is, closer to my age. The Janice Franz who was married to a Viktor Lysenko?"

The confusion on the woman's face disappeared, but something else settled in its place. It was an odd expression; her eyes were sad, but the set of her jaw suggested she expected a fight. "You're confusing me with my daughter—Janice Marie Franz. I'm Janice Lee Franz."

"Oh, I see," I said, unsure. This wasn't going at all according to plan. A white cat with black spots poked his head out the door, snaking his way through the woman's legs. "I thought this was your daughter's house. Is she by any chance living here? Or could you tell me how to get in touch with her?"

The woman's face turned red and for a moment I thought she was furious, but then tears welled in her eyes and she said, "My daughter is dead."

Startled, I blurted "She's dead?" before catching myself and hastily adding, "I'm so sorry for your loss."

"Who are you?" she said. "What do you want with Janice?"

"I'm sorry, it's just—she was once married to Viktor Lysenko, right?"

"Yes, Viktor was her husband, why are you asking?"

"I don't want to bring you more pain, Mrs. Franz, but if you don't mind my asking—how did Janice die?"

"What is this about?" The woman's voice rose. "Why would you come to my house and question me about my precious daughter? Did you know Janice? Is that why you're asking?"

"No, I didn't. I'm sorry, it's just that I know Viktor."

The red on her face deepened and her eyes narrowed. "Did he send you here? He's hoping I'll sell up and retire out-of-state."

"So you're still friendly with your former son-in-law?"

Another snort. "Friendly? If by friendly you mean the court case is over."

"Court case?"

"I'm sure he sent you out here to dig up some reason to make me give up my visitation rights. Well, you can tell him it ain't gonna happen."

"Visitation? I don't know what you're talking about."

The old woman snorted. "You can tell Viktor I'm not talking to his hussy—if he wants to talk with me, then let him come himself." She nudged the cat back with her foot and slammed the door.

Hussy? I was torn between indignation and amusement. As I headed back down the walk, a movement caught the corner of my eye, and I turned to see the old woman yanking aside one of the lace curtains and watching me, another, darker cat cradled in her arms. What if she called Viktor?

Sarah pulled out as soon as I got in the backseat. "I hope she didn't see my license plate," she said as we drove over a hill and the house disappeared from view. I told them what the old woman had said and how she'd reacted when I mentioned Viktor.

"It's not like we're breaking any law," Sarah said, and she sounded like she was trying to convince herself. "It's a free country—it's perfectly legal to ask any question we want."

Yes, but legal and explainable could be two very different things. Had I told Janice Franz my last name? I hoped not.

"Any evidence Viktor abused her daughter?" Alison said as she pulled out her phone to search for the obit.

"I don't know, but she really seems to hate her ex-son-in-law."

"You said there was a court case?" Sarah said as Alison typed rapidly on her phone, muttering "damn autocorrect." She looked up as Sarah braked hard at a stop sign. "What were they fighting over?"

"Visitation," I said. "Whatever that means."

"That can't be right—visitation's about kids," Alison said. "Unless Viktor has another child?"

"I have no idea, but I'm not going back to ask her. Janice made it pretty clear that she's done talking."

"It could also be about a pet—you'd be surprised what people go to court over," Sarah said, accelerating again.

"Do they have any pets?" I asked, trying to recall if I'd ever seen a cat or any other creature at the Lysenko house. It certainly never smelled like Viktor's ex-mother-in-law's place.

Alison stared intently at her phone. "Janice Marie Lysenko? Found it. I can't believe you didn't spot this the first time you searched, Sarah."

"I guess I don't have your superior Googling skills," Sarah said with as much sarcasm as she could layer in her voice.

Alison ignored her, scrolling through the obit in silence for a moment. "Interesting—there's no cause of death listed."

"Do you think it might have been a suicide?" I said, distressed at the thought. "They usually keep that out of obits."

"Or he made it look like a suicide," Alison said.

Sarah shot Alison a quick look, but she didn't refute her. I couldn't either.

Alison kept tapping on her phone; I sat forward, trying to watch over the seat as she opened window after window, following links so fast that I couldn't keep up. "Here we go," she said, "another obit from the *Penn Hills Progress*. 'Died unexpectedly'— well that's not a lot of help."

"It rules out cancer," Sarah said. "Could be a heart attack, I guess, but usually they'd just say if it was a sudden illness."

"It doesn't rule out an accident," I said. "It definitely could have been a car accident."

"Or it could have been made to look like an accident—" Alison stopped short.

"What?" I said, but Alison didn't answer for a moment.

"What is it?" Sarah demanded, looking at her and then the road and back again. I tensed in my seat, just as anxious.

Alison read from her screen: "'Survivors include her husband, Dr. Viktor Lysenko; mother, Janice Lee Franz; and son, Daniel Michael.'" She swiveled in her seat to look at me and Sarah. "Daniel is from Viktor's first marriage. He's Janice's child, not Heather's."

chapter eight

The shock of finding out that Daniel was not Heather's birth child was as great, in many ways, as seeing that vast and lovely kitchen covered in broken glass. Sarah swung the car off the side of the road, screeching to a halt along the berm, before reaching for my phone to confirm for herself.

"You'd never guess," Julie said hesitantly, the first of us to break the silence. She meant that Daniel looked like Heather's biological child; they were both blond, for instance, while Viktor had brown hair. I couldn't believe that we'd known them for more than two years and she'd never mentioned it.

"So I'm guessing that Janice's mother sued Viktor over getting visitation with her grandson," Sarah said.

"We need to compare the dates," I said, nudging Sarah for my phone. "When did Janice die and when did Viktor marry Heather?" I pulled up Heather and Viktor's wedding announcement and compared it with Janice Franz's obit. The same, sickening feeling that I'd had two days before in Heather's kitchen returned. "Eleven months apart," I said, doing the math. "He buried his first wife and married a second in less than a year."

The implications of that hung in the air for a moment, heavy and silent, before Sarah abruptly jerked the minivan back onto the road, driving fast while all of us began talking at once, tripping over one another's sentences. Had Heather known about Janice? She must have, yet she'd never mentioned her or the fact that this was Viktor's second marriage.

"Do you think Viktor killed Janice?" I finally said.

"Don't even go there." Julie sounded shocked.

"Why not?" Sarah said. "It's the question begging to be asked here, isn't it?"

Julie didn't say anything, but I could see her lips purse the way they did when she was upset.

I did another search, but still couldn't find any more information about Janice's death. Her employment history popped up—she'd worked in sales for a medical-supply company, which was probably how she'd met Viktor—but there were no articles about fatal accidents and no mention of donations made in her name to organizations for cancer research or other incurable diseases. Viktor's first wife's death looked murky, but we had no real evidence.

"We could visit her old company," Sarah suggested. "Maybe one of her former colleagues knows something."

Great idea, if only the medical-supply company hadn't gone out of business. After discovering that, I spent a fruitless fifteen minutes trying to track down somebody—anybody—from the defunct company, without any luck.

"We need to talk to Heather," I said after exhausting my search efforts. "We need to ask her about Viktor's first marriage."

"Oh, God, I don't want her to think we're gossiping about her," Julie said.

"We're not gossiping, we're trying to help because we're concerned," Sarah said. "There's a big difference."

"Fine," Julie said. "But I don't want her to know that I'm the one who told you about Viktor's first marriage."

"Agreed," I said quickly, afraid she'd change her mind. "But we need to get her away from Viktor and their house so she can talk freely."

I offered to host a girls' night in at my house the following weekend. Wine and snacks, perhaps watch a chick flick—this was how we presented it to Heather. Looking back, I think that what we planned was too much like an intervention. I, for one, was so focused on wanting to get Heather away from Viktor that I didn't stop to think about what kind of support Heather might actually have wanted and needed.

My house was a safe, relatively neutral setting. The coffee shop would have been better in that sense, but it wasn't private and we needed privacy for this. Michael took Lucy and Matthew to visit his family for the weekend, ostensibly so I could get the peace and quiet necessary to complete a big project that I'd gotten behind on. He'd even taken George, our lovable but noisy and demanding chocolate Lab, so I wouldn't be distracted. He and the kids, with George, had driven off in the Volvo the afternoon before, loaded down with books and crayons and snacks and a fully charged tablet stocked with cartoons—Michael had made sure of that, panicked at the thought of six hours in a car without any electronics to distract them. It was the first long trip they'd taken without me, and I'd seen the slightly crazed look in Michael's eyes as he backed down the driveway, the kids waving frantically out the window. A wave of emotion had come over me as I watched the car speed down the street and disappear over the hill. "Wait, come back," I'd wanted to call after them. "Take me with you."

The house seemed so quiet, with only the little sounds usually drowned out by the great cacophony that is life with children. Various creaks and groans, the rumble of the furnace coming on, a steadily dripping tap. I sat in my upstairs office trying to concentrate on work—the project was a beast and I really was in danger of missing the deadline—but I couldn't focus. Instead, I found the numbers for various domestic-violence hotlines and safe houses and made lots of phone calls, looking for help in getting Heather to leave and finding her a place to hide from Viktor. By the end of the afternoon I had over ten pages of notes and numbers, which I compiled into an orderly list to present to Heather.

"Not right away," I reassured Julie when she arrived early that evening and balked at the stack of papers. "I'll wait until later, after we're done talking."

"I just don't want her to get scared off," Julie said apologetically. She deposited a bottle of pinot grigio on my counter along with a string bag that held various bundles wrapped in butcher paper. "I've brought goodies from that great French store—there's a soft goat cheese and a smoked Gouda plus these delicious crackers and olives, those delightful little Niçoise ones— I just love those, don't you?" She prattled on about the food while I uncorked her wine and my own bottle of red and took glasses and plates down from the cupboards.

We might have been prepping for a party; it certainly would have looked that way to others. Chastened by her concern about the list, I put it out of sight while Julie moved refreshments to the glass-topped coffee table in my living room.

From the outside, my house looked like the quintessential cottage, a lovely stone-and-siding turn-of-the-last-century two-story with an actual white picket fence around the front yard and a climbing rose growing along it. This was what had attracted us when we'd first visited. Michael and I had ignored the poky rooms and windows so old and thin that the wind that blew through couldn't be called a draft, but a gale. We'd spent the first year of home ownership, and the better part of our savings, knocking out walls and bringing the electrical up to code and replacing every window and fixture in the house. The inside finally had enough charm to match the outside—an open entertaining space with a wood-burning fireplace and an updated kitchen, and we'd furnished it in comfortable cottage décor, helped along by lots of white paint, spackle, and sales at Pottery Barn. As I liked to tell people, we were lucky that "distressed" was officially a style.

Julie was plumping the pillows on my worn velvet sofa when Sarah rang the bell. She had the look of someone arriving last-minute to a surprise party, darting glances behind her and pausing to peek out a window as she slipped off her coat. "Sorry I'm late," she said. "Of course Eric didn't get home until ten minutes ago."

"You look like Little Red Riding Hood," Julie said with a laugh, taking in Sarah's hooded wool coat and the large-handled wicker basket she'd hauled inside.

I reached for it and wrenched my shoulder. "What on earth did you bring—this weighs a ton!"

"Just some bread and olive oil to go with it. Oh, and some wine, too."

"Some" bread turned out to be two homemade loaves, and there were three bottles of olive oil that she'd personally infused with different seasonings, plus two bottles of wine. Count on Sarah to make the rest of us look and feel like slackers. "Do you think she personally stomped the grapes?" I whispered to Julie when we were alone for a minute in the kitchen, and she laughed, turning it into a cough as Sarah joined us. I took out bagged salad and a wooden bowl to toss it in, sensitive to her watchful eye. Had Sarah just sniffed at my lame offering?

"Heather should be here soon," she said, pouring herself a large glass of wine from the bottle of cabernet I'd opened.

Julie poured herself a glass. "Brian is going to feed the kids, because they were playing when I left. What's that saying—never disturb a sleeping child? I'll amend that to never disturb a contently playing child." She laughed nervously, fidgeting with the gold bar pendant hanging around her neck.

The doorbell rang and we all flinched. I was tossing dressing on the salad, so Julie offered to get the door. I heard the sound of the floorboards in the hall creaking, and then we could hear Julie greeting Heather: "Come in! Come in! It's so great to see you!" Her usual enthusiasm, but I heard a nervousness that seemed to crackle like static in the air. There were the sounds of the coat closet opening, hangers tinkling, and chitchat about Daniel. Then they both appeared in the kitchen doorway. "Heather's here," Julie said unnecessarily, in a voice that sounded even higher and brighter than usual.

"Hi," Heather said with a smile, depositing a box of chocolate truffles on the counter and looking at Sarah and then me. "Can I help with anything?"

"No, we're all set." There was a slight tremor in my hand as I reached for a wineglass. I did my best to steady it and my voice, fixing my expression in a smile. "Red or white?" I said, indicating the bottles.

"White. I thought I'd be the first," Heather said, "but I can see that I'm actually the last—did I get the time wrong?"

"Oh, I just got here early because I came straight from the store," Julie said, busying herself with finding bowls for the salad.

With a brittle laugh, Sarah said, "I had to escape my children." She reached for the bottle of wine and poured herself another glass. I had a fleeting thought about what my husband's reaction would be at not finding any of his favorite red left when he came home.

I put the bread and oil on a tray and Heather offered to carry it, holding it steadily and walking gracefully, her nonexistent hips swaying slightly as she walked into the living room. We followed her with the rest of the food, like ladies-in-waiting, agitated and heavy-footed and altogether less graceful.

We took seats around the fireplace, the log fire warming the room and creating a coziness belied by the purpose of the evening. But where to start? What had seemed like a good idea ahead of time now felt daunting. She'd gotten so upset the last time we'd tried this conversation.

We avoided the topic by passing around the food, and then passing around compliments about the food, all of it stiff and polite and unlike any other get-together. But it was easier than bringing it up. For a moment I thought that maybe Julie was right and we should just pretend that we hadn't seen anything. Let it go. Don't ask. This was someone else's marriage and we were about to cut it open and examine its contents, and how was that an okay thing to do?

It was only when I saw Sarah and then Julie giving me pointed glances that I finally turned the conversation. "Did you get your kitchen back in order?" I asked Heather, trying to sound casual, but my hands felt suddenly clammy and I had to work to look directly at her.

She was eating a piece of bread with small, mouse-like nibbles and she'd barely touched her wine. I knew she was one of those women who chewed each bite of food dozens of times in order not to overeat. A leftover from her modeling days, when gaining weight meant losing work. She paused, holding the bread near her lips. "Yes, it's fine."

"Is Viktor okay?" It was a stupid question and it came out squeaky, because I couldn't think of another way to ask.

Heather swallowed hard—I could see the movement in her slender throat—and she let the hand holding the bread drop to her lap. It took her a moment to answer, but when she did, all she said was, "He's fine," her voice so quiet that we could barely hear her.

Even less sure than I'd been when I started, I said, "I didn't realize, that is, Julie said that Viktor was married before."

Heather's head shot up at that and Julie positively gaped at me. "What are you doing?" she demanded, and then said rapidly to Heather, "I didn't know you hadn't told anyone else—I thought it was common knowledge."

"We're just concerned about you," Sarah added, and that was the end of any pretense that this was just a regular girls' night.

"What is this?" Heather asked, still in that quiet voice, but there was something in the way she looked at us—anger? Agitation? I couldn't read her expression, but her eyes were alert and very focused. "Why are you asking me this? I told you things are okay with Viktor."

"It's obvious that they're not okay," Sarah said, with her usual directness. She downed the rest of her glass of wine as if it were a shot.

Heather stiffened, but before she could respond, I asked, "Did Viktor have issues in his first marriage?"

"Issues?" Heather sat back in the sofa and crossed her arms protectively across her chest.

"Did he have anger-management issues back then, too?"

"I don't know. Obviously, I wasn't married to him then." She sounded annoyed, but she was repeatedly and unconsciously pinching her forearms, that pale, perfect skin turning pink, then red.

"Did Viktor, um, that is, did he get a divorce?" Julie asked as if we didn't know.

Heather gave a single, brief shake of her head. "No. His wife died."

"How?" I asked, coming too fast on the heels of what she'd said.

She was clearly startled, her eyes widening, but after a moment she said, "It was an accident."

"Car accident?" Sarah asked.

Heather shook her head. "She fell. She was home alone with the baby—" She stopped, realizing what she'd revealed, and for a moment nobody spoke. "Daniel is my stepson," she continued in a low voice. "His mother, Viktor's first wife, died when he was about six months old. Daniel doesn't know, not yet at any rate." Her face was flushed and she looked at all of us with her chin jutting forward defensively. My heart, already hurting for her, ached even more.

"She was home alone with the baby . . ." I prompted softly.

"She was home alone and Viktor was at the hospital," Heather continued. "Janice was upstairs, exhausted from caring for an infant, and they think she must have slipped coming down the stairs. She fell two flights. Cracked her skull."

"How awful!" Julie said.

Heather nodded. "I think Viktor was the one who found her."

Sarah and I exchanged a quick look. I asked, "Was there an autopsy?"

"I don't know; it was an accident." She relaxed just a little, leaning forward to pick up her wineglass, but she twirled it by the stem without taking a sip. "It was sad for Viktor." She looked up at us when she said his name.

It was easy to picture it, Viktor hitting his exhausted wife and her either falling or being given a shove over the edge of the stairs, tumbling head over heels, cracking her skull against the sharp edge of a stair or a hard floor. I suppressed a shudder, picturing him standing by and watching her bleed out, knowing precisely how long he had to wait until calling the police. Obviously, nothing had happened to him; the police had just accepted his story that his wife had fallen when he wasn't home, leaving Viktor free to play the mourning widower and move on to another vulnerable woman.

"Do you think he had anything to do with her falling?" Sarah asked the question we were all thinking.

"Of course not," Heather said, but her voice lacked conviction. She huddled deeper into the couch. "He loved her."

"Just like he loves you," I said. "Yet he trashed your kitchen the other day."

"He was upset," Heather said. "He's been under a lot of stress at work."

"And he's grabbed you so hard he's left bruises," I said.

"He just doesn't know his own strength," she said, her voice pleading.

"Has he ever hit you?" Julie asked. I could tell just from looking at her that she was hoping against hope that the answer was no.

Heather hesitated, and then she broke, her placid expression crumbling and a single sob escaping before she brought up her hands to hide her face.

Julie moved first, leaping up to embrace her. "It's okay," she said in her most soothing motherly voice. "It'll be okay."

"It's not what you think," Heather said, the words muffled behind her hands. "He doesn't mean to hurt me."

"How big of him," Sarah said darkly.

Heather accepted the tissues that Julie offered and sat back, swiping at her face and blowing her nose. "There's so much pressure in Viktor's job and he says he needs to come home to a clean, quiet house. He can't handle mess or arguing—he gets so much of that at work."

"Yeah, well that's called real life," Sarah said. "He doesn't get to live in a bubble at home—life is messy and noisy and life with children just means double the chaos."

I wouldn't have put it that way, but Sarah was right. We are always trying to order our lives—writing to-do lists and making schedules, perpetually watching the clock and breaking time into tidy segments—but there are always interruptions and disruptions to our carefully made plans. A child's sudden fever as you are on your way to a party, a bill that you thought you'd paid that somehow slipped past, the flights delayed, the jobs lost.

It was clear that Sarah didn't know what it was like to live with someone who couldn't tolerate any deviation from the schedule, someone who refused to accept that interruptions and disappointment were a natural part of life. I knew what that was like. I pressed a hand against my forehead trying to push back the memories. *"Sir, step away from her right now!"* Blood spattered and sticky on linoleum. I blinked rapidly to clear the images. As Heather sat there, damp eyes wide and doe-like, I thought of that purpling bruise on her arm, of the large welt on her side, and wondered what had happened when she'd gotten them. Had dinner been late? Had she paid too much attention to Daniel and not enough to Viktor? Had she dared to contradict him when he'd told her that she didn't work hard enough to make things easy for him?

"He doesn't mean to hurt me," Heather said. "He's a good man—he is!" She directed this last at Sarah, who'd snorted when she said it.

Were Julie and Sarah wondering, as I was, what marks this "good man" had left on Heather's body that morning? She wore a loose, long-sleeved blouse with a sweater and jeans. It was easy in the winter to cover up the evidence of abuse, but what about in the summer? I tried to think back and remember when she'd worn too much or acted differently, and I suddenly recalled how many times Heather had begged off, last minute, on get-togethers. How often had we planned things only to have her cancel? It all made sense now, and I regretted having been annoyed with her for being so distracted.

From the outside, Viktor, Heather, and Daniel appeared to be the perfect family. The successful doctor, his beautiful wife, and their precious child in their lovely house on the hill. I should have known better.

You never know what happens behind closed doors.

"Viktor needs to get help," Julie said. "He's got to realize that this isn't right."

"Heather is the one who needs help." I stood up and fetched the papers from their hiding place, handing them to Heather. "You need to leave him—I compiled a list of different agencies and safe houses that can assist you. And, of course, we'll help you."

"I can't leave," she said.

"I know you're worried about Daniel," I said, "but if you go to the police they could help you, arrange for you and Daniel to go to a shelter, and then you could try and fight for custody."

Heather shook her head. "You don't understand," she said. "I can't leave. Not now."

"You're the only mother he's ever known," Sarah said. "We'd testify on your behalf."

"It's not just Daniel," Heather said. "I can't leave Viktor."

"Has he threatened you?" I said. "You can file a restraining order."

But Heather was shaking her head. "It's not that."

"What then?" Julie asked.

"I'm pregnant."

chapter nine

SARAH

There are certain moments in life that you can remember with all the clarity of a photograph—where you were and who you were with and how the place looked or sounded or smelled. I can see us just as we were, the four of us sitting in Alison's living room, Heather hunched over on the sofa, hands cradling her midsection as if holding a child, Julie in the chair closest to her, unconsciously tearing a napkin to shreds in her lap, and Alison, so startled that she'd stopped talking, her mouth falling open. Everyone so shocked by what Heather had revealed that for a long minute the only noise you could hear in the room was the faint hiss and pop of logs burning in the fireplace. These are the things I remember with perfect clarity: The slight smell of woodsmoke, the taste of cabernet, dark and dry, the table lamps casting shadows on the walls. The light from the fire illuminating the wine as I refilled my glass, a gush of liquid splashing, deep red, like blood pouring from a wound.

"Well, congratulations," Julie said at last, voice faint and smile forced, but at least she'd thought to say it.

"Yes, that's wonderful," Alison said, and I echoed her, both of us trying to summon an enthusiasm we didn't feel.

"How far along are you?" Julie said.

"I just found out a few days ago." Heather's cheeks were flushed; was she hurt by our muted reaction? Had she planned to surprise us tonight and instead we'd surprised her?

Alison was the one to ask, "Does Viktor know?"

69

Heather shook her head, giving a tremulous smile. "I haven't told him—not yet."

She desperately wanted us to be happy for her, for them, I could hear it in her voice. "But don't you see, this is even more reason that you've got to leave," I said. "It's not safe for you to stay with him, not for you or your baby."

"He wouldn't hurt the baby." She must have seen our skepticism, because she shook her head, insisting, "He wouldn't. And he's never going to hurt me again—I know he won't." Her voice quavered, but she met our eyes, her own wet, but sparkling with some unspoken emotion—anger? Defiance?

In the silence that followed, there was a sudden and insistent buzzing sound. "That's my phone," Heather said, standing up and swiping at her eyes as she tracked the noise to her purse, which was sitting in Alison's front hall. The phone stopped ringing before she finished rooting through her bag for it. We watched her check it, as another buzz announced the arrival of voice mail and then two pings, text messages arriving, one on top of the other. Insistent sounds. Someone demanding her attention. I wasn't surprised when she said, "I have to go."

"Don't leave," Julie said, getting up, too. "Not like this."

"I have to get home for Daniel," Heather said. "I promised him I'd be home in time to read him a bedtime story and it's already after eight."

I don't think any of us believed that it was Daniel she had to be home for, but we didn't argue. We took turns embracing her at the door, and all of us were tearful by the end. In a shaky voice, she said, "Promise me that you won't tell anyone. About the baby, but especially about Viktor."

"You have nothing to be ashamed of," I said. "It's not your fault."

"But I am ashamed," Heather said, fresh tears in her eyes. "I can't deal with other people knowing. You have to promise not to talk about it, not to anyone."

"It's okay," Julie said, rubbing her back. "You're our friend, of course we won't."

"No one," Heather said. "Please. Not even your husbands. No one knows. Promise me?" Her wide-eyed, desperate gaze fell on each of us in turn.

"All right, we promise," I said in a gruff voice, and Julie made a quick cross over her heart.

"Of course we promise," Alison said after a minute, caught up in the moment, desperate like we all were to stop her tears. "It stays just between us."

The hardest person for me not to tell was obviously Eric, but in some ways he was the easiest, too, because my husband really never asked any questions about my friends. I don't think he gave a thought to them at all, unless I talked about them or he could tell that they had upset me in some way. If Eric noticed anything different about me, it was easy enough to tell him I was tired or not feeling well or was just experiencing PMS—the surefire way to get any man to stop asking questions. It wasn't difficult, in that respect, to keep a secret from him, but it was hard on me emotionally.

One evening, about a week after Heather told us, he came home late from a faculty meeting to find me hunting through old law books in the living room, my laptop open on the coffee table with six different legal websites pulled up in a browser. "What's all this?" he said, padding around the piles of books and a meowing Hansel to drop a kiss on my head. "Taking up the law again?" His hair was damp from the snow, the first flurries of the season, and icy drips fell on me, as if I were standing under a tree after a storm.

"Trying to help a friend with a question about domestic abuse and child custody," I said, hoping he'd follow that up with some question of his own so that I'd have an excuse to talk about the situation, even if only obliquely.

"That's nice," he said, distracted and already moving away from me toward the kitchen. "Kids upstairs?"

"Yep." They were playing in their rooms and I had one ear attuned for periodic thuds or faint yelps from above. I heard Eric open the refrigerator and the cats heard it, too, Hansel abandoning me for the kitchen as Gretel, our black Burmese, came padding silently down the stairs, nose lifted as if she could already smell something good. Moochers. I heard rustling sounds as Eric searched through cupboards, annoyed enough to not offer any assistance until he appeared again in the living room to ask sheepishly whether the kids and I had eaten dinner and if there were, perhaps, any leftovers.

"How could he be so oblivious? Didn't he wonder who I was talking about?" I complained to Julie and Alison when I next saw them, although I was quick to point out that if Eric *had* asked I wouldn't have broken our promise to Heather. From the slightly guilty look I saw Alison exchange with Julie, I knew that I wasn't the only one struggling to keep it.

Perhaps to compensate for our inability to tell anyone else, Julie, Alison, and I now talked about it obsessively, whispered conversations as we huddled on the sidelines at the kids' soccer games, or at the coffee shop if Heather wasn't there, or during long phone conversations with one another that consisted mainly of endlessly reviewing our futile efforts to get her to leave.

Every time I saw Heather now I'd surreptitiously check her for injuries. What was that shadow on her collarbone? Was she limping? Did that sweater hide a midriff covered in welts? If she seemed to have more makeup on than usual, I automatically assumed that she was covering something, searching her face for evidence of a bruise or a black eye.

We decided to take turns doing daily check-ins, so our conversations usually opened with that. "Have you heard from Heather today? No? Okay, I'll call her." Or we'd drive up to her house to check on her in person, trying hard, initially, not to make it seem like we were expecting the worst so she wouldn't get offended and shut us out.

It turned out we needn't have worried. Now that she'd finally shared her secret, it was clear that Heather had been desperate to tell somebody about life with Viktor. It took little prompting for her to reveal the latest horrors happening in her marriage, and they were devastating.

"It was my fault—I forgot to send his shirts to the dry cleaner," she said one afternoon, when the scarf she wore slipped and we spotted a cluster of purple spots on her neck.

"Jesus," Alison breathed, leaning forward to look more closely, her face pale. "If you won't think of yourself, think of your children."

"Oh, he wouldn't hurt Daniel. And he only grabbed my throat," Heather said, as if this were somehow better. "He didn't hit me." Like Viktor should get a medal for showing such restraint.

We were at Julie's house after school, the four of us sitting around in her living room, while the kids were off playing in the toy-strewn family room, tucked out of sight down a hall.

"What did Dr. Banerjee say about the mark?" I said, mentioning the ob-gyn I'd recommended.

"She didn't see it." Heather readjusted her scarf so the bruises were covered again.

"Didn't you have an appointment yesterday?"

She hesitated, before saying in a light voice, "Oh, I canceled."

"So she wouldn't notice?" Alison said.

"She would have reported it," I said. "You should let her see because then it wouldn't be you telling anybody, it would be her—she's required by law to report abuse."

"How would that help me?" Heather said. "If Viktor's arrested, he could lose his job and then how would I support myself?" She spoke as if she'd be destitute and I wondered if this was something Viktor had threatened to keep her quiet. "There's just a lot of pressure at work right now, but it won't last forever," she said. "He's promised he'll cut back on his hours."

"Then at least move out until your due date," Julie suggested. "What about your parents? Can't you go stay with them for a while?"

"God no," Heather said, giving a bark of laughter. She shook her head, clearly adamant. "I am never going back there."

We knew Heather came from a small town in West Virginia, and once, maybe two years earlier, her parents had come to visit for Easter. I recalled running into them along Broad Street. They were in their early sixties, but had seemed so much older. They'd looked out of place, too, her father wearing a clip-on tie and a cheap sports coat as if someone had told him the town had a dress code, and her mother, a husk of a woman with traces of the looks that she'd passed on to her daughter—those cheekbones, the pale, catlike eyes—but the beauty obscured by a tight home perm and frumpy dress. I hadn't seen them since and Heather didn't talk about them much. Was she ashamed of them or was their absence from her life Viktor's doing?

"Check into a hotel then," Alison said. "One of those Residence Inns. Or what about renting a place? That might be nicer—cheaper, too."

Heather shook her head. "I can't."

"Why not?" I said. "I've seen some great places online."

Her face flushed and she looked away as she said, "It's not about the place, it's about the money. My cards are tied to Viktor's accounts. Everything is in his name. Everything. He wouldn't pay for it."

I was stunned—I think we all were. I thought of all the times I'd seen her wearing a new outfit or off for another day at the spa and envied her financial freedom. I hadn't realized it came with such tight purse strings and that she didn't hold the purse. "You need to divorce him," I said. "I can connect you with a great attorney. I'll call her for you."

"No!" Heather cried, before repeating it in a lower voice. "No. Thank you. But I already told you—I'm not leaving him, I can't."

"Don't be so stupid," I muttered.

"Sarah!" Julie was aghast.

"I'm sorry, but c'mon! We all think she should leave him."

"It's not our decision to make," Alison said, but her voice was very sad. "It's Heather's choice."

There was an awkward silence, and then Julie said gently, "Well, you're always welcome to come and stay with me." She smiled at Heather and took another sip of the green tea smoothies she'd made for everybody. I would have preferred some wine to help cut the stress we were all under, but apparently since

Heather couldn't drink, none of us would out of solidarity. I sipped my own smoothie, peering around at Julie's house and wondering what it would be like to live there—probably like staying at a hotel, or a modern art gallery.

The first time I'd been to Julie's, back when our older children were babies, I'd been intimidated by her ultramodern and immaculate house, a plaster-and-steel series of stacked cubes designed by an architect that she'd met when she'd sold him some investment property. "He studied with Philip Johnson," she'd told me as she led me across pale hardwood floors enlivened here and there by colorful rugs that she casually informed me had been picked up when she and Brian vacationed in Turkey.

With the designer furniture and refined, minimalist décor, the house had not screamed kid-friendly, and I remember making a silent prediction that in six months the matching set of dove-gray modernist sofas and hexagonal glass coffee table would be covered with sticky little handprints and stains.

Fast-forward nine years and I was sitting on that same sofa, which Julie had recently talked about replacing, but only because she'd grown bored with the look; the dove-gray wool was still immaculate, the glass in the coffee table shining in a way that nothing ever did at my house. Of course, Julie's secret weapon was the high-end cleaning service that came weekly.

"Thank you," Heather murmured. "That's very nice of you to offer."

"You can stay with me, too," Alison said. "Although given the clutter at my house I think I'd take Julie's offer."

"Ditto," I said, an easy offer to make because I knew, we all knew, that Heather wasn't going to accept.

We were silent for a moment, sitting around the gas fireplace, also ultramodern, a line of blue-tipped flames dancing above a row of smooth river rocks. A large abstract oil painting, done by some apparently "well-known" artist, hung above the fireplace, its violent red slashes always striking me as incongruous—as did the whole, cold house—with Julie, who was so warm, so down-to-earth, so bubbly.

"What if you told Viktor you need some time away to rest because of the baby," Julie said. "Like you said, he wouldn't want to hurt his own child."

Heather looked up at us, mouth opening like she was going to say something, but then she closed it and looked back down, fiddling with the straw in her drink.

"What is it?" Alison said, and then her voice darkened. "Did something happen?"

Heather looked up, large tears welling in her eyes. "I haven't told him."

"About the baby?" I said, surprised. "Why not?"

"He told me he doesn't want more children," she said, swiping at her eyes. "He'll want me to get rid of it."

"Oh, I'm sure that's not the case," Julie said, rushing to embrace her. Alison and I exchanged a look as we joined them on the couch.

"You're so kind," Heather said, looking at each of us in turn. I'll remember forever how she looked, leaning forward in her seat, her face luminous, hands clasped together on her knees, both intent and nervous, her lovely smile a little strained but sincere. "I'm so lucky," she said, a word that was jarring given the circumstances. "I'm so lucky to have you for my friends."

Again, she was the first to leave, making excuses that none of us believed. Daniel was engrossed in playing Hungry Hungry Hippos in the family room, and was so angry at being interrupted that he aimed a kick at the game, scattering the board and the pieces. I'm sure I wasn't the only mother wondering if he'd inherited that temper from his father. And also just like Viktor, a few minutes later Daniel presented as a smiling and happy little boy, cheerfully trotting off to the car with his mother after she'd bribed him with the promise of a stop at the frozen yogurt shop if he came away quietly.

The specter of fear descended on us, our phone calls increasingly frantic, the litany of Heather's injuries piling up: The black eye that she said she'd gotten running into a door. The cut on her lip that she insisted she'd done herself. The limp she had because she'd "tripped." The series of spots on the inside skin of her forearm that looked suspiciously like cigarette burns. That last injury marked a turning point for Julie. She'd still believed that something could be done, that if Viktor "got help," then everything would restore itself in that marriage, but no longer. Cigarette burns were so obviously and deliberately cruel; they were also impossible to explain away as an accident.

"They were right there," she said in a tremulous voice, holding out her own arm and pointing with a shaking hand. "He isn't going to stop until he's killed her." She looked so stricken that both Alison and I hugged her, the three of us holding on to one another for a long moment, helpless.

"Why doesn't she fight back?" I said. "If she won't leave the bastard at least she could defend herself."

"She's afraid of him," Alison said. "He makes her feel powerless."

"Then we've got to give her the power," Julie said, taking the words out of my mouth and sounding surprisingly determined for someone who until recently had been eager to accept Heather's excuses as reality.

"You've got to keep a record of what Viktor's doing," I said to Heather the next time we were all at Crazy Mocha. "Take photos of your injuries."

"Shh." Her gaze darted around the shop, anxious that someone might overhear our conversation. She whispered, "Viktor checks my phone—he doesn't trust me."

"Then use this," Alison said, pulling a small digital camera out of her purse. Heather didn't ask why Alison just happened to be carrying a camera with her, and none of us volunteered that we'd talked about it beforehand and come up with this idea. We'd anticipated that she might argue with us, give us some reason she couldn't take the photos, or deny again that things were that bad, but she just took the camera from Alison and quickly shoved it in her purse.

We berated ourselves for the injuries that had gone unnoticed, like the broken arm from a year ago that Heather said came from a holiday skiing accident, which we now knew had been broken by Viktor. I thought of us all writing happy phrases on her cast and felt sick. Even worse was remembering how once I'd seen a huge bouquet of dark pink roses at her house and teased her, "Oh, look how sweet—someone must love you very much," completely unaware that these were a guilt gift from Viktor.

Sometimes I look back and wonder how things might have been different if we'd just pulled up outside that enormous house on the hill and packed up Heather's belongings, hers and Daniel's, ignoring her protests, sedating her if necessary, and driving them away to Julie's house, or Alison's, or mine. But none of us did that. We were polite women living in a civilized society where people rarely did more than whisper about one another's marriages. We tried reasoning with her and spent hours worrying about her, but ultimately we did nothing, watching from a distance like movie-goers at a disaster film, tense and expectant, waiting for the awful yet inevitable conclusion.

chapter ten

I think about leaving all the time, but where would I go? Back to West Virginia and coal country? Back to living at my mother's house as if I'm fifteen again and not thirty? He'll follow me there; he's said he would. He likes to tell me that now that he's got me he's never letting go.

Sometimes when Viktor's at work I take one of the large suitcases out of the closet in the guest room and open it on our bed. I bring out my clothes from the walk-in closet, folding them carefully, stacking them in as tightly as possible. I plan as I pack: I will take all the jewelry that he's given me, the necklaces that weren't my taste, and the rings he chose because *he* liked the stones. I will take the emergency cash that he keeps in a drawer in his desk and the money that he's left for the cleaning people. I will call for a taxi and have them drive me to the bus station. Not in Pittsburgh, that is too close and he'd think to look there. I will have the driver take me to the bus station in Greensburg and from there I will board a bus for Georgia or somewhere that is warm, but not a tourist destination. A place he wouldn't think to look for me.

But as I stand there packing I'm already seeing the flaws in this plan—there isn't enough cash to get far. Even if I take the money in Daniel's clown-shaped bank, I would have barely enough to afford the bus ticket to Georgia. That isn't enough to begin again; I'd have to sell the jewelry first. Viktor might think of this, too. He might have the police put a trace on the jewelry, or claim that

79

it wasn't mine to sell since he purchased all of it. He'll have the receipts to prove it because he's a details person—meticulous, orderly, bothered by things that aren't neat and tidy. Even if I did manage to sell to a pawnshop or a private buyer, how much am I really likely to get from all of it? It's not nearly enough to live comfortably.

I can't do it, I can't leave. I unpack the suitcase and put it away before he gets home. The clothes are back in the closet, the money back in the drawer. His tires are snaking up the drive as I look around frantically to make sure that there is no sign that I was considering departure.

"You're home early," I say, trying to sound excited.

Daniel is at his grandmother's. It turns out that Viktor has arranged this ahead of time—a special night just for us. "I want to spend time with my wife," he says, speaking of me, as he often does, as if I'm a possession. He leads me to the bedroom where at his direction I put on the silk negligée he bought me, an ugly shade of salmon pink that was his choice, not mine. He is ready before I am, sitting there on the side of the bed in his briefs and socks, the dead-white skin of his chest stark under the full light that he likes. I imagine that it reminds him of an operating room. When he pats the center of the bed, I dutifully cross the room and climb on to it before presenting myself like a patient, because that's what he wants, lying still on my back while he runs his cold hands over my body. He straddles me on the bed and I close my eyes, removing myself from this place, but he says, "Look at me, I want you to look at me." So I open them, but I can't meet his gaze, looking away from the intensity in his eyes to focus on a spot on his forehead. He examines me the way I imagine him checking his patients on the operating table, carefully perusing every inch of me through the reading glasses he sometimes wears, even in bed. I imagine what he would think if I suggested Botox for the thin trenches running across his forehead.

The bruise on my arm is an interruption in this fantasy he is enacting, a blemish on the blow-up doll beneath him. He runs a finger lightly across it, once, then again, watching my face, waiting for each wince. "How did this get here?" he says, but of course this question is rhetorical. He isn't really asking, because he's too busy erasing the mark, reshaping my arm mentally without it. But it won't go easily, he can't ignore it. He cups his hand over it—out of sight, now out of mind. It clearly disturbs him, this mark, and he keeps coming back to it, finally kissing the spot too hard several times. "There now, all better," he says at last, like an owner soothing a pet he's stepped on.

chapter eleven

JULIE

I'd always been a good sleeper, the person who takes forever to finish the book on the nightstand because she barely gets through two pages before nodding off. How many nights had Brian tugged a novel gently out of my slack hands and pulled up the covers, all without me waking? This changed after we found out about Heather.

Every night I'd lie there in bed, unable to stop my brain from cycling through Heather's situation over and over again. I'm a planner and a problem solver—a keeper of daily lists that can be neatly checked off, a person who says yes where others say no, a certificate-bearing graduate of multiple, expensive motivational seminars. I'd fire-walked for goodness' sake, practically skipping across the hot coals while fellow attendees with near-religious devotion chanted "Believe and do! Believe and do!" to the beat of a goatskin drum. But this was a situation that I couldn't fix, and so I chewed at it in my mind, over and over, tugging and pulling, like a terrier with a rat, trying to conquer it.

"What's going on?" Brian asked one night after weeks of my insomnia. In stereotypical fashion, it had taken him that long to notice something was up. He's on the road so often, and when he is home, he's got his head stuck to his phone or focused on his laptop. I once experimented with being a brunette and it took him five full days to realize that this change from red hair to brown was what had been throwing him off.

It was the Saturday after Thanksgiving. The holiday had passed in its usual bustle of shopping and traveling to Grandma's house. It wasn't over the river or through the woods, but my mother's house was far enough away that I'd worried about what would happen if Heather needed me. My mother always insisted on hosting Thanksgiving dinner, even though her house was so small that we had to set up separate card tables in the living room to seat everybody. I'd endured the usual jokes from my aunts and cousins about being assigned to bring the store-bought rolls and drinks because "everybody knows that Julie doesn't cook," while ducking periodically into the privacy of my mother's bedroom to check my phone.

"I'm fine," Heather said, sounding impatient but unharmed when I'd finally reached her. I could hear some fast-paced, Eastern European–sounding music in the background. "We're at his aunt's house," she said when I asked. And then she whispered, "It's okay—he's in a good mood."

The way she talked about Viktor's moods reminded me of a weather forecaster. I felt a momentary relief at hearing that things were fine, but of course he'd be on his best behavior out in public. Sarah had read some articles about how abuse could actually get worse over the holidays because of the additional stress. Christmas was coming and Viktor was likely to be around more.

I was worrying about this as Brian and I sat side by side in bed, when he looked up from the news he was scrolling through on his tablet and asked me what was going on. Apparently I hadn't turned a page in my romance novel in a while. "How come you're not conking out like you usually do? Is something wrong?"

I gave up any pretense of reading and tossed the book aside. "No, I've just got a lot on my mind."

"The McCormick sale?" he asked with understanding. He put his tablet aside and drew me into his arms. "You'll get them to the closing table eventually, babe. You always do."

I stiffened as his strong arms came around me, feeling slightly panicky as they wrapped around my midsection. *Viktor grabbing Heather at the party, Viktor's finger marks on her neck.* "Hey, you really are stressed," Brian said with surprise, feeling my re-sistance. "It's just one sale, hon, you've got to let it go."

If only it were about a sale. I could only look back with won-der at feeling so much anxiety over something so trivial. No one was going to lose his or her life over a house sale.

"It isn't about the McCormick house or any other sale," I said, turning to him in bed, thinking that this was it—he'd asked and I was going to tell him. "It's about a friend—she's being hurt—"

At that moment, we heard Aubrey cry out, a prolonged, high-pitched sound that startled both of us. She'd been waking from bad dreams recently and I'd wondered if she was somehow chan-neling the anxiety I was feeling. "My turn," Brian said, throwing back the covers. "Back in a few—just hold that thought."

Before he'd even made it out of the master bedroom, I knew that I couldn't tell him. I'd made a promise to Heather and felt ashamed that I'd almost broken it, and for no better reason than *my* own fear, which was nothing compared to what she had to be feeling. There was nothing Brian could do about it anyway; there was no point in telling him. I switched off the lamp on my nightstand and rolled onto my side, closing my eyes and willing myself to be asleep before he came back. It didn't work—I was as fully awake as I'd been every other night for weeks—but I kept my eyes closed and my breathing even as he got back into bed, feeling him hover over me for a second before his lips gently grazed my cheek. He was engrossed again in his tablet in a min-ute and missed the tears that I couldn't stop from slipping sound-lessly beneath my closed eyelids.

Being so sleep-deprived can do odd things to one's perception. I tapped the fender of the car in front of me one morning as I waited to merge onto Route 65 because I swore I'd seen his car moving. The irate driver sprang from his car yelling, "You! This!," waving a hand at me and then at his car's rear end and back again, while I tried to apologize and riffled through my glove box for insurance information, the traffic swelling behind us, a cacophony of angry voices and car horns.

A few days later, I thought I spotted Heather at the Whole Foods in the city, where I'd stopped after a realty meeting. Pushing my cart slowly through a maze of organic, vegan, and gluten-free shelves, I came around a corner and spotted a familiar figure at the other end of the aisle. She had her back to me, but I knew it was her, that lithe body and messy blond bun, the thin legs in yoga pants and an oversize sweater. She was talking to someone as she rounded the corner, and I swore I recognized that languid, lilting sound of her voice, but when I turned the corner after her, I saw that it wasn't Heather, but another woman altogether, part of a couple, the dark-haired, muscular man she was with resting a brawny arm protectively across her shoulders and bending to kiss the bare skin at the nape of her neck.

A week went by, then another—time passing in the whirlwind of activity that is life with a job and children. I'd wonder how it came to be Friday when it felt as if I'd just woken up on Monday morning, and the struggle to stay on top of all my responsibilities, in addition to worrying about Heather, had left me seriously exhausted. That's why, while I realized that things were getting worse, I didn't understand just how bad, and by that time it was too late.

The day before it happened was a Tuesday. I remember waking that morning with the same drugged feeling I'd had every morning of late. Unable to sleep for most of the night, I'd finally fall into a slumber so deep that when the alarm went off it felt like coming out of anesthesia.

I remember dragging myself out to the bus stop with Owen and Aubrey while gulping down a cup of coffee, and once the children had been successfully loaded on the bus and waved off, having a quick conversation with Alison. It was supposed to be her turn to check in with Heather, but she asked if I could cover, because she was late on a project. She looked as tired as I felt, shadows under her eyes, clothing and hair both rumpled as if she'd gotten out of bed and come straight there, which perhaps she had. I glanced at my watch; my closing wasn't until ten that morning. "I can do it. I've got a form for the fashion show that I need to give her anyway, so it's an excuse to drop by."

The drive to Heather's took me no more than ten minutes, and only because I slowed down for lights. After the minor fender bender, I wasn't risking any more accidents, but I also hoped to arrive after Viktor had left for work. When I turned in through the two stone pillars at the end of her driveway, the radio was playing some pop song by a singer I didn't recognize, whose refrain, uttered in a low, mournful voice, was "Why did you have to hurt me?" I pulled up in front of the house and stopped the car, the voice cutting off abruptly at "why." The only other sounds—the knocks and bumps of the engine as it cooled off and the slam of the car door as I got out—suddenly seemed very loud. There were no other cars on the driveway, but to the right of the house was a three-car garage, ample storage for Viktor's beloved bottle-green Mercedes as well as Heather's BMW. I was conscious of my heels clicking on the stone pavers as I walked to the front door, practically tiptoeing in an effort to avoid the noise. I had to ring the bell three times, listening to the faint melodious chime, before Heather finally answered the door, breathing hard and tying the strings of a filmy silk robe around her. Apparently I'd gotten her out of bed. "What time is it?" she said, stifling a yawn as she leaned forward to give me a kiss. As I stepped past her into the hall I caught a whiff of cigarette smoke.

"Is Viktor here?" I asked in a low voice.

She shook her head. "He left a while ago."

"How are you?" I asked as she closed the door, trying to act as if I weren't scrutinizing her. She was sensitive to it; she'd asked me multiple times not to stare at her.

With the door closed, the hallway was dim. Her skin, always pale, looked practically translucent in this light. It was hard to tell whether the purple smudges under her eyes were shadows or souvenirs from Viktor's fist. She wandered down the hall, a ghostly figure, and I followed after her into the kitchen.

"Can I get you some coffee?" Heather asked, yawning again as she opened a cupboard.

"Yes, please, that would be great," I said, amazed that my voice could sound so normal when my mind kept showing me shattered glass, cupboard doors hanging open like hairs standing on end.

There was something off about the house, the stillness. Of course, I've been in hundreds of houses—some places so cluttered that I practically need a hiking stick to fend my way through mountains of junk, and others that are absolutely vacant, where dust balls linger in corners and even whispers echo. Homes have an energy that you can feel the moment you walk in the door. Some people pooh-pooh this and laugh at any mention of feng shui or bad flow, but as a Realtor I take these vibes seriously, so trust me when I tell you that there was something different in the house that day, some negative energy.

"I just wanted to drop off the fashion-show form," I said as I pulled it from my purse.

Heather used her expensive espresso machine to make me a cup and then pushed the buttons again for hers.

"Are you allowed to have caffeine?" I asked, surprised. "My doctor always said no."

She stopped short, jerking the cup back out as the machine continued to fill, and pouring it down the drain. "I forgot," she said with a rueful smile. "Good thing you're here." She took a bottle of water from the refrigerator and the form from me. "I told you that I don't think I can do it."

"You don't have to answer now—just give it some thought."

Her eyes betrayed her skepticism, but she said nothing, just laying the form on the counter between us, before taking a long swallow from her water bottle. My own nervousness made me prattle on about the fashion show, desperate to try to ease the tension that hung in the air. Heather didn't seem to notice. I hid behind my coffee, my eyes darting from her to the rest of the house, while she stood there fidgeting with the cap on her water bottle. Could she have lied? Could Viktor still be there, lurking upstairs, waiting for me to leave?

This is what I'd berate myself for later. This moment. I'd known things were getting bad, but I didn't realize just how bad they were until that morning in the house—the feeling of someone there, of some malevolent presence. I should have done something, but instead, after a few minutes, I said my good-byes, gulping in the air when I was on the other side of the door as if I'd been unable to breathe.

chapter twelve

ALISON

The strange thing about a secret is it longs to be told. Someone can confide personal news—a terminal illness, having
lied on a job application, even an indiscretion with a stranger—
and you might simply focus on the story itself, the details and
the implications, but if they add that caveat "don't tell," then suddenly that's all you can think about doing.

At least that's how it was for me. At the bus stop in the afternoons or at the soccer pitch on Saturday mornings, I'd wonder if
any of the other parents suspected anything. "Have you ever noticed anything odd about Viktor?" I always wanted to ask them.

Finally, desperate to talk to someone besides Julie and Sarah, I
drove one morning to Indiana, Pennsylvania, to talk to my
brother. Sean is a police officer there, a job he's held since he
graduated from the academy back when he was nineteen. It was
over an hour's drive and I was behind in work, but I justified the
trip and telling him because as a cop he'd be able to offer some
real help. The truth was that I just needed to tell someone.

Sean is four years older than I am and it's always been the two
of us against the world. Our mother's family came from Indiana
and some of my happiest memories are of time spent there, the
two of us playing in the summer with cousins, or visiting at
Christmastime. I know this is what brought Sean there—a happy
place, the chance to build the life we'd never had. Stability.

He was out on a case when I arrived, so the desk sergeant

ushered me into a comfortable meeting room, joking that he could let me wait in a holding cell if I preferred. The secretary brought me coffee a short time later. It was all very friendly and yet just being in that building made me feel tense.

As time ticked away I thought I'd made a mistake by coming. What if my brother asked for Viktor's name? Or wanted to contact Heather? Just as I was standing up to leave, Sean opened the door.

"This is a nice surprise," he said with a big smile, giving me a hug. He looked good in his uniform. Sean had been promoted to lieutenant a year earlier and I wondered how many women he'd turned down over the years. "What's up? You've been ducking so many of my calls that I thought you'd crossed me off your Christmas list." He laughed, but I winced.

"Sorry, I know, I've been busy," I said, glancing at my watch to avoid meeting his gaze. "I just wanted to say hi, but I should get back. I need to pick up the kids."

"Hey, I was just kidding. You can't leave yet—I just got here. Sit down for a minute." He took a seat at the table and I sat back down across from him. He nodded at my mug. "You want some more coffee?"

"No thanks."

"I know it sucks. I'm trying to get the department to cough up money for a Keurig." He sat back, folding his arms across his chest. "You got the latest letter?"

I should have known he'd bring it up. That's why he'd been calling. That's why I'd been avoiding him. Heather's situation had distracted me from my own problems. I nodded, shifting in my seat. "They always show up, just like a bad penny."

He laughed, but his warm brown eyes weren't smiling. "Did you read it?"

"Yes."

"So you know about the cancer?"

I nodded again. He didn't say anything and I knew he wanted me to speak, to ask questions or express concern. I felt that familiar acid wash down my throat. "How long?"

"They don't know." Sean shrugged. "Six months? A year? Might be longer, but the health care's not that great, you know?"

"Do you expect me to feel sorry about that?" I snapped.

"Of course not. C'mon, Alison, I'm not the enemy."

"No, you just want me to talk to them." I stood up and shouldered my purse, heading for the door. Sean came after me, touching my arm. The lightest touch, but it stopped me. He didn't grab me; he'd never do that.

"I don't want to talk about it," I said without turning, trying to steady my voice. "I can't."

"Okay, I know, it's okay." He moved his hand to my shoulder, a gentle squeeze. "But don't leave, not like this. Please?"

It was the sadness in his voice that made me come back to the table and sit down once again. We disagreed fundamentally on this issue, but I knew it was as painful for him as it was for me. He was my big brother. He was the one I'd reached for when I was little and scared and he'd never failed to return that trust, his hand always closing protectively over mine.

He rubbed a hand over his cropped brown hair and smiled, trying to start over. "So if you didn't come here to talk about that, then why did you come?"

I cleared my throat, fiddling with my purse straps. "I wanted to ask you about a friend of mine. I think she's being abused by her spouse."

Sean's face registered surprise for a second before he frowned, hands clenching into fists. "Is this really a *friend*? Is Michael hurting you?"

"No, it's not Michael—how can you even think that?" As soon as the words were out of my mouth I knew how foolish that sounded. He shot me a look that said as much. "It's not Michael," I said. "I'm not the one being abused."

"Swear," he said. "Swear on the kids that you're telling the truth."

I held up two fingers like a Boy Scout. "I swear on the kids."

He looked only slightly mollified. "What's going on with your friend?"

I filled him in on Heather's situation and he listened, asking a few pertinent questions. When he asked for Viktor's name, I shook my head.

"I can't tell you that—I promised not to."

"If I knew who it was, I could call the Sewickley police and they'd send someone to talk to him. They wouldn't say it came from you—it could be an anonymous tip."

"She'd know it was me. I can't do that."

He nodded, running his hand over the fake grain in the laminate table. "It doesn't work most of the time anyway. It might even backfire—he might hurt her worse for telling someone. There are a lot of shelters she could go to."

"I know, I've given her all that information, but she won't leave him."

"Does she know she can file a restraining order against him if she does? Because that's what I'd advise her to do."

I shook my head. "She won't do it; he's got a prominent job and she's afraid of losing her stepson."

Sean shook his head. "There's not a whole lot that can be done if she won't take that initial step. She's got to leave and file a restraining order. Even if someone else called the police on him, you know as well as I do that victims usually won't press charges. And you can't force them to leave—it doesn't work. She's got to make that decision."

He changed the subject after that, talking about the holidays and what he wanted to buy the kids, and whether he'd make it to Sewickley on Christmas day itself or the day after, depending on his work schedule. As he walked me out to my car he brought up Heather again. "Cheer up, sis. She could leave him—she might be stronger than you think." He shrugged, shaking his head in a knowing fashion. "If there's one thing I've learned in this job it's that people can surprise you."

I tried hard to believe what Sean said, to convince myself that Heather would find the strength to leave Viktor and everything would be okay. It didn't work—I'm not that optimistic by nature.

Christmas came and went, a flurry of decorating and gift buying that seemed more frenzied that year than ever before, but maybe it was because I couldn't focus, jumping every time the phone rang, expecting the worst.

On New Year's Eve, the four of us met at Crazy Mocha in the afternoon for a quick get-together without the kids. I left Michael at home staring at college football on TV with the dog sprawled at his feet, while the kids ran in and out of the house, setting up sand buckets and plastic cups on the back porch to catch enough lazily falling snowflakes to "make snow cones."

"Have you told him about the pregnancy yet?" Sarah asked Heather when she waved away the gingerbread man that Sarah offered, saying it made her queasy.

"Not yet," she said, "I'm planning how to do it." She'd been the last of us to arrive, hurrying in looking pale and wan, buying only bottled water. She'd lowered herself carefully into her seat, but she had no visible marks that day. Of course, with her high-necked sweater and jeans, there wasn't much skin to see.

"You've got to tell him soon," Julie said. "You're going to start showing."

"I know, I already am," Heather said, and she smiled at that, looking around to make sure no one was watching before lifting the hem of her baggy sweater so we could admire her nonexistent "baby bump."

"That's not a bump, it's barely a burp," Sarah said, and Julie and I laughed weakly, but Heather looked kind of offended.

"What do you think of Abigail?" she asked. It was only when she added "Or Zoe?" that I realized she was talking about baby names.

"Those are pretty," Julie said, nudging me, and I nodded, trying to summon a smile, though my own stomach felt suddenly queasy.

"It could be a boy," Sarah said, tearing off the gingerbread man's head. "Daniel might like a brother."

Heather ignored her. "I really like Emma, but it's been used too much, don't you think?"

I thought the whole conversation was surreal, but I couldn't bring myself to say anything to upset her. She reminded me of a child at that moment, sitting there talking about this name or that, while nobody spoke about what we all feared would happen when her husband finally found out about the baby.

As I walked home through the snow, I had a sudden memory of another New Year's Eve, long ago in Braddock, when my mother had let Sean and me stay up past midnight, handing us wooden spoons and pans to bang. "It's going to be a good year," she'd said to us after the ball dropped, her eyes wide and painfully bright. "It's going to be so good—just you wait and see."

I spent the New Year and every day for the first few weeks in January dreading that phone call telling me that Viktor had killed Heather. Yet the night the call finally came I wasn't at all prepared.

Buzzing. In my dreams I waved at my face, chasing away a wasp, but the noise persisted. I woke in the dark, disoriented. My cell phone buzzed again. I fumbled for it on the nightstand, answering without looking to see the ID of the caller. "Hello?"

"Alison?" The voice was panicked; my name ended on a high-pitched sob. "Help me!" A shriek.

I sat straight up, looking toward Michael, but he took a sleeping pill most nights and didn't stir. "Heather?" I whispered. "Is that you?"

Instead of answering, she sobbed again. "Help me! Please, I need you to help me! Hurry!"

"I'll be right there," I said in a low voice, slipping from my bed to the closet, struggling to change out of pajamas while balancing the phone. That son of a bitch had finally gone too far. "Have you called the police? Call them right now, Heather."

"I can't." Her breathing was ragged and hiccupping. All I could hear was her wild sobbing, as if she had her hand cupped around the phone.

"I'll call them," I said. "I'll call them and I'll come over."

"Don't!" she wailed even louder. "No police; just you!"

Michael made a snorting sound and I froze, looking back

toward the bed, but he'd merely been rolling onto his side, his breathing once again deep and even.

"What did he do to you?" I said to Heather, picturing her hiding from Viktor. "Are you bleeding badly? Can he get to you?"

"No!" A long, drawn-out wail.

"Where is he?"

She didn't answer, her sobs increasing. I tried to listen for background noise, expecting to hear Viktor pounding on their bedroom door, but it was impossible to make out any sounds beyond her wails.

"Heather, where is he? Where is Viktor?"

"He's dead!"

chapter thirteen

ALISON

What is it about the dark that transforms the ordinary into something frightening and otherworldly? The plane trees along the narrow, winding road were ghostly in the headlights, their branches outstretched like arms reaching to stop me as I raced toward Heather's house. My pulse was racing just as fast. At a traffic light I cried out at the sudden flutter of a large gray moth batting against my windshield. How was that creature alive in this cold? How could Viktor be dead? I struggled to believe it. Julie didn't seem to believe it either. "*He's* dead?" she repeated when I called her from the car.

"I don't know—that's what Heather says. I'm on my way to her house. Call Sarah, okay?"

"Yes, of course. Maybe it's a mistake?"

"Maybe."

But Julie hadn't heard Heather's voice, her panic. "Hurry," she'd sobbed on the phone to me. "Hurry, please!"

I almost missed the entrance to her house; the gas lamps that topped the stone pillars weren't lit. Braking hard, I quickly reversed and jerked the wheel to turn onto her drive, the grind and groan of my car's engine jarringly loud. The lights that lined either side of the road weren't lit either, and I jumped as a branch from a bare forsythia bush brushed against my car.

The drive wound up and up, seeming twice as long as it did in the daytime, and I felt a slight panic that it would go on forever. Finally I reached the top of the hill and the house came into view, lights blazing from the first-floor windows and pouring from an open bay in the three-car garage to the right. As I parked, I saw a dark shadow step into the light of the open garage door, a figure in black, pacing nervously. It was Heather, wearing jeans and a black turtleneck, her blond hair in disarray.

"What happened?" I said breathlessly as I got out of the car.

She pointed toward the open garage door, giving me an unblinking stare, clearly in shock. As I hurried toward her, another car crested the hill, the sweep of the headlights startling both of us. It was Julie, and as she stepped out of her car, Sarah's car pulled in behind her.

"I shot him," Heather said, and then she just kept repeating it, "I shot him, I shot him," her voice as blank as her face, while she tugged at the fingers of one fine-boned hand, then the other.

Sarah pushed past her into the garage, and I called after her, "Careful! Don't touch anything." Julie looked from Heather to the open door and back again. Then we heard Sarah moan, "Oh, God," and Julie followed me as I headed into the garage.

Viktor's bottle-green Mercedes was parked inside, but the lights were on, and now that I was close I could hear the faint *ping*ing of a key left in the ignition. I saw a foot first, clad in a black leather men's dress shoe, sticking out of the open driver's door. As I got closer, I saw Viktor's body slumped sideways in the driver's seat, his head falling forward onto the passenger side. He might have been napping except for the gaping wound in the back of his head. Blood and what I guessed was brain matter, a dark, sticky mass in his light brown hair, dripped in rivulets onto his face and pooled on the leather passenger seat. There was an overpowering smell, like raw meat, with a faint rotten-egg odor on top of it. I gagged, rearing back and covering my mouth.

"Jesus!" Julie cried. "What happened? What did you do?"

"I had to do it, he was going to kill me," Heather said in a dull voice behind us.

"Where's Daniel?" I asked. I looked around, terrified that he'd seen this final, awful violence between his parents.

Heather was staring at the car. Up close, under the garage lights, we could see that she had a fine mist of blood freckling her face and hair and spattered across her shirt.

"Heather?" Sarah snapped her fingers in front of the blank face. "Daniel. Where's Daniel?"

"He's not here." Her voice was a scary monotone. A new chilling fear swept through me—had she killed him, too, in some misguided act of motherly love?

"Where is he?" I persisted.

She finally blinked, looking away from the car to me. It seemed to take her forever to form the words. "He's with Viktor's mother."

"Thank God," I said. She was trembling and I reached to try to comfort her, only then realizing that I was trembling, too.

"Where's the gun?" Julie asked.

Heather slowly raised a finger, pointing, and we saw a small black handgun lying in a corner of the garage floor as if it had been tossed or kicked over there.

"We need to call the police," I said. "This was self-defense, the police will understand." I pulled out my cell phone, only to have it snatched away by Sarah.

"Don't," she said.

"We have to call now," I said, trying to take it back from her. "The blood is congealing."

The word made Julie moan, but Sarah only shook her head. "Not yet. Not until we know what happened."

I realized she was right. What would the police say if they saw Viktor's body and his blood spattered all over Heather? Sarah gave me back my phone and I slipped it into my coat pocket as she leaned into the open driver's door, careful not to touch anything. "Where were you standing when you shot him, Heather?" she asked as she stepped back, crossing around the front of the car to peer in through the passenger window.

"Over there," Heather said, pointing to a spot about five feet from the car where Julie was standing. Julie immediately moved away, as if that spot was tainted.

Sarah stepped back around the car to us and said to me in a low voice, "He was shot in the back of the head."

"Did Viktor hit you?" Julie said, sounding desperate. "Is that what happened? He was hurting you?"

Heather nodded slowly. "He was going to kill me."

I looked around the garage, trying to make sense of it. It was the closest bay to the house, with a connecting door, and against the back wall, beyond Viktor's car, was a workbench with drawers and some tools mounted with hooks. It was hard to imagine Viktor, much less Heather, using any of them; they looked untouched. Viktor was inside his car and nothing else seemed out of place. "Did he have the gun?"

Heather shook her head, clearly still dazed.

"Listen, you need to start at the beginning and tell us everything," Sarah said. "Now, Heather!" The last came out as a snap and Heather flinched.

"Sarah, don't," I said in a reproving tone, but she wheeled on me.

"We don't have time to waste," she barked, eyes wild and small body trembling.

That was when I noticed just how cold it was in the garage. The rest of us had coats or down vests over sweatpants or pajamas, but Heather didn't and her feet were bare and almost blue with cold against the concrete floor.

"She's in shock, I'll go get her a coat and shoes," Julie said, starting for the door into the house. I stepped in front of her.

"Wait, this is a crime scene. We can't touch anything."

As I said that, Heather started talking, the story spilling out in a monotone. "I was going to leave him. He was supposed to be at the hospital late—an emergency surgery—so I sent Daniel to stay with his grandmother while I packed. But the surgery was canceled and Viktor came home early. When he saw the suitcase he started yelling—he shoved me up against the wall and said the only way I was leaving him was in a body bag."

Julie inhaled sharply and Heather paused for a second, but Sarah urged her on, voice impatient. "What happened next?"

"He knocked me down," Heather said, her face losing some of that slack expression. "And then he said he was going to go get Daniel, that I was a horrible mother, and that I was never going to set foot out of the house again. That he'd kill me first."

"Is that when you got the gun?" I asked.

She nodded, face pale and eyes huge. "I went to the hiding place in the closet and took the gun down. I thought I would just hold it, just hold on to it so he'd let me leave."

Her voice had dropped to a whisper; there was no other sound in the garage except the insistent pinging of the ignition.

"Somebody shut that damn thing off," Sarah said before doing it herself, reaching in past the body and using a sleeve to turn the key to avoid leaving fingerprints.

"So you showed Viktor the gun?" Julie prompted.

"He said, 'What the hell do you think you're doing?' I said I was leaving and he couldn't stop me. But my hands were shaking and he started walking toward me. He said, 'You're not going to shoot me.' And I couldn't do it—I was too scared."

Heather started speaking faster and I could feel my heart rate quicken in response, reliving it with her. "He yanked the gun from my hand, slammed me up against the wall, and then he pointed it at me. I begged him not to shoot me." Her voice climbed. "I begged him."

"How did you get the gun back?" Sarah asked.

"He tossed it on the ground." Heather flung her hand out in imitation, her voice incredulous. "I thought I was going to die and he just laughed. He said, 'You're never going to leave me— you're nothing without me.'

"I picked the gun up off the floor and followed him out to the garage." She held up her hand as if she were still holding the gun. "He was looking away and I thought, *This is it—shoot him now before he kills me*. And it just went off. Bang!"

We all jumped at her shout.

"It's self-defense," Julie said. "We call the police and explain it to them."

"She shot him in the back of the head," Sarah said, running a hand through her hair. "It doesn't look like self-defense."

"We can tell them what happened," Julie said. "Tell them how abusive he's been."

"Did he hurt you today?" I said. "Do you have any bruises right now?"

Heather slowly looked down at her body, staring for a second at her hands, which were speckled with her husband's blood, before plucking at the bottom of her shirt, lifting it up so that we could see the pale skin underneath. She turned, trying to check, and we looked, too, circling her body, and I thought how different it was this time because now I was hoping to find a bruise or torn skin. Anything to prove that he'd hurt her.

But there weren't any marks. Only a faint smudge of the palest lilac on her upper torso—barely a bruise at all. She yanked her arms out of the sleeves and we checked that skin, too. The red at her elbows was just from the cold, and her skin was so pale that I could practically see the blood running through her body, like veining in marble. We found a second, much smaller bruise on her left forearm, this one yellow and green. Also old. She became slightly panicky—we all were—hurriedly unzipping her jeans, jerking them down and her small lace panties with them. She let her clothes puddle around her ankles and stood there, naked and shivering, so we could scan her for evidence of Viktor's abuse.

A faint scratch from a nail around her ankle, a nick around the knee from a razor—there was nothing else, no other injury. "Only those two bruises," Julie said, "and they're old marks."

"Psychological abuse is just as real as physical," I said, but I felt the same sinking feeling that I could see on Sarah's face.

"There's no evidence of abuse," she said, as Heather fumbled back into her clothes. "We need evidence."

"We can tell them," Julie said. "The three of us. We can tell them what happened, what's been happening. How he hurt Heather, terrorized her."

"What Heather told us is hearsay," Sarah said. "Inadmissible."

"The bruises we saw aren't hearsay," I argued. "The kitchen wasn't hearsay. We saw those ourselves."

"But we have no proof of that, do we?" Sarah said, sounding despairing.

She was right—why would they believe us any more than Heather? "Why didn't we think to—" I stopped short and looked at Heather. "Did you take the photos like we suggested? Photos of what Viktor did to you?"

"Yes," Heather said. "But Viktor found the camera—he destroyed it."

"Maybe the photos themselves are salvageable," I said. "Where is it?"

"Inside," Heather said, heading for the door, but I stopped her.

"Let me go. You've got blood on you." I pulled open the door, careful to use my sleeve on the knob. "Where do I look?"

"In the kitchen."

There was a light on in the mudroom, which opened up into a laundry room, and I ran through them both. The rest of the house was dark, silent. There were signs of a struggle—a laundry basket tipped on its side, clothes spilling out onto the floor, and beyond that, a black suitcase lying facedown just outside the door. I stepped around them, hurrying into the kitchen, my footsteps thudding on the tile. I switched on a light, blinking in the sudden brightness. A purse had been upended over the island, its contents scattered across the marble and onto the floor below. A leather wallet had been literally torn open, Heather's face smiling up from her driver's license, which was falling out of a ripped plastic sleeve. Receipts fluttered as I scrabbled through her makeup, mints, and keys, but I couldn't see the camera anywhere until I thought to check the rest of the floor and that's when I spotted the gray plastic shards near the sink. The camera had been smashed into little bits, beyond recognition unless someone knew what they were looking for. I got a paper towel and sifted through the mess, careful not to touch anything directly, but the SD card was missing. I checked the sink. It was damp and there were still tinier bits of plastic near the garbage disposal. If he'd sent it down the disposal, there really wasn't any hope of finding those photos, but I gingerly reached a hand down inside, hoping against hope that I'd find the little card intact.

All I did was prick myself on a fine shard. "Shit!" Jerking my hand back out, I ran it under cold water for several seconds, only to realize that I'd forgotten to use a paper towel. I hurriedly grabbed one to wipe down the faucet.

"It's no good," I said once I was back out in the garage. "Those were the only photos you had?"

Heather nodded, patting her jeans pockets with shaking hands as if she'd find a photo hidden there.

Julie suddenly started patting her own pockets. "No, they're not. I took some on my phone—it's in the car." She ran out of the garage and a few seconds later came back clutching her iPhone. "Here," she said, breathless, holding it out. "Look, they're a little blurry, but it's proof, right?"

Sarah took the phone and peered at the screen, frowning as she scrolled through them. "What is this a photo of?" she said, holding the phone out to Heather. Julie and I leaned in to see as well.

"I think it's my stomach. He punched me here once." Heather pointed toward her side and I looked from where she was pointing to the photo, which was hard to comprehend. It looked like a Rorschach test—a white background with what appeared to be an irregular pattern of blue-purple ink across it.

"There's no way to tell what this is," Sarah said. "It could be a bruise or it could be a watercolor." She scrolled through to another photo. In that one, at least, you could see that it was a person. It was half of a female upper torso, and you could clearly see the strap of her bra, the shadow at the dip in her throat, the tight line of her lower jaw. Less clear was the faint discoloration around her visible shoulder.

"That could be a mark left from CrossFit or rough sex," Sarah said. "It doesn't look like much of anything."

"There's got to be a better one." Julie snatched it from Sarah's hand, frantically scrolling through her photos, but there were only four or five and none of them proved anything.

"We can testify to what we saw," I said. "The police will talk to us—we'll explain it to them."

"It's going to be her word against the man she killed," Sarah said. "It'll depend on the lawyer she gets, the jury."

"Jury?" Heather said. She stared at Sarah, seeming not to fully comprehend the situation she was in. "It was self-defense," she repeated. "I had to kill him."

"Except you didn't," Sarah said bluntly. "You should have called the police, or us, and that's what they'll say, that you could have called for help."

"She was terrified," I said. "It's a valid defense."

"She shot him in the back of the head," Sarah said. "You know as well as I do that even with strong evidence of abuse they'll arrest her and charge her with murder."

"I can't go to jail!" Heather began screaming. "I can't go to jail!"

"Shhh!" Sarah hissed. "Someone will hear you!"

"We've got to do something," Julie said above her cries. "We can't just let them arrest her."

"We don't have any other option," Sarah said.

"We could dump the body somewhere else," I said, thinking out loud, but Heather stopped midscream, and everyone looked at me.

"Yes, yes," Julie said, sounding relieved. "That's what we need to do—just put his body somewhere. They'll think he was shot by someone else."

"Where?" Sarah demanded, full of skepticism. "Where on earth would we put him and what about the car? What do we do with that?"

"Carjacking," I said, thinking of a recent case. "We could make it look like a carjacking."

"Yes, that's perfect," Julie said eagerly, Heather nodding in agreement, but Sarah shook her head.

"There are cameras everywhere," she said.

"Not on the back roads," I said. "We could leave him on one of those isolated wooded roads. Nobody's out this late—not on a weeknight."

"Including a carjacker," Sarah said. "Who gets carjacked in the middle of nowhere?"

"He could have been followed off I-279," Heather said, her hysteria morphing into an eagerness to make this plan—or any plan—work.

Sarah stared at the car, considering. "We'd need to leave the gun with the car, too," she said after a moment. "We could make it look like the carjacker turned Viktor's own gun on him." She turned to Heather. "Is the gun registered to you or to Viktor?"

"Neither of us," Heather said.

"Then where did you get it?" I asked.

She hesitated, gaze skittering away from mine, but before I could ask again Julie gave a short, sharp cough and said, "From me."

chapter fourteen

Alison and I stared at Julie in stunned silence for what must have been only a few seconds but felt much longer. "You gave her a gun?" I demanded. "What the hell were you thinking?"

"She needed to defend herself," Julie's voice rose. "*You* were the ones who said she needed some self-defense."

"Yeah, like karate or something, not a gun," Alison said. "Holy shit!"

"It's not her fault," Heather said. "She was trying to help me."

"That doesn't make it better—she can be charged as an accessory," I said, and then to Julie, "I didn't even know you owned a gun."

"It's to keep me safe. For protection when I'm showing houses alone—just in case."

Alison gave a bitter laugh. "And you've just demonstrated why owning a gun *isn't* safe. Now we've got to dump the gun, too."

"Won't Brian notice it's missing?" I said.

Julie shook her head. "He doesn't know. Nobody knows I have one."

"Well, thank God for small favors," I said.

It was just after two A.M. "We don't have much time," Alison said. "If we're really going to do this, then we need to pick a deserted spot, someplace a carjacking could realistically happen."

"How about somewhere along Fern Hollow Road?" Julie suggested. "It's not far off I-279."

"Yes, there, that's a good place," Heather said, eager to go with

109

any plan that didn't involve prison. "Viktor drives home that way sometimes."

"They could have followed Viktor off the interstate and waited until he was on that stretch," Alison said.

"Someone is going to have to drive the car," I said, "and what do we do with his body in the meantime?"

We all stared at the car. Viktor was over six feet tall and now he was literally dead weight. "Leave him where he is," Alison said. "We can't move the body out of the front seat and then put it back—the police will be able to tell. For this to work we have to leave everything as is as much as possible."

"How can we drive the car with *him* in it?" Julie said, her voice dipping on the personal pronoun as if she were afraid that uttering Viktor's name would somehow bring him back.

"What if we covered him with a plastic bag so we didn't leave any fibers," Alison said slowly, staring at the car. "And then one of us could perch on the seat in front of him and drive that way."

She looked at me, Julie and Heather following her gaze. "No way," I said. "I don't want to drive the car."

"You're the shortest." Alison used her hands to approximate the available space. "It makes the most sense."

The thought of having to touch Viktor's body made me shiver. "Absolutely not."

"No one else is small enough," Alison said.

"Just shift the seat back and let her drive," I said, pointing at Heather. "She's the one who shot him."

"She's not fit to drive and shifting things would be bad," Alison said. "We don't want to move anything in the car if at all possible."

"C'mon, Sarah," Julie said. "We need you."

She and Heather gave me pleading looks, while Alison pulled out her phone again. "We don't have time to argue—if we're going to do this we have to get going."

"Fine," I said, unable to think of another, better way. "But I'm not getting near that car without gloves."

"I have some." Heather hurried to the back of the garage and fetched a box of disposable latex gloves from a cabinet above the workbench. "Here, we can all wear these." She put on a pair and passed the box around.

I pulled on a pair and felt strangely guilty, as if I'd fired the gun myself. And what about that gun? "What are we going to do with it?" I asked, pointing.

Alison slipped on some gloves before squatting down to carefully pick it up, quickly and expertly emptying the chamber.

"Wow, you know how to handle guns?" I was surprised.

"The things we learn about each other," she said sardonically.

I tentatively pressed a gloved hand against Viktor's leg. It moved slightly and I reared back, crying out. Heather shrieked and Julie and Alison turned to look.

"Sorry, it's okay, he isn't alive," I said. "I'm just checking to make sure we can still bend his leg to get it in the car."

"Do you have any large plastic garbage bags?" Alison asked Heather.

"They're in the house, under the kitchen sink."

"I'll get them," Julie said to Heather. "You should go shower." She headed inside, but Alison stopped Heather from following her.

"Take off your clothes here so you don't get any blood inside," she said. "And after you shower you've got to pour bleach down the drain."

Heather stripped and collected her clothes. "I'll throw these in the wash."

I shook my head. "It's too risky—the police might be able to tell that you ran the machine. You have to get rid of them."

"What a waste—I liked these jeans," Heather said, letting the clothes drop. It was jarring to hear her say that with her dead husband just a few feet away. But she was in shock—I think we all were.

As she hurried inside, I found a large pair of scissors and a roll of duct tape on the workbench. Alison peered inside the car, bending down to look at the driver's-side floor.

"Good, I don't see any blood here, so we don't have to worry about tracking it." She stood up just as Julie returned with a box of black trash bags and a handful of small blue plastic grocery bags. "We'll cover both of you," Alison said to me, plucking a black bag from the box and cutting a scoop out of the bottom and on either side. "Here." She tossed me the altered bag. "Pull this on over your head."

We worked at a frantic pace, barely speaking, a tense silence punctuated by sounds of ripping plastic and duct tape. Julie helped me pull the bag on over my clothes while Alison made plastic sleeves that they then duct-taped to the shoulders of the bag and then around the wrists of my latex gloves. Plastic pants followed and then they taped smaller blue plastic grocery bags to my feet. Alison cut another large plastic bag and draped it over Viktor's body.

"I feel like the Michelin man," I said, crinkling as I moved. "How am I supposed to drive like this?"

"We don't have an option," Alison said, "so you just have to make it work."

Heather returned in new jeans and a shirt, damp hair pulled back in a ponytail, and she'd put on shoes. "You need to cover your hair," she said as I moved closer to the car. "I'll get you one of Viktor's hats." She came back with a knit cap, which they pulled on my head because I couldn't raise my arms high enough to do so without tearing the plastic suit.

"We'll lead the way in my car," Julie said. "That way, if we see any traffic or a police car—God forbid—we can distract them so you won't get stopped."

I felt squeamish as I stepped over Viktor's extended leg and sat gingerly on the slim bit of driver's seat not occupied by his body. I slid against the plastic covering it and grabbed the steering wheel to try to keep my balance, pushing back to maintain a grip on the seat and coming up hard against his body. I cried out involuntarily as Alison carefully bent Viktor's leg, folding it up into the car, where it rested uncomfortably against mine. She closed the door and I struggled not to panic, breathing shallowly, trying to avoid sucking in the overpowering scent of blood. It was like a butcher shop. I hated the smell of raw meat, and this was meat that was starting to rot. Was this how an operating room smelled? Had Viktor been surrounded by this odor every day?

The keys were in the ignition. Blood had hit the embossed leather fob and it smeared against my glove as I turned the key and switched on the lights. The sound of the engine seemed too loud as I backed slowly out of the garage. Alison, Julie, and Heather followed me out and closed the garage door before getting into Julie's car, and I let them lead the way slowly down the drive.

It was 2:30 A.M., the time of night when it's utterly and completely dark, the heavy blackness penetrated only by the occasional security light on the houses we passed. In Sewickley Heights these were spaced few and far apart and well off the road. There weren't streetlights out here like there were in the village, no sidewalks for late-night dog walkers. It was too early for the crazy runners who risked life and limb to run along these narrow, winding, hilly roads, and too late for the drinkers who'd already closed down the bars in town. The empty roads made it safer for us and yet I was terrified of the dark and the body pressing against me, only the lights from Julie's car to let me know I wasn't utterly alone.

I kept a few car lengths behind, careful not to let her car disappear over a hill and out of sight, but equally careful not to get too close. Julie was staying at the speed limit and I knew it was wise, but I still wished that she would just floor it and we'd get to where we were going as fast as possible. The knit hat was itchy and I felt claustrophobic, fighting a desperate need to get out of the car, away from that horrible stench of blood and decay, and tear all of the plastic off my body.

The brake lights suddenly went on ahead of me and I slammed on my brakes, too. I immediately reversed, jerking the car onto the side of the road and switching off the lights, straining to see what had stopped them. They didn't move for a minute. If it were a cop, wouldn't they have been pulled off to the side?

My palms were sweating and I instinctively rubbed them

against my thighs, forgetting how I was dressed until I felt that awful sticky rub of plastic against plastic.

Some movement caught my eye, and then a raccoon scuttled into the glow of Julie's headlights. "Everything's A-okay, Viktor," I said with a nervous laugh that fell flat in the deafening silence of the car. I swallowed down a wave of nausea, switched my lights back on, and cautiously resumed following Julie.

Several minutes later Julie braked abruptly again, before jerking her car to the side of the road. I was quick to follow suit, dousing the lights and the motor, and in the silence was suddenly aware of the loud hum of another engine before I saw the distant headlight glow and then a darker shadow as another vehicle passed by on the cross road about a hundred feet ahead. This time Julie waited longer to start driving again, clearly wanting to put distance between us and that other driver.

We followed a circuitous route for several more minutes, a blur of winding streets, before finally turning on to Fern Hollow. Tree-covered hills rose on either side of us, and we drove for only a few minutes more on the deserted two-lane road before Julie slowed and put on her turn signal to indicate that I should stop. I pulled Viktor's car over to the side of the road, tires crunching against the pebbles and dirt. It sounded so loud—had anyone heard it? I peered out the windows and checked the rearview mirror as Julie pulled her own car over about twenty feet ahead. When I switched off the car, the headlights stayed on. As Alison and Julie hurried toward me, racing on tiptoe, I tried to carefully open the driver's door without disrupting the body.

At that moment, we all heard the low rumble of an approaching engine. Julie stopped short, looking wildly around, while Heather headed back toward her car and Alison ran off the road and into the woods. I closed the car door quietly, fumbling for the light switch. The noise seemed to get louder for a moment and then it just stopped. No one moved for a long minute, all of us listening.

"Where is it?" I hissed as I quietly cracked open the door again, looking around for the source of the noise. "I don't see anyone."

"It must have turned up one of the other roads," Julie said, opening the door the rest of the way, while I switched back on the lights and Alison stepped forward to catch Viktor's foot, angling it so it hung out the door just as it had before. She then reached out a hand to help me out of the car, the sickening peel of the plastic too loud in the stillness.

I gulped the clean, fresh night air like a swimmer coming up from some deep, dank pond. Julie and Alison were lifting the plastic bags off Viktor's body and folding them hastily into a trash bag they'd brought with them. I moved away from the car and began stripping off my plastic suit. "Be careful," Alison hissed. "Don't leave anything behind."

"Should we leave the headlights on?" Julie whispered.

We debated it for a precious minute, trying to decide which way would make it look more like a carjacking. As we were arguing in whispers, the car suddenly answered the question itself, the lights switching off automatically.

A last-minute check of everything. Alison ran a cloth over the door handles and the steering wheel, because she assumed a carjacker would remember to do that even in a botched attempt. I bundled the pieces of my plastic suit into the trash bag and then we ran back to Julie's car. I climbed in the back after Heather, who was nervously tugging at her hands. We had just pulled onto the road when Alison said, "Our tire tracks!"

Julie put the car in park in the middle of the road and fetched an ice scraper from the trunk. She used the brush to swipe the side of the road ahead of Viktor's car, trying to erase any evidence of her car and our footprints.

When she came back to the car, she added the scraper to the trash bag. "We need to find an isolated garbage dump or Dumpsters somewhere," she said.

As we pulled away the second time, I turned to look out the rear window, capturing forever the scene that I would I visit over and over again in my dreams. The isolated stretch of road on that murky night, the black spires of trees looming above it, and that bottle-green Mercedes. Its jewel color glinted in the taillights, and

I could see the driver's door ajar and picture Viktor's foot dangling over the side, its dead weight brushing the ground. I watched the car shrink as we sped away, until it disappeared from view, swallowed up by the darkness.

We took different roads back to Heather's house, Julie purposely changing the route. Along the way we passed an old industrial park, and when we couldn't spot any cameras, she pulled into the back and Alison threw the bag into a huge metal Dumpster.

"We still have to get rid of the gun," Alison said. "You're sure Brian doesn't know you have one?"

Julie shook her head. "No. He's anti-gun."

"Yeah, me too," Alison said in a dark voice.

It was almost three. What if Olivia woke up, or Eric, and found me gone? When I'd left home, my daughter had been asleep in our bed after crawling in with us sometime around midnight. Soon after, her father had given up trying to sleep with three of us crowding the queen-size bed and had decamped to her room. Both of them had been sound asleep when I tiptoed out of the house, but what about now? Would Eric call 911 if he woke and found me gone and couldn't reach me on my cell phone? In my haste to help Heather, I'd left it in my car. I pictured the police swarming over my house, Sam greeting them at the door in pajamas, Olivia and Josh wailing. My throat constricted.

"We can ditch the gun in the river," I suggested.

"I'm afraid of being spotted on a security camera," Alison said. "We can't risk being seen throwing something off the Sewickley Bridge."

"Well, we can't hold on to it—we've got to get rid of it," Julie said, as if she weren't the one responsible for the gun.

"Maybe we could bury it?" I said, but where would we do that without being spotted? I pictured us trying to hide it at the park and some enterprising dog digging it up.

"Let's find another Dumpster," Alison said, but we'd moved away from the river and were driving along one of the winding back roads between Sewickley and Edgeworth, and there weren't any businesses with Dumpsters in sight.

Feeling queasy from all the twists and turns, I didn't realize we were crossing over a creek until Julie stopped the car. "What about here?"

We were on an old stone bridge that covered a steep embankment with a creek running through the middle. We got out of the car and looked down at the water below. It looked like an oil slick in the moonlight, a fast-running greasy stream. Someone had thrown a bag over the side, spilling pop and beer cans. Brush and silt had accumulated like mortar up and around them, creating a dam. "Someone will come by to pick up this trash and they'll spot the gun," Alison said. "The water's not deep enough to hide it."

"The water's moving further out," I said, pointing at a spot through brush and scraggly trees where I could make out a thin line of dark water. "No one will look there," I said to Julie. "Just be careful on the hill."

"I don't want to climb down there through that muck," Julie said.

"It's the best place we've found."

"Then you do it."

"It's your gun," I snapped. "We wouldn't be in this mess if you hadn't given it to Heather in the first place."

"We don't have time for this," Alison growled, moving toward the edge of the bridge. "I'll climb down and one of you can pass me the gun."

chapter fifteen

I didn't wait for their agreement, conscious of the time and terrified that someone could drive along this stretch at any minute and spot us. Switching on my iPhone flashlight, I took a closer look over the edge of the embankment. It was a steep slope, made slippery by the soft mulch created from years of fallen leaves, plus the recent rain and snow. At least it wasn't raining at that moment. The clouds shifted, the moon disappearing, making me hesitate, before it reappeared a minute later. It seemed like a sign. Shoving my iPhone in my pocket, I used the edge of the stone bridge for support and picked my way down the hill before switching my grip to the trunk of a skinny, stunted tree. I looked back up to see Julie, Heather, and Sarah leaning over the bridge. Clearly panicky, Julie didn't come close enough to pass me the gun, but instead just tossed the towel-wrapped weapon over the side to me. I missed and it slipped from the towel as it hit the ground beyond me, sliding forward into some leaves. I dug through them to retrieve it, gagging on the smell of wet rot and wood mold, and the awful, clammy feel of it, which thin latex gloves couldn't fully block. Hastily bundling the gun back in the towel, I plodded through the soft ground, picking my way toward the creek and following it along the bank until it widened and the sound of water rushing over rocks grew louder.

It was so cold out I could see my breath. I unwrapped the gun, wiping it down one more time, just in case. It felt surprisingly heavy for something so small. An iron weight in my gloved palm.

I hefted it and then threw it as far as I could downstream, aiming for the center. I heard the plop as it hit the water, a distinct noise in that awful darkness.

I hurried back up the way I came, moving so fast that I slipped and fell, hands sinking through the morass, palms scraping against the ground. Scrambling to my feet, I plowed on, frightened by the darkness, certain that someone was watching, that there were dark shadows sliding in and out of the trees. It was harder getting up the embankment than it had been going down. Julie reached out and helped pull me the rest of the way up.

"You've cut yourself," Heather said, using a tissue to dab lightly at my face, holding it out with her gloved hand so I could see the dark spots of blood.

"Do that in the car," Sarah said. "We've got to go."

We drove back to Heather's house in silence, Julie taking the curves as fast as she dared, all of us painfully aware of the dashboard clock relentlessly ticking away. It was almost four A.M. by the time we drove back up Heather's driveway.

"Shit! What about the security cameras?" I said as we pulled up, scanning the corners of the house and the garage. "We'll be caught on tape—we need to find that and destroy it."

"No, it's okay," Heather said, delivering the only good news of that night. "Viktor disabled the cameras a while ago."

She typed in the key code for the garage and the door to the bay that had held Viktor's car rose, the rumbling noise so loud that I looked around, afraid of being overheard.

We all stripped off our latex gloves and added them to the trash bag and then three of us put on new pairs, but Heather didn't need to. This was her house—the police would expect to find her fingerprints here.

I kicked off my muddy shoes so I could follow the others into the laundry room. I felt a sudden yearning to be home and doing laundry, a mundane, safe task that I would never complain about again, no matter how many dirty clothes the kids seemed to accumulate.

Julie righted the chair in the hall and I picked up the suitcase.

"You need to unpack and put this away and clean up the kitchen," I said. "Do you want us to do that for you?"

Heather shook her head, taking the case from me. "No, I can do it."

"What about the garage?" Sarah asked. "We should check it for blood."

There were a few tiny spots and Sarah poured bleach on each one while Julie and I scrubbed the concrete with a sponge until we couldn't see anything.

"You have to get rid of the smell," I said. "They'll be suspicious of that. Do you have any scented candles? You need something strong to cover the bleach."

Sarah knelt next to the damp spots to get a closer look. "I think we got all the blood, but you need to dry these spots otherwise it'll be a red flag."

"Okay, candles and a hair dryer—got it." Heather ran back inside.

"That's a relief," I said once she was gone. "She couldn't have fooled anybody the way she was acting before."

"I guess she should call the police right after we leave," Julie said.

"No, absolutely not," Sarah said. "She goes to bed and she doesn't realize her husband isn't home until she wakes up later this morning—that's when she calls."

"And she should call the hospital first," I said. "Or better yet his cell phone, which we know is going to go to voice mail, and then she should call the hospital." I was trembling and it wasn't just from being cold.

Heather came back with the dryer and a large white jar candle. "I'll dry," Sarah said. "You light the candle."

Julie and I paced, pausing only to check the concrete floor with Sarah every few minutes. It took an interminable ten minutes before the damp spots were gone. The smell of bleach was overlaid with the burning odor from the hair dryer, but soon the sickly sweet aroma of vanilla-bean-scented candle began to overpower them.

There were a few tiny brown specks left on the concrete, but the largest of them was the size of a pinhead. No one would notice.

"Your hands," I said, suddenly remembering. "Scrub them again with bleach and your fingernails, too, just to make sure there's no gunshot residue. They probably won't check, but better safe than sorry."

Heather frowned and Sarah said, "Hopefully it won't come to that and they won't check you, but you've got to be prepared."

"And make sure you've poured bleach down all the drains you used," I reminded her. "Bleach and hot water."

"Okay, we need to leave," Sarah said, checking her watch. "Especially Alison—she's got to wash her clothes."

We reviewed what Heather should do one more time: sleep if she could for a few hours and then wake at her usual time, seven A.M., and pretend that this was when she realized that Viktor never came home. Call his cell phone and leave a message. "You want to sound concerned, but not overly concerned, not yet," I said. "He's been gone all night before, right?"

Heather nodded. "Not often, but sometimes he'd spend all night at the hospital."

"So you're just calling to check in and you can express surprise and a little concern that he didn't come home, but not too much," Sarah said.

"Save the concern for the call to the police," I said. "After the hospital tells you he isn't there, then you call the police." I thought of something else. "When is Daniel coming home?"

"Sometime tomorrow." Heather shrugged. "Anna never specifies—she wants it to be inconvenient for me."

"Should Heather call Anna and tell her about Viktor?" Julie asked.

"Yes, good idea," Sarah said. "You call Anna before you call the police—ask if she's heard from her son. But before you call her, call his cell phone again after you call the hospital. Leave a frantic message."

"Wait, it's too many things to remember," Heather said. "I

need to write it down." She went back inside to fetch a pen and notepad and we followed her back into the laundry room while she made a list.

"Burn that paper after you're done with it," Sarah said. "And two sheets underneath it, too. You don't want any impression left for the police to trace."

Julie glanced at her watch. "It's almost half past."

I shivered. "We have to leave."

We stood there for a moment and then spontaneously moved together for a group hug—clinging to one another tightly. Something we would do for fun at other gatherings. *"C'mon, group hug, let's all sing 'Kumbaya!'"* Joking and laughing.

No one laughed now.

As three of us walked out to our cars, Sarah suggested that we rehearse what we were going to say if anyone at our houses was awake and asked where we'd been. "No need for me to have an excuse," Julie said. "Brian's at a conference in D.C."

"You left the kids alone?" Sarah looked at her askance.

"They're deep sleepers," Julie said, unconcerned. "I left a note with my cell number in case they woke up."

"What did the note say? Mommy had to go hide a body?"

Julie ignored her, turning to me. "You can both say you were at my house if Michael or Eric asks."

"In the middle of the night?" Sarah said. "We'd need some reason."

"Say that I heard some noise and with Brian out of town I was afraid to be alone."

"And what if the police pull Heather's cell-phone records?" I said. "They'll see that she called me."

"With any luck it won't come to that," Sarah said. "But if they do, then you can say the same thing—Heather called because she heard a strange noise and her husband wasn't home to reassure her."

There were so many pieces to remember, so many threads. The adrenaline was passing; I yawned as I got behind the wheel of my car. I already had the beginnings of that sinking feeling in my stomach, that sense of regret at having done something that I couldn't undo.

The house was silent when I got home. It was so late that even George barely stirred, merely lifting his head from his dog bed to stare at me with big, questioning eyes. I stuffed the clothes I'd been wearing in the wash, grateful that I tended to procrastinate putting away laundry so there was a basket of clean clothing, including a nightshirt, which I slipped on before padding as soundlessly as possible upstairs to bed.

There was no noise on the second floor. I listened outside the kids' bedrooms, but didn't hear anything. I used my iPhone flashlight to find my way down the dark hall to the master bedroom, and slipped under the covers next to Michael. He stirred, making a grumbling sound at the rush of cold air that came in as I lifted the covers, but didn't wake. I thought I'd have trouble falling asleep, but exhaustion overcame fear.

"Ali? Alison? Wake up, honey." Michael was gently shaking me. I rolled onto my back and blinked up at him.

"What's going on? Why are you up?"

He smiled. "It's after eight. I let you sleep as long as I could, but I've got to take off." He walked over to the windows and pulled back the heavy drapes. Filtered light poured in through the sheers, still bright enough that my eyes automatically shut, but not before I saw that he was ready for work in a suit and tie. "The kids are fed, and I packed them lunches, but the kitchen's a mess. Leave it for me—I can get it later." He bent down to give me a quick hug and kiss and I could smell coffee on his breath. "Hey, what happened here?" he ran a finger lightly down the side of my face and I winced. "You've got a scratch—how did you manage to do that?"

"A nail, I guess," I said, trying to shrug.

"You feeling okay?" He stroked the hair back from my face. "You were out like a light."

I nodded, trying to return his smile. "Yes, I'm fine. Just tired, I guess." I swung out of bed, wondering if he'd also notice that I'd changed pajamas, but he didn't.

He checked his watch. "It's cutting it close to make the bus on time; can you drop Lucy off this morning?"

"Of course." I tried not to stare at the clock on my nightstand as I threw on clothes and pulled my hair back in a ponytail. Heather would have called the hospital by now, then her mother-in-law. Had she phoned the police yet? I splashed water on my face in the master bath, looking at the thin scratch a branch had drawn down my cheek. I couldn't face my own eyes in the mirror.

The kids were downstairs, dressed and waiting. "Mommy!" Matthew ran full-force at me on his small, socked feet, smacking against my legs.

"Oomph. Careful, baby." I lifted him up, hugging him tight. "Ready for school?"

"Yes, Daddy made sandwiches for lunch!" He put a little hand against my face. "Oh, poor Mommy—you've got a boo-boo. Want to me to kiss it?"

I smiled. "Yes, please."

He solemnly planted a gentle kiss on my cheek. "There, all better."

I held him close, overcome by the desire for that to be true— for a kiss to make it all magically better, for what happened last night to be nothing more than a bad dream.

chapter sixteen

I t was an ordinary morning. It was only me that had changed. It felt bizarre to load the kids in the car and drive them to school. They chattered happily the whole way and I let it wash over me, smiling and nodding at them in the rearview mirror, making the appropriate sounds. Had the police found Viktor's body yet? It wouldn't take long. I thought of that slide down the embankment, of the heaviness of the gun in my hand.

"You passed it, Mommy!" Lucy cried and I saw that I'd driven right past the entrance to the elementary school. I abruptly stopped and then reversed, forcing the line of cars behind me to follow suit, a symphony of squealing brakes and honking horns.

"That was dangerous," Lucy declared in her most censorious voice.

"Dangerous," her younger brother chimed in.

"Sorry, sweeties." I waved an apology to the other drivers as well, my hands sweaty on the steering wheel. For goodness' sake, hold it together. I slowed the car, concentrating on not causing an accident in the queue of cars pulling up to the school's front doors.

Kids were being ushered into the building and I got out just long enough to make sure Lucy joined the other third graders and to hand Matthew over to one of the kindergarten aides, a twentysomething young woman whose name I couldn't remember. "Have a great day!" she said with a cheerful smile. It sounded ominous to me; I had to force a smile in return.

As I pulled out of the school I switched on the radio, rolling through stations for local news. A multi-car traffic accident on the Parkway East was top of the news, followed by a house fire in Brighton Heights. A shooting overnight—these words made me stiffen in my seat—but far away in Hazelwood, and they had the suspect in custody. I shut off the radio and called Julie. The phone rang and rang; just as I was about to hang up she answered. "Hi." She sounded stilted, her voice higher than normal. "How are you?"

I broke into a sweat. "Is someone there?"

"Yes. Can I call you back?"

"Okay." I hung up and immediately called Sarah.

She answered on the second ring. "Any word?"

"I think the police are at Julie's."

"What? They can't be."

"I just called her—she sounded odd and couldn't talk."

"It could be anybody," Sarah said, but she sounded unsure. "There's no reason the police would be there."

"Unless Heather told them."

"She wouldn't do that—would she?"

"I'm on the road; I'll drive by Julie's house and see who's there."

There was an unfamiliar dark SUV parked in the driveway. It could be an unmarked car. The police could have sent someone to talk to her. What if Heather had told them? What if they were coming to my house next? I wanted to floor the accelerator and flee, but what if someone spotted me? As I drove slowly past I saw the realty-company logo on the car's side. I sagged in my seat with relief and called Sarah back, feeling foolish.

"I knew it couldn't be the police," she said. "There's been nothing on the news yet."

We were both being careful not to say anything too direct, just in case someone was listening. "Do you think Heather's got company?"

"Possibly. Look, we shouldn't stay on the phone. Call if you hear anything and I'll do the same."

I didn't want to hang up; I didn't want to be alone with my thoughts. After driving home, I made a cup of coffee. The sound of it pouring into the cup reminded me of the rushing noise of dark water in the creek. I closed my eyes and heard the splash of the gun.

Focus on work. I carried the coffee into my office and opened my laptop, trying to absorb myself in the projects that were piling up. I would work for thirty minutes before taking a break. I set a timer, one of the many tricks I'd learned long ago when I'd just started working from home and setting my own deadlines. It forced me to start, but I couldn't concentrate. I kept thinking about Heather; we'd agreed that none of us could call her, not right away.

When twenty minutes had passed, I got online and checked the local news. Nothing; no mention even of a car being found. Shouldn't someone have noticed the green Mercedes by now? It wasn't as if we'd dumped it—him—out of the way, though maybe we should have. I ruminated yet again over what we'd done. It was stupid, just plain stupid to have tried to make it look like a carjacking. If we'd called the police first, if we'd waited with Heather and told them how scared she'd been, wouldn't that have been smarter? But no, they wouldn't have believed her, or believed any of us, not without some tangible proof. Sarah was right—she would have been charged with murdering Viktor. Why hadn't Heather taken better photos? Why hadn't we? We could have taken photos of her kitchen, for instance. Stupid, so stupid not to have thought of doing that, because we were so focused on convincing her to leave him.

It felt as if an enormous amount of time had passed, but when I glanced at the clock it was barely half past ten. I gave up and left my desk, circling around the house because I had too much nervous energy. At eleven, on impulse, I called my brother at work.

"Indiana Borough Police." The desk sergeant's voice was blandly professional.

"May I speak with Lieutenant Sean Novak, please?"

"One moment, I'll put you through to his office."

I almost hung up while the phone was ringing—what could I possibly ask him—but before I could he answered. "Hello, this is Lieutenant Novak."

"Hi, it's me."

"Hey, Ali." He sounded happy to hear from me, which despite my stress made me smile. "Everything okay?"

"Everything's fine. I just thought I'd call and say hello."

"Kids okay? Michael?"

"They're fine, thanks. You?"

"Oh, fine. Too much paperwork, but other than that." He laughed and I joined in, but it sounded hollow to me. He said, "So what's going on with you?"

"Not much—just busy as usual." I chatted with him about what the kids were up to for a few minutes and then I tried to casually bring the conversation around to crime.

"You know those police scanners? Do you hear news reports on things happening everywhere? Even in my neighborhood?"

"Sometimes. Why? What's up?"

"Oh, it's nothing, really, I just heard some sirens earlier and wondered what was going on."

"Close by? Are you worried about the kids? Don't worry, most schools have good security and emergency-response measures these days. They're really sensitive because of all the shootings—" He must have thought my intake of breath was a gasp, because he stopped talking, although I could hear him clicking keys on his laptop. "I don't see anything; it was probably a false alarm, people are always calling those in."

What about carjacking, I wanted to ask, but didn't. We chatted for a few more minutes and then just as I was about to hang up he asked, "Say, whatever happened to your friend, the one being abused? Did she leave him?"

Shit, why was he asking about her now? "Oh, she's good. I mean, she's dealing with it. Hey, that's my call waiting—I've got to go."

"Sure, nice talking to you, sis."

My palms were sweating as I hung up the phone. When they found Viktor's body—if they ever found Viktor's body—would Sean make the connection? I hadn't told him their names, but had I said anything else? Given out any other identifying details?

There was no mention of a carjacking, or a body, all day. At three P.M. I drove to the bus stop to wait for the kids, and five minutes later I spotted Julie's car pull in a few cars behind mine. There was always a queue of parents waiting to pick up the elementary school kids in the afternoon. Aubrey had started kindergarten that year along with Matthew, so Julie was child-free during the school day, too, usually coming straight to the bus stop from showing houses or dealing with clients. I felt desperate to talk to her, eager to know if she'd heard anything or seen anything. I had no reason to drive near Sewickley Heights or the roads beyond it, but she had the perfect excuse.

Usually, she came to me, because I was always closer to the front of the queue, but this time I didn't wait. After zipping up my coat, I opened the door, feeling the sting of the cold air against my face. As I walked back toward Julie's car she got out to meet me, only to be intercepted by a mother in one of the cars behind mine. The woman greeted her effusively, but the smile on Julie's face seemed forced. She kept darting glances at me over the woman's shoulder. I could hear snatches of the conversation, something about a house for sale by one of Julie's competitors. "Shut up already," I muttered. "C'mon, Julie, just end it."

That distinct sound of a heavier engine turned everyone's attention to the road as the bus rumbled into view. Julie broke free of the other woman and came toward me as the bus wheezed to a full stop and the doors opened. "Sorry about that," she said in a low voice. "Heard anything?"

"No, you?"

The kids were streaming off the bus. I saw Lucy pause in the door and look for me before she stepped down, and I waved my hand, getting a sweet smile in return.

"No, nothing. Poor Heather—I hope she's okay."

That was all she had time to say before Owen and Aubrey were upon her, clamoring for her attention.

Matthew came off the bus after his sister. "Mommy, look at my moose-a-ick," he said as he reached my side, holding aloft a large piece of construction paper to which a colorful mix of smaller pieces of paper had been arranged in a pattern that vaguely resembled a cat. Or a dog. Or some other creature altogether. I'd learned it was better not to make assumptions.

"Is this your mosaic? It's beautiful. I love the colors. Did you choose those?"

"Yes, purple is my bestest color."

"Best," Lucy corrected him. "There's no such word as 'bestest.'"

"Hon, let him tell his story."

"Well, it's not a real word." She fixed us both with a reproving look, but Matthew ignored her.

"Daniel said it was dumb because there is no such thing as a purple cat, but I said he was dumb because it is my moose-a-ick and I can make it whatever color I want and the teacher said I was right because it was my 'magination."

We walked back to the car, my arms around both kids' shoulders. I felt as if I were playing a role, part of me listening and giving the appropriate responses, while another part of me was wondering why there was no news about the carjacking. It was a gray afternoon, dark clouds hovering in the sky like an omen. I helped strap Matthew into his booster seat, while Lucy insisted on buckling herself in. As I pulled back onto the street, I glanced in the rearview mirror, and for a moment what I saw wasn't the residential street but the last look I'd taken of Viktor's car disappearing into darkness and shadow.

The discovery was announced late on the six P.M. newscast. I was prepping dinner and had the kitchen TV on low so the kids, who were running in and out, wouldn't hear the litany of scary and depressing things that dominated every broadcast.

"And in breaking news, police are reporting that a UPMC physician was killed last night in Sewickley during a carjacking. The Allegheny County police report that Dr. Viktor Lysenko was found in his car on Fern Hollow Road sometime this morning, the apparent victim of an attempted carjacking. With more on that story, we turn to KDKA reporter Todd Holmes."

The knife I'd been chopping vegetables with clattered onto the cutting board. The camera switched to a man standing on a familiar-looking road overhung by trees, the lights from his camera casting the police vehicles and crime-scene tape behind him in an unnatural light. It was only just dusk; the front of Viktor's car was clearly visible, but there were police officers and cars blocking the rest of the view. My pulse pounded in my ears. "Police report that a local resident alerted authorities after spotting Dr. Viktor Lysenko in his car, a Mercedes, on the side of the road this morning. We don't know all the details yet, but we've been told that Dr. Lysenko was shot during what appears to be a botched carjacking. According to the Allegheny County police, Dr. Lysenko was pronounced dead at the scene. The medical examiner has not yet released the cause of his death."

I tried to pick up the knife again, but my hands were shaking. Of course, Michael chose just that moment to walk in the door. "Daddy!" Lucy cried, and I could hear two sets of small feet pounding down the hall toward him.

"Hello! How was school?" Michael made loud smooching noises. "Oh, you're getting so big I can barely pick you up." Lots of giggling. "Let me hang up my coat."

The hall closet opened and I could hear the ping of hangers. I tried to pull myself together, turning on the tap to try to fill a glass of water, but my hands were shaking so badly that it dropped and shattered in the sink.

"Shit!" My curse brought Michael to the kitchen.

"Hey, what's going on? Are you okay?" His voice was gentle and kind, yet so unwelcome at that moment.

"It's nothing. I broke a glass, that's all." I knew I sounded gruff, but I couldn't help it. I grabbed paper towels and began swiping the pieces of glass together.

"Don't cut yourself," Michael said. "Here, let me help." He touched my arm and that's when he realized I was shaking. "Ali? What is it? What's wrong?"

I tried to think of what to say, but before I could get the words out the TV did it for me. "Sewickley police are asking anyone who drove I-279 between the hours of ten P.M. Wednesday night and two A.M. Thursday morning and might have seen the Mercedes driven by Dr. Viktor Lysenko to contact them." A smiling headshot of Viktor appeared on the screen.

"What the hell?" Michael grabbed the remote, turning up the volume, but Viktor's picture disappeared, replaced by a temperature icon and a snowflake. "There's snow in the forecast, folks! Our meteorologist, Tina Cho, will tell us how much we can expect. That's up next, so keep watching *KDKA News*."

"Wasn't that Heather's husband?" Michael turned from the screen to me. "Did you hear the whole story—what happened?"

"Apparently he was the victim of a carjacking," I said, trying to keep my voice even.

"Oh my God! Have you spoken to Heather?"

"Not yet," I said before suddenly bursting into tears. I couldn't have planned it better, but there was no pretense. Michael wrapped his arms around me and pressed me against his chest.

"It's okay, it's going to be okay," he murmured, stroking my hair. He rocked me a little in his arms and I wanted to stay there forever, hiding from the world, but of course the children interrupted. Matthew rode his scooter into the kitchen and stopped short at the sight of us.

"Why sad, Mommy?" He always reverted to his most babyish when he felt anxious. I pulled away from his father, wiping my eyes with my hands.

"I'm okay, sweetie," I said, giving him a tremulous smile.

"A friend of Mommy's got hurt," Michael said. "But Mommy's okay."

A friend. He hadn't been a friend at all; he was a monster. I wanted to correct Michael, it was on the tip of my tongue, but I caught myself just in time. I couldn't say anything negative about Viktor—not now, not ever again.

"Let me finish up in here, you go call Heather," Michael offered. It was exactly what I'd wanted to do all day, but now I had a legitimate reason to do so. I gave him a grateful smile and carried my cell phone upstairs to the bedroom to talk, ostensibly so I wouldn't disturb the children.

It was the first time I'd ever been nervous dialing her number. I swallowed hard as it started ringing. Three, six, nine rings and no one had picked up. Maybe she was talking to someone else. I went to push the off button and that's when I heard her breathy "Hello?"

"Heather? I just heard the news. I'm so sorry." My voice sounded stilted, false—it was harder sticking to the script we'd all agreed on than I'd thought it would be.

"Hi, Alison. Thank you. Hold on a second." A muffled sound and I heard her say to someone else, "It's a friend calling—I'm going to take it upstairs." Then back to me. "You heard the news? They think it was a carjacking."

"What on earth happened?" I played along, letting her spin the story we'd created for her to tell the police. How she fell asleep before Viktor came home, just like she did many nights, and how she didn't realize he hadn't made it home until the morning. How she'd assumed it had something to do with a patient, but then she'd called the hospital and he wasn't there either.

"That's when I started to worry," she said. I heard the sound of a door closing, and then Heather's voice dropped to a whisper. "It's okay, I'm alone now."

"What's happening? Are the police there?"

"They've gone for now. They might come back tomorrow to give me more details on the investigation. Viktor's mother is here and his aunt."

"Oh God. How's that going?"

"It's okay; they're watching Daniel."

"How was it with the police?"

"They asked a lot of questions. A lot. About Viktor's schedule, about when he usually got home, about why I didn't call until the morning."

"You explained that, right?"

"Yes, of course. I said everything we talked about."

"It shouldn't take too long then; this will all be over soon."

"Yes, soon." She yawned. "I'm beyond tired. How about you?"

"Going off adrenaline. Did you have to identify the—that is—Viktor?"

"Yes." I thought I heard a hitch in her voice, but Heather held it together.

"Just hang in there; I know it's hard. When will they release his body?" My voice dipped on the last words; it felt awful to refer to Viktor that way even though he'd been such a rotten person.

"Not until after the autopsy," Heather said. I heard a knock and Heather said in a normal voice, "Come in." In the background I could hear a thickly accented female voice say, "Daniel needs his mother," before Heather said back into the phone, "Thank you for calling," and hung up.

The autopsy. I hadn't thought about that, but of course there would have to be one. I tried to picture Viktor lying on a medical examiner's table, but all I could visualize was a pale, waxy, male figure, his features blurred so that I couldn't really see him. Death had reduced him to an object—a body, not a man.

chapter seventeen

JULIE

By the next morning, the news of Viktor's death was all over town. A mother I barely knew flagged me down in the queue at the bus stop to ask breathlessly if I'd heard. "It's just terrible," she said, although her eyes were alight with the excitement of having something this juicy to discuss. "Can you believe it was a carjacking? In Sewickley?" Her tone suggested that things like that were never, ever supposed to happen here. That was for other neighborhoods, not ours. When I broke the news to Brian, he offered to fly home immediately, but I dissuaded him. "It's just a few days," I said, as if I wanted him with me, when having him gone actually reduced some of the stress. With him out of town, I could talk freely with my friends without worrying about being overheard.

"Viktor can't be dead," he kept repeating in a stunned voice. "I just saw him last month at that dinner—you remember, that cancer fundraiser? I hope they catch the son-of-a-bitch who did this." I was glad he couldn't see me blanch.

I made a quick stop at the office to pick up some OPEN HOUSE signs, and one of the other agents saw me from across the room and came scurrying over so fast on her high heels that I was surprised she didn't twist an ankle. She insisted on repeating every detail from the news coverage of the crime even after I said I'd heard. "You're friends with his wife, right?" she said. "Have you talked to her?"

"Not yet." I'd tried to call, but Heather hadn't answered her phone and I was afraid any voice mail I left would sound fake. A sweet smell of sugar and grease wafted from an open box of doughnuts on the front desk. I grabbed one mindlessly, taking a big bite as if that could quell my fear and frustration.

"I just don't feel safe anymore," the agent said, looking nervously around our bland office as if she expected a carjacker to leap out from behind someone's desk or one of the potted ferns. I didn't feel safe either, but for entirely different reasons. What I wanted to do was go home, lock the door, and hide until Viktor Lysenko's death was long forgotten. But I couldn't do that. I had appointments and I had to keep up the pretense that my only involvement was as someone deeply sorry for my good friend's tragic loss. As I pulled back into my driveway around lunchtime, I spotted my neighbor, Christine Connelly, shivering outside on her lawn with her little dog. She took a hand out of her parka to wave, and it was too late to pretend I didn't see her. She's sixty-something with grown kids, an irritating woman at the best of times, nosy about my family's comings and goings, always making cryptic comments that leave me feeling off-balance. The kids love her, though, because she gives out lots of candy at Halloween and her Yorkie is adorable.

"Julie, hi!" she called, tramping across the remnants of snow to my driveway in fur-lined boots as I got out of my car, while Cinnamon trotted more gingerly behind her. "Glad I caught you," she said, pushing back blowing strands of her salt-and-pepper hair. "I wanted to talk to you about something."

"Hi Christine, I'm in a hurry today," I said, glancing at my phone, trying to pretend that I had urgent business to attend to, but she didn't budge.

"It'll only take a minute," she said, and I braced myself to hear about the carjacking for the third time, but she surprised me. "I saw you the other night and I just wanted to make sure that everything's okay."

The chill wind felt as if it had gone right through me. "The other night?" I managed to say, my tongue suddenly heavy, my mouth dry.

"Yes, I saw you leaving. After midnight, wasn't it? I was out with Cinnamon and I saw you pull out and you were going so fast I just knew something had to be wrong."

For what felt like an endless moment, I just stared at her, before self-preservation kicked in. "Oh, yes, the other night. I had to take Aubrey to the ER—she had a fever." Borrowing one of Owen's recent stories about a classmate.

"Oh, my! Is she okay?"

"Yes, she's fine," I said. At least that wasn't a lie. "It spiked really high. Over a hundred and four. I was worried."

"Of course you were," Christine said. "What caused it?"

"They don't know, but they gave her antibiotics." I bent down to pet Cinnamon, desperate to change the subject. "How is this little sweetie handling the cold?"

We'd agreed not to call Heather constantly and to make sure we were careful about what we said. But the brief conversation I eventually had with her that first day didn't do anything to relieve my nerves. On the third day, desperate to know what was happening, I took a casserole over to Heather's after a house showing nearby. There was an unfamiliar SUV parked near the garage; otherwise everything looked just as I'd last seen it. I couldn't help staring for a moment at the garage bay closest to the house, picturing Viktor's car. And his body.

An older and heavily made-up woman answered the front door, startling me. "Oh, hello, I've come to see Heather," I said, holding aloft a white porcelain dish that held some concoction of meat and potatoes that I'll admit was actually made by one of the nannies from the service I sometimes used. I'll also admit that I'd called them with this in mind, asking the agency if they could send someone who cooked. I've never made a casserole in my life, but it seemed like the thing you did after someone died. "Are you a family member?"

The woman didn't return my tentative smile, looking me up and down with a grumpy expression. "I'm Anna," she said in heavily accented English. "Vitya's mother."

"Vitya?" I said, confused, lowering the casserole dish and trying to look over her shoulder to spot Heather.

Her frown deepened. "Viktor. My son."

"Oh, yes, of course. I'm Julie, a friend of Viktor and Heather's. I'm so sorry for your loss. This is for you." I thrust the dish at her, babbling in my nervousness. "For all of you."

The corners of her mouth turned ever so slightly upward in a sour, Grinch-like smile. "How kind of you, Judy."

I'd heard about Heather's mother-in-law, but Heather's descriptions hadn't fully done her justice. Anna Lysenko was in her early seventies, a short, squat woman with very bleached-looking blond hair, styled in a strangely coquettish long bob with a Veronica Lake–inspired swoop down one side of her face. She wore a tight, shiny black polyester suit with a ruffled white shirt.

"It's Julie," I said with my own forced smile. "It's the least I could do. I'm so sorry for your loss." I leaned toward her to exchange a quick air kiss.

"He was a wonderful man," she said, delivering accolades ahead of me. "An amazing son and father. My only child." Tears spilled over, creating tracks through a heavy layer of rouge and powder and reddening her nose. Sympathetic tears welled in my own eyes and I swallowed hard, reminding myself that her son had been a bully and a brute.

She was still blocking the doorway, and I realized that Anna thought I was just dropping food off and leaving. "Um, is Heather home?"

A quick nod. "She's busy now; I'll tell her you stopped by." She shut the door in my face.

I stood there, too dumbstruck to protest, but just before it slammed, I heard Heather call, "Who's there, Anna?" and a moment later the door opened again.

"Julie! I'm so glad you're here." She sounded so pleased to see me—too pleased, I thought, catching the narrow-eyed appraisal that Anna gave her. Or was I just being paranoid?

"I'm so sorry for your loss," I said quickly, pulling her into an embrace. She clung to me for a moment, sniffling, which surprised me, but perhaps shouldn't have. This was stressful and he was, after all, her husband, even if he'd been a wife-beating ass-hole.

"She brought food; you should put this in the fridge," Anna interrupted, pushing the dish at her daughter-in-law. Heather pulled back, swiping at her eyes, but I noticed, startled, that there weren't any tears. So that was all an act—I hoped it fooled her mother-in-law as well as it had fooled me.

"Come in, Julie, come in," Heather said as she took the cas-serole dish with one hand and pulled on my arm with the other. I could feel Anna Lysenko's disapproving gaze on us as I followed her daughter-in-law into the house.

The kitchen island was covered with other casserole dishes, plus plates of cookies and at least one cake. My offering—the nanny's offering—seemed somewhat pitiful. "Strange, isn't it?" Heather said as she added my dish to the pile. "This custom of giving food when people die—I've never felt less like eating."

"I'm sorry, I should have realized you wouldn't want—"

"No, I didn't mean that," she cut me off. "I'll serve yours to-night. I'm very grateful—truly."

"How's Daniel?" I asked, glancing around, surprised not to at least hear him.

"As well as can be expected." Heather shrugged. "He's visiting Viktor's cousin right now." She must have seen the surprise on my face, because she added, "I didn't want him here with the police and everything."

And everything. From where I was standing I could see down the hall into the laundry room and I had a sudden vision of Heather standing, blood-spattered, in the doorway out to the garage. I forced the image away, turning back to see Heather making me coffee, her hair and clothes clean. She was dressed casually, as always, her jeans and T-shirt a stark contrast to her mother-in-law. The only visible signs of stress were the gray smudges from fatigue under her eyes. "I think you could wear a burlap sack and still look pretty," I said as she handed me the coffee. She smiled, but it vanished as she looked over my shoulder at something.

I turned to see Viktor's mother talking to another short, older woman, this one wearing large round glasses that seemed even larger because her silver hair was pulled back from her round face. They were whispering and shooting hostile looks at us.

"Who's that?" I muttered.

"Viktor's aunt. Olga. Yes, that's really her name. She came yesterday—she brought Anna—and she hasn't left except to drive Daniel to her daughter's house." She raised her voice and said, "Do either of you want some coffee?"

Anna shook her head, but the other woman just stared, giving me a once-over before she turned her back and stalked away down the hall. Her sister hurried after her, the two of them reminding me of bugs scuttling back to a hidey-hole.

"Charming." I rolled my eyes and Heather grinned.

"Aren't they? His whole family is like that. I don't know if that's just an Eastern European thing, not smiling, but they all seem like depressives. The only positive is there aren't too many of them."

"Do you think they suspect something?"

"I don't know. I hope not."

"Did they know about Viktor?" I asked hesitantly. "About the abuse, I mean." I was afraid of upsetting Heather, but she just shook her head.

"No. I never told Anna—she wouldn't have believed me. As far as she's concerned the world has just been robbed of the most wonderful, amazing son and father." Her voice was bitter, and I reached out to pat her arm.

"You're free now," I said in a low voice. "Just remember that."

"Not yet. Not until the police stop investigating and release the body."

She seemed a bit calmer than she had two nights ago, sitting there sipping coffee. "It's decaf," she whispered when she saw me looking. She looked around again before adding, "Don't say anything about the baby."

"You haven't told Anna?"

"Absolutely not," she said before adding, "It would just upset her."

I thought it might give Anna something to look forward to, but I didn't say that. Heather was already dealing with enough; she didn't need her overbearing mother-in-law trying to micromanage her pregnancy.

"What are you going to do about the funeral?" I asked.

"His mother's taken care of that—she called the funeral home and is arranging a service at a Ukrainian church."

"Has she asked for your help planning the service?"

She gave me a small smile. "Of course not."

Her casualness about this concerned me. I didn't blame her for not caring, but she needed to grieve publicly. We hadn't factored in problems with Viktor's family and how it would look if they seemed more upset than she did. "You should pick some special hymns or something like that," I whispered. "Claim they were particular favorites of Viktor's or something. Make sure everyone sees the great loss you've experienced."

"How about 'These Boots Are Made for Walking'?" she said.

Surprised, I laughed out loud only to promptly clamp a hand over my mouth, swiveling on the kitchen stool to see if Cruella and her sister were listening. Thankfully, the hall was empty. "Maybe 'Gone, Baby, Gone,'" I said, and this time Heather snorted.

"'Forget You,'" she said.

"'Goodbye Earl,' I mean Viktor."

"'I Will Survive.'"

We were overcome by fits of giggles and didn't hear the doorbell. Heather's aunt-in-law suddenly appeared in the kitchen doorway with Sarah in tow. Quick as you can, Heather and I pretended to be crying, swiping at eyes teary from laughter, as I said loudly, "I'm so, so sorry." Olga gave us a sour look, her suspicious gaze magnified by the enormous glasses.

"Another friend of yours is here," she announced, her tone suggesting that we were throwing a party.

"Thank you, Aunt Olga," Heather said, and the older woman made a noncommittal sniffing sound and didn't move from the doorway.

Sarah placed the wicker basket she was carrying on the marble island and hugged Heather. "This is just so awful," she said. "I didn't know what else to do, so I brought you some food." She unpacked the basket, all of us aware that Viktor's aunt was still standing in the doorway, watching. "Here's some chicken soup and a loaf of bread to go with it." Of course Sarah had made them both; I hoped she wouldn't ask about the nanny's casserole.

"Thank you," Heather said. "That's very kind of you."

"I'm so sorry about Viktor—so sorry for you and Daniel."

Their conversation sounded stilted and I tried not to glance at the doorway to see what the Ukrainian woman was making of it. We chatted like this for several minutes, a conversation so mundane that eventually it must have bored even Olga, who extracted a cell phone from some pocket and began texting as she clomped away.

"I'm surprised the police aren't here," Sarah whispered. "I was afraid of running into them."

"They've been and gone," Heather said, turning away to pour a cup of coffee for Sarah.

"When was that?" I asked as Sarah said, "Do they think it was a carjacking?"

"A few hours ago, and I don't know. I think so." Heather handed a mug to Sarah, who took it without looking and just as automatically set it down. "They didn't say much about it; they were asking a lot of questions."

"What? What did they ask?" Sarah's voice rose and she sounded incredibly nervous.

"Calm down," I hissed, glancing around. "We don't want to attract attention."

Heather didn't answer and looked down at her watch. "Do you think they'll have finished the autopsy by now? What if they can tell that the body was moved?"

"What did they want to know?" Sarah persisted.

"Don't ask too many questions in case the in laws can hear us," I whispered. "It will look suspicious."

This time we all heard the doorbell and Heather moved toward it. She came back in the kitchen a few minutes later with one of the other mothers from school. Terry Holloway was carrying a large aluminum pan. "Oh, hello," she said when she saw me and Sarah, her small, probably fixed, ferrety nose sniffing the air while she darted beady-eyed looks about the room. I doubted she'd ever been in Heather's house before—she was an acquaintance rather than a friend, one of those women who believed that personal power came from the collection, and distribution, of gossip.

"This is for you and Daniel—it's lasagna," she said to Heather, holding her pan aloft. "You can freeze it, which you probably should given everything here." She headed for the large stainless-steel refrigerator without waiting for Heather's reply, taking it upon herself to shuffle the food in the freezer to make room for her dish.

After that she circled the island, examining the other food with a proprietary air, shifting dishes and lifting lids to get a better look. "What on earth are you going to do with all these cookies and cakes?" she said to Heather. "You can't eat all this sugar and stay so skinny." A short laugh followed that sounded like a squawk. It seemed to echo off the tile.

A scraping sound punctuated the awkward silence as Terry stepped on something. We all looked toward the floor, but she bent down first. "Where did this come from?" she said, holding up a silver disk. I recognized it immediately—it belonged to Viktor.

The shocked look that flashed across Sarah's face told me that she'd recognized it, too, and Heather seemed downright panicky for a moment.

"Oh, what is it?" I asked, leaning forward to look, hoping Terry would focus on me and not the others, forcing my interest to sound casual.

"It's a saint's medal," Heather said, and her voice was smooth.

She picked it up and slipped it into her pocket. "Viktor gave it to me."

We avoided each other's eyes. Viktor always wore that medal. It must have come off that night when he and Heather struggled. What if it could be seen around his neck in footage from the hospital? Would anyone notice that he'd been wearing the medal earlier that night, but wasn't wearing it when he was found?

Was it my imagination, or was Terry giving Heather a knowing look? "Aren't you missing someone?" she said after a minute, looking from Sarah, to me, then Heather. "Alison Riordan," she said when none of us said anything. "You four do everything together." Another squawk of laughter. What was that gleam in her eyes about? Even her smile seemed menacing.

"I'd better get going," I said, desperate to get out from under her gaze. I gave Heather another quick hug. "I'm so sorry about Viktor. Call me if you need anything—anything at all."

But it was Sarah who called later. "I can't believe Heather didn't find that when she cleaned up," she said. "And of all the people to find it, of course it had to be Terry Holloway."

"It could be worse," I said. "It could have been Viktor's mom who found it."

"Or the police."

"What if Terry tells them?"

"I don't think she recognized it," Sarah said. "But that busy-body would love to have something to share with the police."

Sarah had also encouraged Heather to get involved in the funeral planning. "I know it's hard to act as if he was this incredible, loving husband, but I hope she can fake it or the in-laws—and all the other people like Terry—are going to start asking questions."

chapter eighteen

HEATHER

No one must know. This is what I tell myself over and over again, afraid that I'll blurt it out, that I'll scream it in the funeral home, that I'll tell the director or all of his helpers, with their dark suits and bland faces. I feel as if I'll babble it to anyone who comes to express his or her sympathies. It was me, I'll say. I did it. I shot him.

You're hysterical. Pull yourself together. Stop blubbering. All the things he would say, but of course he isn't here to say them. Not now. My cheeks throb and I can still feel the last time he slapped me.

The funeral home collected his body, so I didn't have to see Viktor postautopsy, which was a relief. It had been hard enough to identify him at the morgue. I'd practiced in the mirror to look appropriately shocked, but as it turned out I hadn't had to fake it. The dead man on the metal slab didn't really look like Viktor at all, at least not at first glance. It took me a minute to see beyond the swollen face and redness and other odd marks. He'd been contorted in his precious car for so long that the blood had rushed to certain areas and not to others. No matter how prepared I was, it was still a shock to see him lying there, naked and dead. I half-expected him to sit up on the table and point a finger accusingly at me. I remembered to ask how he'd died, to act as if I didn't know. I didn't have to force a reaction. I shook and wept, not from sorrow, but from fear.

It took them forever to release the body. Apparently that's

pretty standard in cases like this, or so the police told me when I called every day to check. I wanted him to be cremated. Just get it done so I could get on with the business of forgetting. Of course, his mother wouldn't accept that, she wants a big funeral, and I am afraid to protest. She insisted on being part of the planning, which meant that she picked the most expensive coffin available, but I let her have it. After all, she'll be the only truly sad person in the room. I made sure to watch clips of sad movies on my phone so I could be red-eyed and puffy when we arrived at the funeral home to make the arrangements, and I kept up the pretense, dabbing at my eyes as we discussed the coffin, the suit Viktor would wear, the schedule for the visitation, while Viktor's mother sobbed, using up an entire box of the funeral home's tissues. The director, a dapper little man who smelled of hair gel, kept passing it to her, his face downcast as if he was moved by our loss, when I suspect the only emotion he truly felt was impatience at how long the process was taking. I was impatient, too, desperate to get out of the place. As we were leaving, Anna bustling ahead of me out of the funeral home, I turned back and quickly handed Viktor's medal over to the director.

Worse than that first visit was having to return two days later, ahead of the official visitation, to admire the work they'd done. I wanted a closed casket, but of course Viktor's mother wouldn't hear of it. "Don't worry," the director said to me, "none of his, um, injuries, will show." I still hesitated to approach the coffin, feeling almost as fearful as I had that night, standing by the door out to the garage, the gun trembling in my hand.

All Viktor's swelling and redness was gone. Now my late husband was a waxy department-store mannequin, his skin so pale that they'd added makeup. I could see a knife-thin streak of foundation near his collar and knew that the faint hint of pink in his cheeks came from rouge. The medal was around his neck, lying on the outside of his expensive shirt and silk tie in a way that my husband never wore it, but his mother seemed pleased. The coffin was a huge, satin-padded mahogany box, Viktor tucked into its folds like a piece of expensive mail-order fruit that got delayed somewhere in transit, polished and presentable, hiding a rotting core.

There was a cloying, heavily perfumed scent in the room from the dozens of flower arrangements that had already arrived, drooping lilies and overblown roses, spider-like chrysanthemums and fussy white carnations, alongside pots of ferns and other green plants. But it wasn't the odor from the flowers catching in my throat, making me gag. It was the blood.

The smell isn't real. It can't be. There is no reason to still have that salty, sweet-sour, metallic taste in my mouth, or feel that spray of blood and bone matter coating my body.

I'd been afraid that I wouldn't be able to go through with it, afraid of what would happen if he saw me with the gun, afraid of him grabbing it from me, but when I held the gun I realized I was tired of feeling powerless.

Pinned against the wall, hand tight on my throat, his eyes boring into mine. "No one will ever love you like I do."

Viktor turned his back as he got into the car and that's when I fired. He jerked forward, head dropping, and for a moment there was nothing but that fine red mist, the ringing in my ears, and a faint puff of gray-white smoke.

Every time I close my eyes I replay the shower I took that night, all that blood circling down the drain, as if I were Janet Leigh in *Psycho*. Except *I* am the killer. Is this why the smell of blood lingers? Why aren't I smelling the bleach that I scrubbed over every affected surface, including my own body?

I was afraid Anna would smell the bleach when she came to the house, but she didn't say anything. Maybe the candles had covered up the scent. Or maybe she assumed it was from the cleaners. She is suspicious anyway. She's never liked me; she didn't like Viktor's first wife either, all of her supposed devotion to that woman's memory just a way of irritating me. Anna wanted a good Ukrainian girl for her son and she'd been convinced that she could just wait out this marriage. But it's her son who has timed out, not me. Looking down on Viktor in his coffin I wondered if I'd ever truly loved him. How do you separate love from need? Or fear?

I kissed my fingers and pressed them to his cold lips, playing the grieving widow. No one else can know the truth, about him, about us. There are secrets in every marriage. This is my secret, Viktor's and mine, and he's taken it to the grave. No one must know.

chapter nineteen

SARAH

I didn't tell the others, but Viktor Lysenko's was not the first dead body I'd seen. When I was in my twenties and fresh out of law school, I worked briefly for a local defense attorney who handled a lot of high-profile and controversial cases.

"This isn't right," my boss said one day, waving around the autopsy results the medical examiner's office had just faxed over. "He's saying the marks are consistent with the knife found in possession of our client—that's got to be some bull that the DA talked him into."

He had to be in court, so he sent me, the fresh-faced twenty-six-year-old who'd cried when she accidentally ran over a squirrel, to talk with the medical examiner at the county morgue.

"There is no error," the medical examiner said when I stumbled through why I'd been sent to see him. I made the mistake of implying that *he'd* made a mistake, and he traded the paternalistic smile he'd greeted me with for a frostiness that made me feel even smaller than I am. "The stab wounds are three centimeters long and jagged—apparently this is consistent with the weapon found in possession of your client." He stood up from his desk. "Come along—I'll show you."

If the same thing happened today, I'd say no or walk out. But I was young back then and susceptible to bullies. He led the way into a chilly room with a long row of stacked stainless-steel drawers and yanked one open. "This way," he said, gesturing impatiently with his hand, when he turned to see that I hadn't

151

moved from my position near the door. "Come here and look at the wounds yourself."

I inched my way toward the open steel drawer and the waxy-looking figure lying upon it. It was a woman of about my own age and weight, who'd been stabbed and had her throat slit by her boyfriend because, or so he was insisting, she'd attacked him. She was lying there on the slab naked, her pale, fragile body completely exposed. I could see the wounds clearly, though they were no longer bloody, just gashes, as if she weren't human, but some stuffed upholstery that had split open, an impression reinforced by the rows of even stitches made postautopsy. There was a line across her forehead, and it took a moment for me to realize that they'd sawed open her skull.

I can remember that there didn't seem to be enough air in the room, that I struggled to breathe. I can remember looking away from the body, gazing frantically at the medical examiner's dispassionate expression, before glancing up at the lights. The next thing I knew I was sitting in a hallway being told to breathe into a paper bag. Hyperventilating from stress, the medical examiner said. "Tell your boss to come himself next time," he said when I'd recovered enough strength to leave.

At the visitation, more than ten days after his death, Viktor's head didn't show this line. It had been covered by heavy makeup, all evidence of the postmortem carefully concealed, just like the gaping wounds the bullet had left in the front and back of his skull. But I knew they were there, and at first, as I stared down at him in his coffin, I felt that same panicky struggle to breathe.

The visitation was in an old brick building in Ambridge, the choice becoming clear when I saw the name, Beresko Funeral Home, embossed in gold on the outside. It was Ukrainian. The narrow building had old rooms made up in heavily patterned, jewel-toned wallpaper, as if they were *pysanky*.

Viktor didn't look like he had in real life, despite the comments so many people were making as they passed his coffin, a heavily polished dark wood with large brass handles and lined with puffy cream-colored satin. "He looks so handsome," I heard one older woman murmur to Anna Lysenko. "Just like he always did."

But to me, there was nothing natural-looking about him. Viktor hadn't worn makeup when he was alive, and no amount of foundation or blush can simulate the glow that blood flow brings to the skin. There were visible comb marks in his short brown hair, which I'd never noticed before. He wore a dark suit and a white shirt with a collar so sharp it seemed to be cutting into his throat. His tie was bright blue and he had a small pin affixed to his lapel—apparently a symbol of membership in some medical organization. The medal that Terry Holloway had picked off the kitchen floor had been attached to a silver chain and was weirdly centered on Viktor's tie. Someone had folded his fine-boned surgeon's hands neatly across his chest. Looking closely, I could see that makeup had been added to this skin, too. He looked so different, and after a minute I realized what it was: He looked vulnerable.

"You'd never guess that he choked her with those hands," Alison murmured after I'd sufficiently paid my respects and joined her standing at the rear of the room among the huge flower arrangements flanking the walls. The cloying and competing scents of dozens of varieties of cut flowers filled the tight space.

"You'd never guess it looking at Heather either," I whispered, glancing across the room where the grieving widow sat in a receiving line, tearfully greeting people, flanked on either side by Viktor's mother and aunt.

"Did you spot the police?" Alison murmured. "They're here."

Alarmed, I tried to look around the room without attracting any attention. I saw mourners, a huge crowd, many of them Viktor's colleagues from the hospital, a few still dressed in scrubs and lab coats. "Where?" I said. "I can't spot anyone out of place."

"The man in the blue suit at ten o'clock," Alison said, "but don't look now. Wait a minute." I kept my eyes down for a moment before moving my gaze up and slowly in that direction. The man was standing by a doorway, not in the line waiting to pass by the coffin, and not in any of the small clusters of mourners.

"He's a detective? How can you tell?" He didn't fit my vision of the police at all, this short, stout man with a bald head and fuzzy fringe of graying hair. I'd met with various members of the police force when I was a lawyer, but none of them had looked quite as, well, nerdy as this guy. He looked like he worked for Charles Schwab, or, given that cheap suit and those orthopedic shoes, I also could have pegged him as a high school teacher. That's who he really reminded me of, one of my high school history teachers, Mr. Fussel, who all the kids had called Mr. Fossil because he was about as lively as one, droning on about supposedly vitally important moments in history without capturing anyone's interest.

"He just looks like one. I'd lay money on it," Alison said, speaking so softly that I had to strain to hear her. "And I'll bet his partner is the guy standing next to the table with the guest book." She didn't have to tell me again not to look; I waited a second and then let my gaze move casually across the space. The other guy was less of a surprise. Young, fit, with a crew cut and an intense look on his face, he definitely looked like cops I'd known. He reminded me of a neighbor's Doberman pinscher— a watchdog on high alert. His eyes met mine and I quickly looked away, afraid he'd read the panic in my face.

I hoped they were here because they thought the carjacker might feel guilty and come pay his respects and not because they were watching us. I was going to ask Alison her opinion, but just then Eric left the conversation he was having and crossed the room to my side. "Almost ready to go?"

Alison smiled at him and moved off into the crowd. I glanced at my watch, surprised to see that we'd been there for almost two hours; we didn't want to pay for too much time with the babysitter. "Sure, I guess. Let me just say good-bye to Heather."

Julie was also there, across the room talking to various people. I'd waved at her earlier, but we'd agreed in advance that it was a bad idea for us to be seen hanging out as a group. That had been Alison's suggestion and I'd been initially skeptical, but not anymore. I was aware of the nerdy detective watching as I cut the line to say a quick good bye to Heather, and I felt his gaze on me again as I joined Eric in the hall and we maneuvered our way through the crowd toward the exit.

"You okay?" Eric put his arm around me and gave me a squeeze. "How's Heather holding up?"

"As well as can be expected, I guess. I haven't been able to talk to her much."

"She's going to need you after this is all over, you and Julie and Alison are her biggest support network."

"She's got other friends," I said quickly, concerned that the Doberman pinscher standing at the exit might have overheard us.

"Yeah, but it's not tight like the bond you four share."

Tighter than he knew. I flushed. One of the hardest parts was not being able to tell Eric what had happened. We didn't keep secrets from each other. Not along the lines of what had transpired at Heather's house and what we'd done. What I'd done. Of course, before this there'd never been anything of this magnitude to keep from him. It was hard to believe it had been barely two weeks since that horrible night.

"I can't believe he's actually dead," Eric said as we walked out to our car. "One minute you're driving along, living your life, and the next minute—bam!"

I jumped, but he didn't notice. "What kind of person would do a thing like that?" he said, shaking his head. "Jesus."

We drove home in a silence that was becoming increasingly common between us. Eric reached over at one point and squeezed my hand. I knew he thought that I was grieving for my friend. He couldn't know that for the last few nights, after turning off the lights and drifting off to sleep, I'd relive that decision, all of us standing around in that garage, staring into the dark cavity at the back of Viktor's head. Sometimes I'd jerk awake to the sound of plastic snapping as Alison shook it out to drape over his body.

chapter twenty

Being at Viktor's visitation felt surreal. I hadn't been at a funeral since I was young, and that time Sean and I had been the ones sitting in the chairs, receiving sympathies, like Heather and her in-laws. The line for Viktor was huge, snaking through the cramped hallway and spilling into the foyer, so that the funeral-home attendants, men in somber black suits who smelled of pomade and cologne, had to take shifts at the front doors. They directed mourners for Dr. Lysenko to the end of the line while ushering a much smaller group of mourners to a side room, where a wizened old woman was laid out in a ghastly white coffin.

There were lots of people from the hospital, of course, plus plenty of parents with children Daniel's age. Multiple young women dressed in scrubs were weeping and I thought of how Viktor had always been able to turn on the old-world charm.

"Oh, God, this is going to take way over an hour," Michael muttered when we joined the line, glancing at his watch. "We should text the babysitter."

That was when I noticed the detectives. The shorter, older one had been lingering near the front door, his hand moving repeatedly between a bowl of pastel mints on the table next to him and his mouth. Toss, chew, toss, and chew as his little eyes rapidly surveyed the crowd.

For a moment I thought about leaving, agreeing with Michael that the line was far too long and we should just move straight to the coffin, pay our respects directly to Viktor, and duck out.

Except that would call attention to us, far more attention than just standing there. Michael was saying something, making a joke about how we could probably take care of all our medical issues by consulting with half the line, but I could barely hear him. I felt as if all sound had faded away as I watched the detective's darting, raptorlike gaze fall on one person, then another. I turned away, smiling at Michael as if I were listening, while I could feel the man turn his scrutiny on me. It felt searing, a brand being pressed against my skin. I actually started to sweat and Michael said, "Are you feeling okay? You look flushed."

Why was the detective still looking? Did he recognize me? The weight pressing against my skin was too much to bear. I turned to confront him, startled to see that the man had his back turned. He wasn't looking at me at all.

"I'm fine," I said, digging around in my purse for a tissue to dab against my face. "It's just hot in here."

By the time we reached Heather I'd adjusted to the police presence; I'd spotted another detective once we'd inched our way up the line and into the viewing room itself. I hadn't adjusted to the soundtrack playing in the background, an Eastern European dirge that someone said was a Ukrainian folk song. "If I have to listen to this for much longer *I'll* incite a revolution," I whispered to Michael.

There was only one couple ahead of us, an elderly man and a woman I'd taken for his daughter until I overheard her murmur a reminder about taking his Viagra. When it was their turn, they took forever talking to Heather, who accepted the odd couple's sympathy with a solemn expression, nodding at their stories, then giving a slight smile when they declared how much they loved Viktor and were going to miss him. "He was one of a kind," the man said, patting Heather's hand. Yes, he was, but not in the way the man meant.

"We're so sorry for your loss," I said when it was our turn, and Michael echoed me. Heather thanked us with the same somber grace, accepting our handshakes and the half-embrace I bent to give her. It felt odd to stand there and pretend that this was the first time I'd seen her since Viktor's death, but she didn't give the slightest hint of pretense. She looked serene, like a Botticelli virgin, yet in her black Chanel suit, patent heels, and diamond-and-pearl necklace and earrings, she was every inch the doctor's widow.

Of course, we'd had to shake Anna Lysenko's hand first, and voice the same sentiments to her. Then there was her sister, Olga, and the sallow-faced younger woman with a dyed black pixie cut, who was introduced to us as Irina, Viktor's first cousin. Far from being serene like Heather, Irina had bloodshot eyes and a sullen, surly expression. "They were very close," Aunt Olga informed me, patting her daughter's hand until the younger woman yanked hers away. "We're so sorry for your loss," I murmured, and Irina teared up and clutched my hand, startling me.

When we finally got out of there, I was surprised to discover that it was still light out, the last of the day dropping off in bright bands of red on the horizon. "God, I thought that would never be over," Michael said, pulling his tie free as we picked our way through the crowded parking lot to our car.

"I'm sorry for Heather," I said. "The line is still out the door."

"What a turnout! All of these people coming to honor her husband—that's got to be comforting."

"Mmm." I tried to sound noncommittal.

"Do you think I'd pull this kind of crowd if I died?"

"I don't want to think about you dying," I said, flashing back to the strong smell of blood in the garage and seeing Viktor slumped over in his car.

"It's okay," Michael said, putting his arm around me as he saw me shudder. "I'm not going anywhere."

It wasn't the thought of *his* death that frightened me, but of course I couldn't tell him.

Michael pulled out of the parking lot as I texted the babysitter to let her know we'd be home soon. "You know, I shouldn't say this," Michael said, "but I never liked Viktor."

He seemed surprised when I leaned over to give him a resounding kiss on the cheek. "What's that for?"

"Nothing," I said. "I just love you."

At home the kids were clamoring for attention, excited because this wasn't an ordinary afternoon and they'd gotten to watch movies and eat popcorn and candy with the babysitter, Kristi, a plump and cheerful high school senior, popular with kids but not parents, because she did nothing but watch TV with the kids and allow them to fill up on junk food. The neighborhood's first choice for sitter had always been Angela, who could tutor your children in Chinese, if you so desired, and had been the first-chair cellist in the high school orchestra, before she graduated and went to study biochemistry at Stanford.

Kristi's one asset was that she seemed to enjoy our kids' company as much as they enjoyed hers. I didn't enjoy the mess that she'd leave in her wake—popcorn kernels scattered across the living room rug, a pile of DVD cases spilled across the coffee table next to sticky juice glasses and crumpled candy wrappers.

"We watched *Finding Nemo* again, Mommy!" Matthew told me for the fourth time since we'd stepped in the door. "Are you sad we watched it without you?"

"No, of course not, sweetie," I said, hugging him with one arm while I tried to slip out of my jacket.

"Mommy is sad because of Daniel's dad, not a dumb movie," Lucy announced in her best imperious big-sister voice.

"It's not dumb," Matthew protested. "Mommy, Lucy thinks it's dumb. *Finding Nemo* isn't dumb, is it?"

"It's not dumb, you are," Lucy said before I could respond.

"Lucy called me dumb!" Matthew wailed, face turning red as he waved his index finger at his older sister as if it were a wand. If only I had a wand to make these arguments magically disappear.

"Don't call your brother dumb," I said automatically, stepping around them to hang my coat up in the hall closet. Michael had

offered to drive the babysitter home, smartly managing to avoid
the chaos. I tuned out the kids' arguing, trying to decide what to
make for dinner. Just as I was closing the closet door, I heard a
pinging sound and realized I'd left my phone in my coat pocket.
A text from Sarah. It said simply Watch this! with a link to a local
CBS affiliate. If I'd gotten it in an email I would have assumed it
was spam and deleted it. I pressed the link and it opened, a
broadcast from last night. "Police are releasing video tonight of
slain plastic surgeon Dr. Viktor Lysenko's final drive—"

"What is it, Mommy? What are you watching?" Lucy hung on
my arm trying to pull the phone down to see.

"—along I-279. Dr. Lysenko was killed in an apparent carjacking over a week ago and police are actively looking for—"

"Nothing, it's not important," I said, quickly shutting it off
and slipping the phone in my pocket. "Let's go see what we can
make for dinner—or are you too full of junk to eat anything
else?"

"Too full of junk," Matthew agreed with a laugh, bouncing
along next to me as I headed into the kitchen. What was on that
video and where had it come from? Were there cameras along
all roads, even the small roads outside of the city? We should
have thought about that the other night, we should have realized
that Viktor's drive home had probably been recorded. And what
about our driving? Had we been recorded? I felt sick as I scoured
the cupboards for something quick to feed my family.

"Mac and cheese?" Michael's reaction wasn't nearly as enthused
as the children's had been. He stood in the kitchen surveying the
empty cardboard cartons that were still on the counter.

"We saved some for you, Daddy!" Matthew exclaimed, waving his spoon around excitedly in the air. Exactly how much
sugar had Kristi given him?

"Thanks, buddy," Michael said with a forced smile, taking a
bowl down from the cupboard.

"There's also some salad," I said, indicating my own bowl of greens. "Of course, you're welcome to make something else." I was proud of keeping my tone light, when what I wanted to do was lash out at him because of the stress.

Michael halfheartedly offered to do the kitchen cleanup and I accepted with alacrity, hurrying the kids upstairs for their baths and feeling very grateful that they were past the age where I had to worry about them drowning. Lucy had refused to keep bathing with her brother almost two years earlier, which meant that I'd usually stagger their baths, but not tonight. I needed some privacy, so I told Lucy to bathe in our large master tub at the same time that her brother was in the bath down the hall. To inspire cooperation and minimize complaints, I said they could each have a bubble bath. It worked. Ten minutes later they were in their respective tubs, happily flicking bubbles, while I pulled out my phone in the privacy of my bedroom and clicked open the link from Sarah.

"KDKA is the first to bring you this footage of carjacking victim Dr. Viktor Lysenko's drive home from Pittsburgh's East End to his home in Sewickley Heights." The announcer's voice was breathless, as if something super exciting were being shown, but all I could see was grainy footage of cars zipping along a stretch of road. This was I-279, the announcer said, before the film slowed down and then I could make out the vibrant green of Viktor's Mercedes. What time had that been? Were they going to talk about drive time between the city and Sewickley and the discrepancy between the times he'd been on that road and when the police supposed the carjacking had taken place?

"Police are hoping that the drivers of the vehicles surrounding Dr. Lysenko's Mercedes, especially this black Ford Escalade," an arrow appeared above an SUV tailgating the Mercedes, "will come forward to help with the investigation."

Wait a minute—did that mean what it sounded like? I peeked into the bathrooms to check on the kids, who seemed fine, although there was an ominous-looking bubble island growing on the tile floor in the main bath. Ducking back into the bedroom, I called Sarah's cell phone.

"Yes, they think that SUV could have been involved in the carjacking," she said excitedly, agreeing with me.

I felt a tiny bubble of optimism forming, but it popped just as quickly. "Aren't those tapes time-stamped? Surely they can figure out that he was on I-279 much earlier in the evening."

"If that's true, then wouldn't they mention that?" She made a sound; was that a hiccup? "Maybe there was no time on the recording."

"Or maybe the police haven't released that information. Anyway, even if they don't know the time, once the other drivers come forward, they'll figure it out."

"*If* the other drivers come forward. That's a big if. The cameras don't pick up the license plates, so the police can't find them that way. And it doesn't mean anything even if they do come forward—Viktor still could have been carjacked by someone else." She paused, and I thought I heard her swallowing something, before she laughed again. "Releasing that video means that they believe it—they think he was carjacked."

"Mommy!" Matthew yelled from the bathroom. "I'm done!"

"I've got to go, Sarah."

"Sure, but cheer up, okay? You're the one who came up with the carjacking idea—and you were right, they believe it. You should be happy."

"I am," I said, though "happiness" didn't really describe it. It was more like a knot being loosened, this slight lessening of the constant tension that had plagued me since that late-night call from Heather.

chapter twenty-one

JULIE

The funeral two days later was mobbed. The viewing had been crowded, but because the service was also being held in Ambridge, ten miles down the Ohio River from Sewickley, I hadn't anticipated the standing-room-only crowd. St. Michael's was a huge old Ukrainian Catholic church, the stone still black in spots from the soot left by long-closed mills that had once blanketed the region. That soot couldn't be simply washed away; it had to be sandblasted off, a costly procedure that often left remnants, black lace etched into the façade. As if to compensate for the stone that wouldn't come clean, there were gold and gleaming onion domes perched on top of the building, like head-lamps on coal miners.

The inside was lit almost solely by candles, waxy pillars on iron stands flickering at the end of every pew and rows of vo-tives glowing like little suns beneath flat-faced, sloe-eyed por-traits of Jesus with his apostles or Mary and her infant son. The stained-glass windows were a riot of jewel-toned colors, and at the front of the church, surrounding a gilt-draped altar, were screens covered with life-size icons of Jesus, discernible from the other pale and bearded men because of the nail wounds.

The sight was quite a lot for people used to the spare décor and simple spires of the Presbyterian Church. Brian and I were as dumbstruck as the kids, staring at everything with the open-mouthed awe of tourists.

We'd come early and gotten a pew toward the front, which

might have been a mistake, I thought as I put a hand once more on Aubrey's leg, quietly urging her to stop kicking the pew in front of us. We'd decided to bring the children because Heather was bringing Daniel and we thought it would be good for him to see his friends. Other people had the same idea; despite the distance, all around the church were familiar faces from the elementary school. Of course, Sarah and Alison were there with their families. I'd seen Sarah and Eric when we walked in, but when Brian started in their direction I hesitated and then led the way toward a pew across the aisle instead.

"What's up?" he asked in a low voice, after we'd excused our way past several old women wearing head scarves and dour expressions. We settled into a pew with the children. "You don't want to sit with them?"

"Might get too rowdy with the k-i-d-s," I said, only to have Aubrey proclaim, "K-I-D-S. Kids!" She looked at both of us with a beaming smile.

"Yes, kids, very good, sweetheart," Brian said.

"Julie, hi!" I heard a stage whisper and I turned to see my neighbor, Christine Connelly, slide into the pew next to me. "Whew, I'm glad I made it—I almost didn't find the place," she said, breathing hard and fanning herself with a program. "This is some church, isn't it?"

I nodded, trying to offer a welcoming smile, while regretting not choosing the seats next to Sarah and Eric. Christine sidled closer on the pew, giving me an expectant look while tucking strands of graying hair behind her ears as if desperate not to miss a word of the conversation I didn't want to have.

"I didn't realize you knew the Lysenkos," I said.

"Oh, I know everybody in Sewickley," she said, waving a little hand airily, before adding in a lower tone, "Or I know of them." She gave me a conspiratorial look. What did it mean?

Christine always made me feel off-balance. Before I could think of a way to ask what that meant, she said, "I see you brought the kids—you don't think all this talk about the d-e-a-d is too much for them?"

"D-E-A-D. Deed!" Aubrey proclaimed.

Before I could stop her, Christine said, "Close, sweetie, but that spells 'dead.'"

Brian and I exchanged a look as Aubrey's eyes widened. She opened her mouth to ask something, but Christine got her question in first, for once saying the right thing. "How old are you now?"

Aubrey ducked her head shyly against her father, but held up one of her chubby little hands like a starfish, fingers splayed.

"Five?"

"Yes!" Aubrey flashed a quick smile. "But on my next birthday, I will be this many." She held up the index finger of her left hand next to the starfish.

"My goodness, six years old!" Christine said, and then to me, "She's clearly feeling better—so it was nothing serious?"

"Serious?"

"Her late-night fever? I saw you leaving for the emergency room that night, remember?"

Color flooded my face—I could feel the heat. I'd completely forgotten about the excuse I'd given her. Worse, Brian was listening to the conversation.

He said to me, "You were at the ER? When was this?"

"It's nothing," I said. "Everyone's fine." I looked past him, feigning concern. "I think Owen might have to use the bathroom—can you ask him?"

Brian looked confused, but he dutifully turned to our son as Christine chattered on, oblivious to my discomfort. "You can never be too careful with a fever," she said. "Could have been meningitis or one of those terrible staph infections. Although you would have been better off taking her to the doctor—you pay so much more if you go to the ER."

"Were you ever a patient of Dr. Lysenko's?" I asked, desperate to change the subject.

"Julie! Really, what kind of question is that?" she said in a shocked voice, giving a flustered laugh and fanning herself again with her program.

"Sorry," I said, "I didn't mean to imply—"

"Not that there's anything wrong with plastic surgery," she said. "No one wants to talk about it, but everybody gets a little work done, don't they?" Another laugh as she self-consciously touched the skin at her temples. She looked around for a moment and then down at her program. It was clear that she was now the one desperate to change the subject. "So sad about his son," she said, tapping the program, which had a grinning photo of Viktor on the front with flowery script below it that read, "Loving son, husband, and father." Anna Lysenko had made it clear that she came first for her son even at the end of his life. "But from what I hear things weren't exactly happy in that marriage."

"Really?" I tried to keep my voice and expression neutral, but I was immediately on alert. "Where did you hear that?"

"Oh, come now, you're friends with his wife—I'm sure you know all about it." She gave me an expectant look.

"I don't know what you're talking about," I said, darting a quick glance around to see if anyone had overheard her. "They seemed happy to me."

"That's not what I heard," Christine said.

Just then Aubrey, who'd clambered up on the pew and was looking toward the back of the church, spotted Daniel entering with his mother. "Daniel!" she shouted, pointing. "There's Daniel! Hi Dan!" Her cries echoed through the church as I pulled her down, clamping a hand gently over her mouth.

"Shh, you can't shout in church," I said, trying to pretend that I didn't see Christine staring at me, waiting.

The organist saved me, playing a few heavy chords, a welcome signal that the service was about to begin. We stood as one, the noise like a startled flock rising, the sound echoing up through the painted wooden beams that crisscrossed the ceiling. A choir entered in a procession, singing a sad song in Ukrainian and then in English, the congregation stumbling through the unfamiliar notes that had been provided in the program. A bishop wearing an elaborate mushroom-shaped crown and flowing gold-embossed robes followed them. He carried a gold shepherd's crook up the aisle, flanked by robed priests swinging metal incense balls from chains, the heavy, spicy smoke wafting over the congregation and setting off a torrent of muffled coughing. Two altar boys came next, bearing gold candlesticks with lit pillars, and then came the coffin, draped in a white cloth that had a red and gold cross embroidered on its center.

Processing slowly behind the coffin, which was wheeled on a metal stretcher by eight pallbearers, were Heather with Daniel and Anna, and then Olga, Irina, and a small group of other people I assumed were the rest of Viktor's family. Viktor had been strikingly handsome, but perhaps his genes had come primarily from his father's side, because Anna stuck out for all the wrong reasons in a shiny, tight black dress and heavy makeup, gold jewelry weighing down her neck and arms, and her head covered with a lace mantilla that reminded me of a Spanish bullfight.

Heather, in contrast, wore a plain black dress, the simple A-line design serving to emphasize her willowy figure, just as her blond hair pulled back in a loose chignon only highlighted her fine, long neck. The only things marring her looks were her red nose and eyes, and she clutched some tissues in one hand and held on to Daniel with the other. As I mentally applauded her acting ability, my gaze fell on Daniel, and sudden tears flooded my own eyes at the sight of this small boy walking behind his father's coffin.

They processed up the main aisle, filing into the front pew. Viktor's mother wept loudly as the pallbearers left the coffin at center stage in the aisle and took their seats.

"Mommy, he's got a funny hat," Aubrey said of the bishop, and a ripple of nervous laughter floated through the crowd around us. "Shh," I whispered, digging in my bag for the books I'd brought to entertain her. "Here, look at these."

There were numerous references to Viktor's happy family life, and Christine nudged me. "Hardly, right?" she muttered, giving me a wink.

It was a relief when the service was finally over and we filed out into the cold, windy day, blinking in the hard light. I tried to lose her in the crowd, but Christine followed close on my heels.

"I don't like to speak ill of the dead," she said in a low voice as we watched the coffin pass by on the shoulders of the pallbearers. "But the living aren't off-limits, right?" She gave me another wink and a little grin. "I know you have some stories to tell." She stared at me with that same glint in her eyes.

"Sorry, Christine, I've got to get the kids home," I said, giving Brian a little push. "Let's go," I muttered.

"What? Don't you want to go to the wake?"

"No, the kids are restless—let's go. No one will notice if we're missing—not with this crowd."

The hot and heavily perfumed air, along with Christine's comments, had given me a headache, which only got worse when I spotted one of the detectives in the crowd as we left. "Let's go," I said, urging Owen to walk faster as I swung Aubrey up into my arms.

"What was Christine talking about?" Brian asked, hustling to keep up with me as I wove between cars in the parking lot. "You took Aubrey to the ER one night?"

"I think she confused me with another neighbor," I said. "She does that all the time—maybe it's early dementia?"

He accepted this, thank God. A momentary feeling of relief washed over me once we were all actually in our car and driving away. Nobody knew anything, I reminded myself. The video Sarah sent proved that. And it was done now. Viktor was gone and buried, and while the police might keep searching for his carjacker, plenty of cases went unsolved. I just had to keep reminding myself of that. Random acts of violence happened every day; why shouldn't Viktor's death just get chalked up as one of those? These first few weeks after his death would be the worst, but the stress was almost over.

I didn't realize until later that day that this was only the beginning.

chapter twenty-two

ALISON

In that sweltering crush of mourners, I'd broken into a sweat, remembering another funeral, years ago, in a church that I could barely remember. It was all just a blur of dark wood and flickering candles, except for my very clear memory of the life-like crucifix hanging over the altar, a frail Jesus dangling from what had looked at a distance like real nails.

"Suffer the little children." I could still remember the breathless voice of a large woman who'd attempted to comfort me and Sean, bending over with clear effort in front of our pew, the skirt of her immense dress fluttering against me like a great black moth as she tried to stroke my head. She'd meant it kindly, but I'd flinched from her, leaning against my brother. I remembered the way she'd exchanged glances with a man standing next to her, and I could still hear that voice, her labored whisper, saying to him, *"See them?"* Pausing to breathe heavily. *"What's going to happen to these poor children?"*

The bishop at Viktor's funeral was also a heavy breather, the microphone picking up every inhalation during his long sermon. There were sniffling sounds as some people quietly wept, and faint rustling as they searched pockets and purses for tissues.

"Viktor Lysenko was a loving son," he said, "a devoted husband and father, a gifted healer, one of a select group of men and women in our world who have been entrusted with easing the suffering of those around them."

I snorted without thinking. Michael gave me a surprised look

171

and a woman in front of me glanced over her shoulder. I quickly pressed a tissue against my nose, pretending to be blowing. *Gifted healer.* Images flooded me—the bruises, the burns, the shards of glass all over their kitchen floor. I squirmed in my seat as I listened to the accolades, which went on and on. After the bishop, the priest spoke, detailing how charming Viktor had been as a little boy new to this country, and telling a story about how as a teenager he'd helped nurse a stray cat back to life and found his calling. His mother sobbed throughout, falling conspicuously quiet only when the priest turned his attention to Heather, re-marking on how Viktor had bloomed again through love after being unexpectedly widowed.

Finally he was done speaking, but the service dragged on and on. After communion, when Lucy stage-whispered "How much longer, Mommy?" just as Matthew started drumming on the pew, I made the snap decision to take both children out.

Nudging Michael, I nodded silently toward the rear of the church before ushering Lucy and Matthew out of the pew and down the side aisle, grateful that we were toward the back and trying to move quietly so we wouldn't disrupt the end of the ser-vice. I'd never seen a church so packed. When my grandmother died, we'd had half as many in the congregation, but that was the difference between dying young and dying in your eighties—there were just more people still around to mourn you. Plus, everyone thought Viktor had been the victim of a violent crime, and that brought out the curiosity seekers and hysterics, people who believed that they were somehow connected to the death of a man they'd never met outside of the local TV or newspapers.

There were dozens of people like that, some clutching bou-quets of flowers, others straining to see past the heads and shoulders of those in front of them. As I glanced at the crowd as we left the church, one familiar face jumped out—the short, balding detective. He recognized me as well, I could see it in his eyes, and I looked away, pretending to be absorbed in helping the children, while I fought the urge to run from the building. What was he doing here?

"It's cold out here, Mommy," Lucy said in a reproving tone as we stood outside on the church steps and I gulped mouthfuls of crisp air.

"Yes, doesn't it feel good?"

"No. It's too cold and I don't have my mittens."

"No," Matthew echoed with a big grin. "I don't have my mittens."

"Stop copying me." Lucy gave him a severe look. "Tell him, Mommy, tell him to stop copying me."

"Stop copying, Matthew," I said, digging in my purse in a vain search for ibuprofen to curtail the headache I could feel mounting. "He copies because he admires you, Luce—you should be flattered."

"No, he does it to bother me," Lucy said, crossing her arms across her chest, a gesture that Matthew promptly copied, putting paid to my theory. She stamped her foot. "Stop it!"

"Stop it!" Matthew echoed.

"Both of you stop it," I snapped. "We're at church, not a playground. You need to be quiet at church."

As I pulled out my cell phone to text Michael for backup, the doors of the church suddenly opened and music poured out along with a parade of people. I hastily pulled the kids off to one side, all of us watching as the coffin was hoisted onto the shoulders of the pallbearers while Heather followed, tears running unchecked down her face.

Was the detective watching that? I hoped so. You had to be extremely cynical not to be moved by this public display of grief from the slain doctor's young, beautiful widow. Even I had to swallow against a sudden lump in my throat.

Julie and Brian passed by on the other side of the crowd with their children, and she waved a hand to me in passing, but didn't stop, heading toward the parking lot with a speed that I envied, especially after we got stuck in the procession, a funeral-home attendant slapping a magnetic flag on our car before we could pull out.

"Oh, well, how long could this take?" Michael said with a

careless shrug completely at odds with the panicked look on his face. The answer to that was forever, an interminable parade of cars moving at a snail's pace all the way back to Sewickley and up a sharply winding hill to the cemetery. Michael stayed with the kids in the car while I picked my way along with others across a snow-covered hillside to the grave site. I kept perched on my toes, trying not to let my heels sink into the damp ground, praying fervently for this torture to come to an end. More incense and droning from the priest—it just went on and on. I suppose as a Catholic I should have felt that this was penitential in some way, or as our yoga instructor Shanti might have put it, karmic. I'd caught a glimpse of her in the crowd at the church, looking exotic in a green silk sari, that bloodred *bindi* a third eye among her crazy blond ringlets.

At last we reached the end, and the coffin was lowered slowly into the ground, at which point Anna Lysenko let out a howl of grief so visceral that it made me shiver. She fell back into the arms of some male relative, almost as if it had been orchestrated, but despite her clear theatrics, tears streamed down my own face. I was a mother, too.

By the time we made it back to the church social hall for the luncheon that followed, the children were snarling at one another and Michael had joined Matthew in complaining about the need to use the bathroom. They disappeared down a hallway while Lucy and I entered a large room with round tables set with white cloths and fake flower arrangements. Along the sides were long buffet tables laden with a strange mixture of American picnic food (potato and macaroni salads and coleslaw, all dripping copious amounts of mayonnaise, plus Jell-O in various Day-Glo colors) and Ukrainian specialties, heavy on meat, cabbage, and potatoes. There was also a separate table piled high with Eastern European pastries, the sight of which made Lucy perk up.

As we joined the buffet line, I realized that I recognized the couple in front of us—neighbors of Heather's, elderly, old-money WASPs, making their way down the line with the focused interest of anthropologists. The silver-haired man paused before each

dish to ask the church ladies serving for the name and ingredi
ents, inquiring, "What is this called again? Ha-lush-ki. And it's
cabbage you say? Why of course I'll try some—just a small serving." And his wife, in a tweed suit with her iron-gray bob held
back by an Alice band, gave each woman a bright smile reminiscent of a lady of the manor visiting tenant farmers, as she murmured, "How lovely this is, just lovely."

Michael joined us in the line, holding tight to Matthew, who'd
spotted a fountain spewing some cherry-red liquid over on a
drinks table. "He tried to dip his hand in it," my husband complained, giving our son a little shake.

"If you don't behave you can't have any cookies," I said to him
and Lucy, resorting to being the sort of parent I'd always promised myself I wouldn't be.

Sarah passed by the buffet line carrying a full plate and raising
an even fuller glass of wine to me. "This makes the whole thing
bearable," she said in a low voice, nodding toward a corner
where a man behind a bar was expertly pouring what looked like
bourbon. We made it through the food line more or less intact—
just a single spilled pierogi quickly squashed under a stranger's
shoe—and wended our way through the crowded room, holding
the plates aloft and instructing Lucy and Matthew to stay close
so we wouldn't lose them. When Michael spotted a table with
four free seats, we took it, and then he went in search of drinks.

The event had the atmosphere of a wedding, albeit more somber, large numbers of unconnected people coming together to
celebrate the life of the man smiling out at the room from a
blown-up headshot mounted on an easel. A special table for
Heather and her in-laws was nearby, and she sat there like a
bride in black, watching with apparently rapt interest as various
people stepped up to the open microphone set up next to the
photo to give speeches about her dead husband. It was mostly
his colleagues, who told long rambling stories of Viktor's prow-
ess as a surgeon, using so much technical jargon that only the
other medical professionals in the room had a clue as to when
we were supposed to laugh or cry.

"To Viktor," each person would say at the end, holding a glass aloft.

"To Viktor!" everyone in the room would echo, glasses raised. Matthew giggled as he held up his glass of punch, his lips already dyed red like a clown's. Lucy disappeared from the table only to come back bearing a plate piled high with cookies, nibbling her way through them like a determined mouse, taking a bite from one and then a bite from another, probably to stop her brother from claiming any.

I drank a vodka tonic in record time and headed to the bar in search of some water, literally bumping into Sarah on the way. Or rather she bumped into me, her second (or was it her third?) very full glass of wine sloshing dangerously. "Watch out," she said with a smile, her speech slurred so that it sounded like, "Wash out."

"Be careful," I said in a low voice. "The police are probably here somewhere."

"Don't worry—I'm fine," she said, waving my concern away, but her smile was loopy and her eyes were glassy.

Seeing Sarah like that should have stopped me, but when the bartender asked what I'd like I found myself ordering another vodka tonic instead of water. I drank the second one too fast, also, sucking on the lime-soaked ice and avoiding Michael's raised eyebrows when I wandered back to our table. On rare occasions I had more than one drink, mostly because I was a lightweight, capable of feeling a pleasant, blurry buzz from a single drink. But if there were ever an occasion to drink heavily, I thought, the funeral of a man you helped kill would be the time. For a moment I thought I'd said that out loud, looking from my glass to Michael's face too quickly, the room spinning. "That was a joke," I said.

"What was?" he said, and my vision steadied enough to see that his expression was confused and I hadn't revealed anything. I shook my head and he laughed. "Good thing I'm the designated driver—I'll get you some water."

He wandered off toward the bar, and the children found friends to play with, including Sam and Olivia. "Where's your mom gone to?" I asked. They pointed vaguely and I craned my head to see, but there were too many people. An older man carrying a plate of food sat down at one of the empty spaces at our table and gave me a polite smile.

"Are you a family member or a friend?" he asked after a minute of silent eating.

"Friend," I said. "Although I'm better friends with his wife."

"Ahh, yes, Heather." He smiled again. He was picking carefully at his plate, cutting a cabbage roll into tidy segments before spearing one with his fork.

"You?" I asked, more to be polite than out of any real interest. "Friend or family?"

"A friend. A colleague, too, actually. I'm a surgeon. Viktor and I worked together."

"Oh, I see." That explained the careful operations he was performing on his plate of food. "One of the rare gifted healers." That came out sounding much more sarcastic than I'd intended—I was as drunk as Sarah. *Careful,* I thought. *Be careful.*

He smiled a bit uncertainly and gave a little laugh. "We try." Another speared bite of cabbage, again chewed carefully and thoughtfully. He was meticulous, like Viktor. Perhaps this was true of all surgeons. I thought of how displeased Viktor would have been by the messy, gaping hole the bullet had left in his skull. All that blood and brain spatter. My stomach suddenly rose and fell, like the tide slapping against a dock, and I swallowed hard, trying to steady myself. The man was looking at me quizzically, his fork poised halfway to his mouth, and I realized he'd said something and I hadn't answered him.

"Pardon?"

"Isn't it sad about Daniel—first his mother dies of cancer and now his father. That's some rotten luck." He popped the bite in his mouth and then shook his head while chewing.

Something in that story—it wasn't right. I shook my head, trying to clear it. "You mean Janice?"

He looked surprised. "Yes. Did you know her? A lovely woman—"

"No, no, I didn't." I shook my head too hard and my stomach protested again. "But it wasn't cancer—her death, I mean. She fell."

He thought about that for a moment, but then shook his head. "No, I'm pretty certain it was cancer."

Maybe that's what Viktor had told his colleagues. He certainly wouldn't want them to know that he'd used his wives as punching bags. Before I could say that, Michael appeared with a glass of water. "Here, drink this while I find the kids. Let's take off before it's time for happy hour."

"I'm not going into work," Michael announced as we drove home. "I'll telecommute for the rest of the day—that was exhausting."

"Yay! Daddy's home!" Lucy cheered, and when Matthew echoed her this time she didn't seem to notice.

"You were well behaved for the most part," I said, filled with sudden beneficence toward them. It was always like that with parenting; when they were being awful you could barely stand it, but then they acted loving with each other and you were besotted all over again, convinced that your children were angels.

"Can we watch a movie?" Lucy asked.

"Sure, why not," I said, and both kids cheered again.

"You're easy," Michael said with a laugh, and then, in a lower voice, "Maybe I should ask for something?" He gave me a wicked grin and this time I laughed.

"Maybe you should."

My phone buzzed silently and I saw a text from Julie: Call me!

I smiled, imagining how she'd enjoy hearing me describe the craziness of the church luncheon. The tension I'd felt for the last week had eased significantly, helped along by the liquor. It felt good to be done with the funeral. And so what if the detectives had been there? There had been nothing and no one to suspect; Heather had performed the role of grieving widow perfectly. The rest of us had stayed away from her and one another. The biggest performance of our lives was over and I felt almost giddy.

As we pulled onto our street, I couldn't help projecting ahead. In a few weeks, we'd be together again at the coffee shop and life would go on, but it would be even better than before because we wouldn't have to worry about Heather. Maybe she'd sell the house on the hill and buy one down in the village. I thought about asking Julie to keep an eye out.

I was humming as Michael pulled into the driveway, still suffused by the pleasant buzz. "I'll get the mail," I offered as he parked the car. "You guys go ahead in with Daddy."

"Can we have popcorn with our movie?" Lucy asked, ever the bargainer.

"Didn't you eat enough cookies?" Michael said.

It was a short walk down the driveway and up the sidewalk to the mailbox at the end of the flagstone walkway that led to our house. The sky was deceptively blue, the sun actually warming my hands as I reached to pull down the little arched metal door. Inside the box was a small pile of mail. I pulled it out, flipping absently through it as I started up the walk. The vast majority was always junk mail. We did all of our banking online, and most of my business correspondence was done online, too. It was rare for us to get real paper mail, so I was surprised to see a business envelope addressed to me.

Tucking the rest of the mail under my arm, I tore open the envelope and pulled out the letter. It was a plain sheet of white paper with a single paragraph of black text. The first line stopped me short: *I saw you and your friends on Fern Hollow Road.*

chapter twenty-three

ALISON

For a moment, I just stood there, staring down at the letter, my skin hot and tingling as if each word were a slap. *You thought no one was watching, but I saw you. I know what you did to Dr. Lysenko and I've got the photos to prove it.* There was a photo at the bottom of the page. I tore my gaze from the text and down to it. A grainy shot, but I knew immediately where it had been taken. I was clearly recognizable, caught in the Mercedes's headlights with a garbage bag in my hand, and Julie stood behind me, though only half of her face was visible. Heather had her head down and turned slightly away, although someone could pick her out from her height and slimness, but Sarah was in the worst position: The camera had caught her standing in front of Viktor's car, yanking free of that makeshift plastic suit.

Who had taken this photo? How? Fern Hollow Road had been deserted—we'd looked around, we'd been so careful.

I will go to the police unless you leave $20,000 in cash at the Kershaw mausoleum in the Sewickley Cemetery on Friday, February 24th, by 10:00 A.M.

My phone buzzed in my pocket and I jumped before fumbling for it. Julie texting again: **URGENT—CALL ASAP!**

She answered on the first ring. "A letter came today," she said before I could say anything, her voice higher-pitched than normal.

"I got one, too—does it have a photo at the bottom?" I said, trying to quell the panic bubbling up to replace my initial shock.

"Yes, yes, that's it. But how? We were so careful." Her voice climbed even higher, edging into hysteria. "No one could have seen us—how could someone have seen us?"

"What about the others?" I interrupted. "Did they get the letter, too?"

"Sarah did, but I haven't heard back from Heather. What are we going to do? We have to talk—"

"Yes, but not over the phone."

"Ali?" Michael's voice startled me. He was standing in the front door.

"I've got to go," I said to Julie, hitting the hang-up button and shoving the phone back in my coat pocket. It buzzed again almost immediately.

"Sorry, didn't mean to interrupt," Michael said as I started toward him, surprised that my legs were holding me up. "Anyone interesting?"

"Just Julie." The phone was buzzing and buzzing. I could feel it vibrating in my pocket. Could he hear it? I forgot I was still holding the letter until Michael said, "What's that?"

"Just junk mail." I shoved the letter into my pocket, too.

"We're out of popcorn," Michael said, holding the door open for me. "So I let the kids have ice cream."

"How can they be hungry after all that food at the church?" I said, surprising myself by how normal I sounded. Was that my voice? I headed automatically toward the kitchen.

"Hey, why don't you stay awhile," Michael said. I turned back to see him standing in the hall, holding a hand out to me. When he saw the confusion on my face he added, "Your coat?"

"Oh, right." I slipped it off, trying not to call attention to the letter in the pocket; I could see a white tip of the envelope poking up. I headed toward the closet, but Michael took it from me.

"I'll get it for you." He gave me a kiss that I couldn't feel as he took the coat from my hands. I hovered for a second, afraid he'd feel the vibrating phone and pull out the letter along with it, but he just hung my coat in the closet and closed the door.

In the kitchen, the kids were chattering happily over bowls of ice cream, while George sat sentinel on the floor between their chairs, looking from one to the other with the hopeful expression of someone fully expecting something delicious to fall. It gave me an idea.

"I think I'll take George for a walk," I said.

"Really?" Michael said, surprised. "We just got home."

"He's been cooped up all day."

"What's the rush? He seems perfectly happy right now." Michael stared at me quizzically.

"No rush." I feigned a nonchalance I didn't feel, leaning against the kitchen island.

"Do you want some ice cream?" he asked, filling a bowl for himself.

The thought of trying to eat anything made my stomach turn over. "No thanks," I said, stepping past him to fill a glass of water at the sink. As soon as I could get a moment alone, I would text Julie and the others. We could meet at the park and figure out what to do. "*$20,000 in cash . . .*" How would we get that money? Where? I gulped the water down, the glass shaking in my hands. I had to set it down before I dropped it, crossing my arms to hide the trembling. I turned back to my family, trying to pretend I was listening to their conversation.

"Are you feeling okay, hon?" Michael asked, reaching over to rest the back of his hand against my forehead.

"Yes, why?" I pulled back, his touch startling me.

"Lucy's trying to tell you something. You're a thousand miles away."

"What is it, Luce?" It took a huge mental effort to focus on my daughter.

She was giving me a mischievous smile, sitting there next to her brother at the wooden table, holding a spoonful of ice cream. Afternoon sun streamed through the windows, catching the gold in her light brown hair. "I know your secret!"

Adrenaline flooded me—now she had my complete attention. Had she been looking out the window and seen me with the letter? I struggled to keep my voice calm. "I don't have a secret."

"What is it?" Matthew said. "I want to know Mommy's secret!"

"She can't tell you, dummy, or it wouldn't be a secret any-more," Lucy said.

"Don't call your brother dumb," Michael said.

"I can so know the secret," Matthew said. "Mommy says not to keep secrets, right Mommy?" Absorbing part of the message I'd tried to impart about not keeping it secret if someone ever tried to touch them inappropriately.

"Yes, that's right," I said, keeping my voice light. "I'd tell you my secret, but I don't have one to tell."

"Uh-oh." Lucy dropped her spoon and scrambled onto her knees on the chair, clapping both hands over her mouth, eyes wide and excited. "Mommy told a lie!"

"Hey, that's enough," Michael said reprovingly, even as my anxiety crossed into panic and paranoia. Could she somehow have overheard my conversation with Julie? Or with Sarah at the wake?

"But she did! She's lying!" Lucy pointed a finger at me, her voice shrill, a small accuser at a witch trial. I suddenly smelled that rank, nose-curdling odor of blood and sulfur and saw Viktor's gaping head wound.

"I don't have a secret," I repeated, even as Michael told Lucy to sit back down in her seat.

"What is it? I want to know the secret!" Matthew chimed in as Lucy sat down but continued to argue.

"There isn't a secret," I snapped. "Aren't you done with your ice cream?"

"Babe, it's okay," Michael said to me, sounding surprised, as Lucy said to Matthew, "She doesn't want to tell you."

"I think snack time is over." I picked up their bowls and headed toward the sink and Matthew burst into tears, not because I'd removed his bowl, but because he thought I wouldn't tell him.

"All right, that's enough," Michael said to Lucy. "Either tell your brother the secret or you can go into time-out."

"It's Mommy's secret," Lucy said, her lower lip jutting out. What had she seen or heard? I tried to think of what I could say to distract Michael, to move them away from this topic, but he was focused entirely on Lucy.

"One," he began, using that old parenting standby, the count-down, to force her to comply. "Two. You don't want me to get to three, Lucy Elizabeth."

"She doesn't have to reveal someone else's secret," I protested, gripping the edge of the countertop. My words were lost by Lucy wailing that her father was "unfair."

"Two-and-a-half—"

"Okay, okay. I'll tell!" Her shriek was piercing.

"Now, please." Michael sounded perfectly calm, but I was as flushed as our daughter, terrified at the prospect of what she'd reveal.

She gave a loud sniffle before announcing in a breathless tone, "Mommy ate ice cream for breakfast."

Michael blinked, startled, and then tried to hide his smile, but Matthew twisted in his seat to look at me, his mouth open with shock. I sagged against the countertop feeling almost weak with relief, the look on Matthew's face making me burst out in slightly hysterical laughter. I'd forgotten that Lucy had come upon me in the kitchen the other morning and caught me mindlessly eating mint chocolate chip straight from the container. I'd given her a taste as well. "Shh, it's a secret," I'd said, forgetting how literal kids could be.

"I want ice cream for breakfast, too," Matthew said, quickly shifting his demands.

"Not a chance," Michael said, sounding exasperated as he helped him down from his booster seat. "Go play and see if you and your sister can manage not to argue with each other for five minutes."

Lucy seemed insulted by his comments and my laughter and stalked out of the room without speaking to either of us. "Kid drama," Michael said with a snort. "I'll get this," he said, heading for the sink to rinse out the bowls.

"Thanks. I'm going to go change." As I headed out of the

kitchen I could hear Michael turn on the TV and the sound of glass clinking as he loaded the dishwasher. The front hall was empty. I checked to make sure that the kids weren't hanging over the banister or lurking around the corner before quietly opening the door and retrieving the letter and my phone, hurriedly texting Julie once I was alone in my bedroom: Borough Park—one hour.

Her reply was swift: I'll tell Sarah, but what about Heather?

I texted back: I'll stop by her house on the way.

George didn't need to be convinced about the park, tripping over his own paws and panting with excitement when he heard the rattle of his leash. Michael was a different story.

"Why the park? Are you okay to drive?"

"Don't be silly—that was over an hour ago." And the letter had completely sobered me up.

"But the alcohol could still be in your system. You don't want to get stopped by the cops."

No, definitely not. "*I will go to the police.*" I swallowed hard, resisting the urge to check on the letter, which I'd zipped in the pocket of the fleece jacket I'd put on over a long-sleeved T-shirt and jeans. Michael leaned on the door out to the garage, watching me load George and his portable water bowl into the car. "Just be careful."

"I'll be fine." I gave him a kiss, pulling quickly out of his embrace, afraid that he'd feel the crunch of the letter in my pocket. As I reversed down the driveway he was still standing in the doorway watching me.

Heather's house was less than an eight-minute drive from mine, but with lights and traffic it could take as much as fifteen. It seemed hard to believe that it had been only eleven or twelve days since I'd responded to Heather's call, making this same drive at manic speed, not caring whether the police stopped me. Now I was scared that they might, careful to drive within the speed limit, but just within, keeping the pressure steady on the village streets but flooring the accelerator on stretches where no one was around, taking the turns as tightly as I dared.

Her mailbox was at the end of the long drive up to their estate, an ornate metal box inserted in a stone pillar adjoining the wall. There was no one in sight and I lowered my car window and gave a quick tug to open it. The box was empty. Shutting it just as fast, I turned in to the entrance and made the long drive up to the house. The place looked deserted, my feet tapping loudly on the stone pavers as I walked from my car to the front door.

In the silence I could hear the muffled sound of the doorbell's complicated peal. George whined softly from the car and a plane droned overhead. I pressed the bell again and, hearing something rustling nearby, turned fast to see a doe come out of the trees bordering the house. It stopped short, clearly as surprised as I was, the two of us staring at each another for a moment. The sound of the lock turning startled the deer and it bounded away into the woods as the door opened. Anna Lysenko stood in the doorway, looking annoyed and very tired.

"Yes?" It seemed as if she'd aged a decade, dark hollows under her sunken eyes, her skin sallow and spotted. It took a second for me to realize that she had no makeup on.

"I'm sorry to bother you—is Heather here?"

"She's out; I'll tell her you stopped by."

Past her shoulder I could see a pile of mail sitting on the hall table. "Do you know when she'll be back?" I stalled, trying to think of how I could get inside.

"She's taken Viktor's son to play at his cousin's. Apparently my grandson had to go there even though he has plenty of toys here to play with." She sounded resentful.

"It's just that I was hoping to get my casserole dish back. Heather said it was okay to drop by today to pick it up." I looked as ingratiating and apologetic as I could.

"Oh she did, did she? On the day of her husband's funeral?" The older woman stared at me sullenly for a long moment before giving a loud sigh. "Okay, come in, come in before you let out all the heat." She ushered me inside and closed the door with a click just short of a slam. "You can wait here. What does it look like?"

"What?" My gaze kept sliding to the pile of mail. "Oh, it's white porcelain, a rectangular pan with fluted edges."

"I was trying to take a nap," Anna said in an accusing tone as she walked down the hall toward the kitchen. "I forgot what it's like having a young child around all hours. It takes a lot of energy."

"It certainly does." I waited until she'd disappeared around the corner before quickly sorting through the mail. There were dozens of sympathy cards, plus some bills and junk mail in Viktor's name. I sifted as quickly as I could and there it was—a white envelope addressed to Heather in a familiar-looking typeface with no return address. I grabbed it, but too fast, spilling the pile of mail onto the floor.

"What did you say it looked like?" Viktor's mother called from the kitchen.

"White porcelain," I called back, slipping the letter into my pocket and dropping to my knees to frantically scoop the mail off the marble tile.

"There are over a dozen porcelain dishes," Mrs. Lysenko said. "What's wrong with those disposable aluminum pans I'd like to know." She came around the corner carrying my dish just as I got the mail back onto the table.

"Thank you so much," I said, giving her that absurd, ingratiating smile as I took the pan from her hands. "Again, I'm so sorry to bother you. Please tell Heather I stopped by."

Anna made a sound suspiciously like a snort. Aware that she might be watching, I didn't even touch the letter until I'd driven far away from the house, parking along the side of the road next to a wide, fenced field where a beautiful black horse quietly grazed, nuzzling the snow in search of dry winter grass.

George pressed up against the window, eager to get out and play, and then tried to nuzzle me into action. I pushed him gently away and pulled both envelopes from my pocket, comparing Heather's with mine, before opening hers and finding a duplicate of the letter that had been sent to me. It didn't get better with rereads. My hands trembled as I folded each back into its envelope and tried to call Heather. It went straight to voice mail. What if the police were tapping her phone? I struggled to keep my voice light. "Just checking in to see how you're doing. If you feel up to it, we'd love to see you—we're meeting for a girls-only walk at the Borough Park at four P.M."

chapter twenty-four

SARAH

The Sewickley Borough Park is a park in the classic sense of the word, a parcel of wooded land dedicated to riding and hiking trails. There's a single paved road through it that dead-ends at a clearing with a glass-fronted trail box containing a yellowed copy of the park rules posted next to a topographical map and some parking spots. On warm, sunny days, people park all along the sides of the road and enjoy picnics and sunbathing and it's a favorite spot where dogs can roam off-leash. I was hoping that the cold and the time of day would keep most of the pet owners away, and not just because I don't really like dogs. We needed a private place to meet and I was glad that I passed only one car as I drove along the road toward the dead end.

There was one car other than Alison's in the official parking spaces and I didn't recognize it. As I pulled in a few spots away, tires skidding on gravel, I heard a dog yipping and saw Alison leaning into the backseat of her car struggling to contain George. The other car was empty. As I got out of mine I could hear Alison saying, "Hold on, settle down," and she didn't hear me coming as she practically wrestled with her dog to get his leash on. If she let George off-leash he'd disappear into the woods in pursuit of squirrels. Apparently he had some pointer blood and it was just in his nature. Well, it wasn't in my nature to chase him through a maze of oak, maple, and birch trees.

"Hi there," I called in greeting, trying not to startle her, but she jumped anyway, whirling around.

191

"Oh, hey, I didn't hear you pull in." She looked pale and frazzled, her blond hair falling out of the neat bun she'd worn at the funeral. George looked far more enthusiastic, large brown eyes wild and even larger tongue dripping slobber. He bounded forward to jump up on me and I stepped back so his paws hit the air instead of my shoulders. "Down, boy!" Alison yelled, yanking on his leash. "George, down!" The dog partially responded, but he couldn't stop moving, bobbing and weaving around Alison like a manic boxer, before bolting toward the open field, dragging his owner behind him.

I hurried after them, the thermos I'd brought bouncing in the bag hanging from my shoulder. The sun was setting and I shaded my eyes as Alison let George lead us around the snowy clearing. He had his nose down and up, sniffing eagerly at every bench and rock, lifting his leg against the wooden post holding the trail map. I checked my watch; it was just after four P.M. I hoped Julie and Heather would get there soon.

As we walked, I saw a man emerge from one of the trails about a hundred feet away with a German shepherd who was off-leash. The dog tensed as it spotted us, but the man didn't react, just kept moving forward with the same steady gait along a path parallel to ours but at a distance. He seemed tall, certainly taller than I was, a broad-chested man with dark hair and mirrored sunglasses. His dog diverted, making a beeline for George, while barking like crazy, and the man didn't say anything, just let him go ahead. I don't appreciate dog owners who let their animals approach strangers without any attempt to curb them.

"Is he friendly?" Alison called as George, goofy, friendly mutt that he was, practically rolled over in front of the shepherd before some canine pride seemed to kick in and he asserted himself with barking, too. The man didn't answer, but he changed direction, walking toward his dog. And us.

Alison kept hold of George's leash, clearly nervous as he and the shepherd engaged in that gross ritual where each dog tries to sniff the other's rear end. The man stopped a few feet away and stared from the dog to Alison and me and back again.

"Cold out today," I said, one last stab at friendliness. He made a sound that might have been agreement before addressing the dog in a deep voice. "C'mon, King, let's go."

The dog didn't listen, jumping and growling as he played with George. Alison had let the leash out as far as it would go and George was jerking her arm as he pulled against it, twisting and running around, tail wagging like crazy even while he barked and growled as if he wanted to tear the shepherd apart. I'll never understand dog behavior. The man was watching; he seemed to be looking us over. "I said let's go," he suddenly boomed, making us jump as much as his dog. He reached into a pocket of his jeans and I caught a glint of metal. For a brief, terrible moment I thought he held a gun. I tugged Alison's arm, stumbling back and pulling her and George back with me, as the man stepped forward and then bent to clip a leash on his dog's collar.

Alison pulled free from my grip, giving me a *What the hell?* face as we both heard the sound of an engine and Julie's car came into view. She pulled into a spot down from mine as King's owner yanked him toward the parking lot and the mystery car. We hurried toward Julie, careful to stay clear of the man's car.

"Sorry I'm late, I couldn't get away sooner," Julie said when she was close. The man loaded his dog into the backseat and then stared at all of us for an uncomfortable minute before getting into the driver's seat. "Who was that?" she asked.

"No idea, but we're glad you're here and he's leaving." Alison led the way to a wooden picnic table off to the side, near some trees, and tied George's leash to one of the metal supports under the bench seats. He whined, pulling against it and shaking the table as Julie and I sat down across from her, brushing off the snow.

"Why was he looking at us that way? I swear, all of this is making me paranoid." Julie looked around once more before saying in a low voice, "Do you have your letters?"

We exchanged ours and they were exactly the same except for the personal address. "Heather got one, too," Alison said, showing us that letter and explaining how she'd gotten it.

"What are we going to do?" I said, pulling the thermos out of my bag and dropping it on the picnic table with a thunk.

"Shh," Julie hissed. "Be quieter for starters. Is that coffee?"

I shook my head. "Something to take the edge off the cold. Here, I brought cups."

Julie and Alison exchanged glances that I chose to ignore, pulling out small plastic shot glasses from my bag before unscrewing the thermos and pouring beautiful golden brown liquid into each one. Alison took a small sip of hers and coughed on the fumes. "Whiskey?"

"The best Kentucky bourbon," I said. "It's cold out here and I can't face another discussion involving Viktor Lysenko without first having a drink."

"You sound like you've already had one," Julie said dryly, but before I could answer we heard another car approaching. I screwed the cap back on the thermos and we put the glasses out of sight, until we saw that it was Heather's SUV. George barked and strained gamely at the leash, tail wagging as she got out of the car and raised a hand to us.

"Hi!" She sounded cheerful—a far cry from the grieving widow she'd presented at the funeral—and she crossed the ground at a good clip, zipping up her down jacket on the way. "Hello, George, hello!" She stroked his head as Alison tried to keep him from planting his dirty paws on her chest. "I'm so glad you called—Daniel's staying over with his great-aunt and I couldn't face being home with just my mother-in-law for company." Her smile faded as she saw our somber expressions. "What is it? What's happened?"

Alison found the letter addressed to Heather and handed it over. She took it from her gingerly, as if it were contagious, looking from Alison to the envelope and then to the other envelopes the rest of us were holding.

"What is this?" she said with a nervous laugh, but when nobody answered she hurriedly took out the letter and read it. She appeared visibly shaken, sinking down on the bench next to Julie and peering in the fading light at the photo on the bottom of the letter. I passed her a shot and she drank it in one go, wiping her mouth with the back of her hand. "Where did you get this? Did all of you get the same one?"

As we passed the other letters for her to compare, Alison explained how she'd taken Heather's out of the mail at her house. "They're identical except for our names," I said. "Who could have written this?"

"How could they have seen us?" Heather said, her breath making little indignant clouds. "That's what I want to know—we were careful. You said no one was around." She looked accusingly at Alison and Julie.

"There was no one around," I said. "We all looked. Someone must have followed us, but I didn't see any other cars on that stretch of road that night—did you see any cars?" I appealed to Julie and Alison.

"No, but obviously this person was out there," Alison said.

"They must have heard the news about Viktor and put it together," Heather said in a dull voice, nervously smoothing the letter against her lap. She looked up at me, then the others. "I was so out of it that night—I thought you were being careful." Her voice held a hint of accusation and I saw Alison stiffen. "How could you let someone see us?"

"We weren't any more careless than you were that night," I said with a growl, before pouring another shot and downing it.

"I don't know, and it really doesn't matter how they saw us," Alison said, "the point is that they did and we've got to figure out what we're going to do about it."

"What if we did nothing," Heather said. "We let this person go to the police—the photo doesn't really show much."

"Oh, that's easy for you to say," I said. "Your face isn't visible in the photo."

Julie said, "The letter said 'photos' plural. This is just one of the photos; who knows what the others show."

Alison took a small sip of whiskey, obviously trying not to

choke on it. "And the photo files will have the time stamp and probably the location as well—if this person takes them to the police then they'll know we were there that night."

"If that happened—if—then why couldn't we just tell the truth at that point?" Julie nervously fiddled with her plastic cup. "We show the letters to the police and explain what happened that night. Viktor was abusing Heather—she shot him in self-defense."

"With your gun? And we were just helping when we made sure he was dead and dumped the gun and his body?" I said. "It's too late for that—we helped her commit a homicide and cover it up. We'd be charged as accessories."

"So what—we just pay the blackmailer? How do we guarantee that they give us all the photos and get rid of any copies?" Alison said. I tried to refresh her shot glass, but she covered it.

I looked again at the photo included in the letter—four of us standing there in the dark by Viktor's car. "We can't guarantee it," I said.

"What if we refused to pay until we see them delete the photos?" Julie said.

"How would we do that?" Alison sounded skeptical.

"The letter says we have to leave the money at the cemetery," I said. "We could stake it out and demand the camera and the photos."

"They're digital," Alison said. "And they've probably already downloaded them. We'd have to take this person's computer, too, and delete their files."

"Then what's your plan?" I snapped.

"I don't think we have much of a choice—we have to pay them."

"I don't know about you, but I don't have a spare twenty grand just sitting around to give away to some shitty black-mailer." I took another gulp of whiskey, feeling my face flush.

"What *do* you guys have?" Alison asked. "Because I think we've got to pool our money."

There was silence for a long moment, but then Julie spoke. "I've got some money stashed away—it's supposed to be our vacation fund. Brian doesn't even know about it; I was going to surprise him."

"Okay," Alison said. "That's a start. I don't have a private fund, but if I added some bonus money I got from work along with other money set aside for emergencies, that would be over two thousand—I can contribute that. Plus, maybe I could sell something."

"Well, I don't even have a thousand," I said in a flat tone, before downing another shot glass. The other three just stared at me and I said, "What? I'm a stay-at-home mom, remember? I don't have the money you three have."

"None of us has that kind of money just sitting around," Alison said.

"What about some of that old furniture from your parents?" Julie asked me. "Weren't you talking about selling that?"

"Yes, but to pay for a surprise anniversary trip for me and Eric, not for this."

"I think he'd be even more surprised if you're charged as an accessory," Alison said pointedly.

I scowled. "It's Heather's fault we're in this dilemma—what's she planning to pay?"

Heather recoiled and Julie made a gasping noise, apparently shocked by my bluntness. She said, "You're being unfair, Sarah."

"It's the truth, isn't it?" I argued. "Besides, she's got more money than all of us combined—why shouldn't she pay the whole thing? She can just say it was for funeral expenses."

"Those costs were already paid," Heather said in a quiet voice. "I can't withdraw that much—the police would notice."

"What about the life insurance?" I said. "I'm sure you're getting a big chunk of change from that."

Julie glared at me, as Heather said, "I haven't got the insurance money yet—it takes time. Look, I can pay you all back."

"Don't be silly, this isn't just your problem—we're in this together," Julie said in a firm voice. "We'll all pay."

"We should split it evenly," Alison said. "If we each contribute five thousand dollars we can pay him off."

"I'll find it somewhere," Heather said.

I snorted. "Oh, I'm sure you've got some portable wealth—all you have to do is sell some jewelry."

"Or we could sell it for you," Julie said. "You have to be very careful that the police don't catch wind of this."

For a few minutes none of us said anything, just sitting there wrestling with the implications of the decision. I poured another shot of whiskey and this time Julie spoke up. "Don't have another one or you won't be able to drive home."

"I'm fine," I said, but Alison snatched the cup away, splashing whiskey onto the wooden table and across the snow-covered ground.

"You're not fine; you're drunk," she said. "You think we haven't noticed? Get a grip and sober up—you're risking everything with this behavior."

"Me?" I spluttered. "How is this *my* fault? If *she'd* just had the common sense to leave him." I pointed at Heather, who flushed under the scrutiny.

"Stop it," Alison said. "This isn't her fault."

"It's nobody's fault," Julie said. "Let's all just calm down." Ever the peacemaker, she didn't point out that I was telling the truth.

Alison closed her eyes, pinching the bridge of her nose. "We have five days to collect the money," she said when she opened them. "It's just one more hurdle—we can't give up."

No one said anything to contradict her, but the light was going, so I put away the thermos and we pocketed our letters and walked quietly back to our cars. "Are you sure you're okay to drive?" Julie asked me. Alison was busy getting George into the back of her car and she and Heather didn't hear me say, "I told you, I'm fine." But I know they all saw me peel out a minute later, leaving sooner and faster than everyone else.

As night fell, so did my mood. I took a long route home, trying to figure out where on earth I could get $5,000 without Eric finding out about it. What had possessed Alison to suggest that we split it evenly? This wasn't some girls' night out, we weren't splitting the cost of dinner or a bar bill—this was $20,000. Julie and Heather could find this money pretty easily, but what about me and Alison? Count on her to act like some goody-two-shoes Girl Scout.

We tended to dance around finances in our friendship. Of course, we all knew that Heather and Julie had more money than Alison and I did, but the closest we'd ever come to having tension over that difference was last year. About six months before our youngest kids were starting elementary school, Heather mentioned that Viktor wanted to send Daniel to Sewickley Academy, a private school, instead of Sewickley Elementary, the public school where all of our kids were enrolled. That got Julie talking about enrolling her kids there, too, even though Owen was already in third grade at the public school. I have to admit that I got a little huffy about that, making a few pointed comments about some people thinking they were better than everybody else. Things had been tense for a little while, but in the end Daniel went to Sewickley Elementary and Julie enrolled Aubrey there as well, and the talk of private school and tuition just died away.

Until that decision to split the extortion cost evenly, money hadn't caused any serious problem among us. Later, Alison texted me to say that if we weren't careful, this tension could cause a crack in our friendship. We had no idea how much worse things could get. And Alison didn't realize that the crack was already there, just waiting for the catalyst to push us apart.

chapter twenty-five

JULIE

There was a part of me that wanted to run away and leave the others to deal with this mess. I'd won one of those top-producer prize packages from my agency—a two-person trip to Cancún—and I called Brian to propose that we use it right away. He'd just gotten back to his hotel room in Kansas City and sounded exhausted.

"Now? Hon, I'd love to vacation with you, but this is the worst time of year for me, you know that."

"Think about it—sand, warm sun, cocktails on the beach. People waiting on us, instead of us waiting on them."

"But what about the kids?"

"Your mom would watch them, or my sister. She's offered before. I know she'd take them if I asked."

"But it's the middle of the school year. Why not wait until summer and then we can all go away together?"

It made perfect sense, of course it did, but I didn't want sense, I wanted to escape.

"Hon? Are you okay? What's with this sudden travel bug?"

"Nothing. I'm just tired."

Brian sighed. "Tell me about it. If I have to listen to another presentation on biotech software I might seriously kill someone."

The word made me recoil; I was glad he couldn't see me. "Would you ever?" I asked on impulse.

"Would I ever what?"

"Kill someone. Would you ever?"

Brian laughed. "What is this? Are you messing with me?"

"No, I mean, it's just a question. Could you ever kill someone? If they were hurting you or me or the kids?"

"I guess I could—especially if you or the kids were being threatened. But seriously, Jules, you're acting weird—what is this?"

"Nothing, it's nothing. Just too much to drink tonight, I guess."

"Yeah, I think so." Brian chuckled a little. "I miss you, hon."

"I miss you, too." My eyes and my voice filled with tears, surprising me as much as him.

"Hey, it's okay, I'll be back in a few days."

"I know, I know."

"Is it the kids? Are they bugging you? Because I'm going to give them holy hell if they're giving you a hard time."

"No, it's not the kids, they're fine. I just miss you when you're away, that's all."

I wanted to tell him—I needed so much to talk to someone other than Sarah, Alison, or Heather—but I couldn't do it. Not now. Not after what we'd done. No one could know.

We had only a week to gather the money. Getting mine was pretty easy; I took $5,000 from the private account that I'd set up as a vacation fund. When I asked for that amount in cash, the bank teller, a blue-haired old woman whom I'd known for years, raised an eyebrow and asked with a cackling laugh if I was planning a little retail therapy. I hoped she wouldn't make that joke the next time she saw Brian.

Sarah was the one I was worried about most. I knew that she and Eric shared all their accounts and he handled all their bills and record keeping. How was she going to manage to pull together $5,000 without him knowing about it? I wanted to offer to pay her half, but I knew that could cause problems between us, and what about Alison? Her finances couldn't be that much better than Sarah's, but it wouldn't have been fair to offer to pay Sarah's share and not Alison's.

Two days after we met at the park I ran into Sarah, relieved that she seemed sober and had taken some furniture she'd inherited to an antiques dealer. "A solid Sheraton dining room set, oak bookcases, and a glass-topped side table and they only gave me twenty-five hundred dollars," she complained. "They're going to turn right around and sell the dining room set alone for over a thousand dollars. Thieving bastards!"

"Can you raise the rest?"

"I'll find it somewhere," she said. "What choice do I have? But I'm screwed if Eric wants to go to the storage locker any time soon. He won't miss the furniture, but he'll sure as hell miss the money I should have from its sale. Last night he asked why I was so jumpy—if he only knew."

"You didn't say anything, did you?"

"Of course not." She gave me a withering look. "I told him that if he'd stop sneaking up on me I wouldn't have anything to be jumpy about."

I smiled at that; typical Sarah. "I guess the best defense is a good offense."

She smiled then, too. "Don't talk Steelers at me. You know I don't like these football analogies."

She'd somehow found all the money by Thursday when we gathered to plan the drop-off. We met at Alison's house in the early afternoon while the kids were still in school and her husband was at work.

"So this is what twenty thousand dollars in cash looks like," Heather said in a slightly awed tone. We were standing around Alison's kitchen table looking at the stacks of bills all neatly lined up on the scarred oak top. "What are we going to carry it in?"

"This." Alison produced a small black duffel bag. "But let's wrap it in a garbage bag, too, just in case anyone looks inside the duffel."

All of us standing around that pile of cash and a duffel bag wearing latex gloves—it was surreal. "I feel like we're playing drug dealers in some police drama," I said with a light laugh, but nobody joined in. Alison kept putting her hand to her mouth, then dropping it, like she was going to bite her nails, but kept forgetting she couldn't reach them because of the gloves. Sarah looked particularly stressed.

"I took the final two thousand dollars from the kids' education fund," she said as she loaded her contribution into the plastic bag. "I just hope Eric doesn't look at that account before I have time to replace the money." She sounded resentful and kept shooting looks at Heather, who volunteered that she'd raised her money by "pawning two bracelets and a ring from Viktor." If she thought this would make Sarah feel better, it didn't; she seemed even more annoyed. Later I overheard her whispering to Alison about not owning anything except her house and her car—certainly not any jewelry—worth that kind of money.

"Did anyone see you?" Alison asked Heather. "What pawnshop did you use?"

"Don't worry, I went to one in the city. I looked around—no one was following me."

"We didn't think anyone was following us that night either," Sarah said darkly. "Maybe the blackmailer was watching you."

"Stop it, Sarah," I said.

"Well, he might have been," she said defensively. "How do you know he wasn't?"

"How do you know it's a he?" Alison said. "The blackmailer could be a woman."

I thought of Christine Connelly's odd behavior at the funeral and broke into a sweat. Could my neighbor have followed me that night? Could she be the blackmailer? I thought about telling the others, but just then Alison's kitchen phone rang, a shrill sound that startled us all, Heather dropping a bundle of money, which spilled across the table.

"Be careful," Sarah snapped, slapping her hand over the bills to stop their flight off the tabletop.

"You be careful," Heather snapped back.

"Shh," I hissed as Alison scrambled to find the phone among a pile of dirty dishes on the counter.

"Hello?" Her voice was breathless as she answered. "Oh, hi." She turned back to us and mouthed, "Michael."

The rest of us didn't speak, quietly shuffling the loose bills back into an orderly stack as Alison carried the phone into another room.

"I need a drink," Sarah said as soon as she was gone, stalking over to the fridge and taking a bottle of chardonnay from a door shelf as if she lived there. "Anybody else?" She wiggled the bottle in our direction. I shook my head, but Heather said, "Sure, why not."

Sarah smiled at that—the first smile I'd seen from her that day—and took some glasses down from a cupboard. "Oh, stop looking so disapproving, Julie," she said as she handed Heather her drink.

"We have to pick up the kids in under an hour," I said, emphasizing the time.

"It's just a little wine," she said, but she left the bottle on the table. "Relax."

I didn't say anything more, shoving stacks of bills into the garbage bag and wishing I'd convinced Brian to leave for Cancún. At that moment, I could have been relaxing on a beautiful beach with a fruity drink of my own, enjoying the warm sun thousands of miles away from all of this.

Alison came back into the kitchen just as we finished zipping the garbage bag full of money into the duffel. "Sorry about that—I got off as fast as I could." She noticed the bottle of wine and she raised her eyebrows but didn't say anything, just pointedly moved the bottle to the kitchen counter. She shifted the duffel to the side of the table and passed out printouts of a map, slapping hers down in the center.

"This is the Sewickley Cemetery," she said, taking a seat. "Our only insurance is to catch the blackmailer in the act. If we can find out who he or she is, then we can at least keep an eye on them and make sure they don't go to the police." The rest of us sat down as well, and watched as she used a highlighter to circle an area on the map. "Here's where Viktor was buried," she said, tapping the location. "And here is the site for the drop-off." She dragged her finger clear across the page to another spot and highlighted it. Had the blackmailer been at Viktor's funeral? Was that why they suggested the cemetery? Alison circled a third spot. "And here is a place where we can stake out the mausoleum."

"Julie can do the drop-off," Sarah suggested.

"Why me? I don't want to do it," I said, alarmed.

"Isn't a client buried there?" Sarah said. "Nobody will think anything of you visiting a friend's grave."

"I can't do the drop-off alone," I said. "I'm too nervous. One of you has to come with me."

Alison shook her head. "It can't be more than one of us—the letter was clear."

"What about me?" Heather asked. "I'll do it."

"*You* can't be there," Alison said. "What if the police are watching you?"

"I'd say I was visiting Viktor's grave."

"Yeah, but we don't want the police anywhere near the black-mailer. And Viktor's grave isn't near that mausoleum. You can't be seen doing anything even remotely suspicious right now."

"Then you drop off the money," I said to Alison. "I'll wait with Sarah in the car at the stakeout spot."

Alison made a sound that was half growl, half sigh. "Fine, I'll do the drop-off. But don't get so caught up in conversation that you two forget to look out for the blackmailer."

Sarah visibly bristled, but I spoke first to head off her angry response. "Don't worry—we'll be watching."

In theory, the whole thing sounded smart and doable. And if things had gone according to plan, it might have worked. But life so rarely goes according to plan.

Alison was right—the letter was very clear. One of us had to come alone to the cemetery before ten A.M., drop the bag at the designated mausoleum and leave. Despite the simplicity, I read and reread the directions numerous times the night before and checked and rechecked both locations on the map. Sarah would pick me up in the morning and we'd get to the stakeout spot more than an hour ahead to make sure that we weren't noticed.

I'd felt jittery all day, as if I'd had too much caffeine, a wired, high-energy feeling that persisted even after we'd turned off the lights to sleep. While Brian was in the bathroom, I got up and tiptoed downstairs to check the directions in the letter one more time and to look at my copy of the map. Both were hidden inside my purse, which I'd left in my car.

"What are you doing down here?" Brian's voice startled me. I dropped my bag and whipped around, slamming the car door closed behind me.

"Don't do that! You scared me."

"You're scaring me," he said. "What are you doing?"

"Nothing. I just came down to find my phone." I held it up to show him.

He looked skeptical, but he didn't say anything until we were back upstairs in our bedroom. He took a seat next to me on the bed as I was setting my alarm. "Jules, I want to know what's going on."

I looked up at him, but couldn't quite meet his gaze. "What? Nothing's going on."

"Don't lie to me."

I flushed and looked away, but he put a gentle hand on my chin and pulled me back, searching my face, staring deeply into my eyes. In that moment I felt desperate to explain it all, to beg him to fix it and make everything go back to the way it had been.

But I thought of the gun, the gun Brian didn't even know I'd possessed, and I knew I couldn't tell him. "It's nothing," I said, my gaze darting away from his. "It's just the stress—the closing I've got in Edgeworth this week."

He looked unconvinced as he held on to my face. "You've never been this stressed about a closing before."

"Yes I have—remember the D'Amicos?"

"That was years ago, when you were first starting out."

I pulled at his hand and he let me go. "This is a lot more money."

He was silent for a moment and then he said in a low voice, "Are you in trouble?"

"What? No. Of course not." As if I were surprised and hadn't known exactly what he meant the minute he asked. I forced myself to look straight at him, struggling to keep the crawling sensation in my gut from appearing on my face.

"Because if you are, I want to know now, Jules. I don't want to find out like last time."

Memories of that day flooded me, snatches of color and sound, the feel of metal tightening around my wrists, the pattern in the cheap carpet that I'd kept my eyes fixed on as I was led out of the office past all those staring faces. I struggled to push the memories down, the sting of humiliation fresh for a moment before I locked it all away again.

"It's not that," I lied. "I promise."

Getting under the covers, I curled up next to him. He's a proud man, so it took me a minute to realize that he hadn't just asked because of the past, he was wondering about the future. Specifically, had I met someone else? I leaned in to kiss him, giving him the reassurance he couldn't ask for, running a hand over his chest and then letting it drop lower.

My worries from the night before seemed to have carried real trouble into the next day. Owen and Aubrey dawdled over breakfast and I burned my hand when coffee splashed over the mug I yanked too fast from under the maker. "Poor Mommy," Aubrey said, offering to kiss it for me.

"Thank you, but I need you to hurry now and get dressed while I find your rain boots, okay?"

Of course it was pouring outside, just something else to make the day harder. I dug in the closet for the kids' rain gear as I heard them squabbling upstairs. "Mommy, Owen stole my car!"

"It's not her car, it's my car—she knows that!"

"C'mon, you two, we don't have time. Leave the cars and get down here." If you think that was effective, then you've never had children.

Only after I'd marched upstairs, physically pulled them apart, and promised that later, after school, I'd use the wisdom of Solomon to determine who the Hot Wheels car belonged to was I able to hustle them downstairs and into rain gear and load both of them and their backpacks into the car.

I'd just fastened my own seat belt when Owen cried out, "Lunch, Mommy! You forgot my lunch box!"

"Mine, too, Mommy!" Aubrey would never be excluded from any drama.

Back into the house to grab the lunch boxes off the kitchen counter, back out to the car, race to the bus stop, keeping an eye out for cops and overzealous neighbors who might report my speeding. I saw Alison's car ahead of me in the queue, but it was raining too hard for anyone to stand outside. Five minutes, eight minutes. The bus was late this morning. "C'mon, c'mon," I muttered while the kids speculated about what the driver could be doing. Finally, mercifully, the bus came up the street, and I opened my big golf umbrella and escorted the kids out of the car and onto it.

Back in the car and a *ping* from my cell phone—a text from Alison to Sarah and me: Good luck; see you later. Home to shower and change, dressing as if it were any other workday. As I applied makeup I tried to stay positive. The worst would be over in a few hours. We'd pay and this troll would go away, slink back under his or her bridge.

Sarah showed up on time, which was a relief. I wanted to drive, but she'd insisted, arguing that since my car was partially visible in the blackmailer's photo it was a bad idea to take it to the cemetery. "Ready to go?" she said, tossing her purse in the back and brushing crumbs off my seat as I got in the minivan. I surreptitiously sniffed, hunting for a whiff of alcohol. Nothing but the unappetizing mixed scents of stale Goldfish crackers and damp gym socks. And breath mints. A wave of mint assaulted me as

Sarah turned her head to back down my driveway. What was she trying to cover? I clutched the door handle, nervous as Sarah pulled onto the street, but her driving seemed steady.

We turned in to the gates of the Sewickley Cemetery just before nine A.M., slowing to a crawl up the narrow, sharply winding road that climbed a steep hillside, eventually reaching the top, where gravestones perched like candles on top of a birthday cake. It looked like a crowded but beautiful final resting spot, although not as much in winter, with the dead yellow grass poking through patches of dingy snow and the black spires of bare trees looking like charred skeletons. Not that I thought much about the landscape in that moment. I was too stressed, checking right and left, while Sarah kept glancing in the rearview mirror. But there was no one out visiting graves this early on a day so rainy and cold.

I'd last been to a cemetery on Memorial Day, making the annual pilgrimage with my mother to put flowers on the graves of her parents, my gram and pap. "She was never the same without him," she'd said four years earlier when we'd buried my grandmother next to my grandfather, who'd died over a decade before. "She missed him every day." She always had pride in her voice, pleased to believe that her parents had been devoted to each other. I wasn't so sure.

By the time I really knew my grandparents, they'd settled into the resignation I've seen in lots of older, long-married couples—general acceptance of the other with occasional bouts of irritation at foibles that had probably once seemed endearing. My grandmother was quick to laugh, but could be impatient with my grandfather's sloppy eating habits. My grandfather once spent an entire afternoon patiently helping me learn to ride my bike, only to snap at my grandmother for being ten minutes late with his dinner. I'd never seen either abuse the other, though. If my grandfather had truly mistreated my grandmother, would she have considered leaving him? Most people didn't in her generation, they just sucked it up and muddled along, convinced by religion or a difficult legal system that they couldn't break their relationships.

Heather wasn't part of that generation, but she hadn't left either, or at least not at first. As Sarah drove past the road that led to the mausoleum, I wished that Viktor hadn't come home early that day, or that Heather had just had the courage to leave him months ago. If she'd only gotten out of there sooner, none of us would be in this situation.

I gave myself a mental shake to focus on the here and now. Only a few more hours and we'd be done with this. We just had to pay the money and it would be all over.

Sarah parked in the spot that Alison had identified, down a road that ran perpendicular to the one with the mausoleum. The view was partially obstructed by pine trees; those hadn't been reflected on the map. "This is going to strain my neck," I said, craning to see past the feathery boughs.

"Don't bother—the road dead-ends up there," Sarah said. "We'll see them coming and going."

When the rain slowed to a mist, Sarah stopped running the windshield wipers and turned off the car. "We don't want to call attention to ourselves," she said, but it got cold quickly without the engine on to run the heater. I burrowed into my down coat and pulled the hood up. Sarah kept popping her mouth above the top of her fully zipped jacket to take sips from a purple travel mug.

"Is that coffee?"

"Yep."

She didn't offer me a sip. Was it spiked? I wouldn't ask. No need to provoke an argument, but maybe I'd insist on driving home. I hadn't thought to bring coffee—or booze—but I took small sips from my water bottle and tried to avoid glancing at my phone. It's amazing how dependent on these things we've become. No need for boredom when you've got an electronic device to distract you, except we weren't allowed to be distracted.

"Do you think whoever it is will notice us sitting here?" Sarah said nervously. "What if they're here right now, watching us?"

I craned my neck to look all around, but the place was deserted. We had only the dead for company.

Time really does slow to a crawl when you're watching it—
9:10, 9:20, 9:30. There was no sign of the blackmailer or Alison.

"Where is she?" I asked, yanking off my hood and looking
around again, trying to see the roads above and below us.

Sarah took another swallow from her purple mug. "She'll be
here."

The letter had said ten A.M. What if the blackmailer showed
up and the money wasn't there?

When it was 9:50 I pulled out my phone and called. It rang
and rang before going to voice mail. "She's not answering." I
hung up and dialed again.

"She's probably driving," Sarah said, but she pulled out her
own phone, checking for messages.

"It's almost ten," I said when it bounced to voice mail the second time. "Where on earth are you?"

The next five minutes felt like fifty. Sarah called, as if Alison
would have been more likely to pick up for her. Voice mail again.

"What are we going to do?" I said, tapping the dashboard.
"We can't just sit here."

"Well, we can't just leave."

"Something must have happened. What if she had an accident?
Oh my God—if she had an accident they could find the money."

At that moment my phone pinged, interrupting my panic with
a text from Alison: The police were at my house.

chapter twenty-six

HEATHER

Viktor is dead. I say that to myself multiple times a day. Viktor is dead and I don't have to worry about him anymore. He can't catch me off guard. I don't have to watch out for his approach or race home to be on time to serve his dinner. I don't have to hide. I should feel free in a way that I haven't in years.

At night I spread out in the bed I shared with him, the bed where I'd done my best to avoid having sex with him, luxuriating in the fact that I no longer have to pretend to be asleep. That threat that hung over my life is gone. When I do sleep, it's more deeply than I have in years.

Of course, the reality is that I am not really free, not now. The blackmail letter has seen to that. What are we going to do if they decide $20,000 isn't enough? And the detectives have been sniffing around. I can sense their presence before they ring the bell, the way a cat is alert to that faint rustle in the weeds before she spots a rodent. I let them into the house every time and try to remain calm in the face of their roundabout questions. They don't fool me—I know what they want.

"Did you and your husband ever argue?" the short one says to me, pen twitching in his stubby fingers. He has come alone this morning, perched on a stool at my kitchen island, reminding me of a troll with his round head and wild fringe of graying hair. There's an oily stain on his cheap tie. I look away from it and up at his broad-featured face. I shrug.

"Of course. Sometimes. All couples argue sometimes." I give him a slight smile. "Are you married, Detective Tedesco?"

He looks discomfited by the question, by this reversing of our positions, but he gives me a sharp nod.

I nod, too, as if we're agreeing with each other. "I'm sure we all argue sometimes with the ones we love."

"What makes you think you can win?" My hair pulled tight in his fist.

The detective slaps his notebook on the marble countertop, startling me. "What about?"

"Excuse me?"

"What did you and your husband argue about?"

"Oh, nothing important." I wave my hand to show him it's trivial. "To tell the truth, Detective, my husband worked too many hours to be home long enough for much of an argument about anything."

"You talk only when I say you can talk." Forcing me down on the bed, pushing my face into the mattress.

"Did you fight about not having enough time together?"

"Viktor disliked arguing," I say, shifting on my stool and hoping the man doesn't notice. "He thought it was pointless."

Daniel runs into the room, a welcome interruption. He woke up with a fever, so I reluctantly let him skip school. Now I'm glad he's home. "What do you need, sweetie?" I stand up to indicate that I'm busy, that I've had enough questions for one day. Tedesco reluctantly stands up, too, flipping his notebook closed and shoving it back in his pocket.

I'm glad Daniel is young enough to be spared all but the most basic questioning. He rarely saw his father, so it's not surprising that he barely misses him.

Viktor's mother is a different story. Her son is dead and she has moved from sadness to anger. She's eager to talk to the detectives, to tell them all about me. About my friends. She is watching me; I'm conscious of her gaze following me when she thinks I'm not looking. She can't know—her son couldn't have told her. She lurks around the house trying to catch me in conversation, and her sister, Olga, is no better, although I think *she's* primarily interested in the insurance payout. The only thing pulling my mother-in-law away from her single-minded focus on me and Daniel is her dog, an elderly poodle named Max, who requires regular walks and chews on the curtains or shits on her cream-colored carpet when he doesn't get enough attention. I've always hated that dog, but now that he's the only reason I get some time away from Anna, I've developed a certain fondness for him. Recently I even bought Anna some dog biscuits she could take to him, hoping that would prompt her to leave right away. She'd eyed the bag and me with her usual sour-faced suspicion. I had to bite my tongue to stop from saying that if I'd wanted to poison her dog I would have done it years ago.

The grocery store is virtually the only place I can go. The police are watching—I catch myself checking my rearview mirror for unmarked cars the few times I drive anywhere. Alison has warned me that the phones might be bugged, our calls recorded, so I can't even text to ask how it's going with the drop-off. I'm as much of a prisoner now as I was before. *"You're not going anywhere. You belong to me."*

chapter twenty-seven

ALISON

It was always so quiet in the house with Michael and the kids gone, but that morning the silence seemed deafening. I tried to do some work online, answering emails, checking to make sure that a project I delivered had been received. The ticking of the clock seemed unnaturally loud. I didn't want to be late, but if I got to the cemetery too early, I'd have to drive around in circles.

I'd just taken my coat from the closet when the doorbell rang, a two-note peal that made me jump and seemed to echo in the quiet house. Fingers crossed it wasn't a neighbor; I really didn't have time to deal with anything else that morning. I pulled my jacket on and held my purse on my shoulder to make it clear that I didn't have time for a chat as I opened the door. I peeped through the side window first, startled when I saw a strange man standing on my front steps.

For a crazy second I thought he might be the blackmailer. I pulled open the door and the man turned—tall, a crew cut. He looked vaguely familiar.

"Alison? Alison Riordan?"

"Yes? Listen, I was just leaving to—" I'm not sure how much I would have revealed if he hadn't interrupted me.

"I'm Detective Jeff Kasper." He flashed a badge. "I wonder if I could ask you a few questions."

"Actually, I'm on my way out," I said. If the detective noticed that my voice sounded squeaky and scared, he didn't react. The minute he said his name I remembered him from the funeral home. He and his partner had been there the entire time, watching and waiting.

"This'll just take a couple of minutes," he said with a smile, but he didn't budge from the doorway.

"Of course, sure. I saw you at the funeral home. Is this something to do with Viktor Lysenko's death?"

He took a step forward, giving me an inquiring look, and I realized that he wanted to come inside. I didn't know how to refuse. "Come on in; I can talk for a minute." I stepped to the side and he brushed past me, the corner of his jacket moving so that I spotted his holstered gun. Without asking he walked into the living room, looking around with an interest I found nerve-racking. Maybe it was supposed to be. "Have a seat," I said, picking a newspaper off a chair and straightening the couch cushions to hide my nervousness. "Would you like something to drink?" I asked, the manners my mother had drilled into me kicking in automatically.

"Sure, got any bottled water?"

Was this some sort of cop trick? Ask for bottled water so he could take the bottle with him and lift my fingerprints from it? "No, but I can get you tap."

"Tap would be fine."

Out of sight in the kitchen, I grabbed a glass from the cupboard and hurriedly filled it at the sink. The kitchen clock ticked away; my window of time evaporating. "Here you go," I said as I came back into the living room, unnerved when I found him standing and looking at the photos hanging in my hall.

"Is this your family?" he asked, pointing at a photo of the four of us from a few years earlier.

"Yes. So what can I help you with, Detective?"

He took the glass from my hand and took a big sip, watching me over the rim, before answering. "You're a close friend of Heather Lysenko, right?"

"We're friends—I don't know how close."

"Been friends for a long time?"

"Several years."

He nodded as if that confirmed something he already knew.

"Yeah, well, we're trying to figure out what happened the night Dr. Lysenko was killed, just putting together a timeline—routine police stuff—and we noticed something." He paused to put the glass down, searching around for a coaster before I handed one to him and he set it down on the coffee table. At any other time, I might have appreciated this consideration, but not at that moment, not when I was desperate to leave.

Hands free, he reached into his jacket pocket and pulled out a small notebook, flipping through it. "We pulled the phone records for that night, and the thing is we found out that a call was placed from a cell phone registered to Heather Lysenko to your cell phone sometime after one A.M." He looked up at me, that benign smile still on his face. "Do you remember that call, Mrs. Riordan?"

"Please, call me Alison." I stared straight back at him, trying to look impassive. "Of course I remember. Heather has trouble sleeping sometimes and she knows I'm a night owl, so she called to chat." This was a preposterous lie; I'm a morning person in fact, in bed and fast asleep by ten most nights. I'd hated this when I was young because I could never stay awake at sleepovers and always missed the best gossip, plaintively asking what everyone was giggling about the next morning over Pop-Tarts.

"Did she talk about her husband?"

I tried to look as if I were pondering. "I don't think so—she might have mentioned that he wasn't home yet. We only talked for five minutes."

"Less than five. It was only three minutes and forty-seven seconds." Detective Kasper glanced down at his notebook for confirmation. "That's a pretty quick chat. Why so short?"

A moment's pause that felt longer as I scrambled to think of an answer. "I'd actually already gone to sleep that night; Heather woke me up. She felt so bad for waking me, that I stayed on for a few minutes to make her feel better and try and help her get to sleep."

He scribbled this down in his notebook, before nodding and standing up. "Great, well that's all the questions I've got at this point."

I stood up, too, feeling more than a little flustered, which was probably the point, so I did my best to hide it. "Have you found the guy who shot Dr. Lysenko?" I asked as we headed toward the door.

"We've got some leads," he said, "the investigation's ongoing." Was it my imagination or had he stared right at me on those last words?

"It's a terrible thing—I never thought something like this would happen in Sewickley."

Why had I said that? I could have bitten my tongue immediately after. I expected him to make a general comment about crime happening anywhere, but instead Kasper said, "Yes, it is pretty unusual."

I waited to leave until he'd pulled away from the curb in an unmarked Ford Taurus. It was five until ten; I had two missed calls from Julie and one from Sarah and I had at least a ten-minute drive to the drop-off point. I shot them a quick text before pulling out of the garage. Even if I raced the whole way, I was going to be late, and I didn't dare speed; I was terrified that the detective or his partner was secretly watching me. Had they been watching all of us all along? What if the blackmail letter was a setup and the cops were waiting to trap us at the drop-off?

Sarah shot down that idea when I called. "There's no way. Think about it—if they sent the blackmail letter, then they have photos of us from that night. If they have photos of that night, then they wouldn't need to set us up—we'd already be under arrest."

"You're right, that's right," I said, but I couldn't shake the paranoia that had me checking all the mirrors in my car every five seconds. "What if we're too late—what if this person goes to the cops because I'm not there on time?"

"They're not going to do that. He—or she—is not a Good Samaritan—they're an extortionist. That greedy asshole will make another attempt to get their hands on the cash before they even think about calling the cops."

It made sense, but I couldn't shake a growing feeling that things were hurtling out of control. What had seemed like a good

decision in the middle of the night looked like a horrible decision in the light of day, and I wished there were some magic
morning-after do-over pill that could reverse everything. If only
I'd insisted that Heather call the cops that night, then we wouldn't
have been out on Fern Hollow Road to be seen by the blackmailer, and we wouldn't be risking our futures trying to drop off
$20,000 to a total stranger.

At least I thought it was a stranger. What if it was someone we
knew? What if that's why he or she had stopped on the road that
night, because they'd recognized Julie's car, or Viktor's, and had
been planning to offer help? That could explain how they knew
our identities, because I was sure, so very sure, that no one had
followed us back to Heather's after we'd dropped off the body.

"Where are you now?" Sarah interrupted my mental spiral.

"At the clock tower. Where are you?"

"In position, where we've been for over an hour," Sarah said
in a withering voice that made me think how much I would have
hated appearing against her in court. Of course they were there;
I knew that.

"They've pulled Heather's phone records—why would they do
that if they think it's a carjacking?"

Sarah didn't have a smart answer for that. She paused for a
moment before saying, "It's routine—they always have to look
at the spouse in a suspicious death. It means nothing." Even she
didn't sound convinced.

As I drove slowly through the cemetery, I wished, more than
anything else, to be back in time, back before that phone call in
the middle of the night, back before we'd made the decision that
had brought us to this point.

I drove along the road in search of the Kershaw mausoleum,
pausing to look at the printout of the map. Behind me a funeral
procession was wending its way up to the cemetery chapel, a
modern building with lots of windows that seemed out of place
among all the old tombstones. The road continued over a hill
and the cars dropped out of sight.

The mausoleum was all the way at the back of the cemetery,

down a little road flanked by pine trees. "Okay, I'm here," I said to Sarah and Julie as I pulled off on the side.

"We can see you," Sarah said, but I couldn't spot them. I glanced around before grabbing the duffel from the backseat and stepping out of the car. There was no other vehicle or person in sight, but I had that neck-crawling sensation of being watched.

It was a short, uphill walk across bumpy ground to the mausoleum, which looked like a miniature stone house, with a peaked roof above the inscribed name and a pair of scrolled copper gates that had gone green with age. Who was Randall Kershaw? Someone who'd clearly had enough money for this monument of a final resting place. Was there anyone left alive to remember him? I looked around surreptitiously, wondering whether the blackmailer had already come and gone, before quickly placing the bag against a back corner of the mausoleum, just as the letter had instructed.

I walked hurriedly back to my car, glancing back only once. The duffel bag was still sitting there. Some movement caught my attention and I turned in that direction, pulse jumping as I thought I spotted a figure darting behind a tree, but it was just a shadow.

We'd agreed that I had to be seen driving away, because the blackmailer was undoubtedly watching the drop-off site. As I came over the hill, the service in the modern chapel had ended and mourners crowded the road. In keeping with the day I'd been having, a woman I knew crossed right in front of my car. She was the mother of one of Lucy's friends. When she spotted me, her eyes went wide with recognition and she waved before saying something to her husband, who also turned to look at me, before she waved again.

I waved back; what else could I do? Would they remember seeing me there if someone asked? The whole day had gone like that, just one mishap after another. As I drove out of the cemetery, I saw four ravens perched on top of a cross held by a downcast stone angel. It felt like an omen.

chapter twenty-eight

SARAH

We'd been sitting there for almost two hours and my legs were starting to cramp, but we couldn't get out and walk around or the blackmailer might spot us. What if we had to use the bathroom? Of course, the minute I had that thought all I could think about was needing to pee.

"I shouldn't have had so much coffee." I squirmed in my seat.

"Yes, better to skip *all* diuretics." Julie looked pointedly at my travel mug. As much as I loved Julie, she could be really annoying. It was the little things she said and did, things you wouldn't notice under normal circumstances, but in a high-pressure situation they seemed omnipresent. Like the fidgeting—I knew she was high-energy, but she couldn't seem to sit still, fiddling with the radio knobs, with the coins in my car's center console, with her earrings. "Where are they?" she said for the umpteenth time. She'd moved on to tapping on the dashboard, drumming so hard on the plastic that I'd thought she'd snap off an index finger.

I ignored her, doing another circuit with my gaze—ahead at the mausoleum, up the hill to the right, down the hill to the left, and behind us. Alison's car was long gone, but still no sign of the blackmailer. She'd mentioned the funeral procession, so I wasn't surprised to spot a handful of mourners in the rearview mirror, carefully picking their way down a snowy hillside in the distance. Dressed in black and other dark colors, they were too far away for us to identify, which meant they wouldn't be able to identify us either, or the minivan. In any case, they were too busy to do more than glance in our direction if they looked at all.

"Maybe he's been scared off by them," I said, pointing over my shoulder at the mourners.

Julie shifted in her seat to see them. "I hope not," she said, before turning her attention back to the mausoleum. The duffel bag was tucked against the stone, but we could still see it. The wind played with the thin straps, lifting one like a black ribbon.

The rumble of an engine made us both sit up. A big yellow backhoe came around the hillside, huge tires crunching down the road, a man in a sheepskin jacket sitting behind the steering wheel stationed high up in the cab.

"I'm guessing that's the gravedigger," Julie said. "It's sure a lot less romantic than two guys with shovels." The backhoe came slowly down the road before stopping adjacent to the road we were watching, the massive machine groaning and sighing, like a dinosaur settling in to rest.

"What the hell," I said. "He's blocking our view."

The mausoleum was now hidden by the backhoe; we could only see a corner of the stone building. For a second I wondered if the driver could be the blackmailer, but he didn't get out of the cab, just lit up a cigarette and sat back, apparently waiting until the hillside service behind us finished to take a left down the road where we were parked.

"C'mon, move it," Julie muttered, stretching her neck to try to see past the machine. "Should we get out and look?"

"No, the backhoe driver will see us, if not the blackmailer," I said. "He didn't stop the machine, he's just paused. He's got to move soon."

A few agonizing minutes later he finally did, the backhoe revving up with a roar before crunching past us, veering onto the grass to do so, while far behind us the little figures in black filed back up the hill.

"Finally," I said, watching him trundle away in the rearview mirror just as Julie said, "Shit!"

"What?"

"It's gone!"

My gaze snapped back to the mausoleum—the black bag had disappeared.

"What the hell? Quick, where are they?" I bolted from the car, forgetting about the possibility of being noticed, forgetting about everything except the need to find the blackmailer. I ran toward the mausoleum, looking around, trying to spot a figure slipping between trees or behind another monument.

Julie came right on my heels. "They're gone—they found a moment and they took it and the money." She grabbed my arm, trying to pull me back. "C'mon, we don't want anyone to see us."

"How could they slip in and out without us seeing them?" I said. "Where did they go?" I scanned the hillside, the trees, the gravestones and other small buildings—it didn't seem possible; this person couldn't have just vanished. All at once I spied a figure in black moving off to the left, running down the hillside. "Down there! Near the trees!" I yelled, stabbing the air with my index finger. "Do you see him?"

Julie shaded her eyes. "Yes, yes!" She ran back toward the car. "Hurry, let's try to catch him."

We drove as fast as we could up the road, around the back side of the cemetery, but it was obvious that we weren't going to catch this guy. He—it looked like a man, but I couldn't tell for sure—had disappeared over the hillside on foot, and he could have gone in any direction. There was no way of knowing where to look. We drove up and down the roads, eventually finding ourselves back the way we'd come. For all we knew, he'd parked a car outside the cemetery property and run back to it.

The disappointment was palpable. "Do you think he could have been working with the backhoe guy?" I suggested as we drove back out of the cemetery gates. "Maybe that guy purposely blocked us in?"

We'd passed the backhoe operator parked along a road near the front of the cemetery; he'd been kicking back, listening to something on his headphones while another cigarette dangled from his lips.

"I don't know," Julie said. "I hope not." She was drumming on the dashboard again.

What if the backhoe guy wasn't the only person he'd told— what if there were others who knew? I hadn't considered the possibility of more than one person knowing or seeing those photos. "We're screwed."

"Don't say that!" Julie said, as I took a left with enough force to pull her sideways in her seat, knocking her hand off the dash. "We paid the money, it's over."

"Is that the way it typically works with blackmail?" I said, unable to contain my frustration any longer. "Do blackmailers typically just take the money and people never hear from them again?"

"I have no idea what's typical," Julie said in a prissy voice, clearly choosing to ignore my sarcasm. "Look, we didn't catch him, but that doesn't mean that everything failed—he got the money he asked for. We just have to stay calm."

"You know, I don't think we're going to be able to fix this with positive thinking," I snarled, accelerating up Blackburn Road.

"Well, we certainly aren't going to fix it with drinking."

"What the hell is that supposed to mean?"

"It means that I know you've spiked your sippy cup."

"It's Irish coffee. Lots of people have it that way."

"Sure. You can explain that to the cops when you get pulled over for speeding."

"Shut up, Julie, okay? Because I really can't take any more crap right now." I was practically spitting I was so pissed off, but I did slow down, my hands knotted on the wheel so tight I could see the bones.

Apparently I wasn't the only angry one: Julie looked like she wanted to hit me, but she crossed her arms instead, turning her back and staring out the passenger window.

"We need to call Alison and Heather," I said after a few minutes of silent driving. Julie didn't respond and wouldn't look at me. Another few minutes passed and I tried again. "It's no use blaming me—it's not my fault this didn't work out."

"No one's blaming you, Sarah, except for telling me to shut up. That I am blaming you for."

I sighed. "Okay, I'm sorry I told you to shut up."

She finally looked at me. "And I'm sorry I commented on your driving."

"And?"

"And what?"

"And you're sorry for commenting on my coffee?"

She pursed her lips for a moment before saying in her most holier-than-thou voice, "If that's what you need to hear."

I laughed. "I'll take that as a yes." I couldn't stop a smile from slipping out. The atmosphere in the car relaxed a little. I made a call to tell Alison what had happened and she sounded almost comically distressed. "Is this guy some kind of ghost? How could he just appear like that?"

"He's not a ninja, he hid behind construction equipment," I said, rolling my eyes at Julie, who laughed, prompting Alison to say over the car speakerphone, "Why are you laughing?" Which only made us both laugh.

"Sorry, we're just punchy," Julie said.

"There's nothing funny about this," Alison said, sounding annoyed before dropping back into panic. "Oh God, the police have pulled Heather's phone calls, they're watching her and us, and now this crazy guy is just out there, a ticking time bomb who can go to the police at any moment." Her voice climbed higher as she wailed, "What are we going to do?"

"Ask for adjoining cells?" I said before bursting out laughing along with Julie, who just lost it, both of us laughing so hard that I had to pull the car off to the side of the road.

"I guess you should consider a career in stand-up," Alison said, tartly. "I've got a project due—got to go."

"She actually hung up on me." I held the phone out to show Julie.

"Oh dear, you have to call her back," she said, still giggling and swiping at her eyes.

"Not until we've stopped laughing."

"Maybe I should call Heather." She started to select her number, but I stopped her.

"No, don't. None of us should call her right now, not so soon after that detective visited Alison."

That sobered her up. "Do you think they're going to want to talk to us, too?"

"Maybe? Heather only called Alison that night—that's why they wanted to talk to her, but who knows what else they've found out."

"There's no proof of anything, aside from the photos," she said. "If this guy keeps his end of the deal we'll be okay."

"There's no reason to trust him, especially after today."

"We have no choice—there's no other option."

The atmosphere had changed again; we were both somber, and we drove the rest of the way in silence, under a sky that was gray and heavy with clouds, seemingly as weighed down as we were.

chapter twenty-nine

Any time the doorbell rang I tensed, convinced it was the police. Every day carried with it a dual threat: The police would find out the truth and come to arrest us, or the blackmailer would go to the police with the photos and then they'd arrest us.

There'd been no more encounters after Detective Kasper questioned me, no sign that they had any interest in Julie or Sarah. Still, I couldn't shake the feeling that we were being watched, that everything each of us did was under surveillance.

Invariably, that tension we all were feeling transferred to our families. No matter that I did my best to hide the stress—I wasn't good at it and my children seemed to catch my mood, especially Lucy, who became irritable and anxious.

"Is this some sort of developmental stage?" Michael asked one night after he'd packed a crying Lucy off to her room to think about why she couldn't just yell at her brother no matter how annoying she found him. "Or should I find a priest willing to do exorcisms?"

"She's okay, it's just sibling rivalry."

He snorted. "It's more than that and you know it."

We were cleaning the kitchen together post-dinner and I turned from loading the dishwasher to look at him. "What does that mean?"

"That this isn't about her and Matthew—she's picking up on

the overall mood in this house." He scraped some plates into the trash and handed them to me.

"And what would mood would that be?" I said, grabbing them from him and loading them noisily into the dishwasher, hoping my obvious annoyance would make him drop the subject.

"Tense. Irritable."

"You mean *my* mood, right? Isn't that what you're trying to say?" I straightened up and looked at him, everything in my face and tone daring him to agree. Emotionally intelligent spouses know how to read the signs, and Michael was usually smart enough to back away from this kind of interaction with me. I've often thought successful marriages are as much about couples knowing how to create space for each other's moods as they are about togetherness and communication.

He paused, but when he spoke again, I could hear his determination to have this conversation. "Yes—it's your mood affecting Lucy."

"Sure, blame the mother." I turned back to the dishwasher, pleased with my deflection.

"C'mon, Ali, you know I'm not saying that."

"Then what are you saying?"

"You're stressed and it's affecting the kids. It's affecting all of us."

"You're working long hours, too, Michael—I'm not the only one who's got stress."

"For God's sake, Ali, you can't even load the dishwasher without slamming things."

He was right, but that only fueled my irritation. I hurled a handful of cutlery into the sink, the sharp clatter echoing throughout the house.

"Mommy, what happened? Are you okay?" Matthew came around the corner, eyes wide.

"I'm fine, sweetie," I said, forcing a smile. "I just dropped some silverware."

"You're yelling? Why are you and Daddy yelling?"

"It's okay, Matt," Michael said. "Your mom and I weren't yelling, not really. We're just talking a bit loud. You know how you talk like that with Lucy sometimes?"

"Like the time she took my soccer ball when I said no you can't borrow it?" he said, looking from me to Michael and back again.

"Something like that," Michael said. "It's okay, bud. Sometimes Mom and I squabble about things just like you and Lucy squabble, but it's okay."

"Mrs. Arnold says people shouldn't throw hard things when they're angry," Matthew said. "Mrs. Arnold says people should only throw soft things, like pillows."

"Mrs. Arnold is a wise woman," I said, a genuine smile slipping out. "Why don't you go up and start getting ready for bed— Dad and I'll be up in a bit to read you a story."

Michael put an arm around Matthew and walked him down the hall to the stairs, while I grabbed a sponge and took out my leftover aggression on the countertops. He came back into the kitchen, but I kept swiping at the stone, not making eye contact.

"I'm worried about you," he said. "You're short-tempered with me and the kids, and you're so tense that you jump at the slightest sound."

"I'm just tired."

"You've been crying out in your sleep, Ali." That surprised me; it was something that I used to do a lifetime ago. I knew I'd been sleeping fitfully, but not to this extent. Seeing the look on my face, Michael reached out to comfort me and I flinched from his touch. An old reflex; it startled us both.

Michael sighed. "Things have been this way since you got that letter."

My hands froze on the counter, a pool of soapy water gathering around the sponge. "What letter?"

"I saw it."

"You did?" My thoughts raced, while everything else seemed to slow. Where had he found it? I'd had it in my coat pocket, before sticking it in a drawer in my desk. He never went in my desk—I should have hidden it better. I looked up from my hands, pressed so hard against the counter that they were a blotchy red and white. "Where? I mean, how did you find it—"

"Sean told me about it."

"Sean?" I frowned, confused.

Michael must have thought I was angry because he said, "Don't blame him, I asked."

And then all at once I realized that he wasn't talking about the blackmail letter at all, but about the letter I'd received back in the fall, the one Sean wanted to discuss, the one I wanted so much to forget. Relief swept through me—he didn't know about the blackmail letter! I started to laugh, totally inappropriate and hysterical giggling that I couldn't contain.

He must have thought this was the beginning of a nervous collapse, because he looked dismayed, coming to rescue me with his arms outstretched. "It's okay," he said, pulling me into an embrace. "It's going to be okay."

Who was he trying to convince? I tried to explain that I was fine, but when I started to speak, the words turned into a sob and suddenly I was clutching him hard and crying.

At Michael's insistence, I called our GP and got a prescription for a sleep aid. The little white pills helped me fall asleep and sleep more deeply, but I felt sluggish and drowsy in the morning and I was plagued by nightmares in which the past and present merged.

I am Lucy's age and hiding in a small dark room, a sharp blade of light under a door, pounding footfalls coming closer and closer. "Come out of there!" Scrambling back, trying to find another way out, but slamming against something hard and slick. I try to climb over it, my hands slipping against plastic, pulling sheeting off a green car. Viktor sitting up, bloody and grinning. "You can't hide from me!"

I woke up from my own screaming, my mouth wide open and a puddle of drool on the pillow, covers twisted like a snake around me. The space next to me was empty, and hard daylight streamed through a gap in the curtains.

"You were sleeping so peacefully I didn't want to wake you," Michael said when I found him downstairs packing the kids' lunches. "You look like you're still tired—I can take them to school if you want to keep sleeping."

"No," I said at once, a bark that made little worry lines appear on Michael's face. Lucy and Matthew were eating breakfast, Cheerios scattered across the kitchen table, a milk carton sitting out and open. A cartoon played loudly on the TV, but the kids were watching us. Matthew tapped his spoon nervously while he looked from me to his father, while Lucy shoveled spoonfuls of cereal in her mouth with grim determination.

"No," I repeated in a quieter voice. "I've got it. You go ahead."

"You sure?" He gave me a penetrating look, but he was already uncuffing the sleeves of his dress shirt and fastening the buttons. I nodded, stretching my lips into a smile in accordance with the positive-thinking tapes a therapist had once recommended: *Fake it till you make it!*

Michael had recommended that I go back to therapy. "If you won't talk to me, you've got to talk to someone."

"I talk to my friends," I'd protested, regretting it when I saw the hurt look on his face. He wanted to be the one I turned to, he shared the good man's fantasy of being his family's savior and protector.

"You've told them about what happened?" he'd asked, sounding both surprised and a little sulky at the idea that I'd share my past with anyone else but him.

"Some of it." Which meant next to none of it.

"They're not professionals," he'd argued. "You need to talk to someone you can tell everything to."

"Maybe," I said. "I don't have time right now—I'm too behind with work."

These half-truths we tell were something I might have talked about once with my friends. At times I passed by Crazy Mocha and felt a wave of longing for the mornings we'd sat there gossiping about other people's lives, before our own became so complicated.

"Have you had any more visitors?" Julie asked every day at the bus stop, the only place where we could talk for a few minutes without concern that it would attract attention. Her way of referring to the police, something that she'd been asking since the detective questioned me. She and Sarah had been waiting for their visit ever since, but it hadn't happened. At least not yet. I knew it wasn't over and the police hadn't moved on. The sound of the doorbell, or even just the noise of a car passing on my street, would send me flying to the window, convinced I'd see a squad car outside, roof lights spinning.

Of course, when I finally did see the police again, I wasn't expecting it at all.

It was a Wednesday afternoon, almost a month after the funeral, a sunny day after a streak of gray ones. I'd driven up to Sewickley Heights because Heather had sent me a text earlier in the afternoon asking if I'd mind picking up Daniel after school. She was running late at the doctor and wouldn't be home in time to meet his bus.

I was happy to do it. I hadn't seen her in well over a week and was eager to see how she was doing. The after-school pickup was fine; she'd called the school and they released Daniel to me without any hassle, my kids running to me while Daniel followed slowly behind them.

"Benjamin Bunny is having a baby!" Matthew announced excitedly as the kids clambered into the backseat of my Subaru.

"Oh, so Benjamin isn't a boy after all?" I asked with a laugh, helping him fasten the straps in his car seat. "What did your teacher say about that?"

"Mrs. Arnold said, 'Wow, now that's a surprise!'" Matthew said, doing a pretty credible imitation of her deep voice.

"You have to give him a new name," Lucy told him.

"I like Benjamin."

"Benjamin is a boy's name and boys don't have babies."

"I know that," Matthew said in a withering voice.

"So you can't call him Benjamin anymore—you have to pick a girl's name."

"No we don't."

"Yes you do."

Just another of their escalating and maddening arguments. Daniel settled in between them, not saying much. Aside from occasional outbursts of temper, he'd always been a pretty quiet little boy, something I attributed to being an only child and not having to fight for attention.

"Mom, do we have to call Benjamin by another name?" Matthew whined, as usual appealing to me to arbitrate the silliness.

"What did your teacher say?"

"She said we need to get a bigger house for Benjamin."

I laughed out loud. "That certainly seems like the more important thing right now."

"You still need a different name," Lucy insisted. "Doesn't he, Daniel?"

Sometimes I wondered if Lucy would grow up to be lawyer. Or a judge. I glanced in the rearview mirror and saw that Daniel wore the look of someone who wished he could be anywhere else.

"Enough, you two," I said as I slowed to turn onto the road leading to Heather's house. "The kindergarten bunny isn't any of your business, Lucy."

"He's the one talking about it," she protested. "It's not my fault his teacher can't tell the difference between a boy and a girl."

"Mrs. Arnold can so tell," Matthew yelled.

"Cannot."

"Can so."

As I slowed to turn left into Heather's driveway, I glanced again in the rearview mirror and saw Daniel pressing two fingers against his forehead as if he were feeling a headache coming on. I could relate. "Be quiet!" I finally snapped, louder than I meant to, feeling guilty when all three kids jumped in their seats. There was silence for a moment as we climbed the winding drive, sun washing the pavers and burnishing the bare forsythia bushes. It was still cold out, but spring would be here soon. "Let's talk about something else," I said in a calmer voice, as we reached the top of the hill. "What else happened today?"

I stopped talking, struck dumb by the sight of a familiar Ford Taurus parked on Heather's driveway.

The short, bald detective from the funeral home was standing on the front steps and he turned to watch us pull up. I fought the urge to flee back down the driveway. There was no sign of Heather's car—she probably wasn't back yet.

As I tried to decide what to do, the detective moved in my direction and I got out of the car, anxious not to speak with him in front of the kids. "I'll see if your mom's home yet, Daniel," I said, turning to the backseat. "The three of you just sit tight."

"Who's that man?" I heard Lucy asking Daniel as I closed the door.

The detective was shading his eyes from the sun, his feet tapping across the pavers. "Alison Riordan?"

"Yes?" I crossed around the car, zipping my coat, and trying to look as if I were having trouble placing him.

"I'm Detective Lou Tedesco," he said, flashing his badge with a small, meaty hand. "I'm investigating the death of Dr. Viktor Lysenko." He paused as if expecting me to say something, but I continued to give him a slightly puzzled look. "I think you met my partner, Detective Kasper?"

"Yes, I spoke with him a while ago."

He jangled something in his jacket pocket, flashing a smile. His teeth seemed too large and too white for his face. "I guess you're here to see Heather Lysenko?"

"Yes. She isn't home yet?"

"No." He continued to stare at me, an occasional breeze flattening the curl from his gray fringe. "Do you know where she is?"

"Doctor's appointment," I said. "She asked if I'd drop off her son from school because she was running late."

"Aah. The doctor." He said the word as if he were testing it out. "You're one of Heather's friends, right?"

"That's right. And her husband's. I was friends with him, too,

I mean." I mentally cursed. Less than a minute in and I was already saying too much. My brother was a cop, for goodness' sake—I knew that when you were talking to the police, the less said the better. Too much information just raised suspicion.

"Right." He jotted something down in a small spiral notebook that he pulled from a jacket pocket. "How long have you known Mrs. Lysenko?"

For a split second I thought he was talking about Heather's mother-in-law. "Oh, you mean Heather? About three years."

"Her husband, the same length of time?"

"Yes. I met Viktor through Heather."

"How would you describe their relationship?"

"Happy. They had a happy marriage." I watched as he jotted this down. "What's this about, Detective? Why are you asking?"

"In any homicide investigation we have to ask a lot of questions." He smiled in what he probably thought was an ingratiating manner, flashing the teeth. They were probably capped.

"I thought Viktor was killed during a carjacking," I said.

"Hmm, yes, well, we have to get as full a picture as possible—it's all routine. Tell me, do you know much about Heather's life before she married Dr. Lysenko?"

Why was he asking these questions? I struggled to look unconcerned. "Not really. She was a model. I know she was doing modeling when she met Viktor."

"And before modeling?"

"Um, I don't know what you mean—"

"About her life in West Virginia? Have you ever talked with her about that?"

"Not really. I know she's from a small town and her parents still live there." Where was he going with this? "But Heather doesn't like to talk much about her past." As soon as I said it I realized it was wrong; it made it appear as if Heather had something to hide. "She's so busy with her life now, I mean, she always said she didn't miss modeling because she loved being a mother." Okay, that was a lie. I'd never heard her say anything of the kind.

I glanced back at the car and saw Lucy's face pressed against the window, staring at me. "Is there anything else?" I said. "I've got to be with the kids."

"Yes, just one more question if you don't mind." Another flash of those teeth. "Did Heather ever mention divorce?"

"Divorce? No, not to me. As I said, she had a happy marriage."

"Hmm, yes, as you said." There was something skeptical in the way he repeated my phrase. "Of course, Heather had a lot of incentive to stay married."

"You mean because of Daniel."

"Well, yes, of course, there's her stepson," he said. "But I was thinking of the terms of her marriage." He flipped his notebook shut. "Thank you for your time, Mrs. Riordan."

He walked briskly toward his car, surprisingly fast and nimble for someone so short and heavyset. I should have been relieved to see the back of him, but I was puzzling over what he'd said.

"The terms?" I called after him. "What are you referring to?"

He turned back and gave me a look of clearly simulated surprise. "You didn't know about the prenuptial agreement?"

chapter thirty

ALISON

A prenup? I couldn't hide my surprise and, even though I didn't say anything, the detective smiled again, his big, capped-teeth grin like a fucking Cheshire cat.

"Thanks again, Mrs. Riordan." He raised his hand in some cross between a wave and a Hitler salute and continued to his car, his footsteps loud against the stone. I crossed to my own car, but waited until he'd driven away to let the kids out.

"Was that the police, Mommy?" Matthew asked. "Daniel says that man is the police."

"Daniel's right." I kept my voice light as I helped all three kids out of the backseat. "Don't forget your backpack," I said, handing Daniel the red bag he'd left in the car.

"Why did he want to talk to you?" Lucy said.

"He didn't. He wanted to talk to Daniel's mom."

"Why?"

"Let's go inside," I said, ignoring the questions and ushering them to the first garage door. Heather had texted me the code for the keypad and I typed it in, mind racing. Was it true about the prenup or had the detective been making things up to goad me? But why would he do that? And why was he asking questions about Heather at all?

I was so jittery that I knocked over some terra-cotta pots stacked inside the garage. One of them cracked wide while another rolled out onto the driveway, and I had to chase after it and put them back into some semblance of order.

Daniel led the way inside, passing the laundry room into the kitchen, tossing his backpack on the tile floor.

"What do you do after school, Daniel?" I said. "Does your mom make you a snack?" It felt strange to be there. I hadn't been in the house since I'd come to retrieve the blackmail letter and then I'd gotten no farther than the entryway. The night Heather shot Viktor seemed a lifetime ago.

"I make my own snack," Daniel said with a casualness that clearly impressed Lucy. He climbed on a stepstool to reach a cupboard, getting out a package of cookies, which he brought over to the island to share with Lucy and Matthew. She was equally impressed when Daniel produced his iPad and brought up some Japanese anime for the three of them to watch.

"Your house is fun," she said, shooting me a look that said I needed to up my game.

I got out some milk and poured them each a glass, noticing the fridge didn't have much in it beyond some Chinese take-out containers, and there were dirty dishes stacked in the sink. Clearly the household's exacting standards had died along with Viktor.

My phone pinged with another text from Heather: **Be there soon—sorry**! A smiling emoticon. While the kids chattered over their snack and video, I walked out of the room and called Sarah. "Did you know that Heather had a prenuptial agreement?"

"Really? I guess it doesn't surprise me." She sounded distracted and I could hear children in the background.

"You don't think it's odd that she never mentioned it? Especially when we were trying to convince her to leave Viktor?"

"It's pretty common in a certain income bracket," she said, adding grimly, "You and I just aren't in that bracket."

"No wonder she wouldn't consider leaving him—she'd get nothing."

"She might have been able to contest it—maybe used the abuse as leverage—but it doesn't really matter anymore."

"Well, the police certainly seem interested."

"What?" Now I had her attention. "How do you know that? What's going on?" She listened intently as I described running into Detective Tedesco on Heather's doorstep, before asking me to repeat what he'd said. "He's just fishing—if he knew anything they would have made an arrest."

"They know it wasn't a carjacking."

"We don't know that. And it doesn't matter. We just have to hold tight and not say anything. You didn't tell him anything, did you?"

"Of course not."

"Good. Good, then we're fine." One of Sarah's children started wailing in the background. "Look, I've got to go, but whatever you do, don't tell Heather what he was asking."

"Why?"

"It'll just scare her. We don't want her making any stupid moves. We just have to stay the course."

She hung up and I paced nervously around the house, unable to sit still. If the police were looking into Heather's background, what else could they know? We shouldn't have been talking about it over the phone. Could the police listen in on cell-phone conversations? Could they have planted cameras in the house?

I thought I heard a noise from upstairs and suddenly remembered Viktor's mother. Could she have arrived while Heather was out and Tedesco didn't mention it? What if she was upstairs lurking, listening in on my conversation? I hurried up the stairs, unable to stop myself from checking all the rooms. It was quiet on the second floor, my footfalls sinking in the plush carpeting. The bed in the guest room was neatly made and there weren't any clothes hanging in the closet. Clearly Anna had left. Could she be the reason there had been a prenup? She didn't seem to trust Heather at all.

I glanced in the master bedroom and saw that the bed was unmade, covers thrown back and rumpled. There were clothes tossed over a chair, as if Heather hadn't been able to decide on an outfit. Daniel's room seemed equally untidy, the bed a tangled mess of sheets, LEGOs, and other toys cluttering the floor. What had happened to the cleaners?

There were family photos lining the upstairs hall, and I was surprised to see one of a dark-haired woman holding an infant. She looked vaguely familiar and I suddenly realized it was Janice Lysenko, Viktor's first wife, with Daniel in her arms. How had Heather felt about having the first wife's picture on display? It would have bothered me. And there was something odd about the photo. Janice was smiling, but there were dark circles under her eyes and what was it about the hair? I peered at it closely. Could that be a wig? I remembered that colleague of Viktor's at the post-funeral luncheon. *"She died of cancer."* I hadn't believed him. I'd thought he was just confusing Janice with someone else or that Viktor had told people a lie to cover up the abuse, but not now, not looking at that photo, at the fake hair and that hollowed face. Could it have been true? Had Janice Lysenko died of cancer?

The noise of a car engine startled me and I hurried down the stairs as I heard the faint whir of the garage door opening. Back in the kitchen, the kids had eaten nearly the entire package of cookies. Matthew gave me a slightly guilty look as he swallowed the last of his milk, his mouth ringed with crumbs. His sister and Daniel were staring, glassy-eyed, at the anime playing on his tablet.

The door from the garage opened. "Hello, hello!" Heather rushed in to the kitchen, her arms loaded down with a purse and a shopping bag. "I'm so sorry I'm late." She gave me a quick kiss on the cheek and then dropped a kiss on Daniel's head. "Oh, I'm glad you found something to eat. This has been such a crazy day." She placed her bags on the free stool at the island and brushed strands of hair off her face.

She looked effortlessly beautiful as she always did—a leather jacket open over a cream-colored sweater and jeans, diamond studs in her ears, a simple gold bracelet dancing from her thin wrist. "Remind me never to hit Nordstrom and the doctor in the same day again," she said with a light laugh. "Foot pain followed by pelvic pain." She unzipped her high-heeled suede ankle boots and wiggled her toes, sighing with relief.

"How are you feeling?" I asked, nodding at her belly, conscious of the kids. At some point she was really going to have to tell Daniel.

"Great, I feel great. Everything's fine so far." She patted her still nonexistent stomach and gave me a secret smile.

She seemed so relaxed, and her skin seemed to glow in the afternoon sun streaming through the kitchen window. It felt oddly surreal, as if I'd imagined everything bad that had happened in this kitchen, in that garage. As if I'd conjured up that grinning detective. My gaze fell on the shopping bag. She was shopping at Nordstrom—what if the detective had seen her with the bag? It wasn't exactly standard grieving widow behavior, and I wondered what Sarah would make of it, when she'd had to sell furniture to raise her $5,000.

"C'mon kids, it's time to go," I said, clapping my hands to pry their attention away from the screen.

"Just five minutes," Lucy pleaded, still staring at the anime. "We're watching something."

"Two minutes—we've got to get going."

"Thank you so much for picking up Daniel," Heather said. "I'm sorry to interrupt your afternoon."

"I was happy to help out," I said. "By the way, you had a visitor."

"Who?"

"Lou Tedesco. That short detective."

"Oh, Jesus, not him again." She sounded more annoyed than concerned. "What did he want this time? Did he say?"

"I don't know." I hesitated, thinking of Sarah's warning, but she hadn't seen how Heather was acting—cheerful and relaxed, going out for a day of shopping as if she hadn't a care in the world. "He was asking a lot of questions—so be careful."

"What kind of questions?"

"About your marriage. Was it happy."

Heather's eyes widened at that and in her nervousness she bumped against the stool, sending the Nordstrom bag sliding. I shot out my hand in a futile attempt to stop its fall just as Heather bent to grab it, and we connected, my hand grazing her face.

"Sorry," I said, flustered, as she put the bag back on the stool, but she didn't flinch, focused on what I'd said to the detective.

"What did you tell him? I hope you told him yes."

"Of course I did. But you should be careful—you don't want to attract attention."

She frowned. "What do you mean by that?"

"Well, maybe you shouldn't do certain things," I said in a low voice, feeling uncomfortable. "Things that could be interpreted as you not mourning your husband."

"Are you talking about shopping?" she said, incredulously, not bothering to keep her voice down. "What am I supposed to do—just sit at home wearing black? I was buying new pants for Daniel. Are you saying that makes me look bad?" I glanced at the kids, concerned they might be listening, but they seemed absorbed in their show.

Heather blinked rapidly, her eyes glistening, as if she was on the edge of tears. It made me feel awful, but so had the detective. "I'm sorry, I didn't mean to upset you," I said, speaking as quietly as I could. "All I'm trying to say is that we need to watch out because the police are watching us."

"Don't you think that's a bit paranoid?" she said with a tiny, nervous laugh.

"Maybe, but why is he asking questions?" I said. "If he wasn't suspicious, he wouldn't visit your house, right?" *And he wouldn't have mentioned a prenuptial agreement,* I thought, but chose not to say.

I said it to Julie instead, calling her once I was back home and the kids were occupied. The minute she answered, I blurted out the same question I'd asked Sarah: "Did you know that Heather had a prenup?"

"What, really?" It was gratifying that Julie sounded more surprised than Sarah had. "How did you find that out?"

"I ran into the short detective." I told her everything that had happened—being surprised by Tedesco, calling Sarah, Heather shopping and seemingly unaffected. There was silence on the other end of the phone when I was finished. "Hello?"

"Maybe the detective just said that to see how you'd react." She sounded defensive. "What are you trying to say—that Heather lied to us? Do you really believe she'd do that?"

Put that way, it sounded so judgmental that I winced. Heather was our friend, she'd been badly abused, how could I believe that about her? "No, I don't know, it's just a big thing not to mention. I mean, if it's true she had a prenup then no wonder she wouldn't leave Viktor. It wasn't just losing Daniel that she had to worry about."

"Look, we know she's embarrassed about being from West Virginia—maybe that's why she didn't tell us. Maybe she felt ashamed of it—like it made her seem like a gold digger or something. That's probably how Viktor made her feel. We don't share everything with each other. I'm sure you have some secrets that you don't tell."

That stopped me; I was glad Julie couldn't see me because I actually flushed. Talking about the past was something I didn't like to do either. Sometimes I'd share snippets from my life before I married Michael, the sanitized bits, the happy times that I could cut from the rest of it, a carefully constructed quilt of memories that made my life sound normal. Ironically, the one friend I'd actually shared more of my past with had been Heather.

Until that moment, I'd forgotten all about a conversation we'd had one day, over a year ago, when Heather dropped by to pick up Daniel after a playdate. Somehow we'd started talking about how lucky our kids were and how much easier their lives were than ours had been. She told me about growing up in West Virginia, how her grandfather had climbed his way out of the coal mines, but her father got stuck as an almost white-collar office worker, moving from one low-level job to another, barely scraping by. And she told me about her mother, a woman so pretty she'd won a local beauty contest. Could have won Miss America, but she'd given up the chance for something better by marrying the first handsome boy she'd kissed, only to spend her days worrying constantly about how they'd pay the bills and keep a roof over their heads. "I didn't want to be like her," Heather had said, a feeling I could relate to.

So I'd told her about my past. Not everything, of course. I had no desire to share some sob story of my life before college and Michael and the kids and moving to Sewickley. I'd said just enough to explain why I'd never wanted to go back to my hometown either. Just enough to tell her what had happened to my mother and her dreams.

Heather had been so kind, listening without judgment. Remembering that made me ashamed. "You're right," I said to Julie, "she was probably embarrassed about the prenup. That's got to be why she didn't tell us."

But after getting off the phone, I kept picturing Tedesco's face when he'd told me—that grin, those hard eyes. And that photo of Viktor's first wife—those hollow cheeks, the hair that might have been a wig. What if Heather *had* lied to us? I couldn't stop thinking about it. This is the problem with doubt: Once a little seed has been planted, it burrows deep into your darkest thoughts and takes root.

Later that week, on impulse, I saw the kids off to school and drove to the city, to Children's Hospital in Lawrenceville, one of the hospitals where Viktor had worked. I'd searched online and found the doctor whom I'd met at Viktor's funeral. Or at least I thought it was him. It was hard to tell from the small head shot, and I couldn't recall his name, but I hoped it was the same guy.

I didn't tell Julie or Sarah, and when Michael phoned I told him I was out running an errand, berating myself for lying once I'd hung up. The entire drive I felt that same crawly feeling, constantly glancing in the rear and side mirrors to see if I was being followed. It was ludicrous—why would the police be following me? Heather, maybe, but not me. Except the detectives knew me by name and they'd questioned me. Were the photos already there, on Tedesco's or Kasper's desk? Had they figured it out and were simply spinning a web to entrap us?

The hospital's parking garage was crowded and I had to circle multiple levels before finding a spot. I checked my makeup in the visor mirror and was startled to recognize my mother's anxious face staring back at me. *"Let's not tell your dad about this, okay? This can be our secret."* Had I become that woman? Running scared and lying to my husband? Who was I to question Heather's behavior?

I almost didn't go inside. Sitting there in the car, I thought about turning back, but I'd taken the parking ticket and it had to be validated inside. Once I stepped out of the car my resolve steadied. I had already taken the time to drive there; I might as well find out what Viktor's colleague knew.

Plastic Surgery was on the third floor. I got on an elevator crowded with a large bunch of balloons that read HAPPY BIRTHDAY and GET WELL SOON in cheerful letters, the two different messages appearing to war with one another, bobbing in and out of front position, as a middle-aged man struggled to contain them.

The hospital was a maze. I took two wrong turns before finally arriving at the doors marked DIVISION OF PEDIATRIC PLASTIC SURGERY. The older woman in scrubs at the reception desk instructed me to sign in when I said I was there to see Dr. Barrow.

"I don't have an appointment," I said, pen hovering over the clipboard she'd handed me.

She looked over her reading glasses at me. "You got to make an appointment or you can't see the doctors."

"I know, but it's not medical, that is, it's a personal matter."

"Personal," she repeated, as if that were a word she didn't understand.

"Yes. I just need to talk to him for a few minutes."

"Is your child a patient?"

"No."

"Former patient?"

I shook my head.

"Well, this is the registration area for patients," she said, taking back the clipboard and holding it against her chest. "I can't help you."

A few people had stopped turning the pages of magazines or watching the game show playing on a large TV and were now staring our way. "Look," I said, moving closer and lowering my voice. "This is a really private matter. Do you know how I can get in touch with Dr. Barrow?"

She sighed, clearly annoyed that I wasn't just going to go away. "You could try his secretary maybe, but you probably still got to have an appointment. Down the hall, third door on the right."

I was halfway out the door when I stopped and went back to her desk. She gave me an irritated look, like I was a fly she thought she'd managed to swat away.

"Can you validate this?" I asked, holding out my parking ticket.

Dr. Barrow's personal assistant was a twentysomething woman with jet-black hair dyed blue at the tips wearing a tight black dress with horizontal stripes of cobalt blue. Behind her was an enormous whiteboard yearly calendar with a neon rainbow of different-colored lines crossed through various weeks each month. Between all the bright colors and the way she stared—head cocked to one side, sharp eyes focused and unblinking—she reminded me of an exotic bird.

"Dr. Barrow's not here on Wednesdays," she said. "They should have told you that—sorry." She shifted that sharp gaze from me to her terminal, reaching for her mouse. "He'll be in tomorrow and we have a cancellation at three and he might have one slot open in two weeks. Why does your child need an appointment?"

"It's not for my child. This isn't medical—it's a personal matter. Is there another way I could get in touch with him? A phone number?"

She looked at me again. "I'm not authorized to give out his phone number. Are you a friend of Dr. Barrow's?"

Had I imagined the emphasis on "friend"? My face flushed as though there were something between us. "Not exactly. I was a friend of Dr. Viktor Lysenko. I met Dr. Barrow at Dr. Lysenko's funeral."

"I thought you looked familiar. I was at the funeral, too." She leaned forward, her face becoming greedy and conspiratorial. "It's a shame about Dr. Lysenko, isn't it? He really loved that car, you know? I mean, not to blame the victim or anything, but when you love something you've got to let it go. That's like karma, you know?"

"Did you know Dr. Lysenko?"

She nodded. "I've been the assistant here for going on eight years, so, yeah, I knew him. I know all the surgeons."

"Did you know his first wife, Janice?"

"No, I don't get to see the spouses much." The disappointment I felt lifted as she added, "Pretty bad luck, though, you know? First she dies young, then he dies."

"Dr. Barrow mentioned that. He said she died of cancer?"

The woman nodded. "Breast. Or was it ovarian? I don't remember—one of those female cancers."

"I heard that she died from a fall."

"Who told you that? No, it was cancer and it took her fast— like six months fast. Oh, wait a minute—I think she did fall toward the end, I remember something about that 'cause Dr. Lysenko had to cancel a few patients that day. She was so weak from all the treatments they tried, that's why she fell, but that was like a few weeks before she died."

A part of me had held out hope that Dr. Barrow had been confused and it was another doctor's spouse who'd had cancer, but another, more rational part of me had known it was true. I'd known it since I saw that photo. Heather had lied to us, but why? I struggled to hide my dismay, but the young woman didn't seem to notice.

"I'll tell you what, he got himself a hot second wife, didn't he? She could be a model."

"She was one," I said distractedly, gazing blankly at the calendar behind her. She saw me staring and said, "This is how I keep track of them all. Each doc's got a different color, so I know when they're not in this office. Dr. Lysenko's color was that bright blue," she said, pointing. "He liked that. Said it was one of the colors of the Ukrainian flag. Now I guess someone else will get that color. I've got to erase him, but it seemed too soon, you know?"

It was odd to think of a life reflected in colored lines. Viktor's blue was visible in virtually every month, stripes of various lengths that suddenly stopped all together a month ago. Here was a life and now it was over, wiped out with the swipe of an eraser. Had his patients mourned for him?

"I was like totally shocked when I saw her," the secretary said, pulling my attention back.

"Who?"

"Wife number two." She hesitated, glancing around, before continuing in a furtive voice. "I'd heard that he was seeing someone else. As in an *a-ffair*." She whispered the word, giving it an extra syllable like she was spelling it out for me. The look on my face must have surprised her, because she quickly said, "But hey, that was just a rumor, and I might have got it wrong. Anyhoo, when I saw his wife, I was like no way is he cheating on that, because it's not like she was one of those women who totally lets herself go after marriage."

"So it's okay to cheat on your spouse if she's let herself go?" The words slipped out without thinking.

She drew back, eyes flitting around again to see if anyone else had heard me. "No, I mean, of course not, I didn't say that." Her voice was huffy and she ran a hand through her hair as if I'd ruffled her feathers.

My chest started pounding as I struggled to find my way through the corridors and back to the parking garage. I paused, pressing one hand against a cool tile wall and rubbing my chest with the other hand, convinced I was about to have a heart attack. Various people in lab coats and scrubs passed by, some giving me sideways glances and a wide berth, but only one actually stopped. A short Indian man who looked far too young to be a doctor asked me in a pleasant singsong voice if I was okay. "Do you need to be sitting down somewhere?"

My heart rate had slowed a fraction by that point and I realized it was probably a panic attack. I used to have them all the time when I was young. I shook my head, feeling ashamed, and pushed off the wall, thanking him over my shoulder as I trotted down the hall. My phone buzzed; it was Sarah, but I didn't answer. I saw that I had multiple missed calls, but I couldn't talk to anyone, not right now. The worst of the panic had subsided, but it was still there, an internal jitter keeping time with the questions beating against my brain. Had Heather really lied? She had to know that Viktor's first wife died from cancer, didn't she?

Only once I was out of the hospital and in my car did I pull out my phone to listen to Sarah's voice mail. It made me jump. She was practically shouting, her voice high and hysterical. And slurred. "Where are you? Did you see the news? It's been on the news all morning—they found the gun!"

chapter thirty-one

SARAH

Two boys fishing in a creek found the gun. That had been almost a week earlier. Somehow we'd all missed that news, though later I heard that the mother of one of the boys had claimed her fifteen minutes of fame by appearing on a local nightly broadcast to crow about her kid's (never mind his friend's) narrow brush with death, neither she nor the reporter bothering to mention that the gun hadn't been loaded. The discovery of a random handgun garnered some attention, but when they linked the gun to Viktor Lysenko it was breaking news.

I saw it on TV after getting Eric and the kids off to work and school. As always it had been a mad rush. Eric's belief in gender equality and sensitivity to the plight of the stay-at-home mother meant that he insisted on helping with breakfast or packing lunches, which satisfied his own sense of fairness, but didn't really make life any easier for me, which was supposed to be the point. Every morning his "helping" would put him behind and there would inevitably be ten to fifteen minutes of panicked, last-minute preparations, Eric buttoning his shirt at the same time that he dashed around trying to find the papers he'd been grading the night before, while I filled his travel mug with coffee, packed up his lunch, and generally tried to help hustle him out to his car. And almost every day, he'd pop back out of his car to say that he'd forgotten his glasses or his laptop cord, or his phone, and one or both of us would run through the house again

trying to find this or that missing item. It was exhausting and
completely avoidable.

By the time everyone was out the door, I often felt as if I needed
a spa weekend. That clearly wasn't possible, but I'd try to re-
create a little of that relaxation by adding some Prosecco to my
orange juice. My own mimosa mix. Suburban moms needing an
escape is almost a cliché, I know, but it's not like I was taking
Valium, so spare me the jokes about Mother's Little Helper. This
was only a tiny bit of Prosecco, not even one-fourth of the glass.
But since Viktor's death that on-edge feeling had gotten harder
to shake, and so sometimes I increased the amount. I was never
drunk though. Not really.

Sitting there that morning on the couch, sipping my mimosa, I
felt the tension easing, edges softening as I stared at the hosts of
a national morning show flip burgers side by side while wearing
ridiculous, poufy chef's hats in a segment on grilling that they
called "Not Too Soon for Summer!" Every sentence they uttered
seemed to end with an exclamation point. The show was abruptly
interrupted just as the female anchor had accidentally-on-
purpose flipped her burger at the male anchor's apron-covered
chest.

A slightly less photogenic local announcer spoke breathlessly
into the camera: "Breaking news out of Sewickley this morning.
Local police have identified the gun recovered from a creek last
week as the same weapon used in the murder of prominent plastic surgeon Dr. Viktor Lysenko."

I choked on my mimosa, orange juice dribbling down my chin
as I reached for the remote, cranking up the volume.

The camera jumped to a press conference. Mostly male police
officers clustered around a podium as a silver-haired white man
identified as the Sewickley chief of police and a dark-haired white
man who was the head of the Allegheny County Police Department vied for equal time in front of the microphone. "Our ballis-
tics experts have provided a perfect match between the barrel of
the recovered semiautomatic and the bullet found in Dr. Viktor
Lysenko."

Julie's cell phone rang and rang before going to voice mail. In desperation I called her home, but the same thing happened. I called Alison, but she didn't answer either. "Oh my God, oh my God," I kept repeating as I paced up and down the living room. An unseen reporter asked, "Were there any fingerprints on the gun?" But the Sewickley police chief would only say, "We can't comment on that at this time, but the investigation is ongoing."

How had they managed to fish out that gun? We should have gotten rid of it somewhere else; we should have sunk it in the river with a concrete block. Or burnt it. Could you burn a gun? We hadn't been thinking clearly, we'd just been desperate to be done with it. So stupid. The whole plan had been stupid.

Finishing my drink with one big gulp, I kept hitting the redial number for Julie. "C'mon, c'mon, pick up already." I left voice mails again for her and Alison.

Would they trace the gun to Julie? I imagined there was a serial number on it somewhere, but I didn't know how that worked. She'd said Brian didn't even know she had the gun. Had she bought it illegally? Wouldn't that make it worse if they found out it was hers? What if Alison hadn't wiped it off carefully—what if they found Julie or Heather's fingerprints on the gun? The thoughts cycled around my head, endless and obsessive without any clear answers.

The TV cut back to the morning show, where the grinning faces of the anchors now felt mocking. I shut it off and hurled the remote across the room as Julie's phone went to voice mail yet again: "Hi! You've reached Julie Phelps. I can't come to the phone right now, but your call is important to me. Please leave your name and number and I promise I'll get back to you. Leave a message after the beep."

"Where are you?" I shouted into it. "Call me as soon as you get this." Finally, in desperation, I called the realty office.

"Gainsborough Realty, where every home is a masterpiece. How may I help you?" The melodious voice belonged to the basset-hound-faced receptionist.

"Julie Phelps, please."

"Ms. Phelps is out of the office at the moment, would you like me to put you through to her voice mail?"

"No," I snapped, adding in a softer voice, "no thank you. I need to talk with her—it's urgent."

"Is this the school nurse?"

"No," I said, and thought better of it. "But this is the school and it's about the kids."

"Oh, I hope everything is okay?" A desire in her voice to hear someone else's bad news.

"I really need to get in touch with her."

"Have you tried her cell phone?"

"Yes, of course, but it's going straight to voice mail."

"Well, I don't know what to tell you—wait, let me see if I can find out where she might be." I heard keys clicking. "Yes, I thought so. Julie's doing an open house at a new development over in Edgeworth. It has really bad cell reception, so that might be why you're not able to get in touch with her."

If I could just beat the police to that development—that's what I was thinking as I clipped the curb turning on to Beaver Street, imagining a convoy of patrol cars, sirens screaming as they made their way to the house to arrest her. I don't remember thinking of the speed limit at all, but I do remember pressing down the accelerator and hearing the tires squeal as I took turns without slowing.

As I flew down a stretch of road outside of town, I heard a siren and thought my fears were being realized, that the police were on their way to arrest Julie. Something flashed in my side mirror and I saw a police car behind me. My foot moved from accelerator to brake and I slowed to a crawl, moving over in the hopes that the car would pass. It didn't. Instead, the driver moved over with me.

Shit! I broke into a sweat as I screeched to a stop along the side of the road, the cop stopping more smoothly behind me. I scrambled around my console in search of mints. It had only been half Prosecco this morning. I was not drunk, but I sucked hard on that mint, while frantically pushing buttons to lower the windows and sniffing the car interior. The smell of one of Sam's abandoned soccer socks was crowding out any other odor as far as I could tell.

A patrolman got out of the squad car and walked briskly up to mine. "License and registration, ma'am. Any idea how fast you were going back there?" He spoke in that cowboy-like drawl that must be taught at the police academy, but he looked about thirteen years old, with a smattering of acne across his ruddy cheeks and forehead.

I passed them out the window, willing my hand to be steady. "I'm sorry, Officer, I didn't realize I was speeding," I said, trying a smile when he glanced from the license to me.

That was when I noticed his name, Derreire. "Say, are you by any chance related to Helen Derreire?" I said. "The one that owns the dry cleaner's?"

He nodded, a little reluctantly. "That's my mother."

"Oh, I thought you looked familiar! I've known your mother for years. She's so proud of you." I babbled on for a few minutes.

I did know his mother, a hardworking woman whose name I remembered only because I'd confused it the first time with "derrière." She'd sighed as if she'd heard that before and simply corrected me, "It's Dare-rare-ee." I remembered nothing more about her beyond the photos pinned to a board behind the front desk, the corners curling from age and steam. "Do you still have that dog?" I said, having a dim recollection of a photo of grinning children around a slobbering beast. I felt like one of those TV psychics, fishing for information to fake a connection.

He smiled at that. "Waldo. He died. We've got Chip now." I listened to a five-minute dissertation about the merits of black Labs versus beagles, uttering sounds of animated interest while I tried not to notice the time ticking away, before he finally handed me back my license. "I'm going to let you off with a warning, Ms. Walker—slow down."

"Of course, thank you so much. I definitely will. Say hi to your mom for me."

I wanted him to pull out first, but he indicated that I should go ahead, tailing me as I drove glacially slowly for the next mile, before he finally passed, giving me a short wave as he sped around and off.

It was only another five minutes before I arrived at the new development and then just a short, albeit confusing drive around the streets before I spotted Julie's car in front of a colonial with a brick front and siding everywhere else.

A couple was coming out of the house as I pulled up out front, the wife heavily pregnant and listing like a ship at sea as she came down the steps, her husband providing support at her side like a tugboat. Julie clicked along on her heels behind them, chattering away in full Realtorspeak. Her eyes widened slightly when she saw me, but my presence didn't slow down her patter and as I opened the car door I heard her saying how great it was to meet them and how excited she was that they'd gotten in to see this *upscale* property before anyone else, and how wonderful it would be to raise their new child in this *exclusive* development.

I waited until the wife had been wedged into the passenger seat of the couple's two-seater sports car (*Say good-bye*, I thought, *that will be a trade-in for the minivan once the baby comes*) and the husband was out of earshot before racing up the front walk to Julie.

"What are you doing here?" she asked. "What's wrong?"

"They've found the gun—they know it was used to kill Viktor," I said without preamble, regretting it when her face literally drained of color. I reached out an arm to grab her, concerned she was going to faint.

"Oh shit," she said in a weak voice. "How did they find—who found—?" She tripped over her words, her mind clearly racing.

I helped her back inside, our footsteps echoing on the bare wood floors, and opened one of the water bottles sitting on a table alongside flyers about the house. "Here, sit down and drink some of this," I said, pulling out a chair and thrusting the bottle into her hands. She took a gulp, then swiped the back of her hand across her mouth. "Apparently some kids found it while fishing."

"Have they traced the owner?"

It seemed an odd way to ask if they knew it belonged to her, but I shook my head. She took another gulp of water. Her hand was shaking. "Was it illegally purchased?" I asked, trying to imagine Julie at one of those furtive gun shows with people dressed in camo and complaining about government interference.

She shook her head. "No, I don't think so." She tapped the bottle slightly on the table, the water rocking back and forth.

"So it's registered to you?"

She shook her head and I let out a sigh, sinking into a chair across from her, feeling dizzy with relief. "Okay, that's something." At least the police wouldn't be arriving any moment.

"What if they find fingerprints?"

"Alison wiped it down," I said, trying to sound convinced, although I'd been scared of just that.

"But we were in a hurry, she wasn't that careful."

"It's been soaking in muddy water for several weeks—surely if there were any prints on it they would have been washed away."

Julie didn't appear to believe this either. I kept thinking of fictional crime shows in which good-looking crime-scene analysts managed to solve cases with what appeared to be the slimmest of evidence—the imprint of a single tooth mark on a pencil, the oily smear that turned out to be from a particular moisturizer. In this high-tech world it was hard to believe that there wasn't some way to retrieve prints from the gun. If there were any.

"So someone gave you the gun?" I said.

"Something like that."

"Is it registered to them?"

She shrugged, tapping the water bottle more and more rapidly, the water jumping higher and higher. "I assume so."

"I don't understand—how did you get this gun?" I said, growing impatient, the drumbeat of the bottle echoing in the empty house. "Would you stop it and answer me!"

Julie slammed the bottle down, the water erupting up and over the sides. She ignored the rapidly spreading puddle, finally looking directly at me. "I stole it."

chapter thirty-two

JULIE

I t's a nervous habit, not so different from Heather's smoking, or Alison's nibbling at her nails, or Sarah's drinking. She had no business judging me. "You stole it," she'd repeated, staring at me with a look of shock and revulsion, as if I'd revealed a forked tongue, or some bizarre body piercing.

When did I first start taking things? This was the question one of the police officers had asked me years earlier, when Brian and I were first married and living in Erie. I'd lied. I'd told him that I hadn't really meant to take my coworker's watch, that I would never, ever take something that wasn't my own. This was before real estate, when I was a claims agent for a local insurance company, just one mouse in a maze of cubicles. It might have worked—I was young and pretty and truly tearful—except it turned out there were security cameras tucked high on the walls on every floor in that office building, and they had footage of me slipping into other people's cubicles and rifling through their drawers.

My mug shot was truly awful, because by then I was openly sobbing, my nose red and my eyes swollen. I was charged with theft and of course I was fired, although I would have quit anyway. How could I have gone back into that building after I'd been escorted out by police in full view of all the other employees? I had to return the stolen property—the total value of which was estimated at $1,249. The sum stuck in my mind because it was so ridiculously specific and paltry. The insurance company was responsible for that amount of legalized theft on an hourly basis, I argued to Brian and my lawyer, who both insisted that I not mention this in front of the judge. "Do you want to go to prison?" Brian had finally yelled. "They are not the same thing at all!"

In the end the case was settled with three years of probation and a hefty fine. "You're very lucky, young lady," the judge had intoned, staring down at me after I'd acknowledged my crime. "This is your first offense—let it be your last."

Of course, he didn't know it wasn't my first offense. Not even close. The first offense had been committed when I was six years old at my grandparents' house, a classic Pittsburgh three-story brick house in the heart of Etna. As a child, I'd been free to wander anywhere in their home, enjoying the sound of the creaking old floors, playing with the hand-tatted lace doilies covering the table-tops, pulling out the ancient, musty books on my grandfather's oak bookcase. I'd climb the carpeted stairs to my grandparents' bedroom, sitting on the stool in front of my grandmother's frilly vanity, with its round mirror and lace skirt, the glass top covered with pretty perfume bottles and a silver-plated toiletry set. One afternoon, I pulled open one of the dresser drawers and found a large green velvet box. In it was a sparkling mass of costume jewelry, and I remember crowing with the delight of a pirate coming upon a treasure chest.

I'd taken each piece out and arranged them on the cool blue comforter covering my grandparents' bed and then I'd tried on piece after piece. Later, I'd gone downstairs with one of my grandmother's satin nightgowns hanging off my shoulders, a matinee strand of pearls around my neck, a pair of dangly gem-stone earrings clipped to my ears, and my face smeared with her lipstick and coated in face powder.

"Oh, look at the fine lady," my gram said with a laugh, but my mother hadn't smiled. She'd wiped the lipstick off my mouth and marched me upstairs, ordering me to take off what wasn't mine and put all of that jewelry carefully away. In my haste, a small gold-and-black enamel bumblebee fell out of the pile and rolled onto the floor. My mother didn't notice and after she'd left the room I'd pocketed the pin. It felt good to have this secret thing, it gave me a rush.

I've taken many items over the years, a bracelet from a friend at school, makeup from other people's lockers, and candy or panty hose from shops. It's not the value of the object that matters— I feel a little guilty if they're worth much—although I do take things that I like. It's the idea of it, the feel of it slipping into my pocket or purse. No one misses them, or if they do they're easy to replace.

My job presents a special opportunity. I'm alone in homes so often, and I have to check each room in the houses that I list to make sure that they're ready for a showing. After Erie, I'd vowed never to take anything again, but that promise lasted only a few years. The first time I took something from a client was when I listed the property of avid collectors in Ben Avon. I took a tiny porcelain Scottie dog that was literally one of hundreds of pieces decorating their home. The thrill came back as strong as ever, my heart racing as I slipped it carefully into the pocket of my blazer. They never missed it. After Erie, I was very cautious of cameras. No one since then had missed anything at all until the gun.

I'd found it almost a decade ago, tucked away in a small wood and metal box that was just waiting to catch my eye as I checked the master bedroom closet in one of my properties. The house belonged to George and Lois Duncan, retirees and snowbirds, who'd tasked me with selling their home while they were in Florida for the winter. They'd lived in their Pittsburgh home for over forty years and had managed to squirrel things away in every corner and crevice. Rooms were obstacle courses of furniture, every closet stuffed to bursting; the first time we'd met I'd advised them to clear out the clutter. This is advice I have to give to most homeowners. People want to imagine themselves in the house, I'll say. Make the rooms look bright and spacious.

The day of the open house was bitterly cold and I arrived early to walk through the rooms one more time. The Duncans had moved some things into storage, but there was still that fusty feel

to the place, enhanced by the dated wallpaper and wood panel-
ing, and there was a musty odor in the basement. I opened every
closet, because this was what potential buyers would do, pleased
to see that they'd at least gotten rid of some of the mothball-
clogged plastic bags with outfits last worn in the 1970s. That
was when I spotted the box, sitting on the shelf in their master
closet.

Snow was falling, soft and thick, outside. I remember looking
out the window before I stood on tiptoe to touch the box with
just the tips of my fingers, dragging it slowly forward until it
toppled over the shelf and I caught it. The box was intricately
carved, that's what had caught my eye, and it looked like it hadn't
been opened in years. I'm not sure what I thought it would contain, but I remember recoiling when I pushed open the lid and
caught sight of the small black handgun nestled in a gray foam
bed, a row of copper-tipped bullets tucked nose-down in the
foam alongside it. After a moment, I traced the gun's clean lines
with my finger, admiring its design. It was an interesting find.

How did I think that its absence wouldn't be noticed? Two
weeks after I'd tucked it in my purse, feeling that familiar thrill,
George Duncan called to tell me that his son had informed him
that something was missing from their home and had I, by any
chance, seen it or let anyone "questionable" walk through the
open house? I played dumb, expressing concern before finally
asking what had been taken. I said I'd never touched a gun and
wouldn't, but I was concerned that someone else might have carried it out of their house. Was it possible he'd put it in storage?
Or could it be somewhere else in the house? I did my best to
erase his suspicion while also giving him the list of visitors to his
home. We'd had a steady stream of potential buyers through the
house. My palms were sweaty at the thought that he might try to
involve the police.

George made a halfhearted attempt to search for the gun and
I got the sense that he didn't fully believe my denials. A few
months later, when the house failed to sell, the Duncans didn't
renew their contract, quietly firing me as their Realtor. That hap-

pens; sometimes an agent can't sell a place because the owner has set the price too high, but somebody has to pay for the wasted time and often it's the Realtor.

That was the case with the Duncans' house, too—they went with a competitor at another firm, but dropped the price by over $50,000. Not surprisingly, they sold the house soon after. So it might have been only that, the case of the football coach for the losing team losing his job, but I couldn't help feeling that it had been personal, that George Duncan went with another agent because of the missing gun. I'd been stupid to steal it; it's not like I was ever planning to use it. But a year later, once the Duncans were permanently in Florida, I had to do an evening showing at a house in an isolated area and on impulse I stuck the box in my purse. After that, I started taking the gun with me to all night-time showings and open houses.

I never told Brian. Over the years he'd given me a small can of Mace, which is illegal, and a high-pitched security whistle, which I couldn't see scaring away anybody but the neighborhood dogs. It wouldn't have occurred to him to buy a gun; he thinks they're dangerous and he's squeamish about blood.

Giving the gun to Heather had been a big mistake. For some stupid reason I hadn't thought she'd actually use it. Maybe because I was so nervous when *I* handled it. Actually, I'd never even loaded the thing. When I passed it on to her all the bullets were still in their little foam beds. I didn't think about what she'd actually do with it, I just wanted to help her in any way that I could. If I'd imagined Viktor's death at all it had been Heather shooting him as he came toward her, the bullets hitting him in the chest, stopping him as he lunged at her. I couldn't have imagined the reality—his lifeless body in the car, that dark, bloody hole in the back of his skull.

Of course the police traced the gun to the owner. There are serial numbers and George Duncan had bought it legally. I had a brief hope that perhaps he'd died—it had been almost a decade ago and he had been elderly—but they found him in an assisted-living facility in Naples, Florida, and while he was riddled with

health problems and confined to a wheelchair, he was still mentally all there.

The day after the news about the gun, the police showed up at
my door. At least thanks to Sarah I'd known they would be coming and had time to prepare. I waited for two peals of the bell
before I opened the door, standing there dressed for work, trying
to project busy professional. Both of the detectives were on my
doorstep this time, the skinny and the fat one, Jack Sprat and his
husband. I've never been much of an actor, but I tried to look
surprised.

Detective Kasper said, "Julie Phelps? We'd like to ask you a
couple of questions."

"Is something wrong? What happened?" I said, faking concern.

"Ma'am, we'd rather not discuss this on your doorstep."

"Come inside." I stepped back, but the fat little detective, Lou
Tedesco, shook his head.

"We'd like you to come down to the station to talk," he said.

That I hadn't been expecting. It wasn't even eleven in the
morning, so the kids were at school, but I tried that excuse anyway. "I need to be home for my children."

"It shouldn't take that long." Tedesco had an odd smile and
the taller, skinnier one tried to mimic it—all teeth, no eye crinkling, a phony friendliness. "You should be back well before
school lets out."

What choice did I have? I tried to hide the panic I was feeling,
my hands shaking as I grabbed a coat and my purse and followed
them out the door. What if Brian called, looking for me? Worse,
what if they arrested me? I experienced a horrible déjà vu feeling
as I got in the back of their car, although at least it wasn't a
squad car and I wasn't under arrest.

The skinny detective drove toward the center of town, while
the fat detective fiddled with the radio station. I tried to slink
down in the backseat so no one would see me. We passed the
Sewickley Spa and I saw the mother of one of Owen's close
friends turning in the door. Another woman I knew was just

coming out of the Penguin Bookshop as we drove by. There were more familiar faces along the street. We parked at the old brick Sewickley Municipal Building on Thorn Street, and as I walked between the two detectives up the path and into the building I saw a client of mine heading into the library. She stopped, shading her eyes, clearly trying to see if it was really me. I looked away.

The conversation, this is what they called it, took place in an innocuous-looking room that might have been any meeting room for a small business. I sat at one side of an oval table with the two detectives across from me, although Kasper kept getting up, first to fetch coffee, then to lower the window shades because sunlight was in his eyes, and then to adjust his chair. He seemed unable to sit still; perhaps that's why he was so thin.

"So I'm sure you heard on the news that we found the gun used in the killing of Dr. Lysenko," Tedesco began, his voice friendly, like a neighbor exchanging gossip. He sat back in his chair, resting his small hands on his round stomach as if he'd just finished a large and delicious meal.

"No, I hadn't heard. That's great." I tried to match my expression and tone to his, staring him straight in the eye and smiling.

"We traced the owner of the gun, Mrs. Phelps. It belonged to a George Duncan. Do you know who that is?"

"Duncan?" I said, pretending to think about it. "It sounds familiar, but I don't think so."

"That's interesting, because you were his real estate agent some years back."

"Really?" I said, faking surprise. "I sell so many homes I just can't remember everybody. George Duncan?"

Kasper gave a sharp nod, while Tedesco just stared at me.

"Duncan, Duncan . . . wait, I do remember him! George and Lois Duncan—they moved to Florida."

Tedesco's expression didn't change. "That's right," he said affably, although his eyes were watchful. "He certainly remembers you. He told us something very interesting—he said that his gun had been stolen."

"Well, that's a relief," I said with a slight chuckle. "I was afraid you were going to tell me that George Duncan had shot Viktor Lysenko."

Tedesco's face soured and he sat up, the affability dropping away. "The gun disappeared from his home in Sewickley while a Realtor was showing his house."

I tried to make my stare as blank as possible. Tedesco looked annoyed. "That doesn't ring any bells? *You* were the real-estate agent, Mrs. Phelps."

"It sounds sort of familiar—I think I remember him calling to say something had gone missing and, now that I'm thinking about it, I do remember giving him the list of names of people who'd been through his house." I sighed. "I'm sorry, but it's too many years ago—I don't keep a record of those names if that's what you're hoping I can help you with."

He looked frustrated. "What I want you to help us with, Mrs. Phelps—"

"Please, call me Julie."

"What I want, *Julie,* is for you to help us understand your connection to the gun that killed Viktor Lysenko. It's quite a coincidence, don't you think?"

"Not really." I shrugged. "Sewickley has a small population— I'm sure everybody's connected in some six-degrees-of-separation way."

"Not everybody is connected to this crime, Mrs. Phelps."

"Connected?" I let my eyes widen. "Let me get this straight— I knew Viktor Lysenko and I knew the man who owned the gun that shot him, so I must be the one who shot him?" I made a scoffing noise, but inside I was trembling. I crossed my arms, trying to hide it.

"Did you?" Tedesco asked.

"Of course not," I said, pretending to be outraged. "Viktor was a friend of mine."

"Was he more than that?"

That question floored me. I didn't have to act confused—I truly was. "What's that supposed to mean?"

Kasper smirked. "You were having an affair with Dr. Lysenko, right?"

The thought was so ridiculous that I burst out laughing, but neither detective reacted. They were clearly waiting for my reply. "That's crazy," I said. "He was my friend's husband—I wouldn't do that to her."

They didn't look convinced. Detective Kasper sat forward, resting his pointy elbows on the table. "Let's look at the facts, Julie—we got a stolen gun, we got a guy shot to death, and we got a woman connected to both." He ticked them off on his bony fingers while Tedesco opened a manila folder that had been sitting on the table when we entered the room.

I'd glanced at it, but had forgotten about it until now, as his stubby fingers struggled to undo the butterfly latch. When he pulled out photos, I froze.

For one horrible moment I thought that this was it—the blackmailer had turned us in and the police had the shots. Tedesco was watching me. I saw him register my shock, and then he turned the photos faceup and spread them out on the table.

They were bright and glossy, not the grainy nighttime shots at all. Photos of me and Brian with Heather and Viktor at one of the fund-raisers for the hospital. There was also a single shot of me and Viktor, his arm loosely around my waist, our glasses raised. We'd been pretty tipsy.

My smile was genuine. "These are from last year's hospital fund-raiser."

"You're clearly good friends with Viktor."

"We gave a lot of money to that event. My husband was the one who took this photo."

The look on Tedesco's face was like someone delivering what they thought was a winning hand only to realize that they'd been outplayed. He scooped the photos up and shoved them back in the manila envelope like a child taking away his game because he lost.

"I don't understand why you're even asking this," I said during the long pause that followed. "I thought Viktor was killed during a carjacking."

The two men exchanged a look before Kasper said, "So you didn't know about Dr. Lysenko's marriage?"

"What about it?"

"He consulted a divorce lawyer."

chapter thirty-three

Julie was a thief? This news made no sense at all to me, coming as it did in drunk and hysterical messages from Sarah. At first I thought her voice mail might have been some alcoholic hallucination, but then I'd Googled the news about the gun, and by the time I actually spoke to Sarah she sounded less hysterical, if not sober. Yes, yes, Julie was a thief, she insisted, detailing her drive to the subdivision and how Julie had admitted that she'd stolen the gun.

"She stole from me, you know," she said. "I thought about it—remember that time I couldn't find my pen? I bet she has it."

"She wouldn't do that," I protested.

"Wouldn't she? Are you kidding me? She stole from clients, for God's sake." This came out as "gosh shakes." "Of course she'd steal from me!"

Then I found myself remembering a little wooden bird that had gone missing a few years ago and how I'd blamed the children, assuming one of them had taken and broken it, although they'd vehemently denied any knowledge of it. And then I recalled Heather's missing sugar bowl. Maybe these things weren't missing; maybe Julie had stolen them.

As much as I was thrown by this revelation, I was more concerned about what she'd say when the police questioned her. She expected that to happen—she'd told Sarah as much. I was sure the police knew more than was being reported. What if they had more than the gun? What if at that moment they were looking at photos sent by the blackmailer?

A day passed, then another. I wondered if Julie had already been arrested and pictured her sitting alone in a cell. No one wanted to call her, just in case the police were somehow tapping her phone. I'd gotten one slightly cryptic text: **Everything's good here. Hope you're well, too**, which could mean any number of things. Everything's good, as in "I've been arrested but won't talk"? Or, everything's good, meaning her old client hadn't remembered that she'd taken his gun?

I wasn't doing well. I was still grappling with what I'd learned at the hospital, struggling to understand why Heather would lie to us about how Viktor's first wife had died. She had to have known it was from cancer, unless Viktor had concealed that fact from her as part of some manipulation. Maybe he'd told her the story about the fall? Maybe he'd wanted her to believe that he'd gotten away with killing one wife and he could do the same to another?

And what about the other details his assistant had revealed? Was it true that he'd been having an affair? Not that it made any difference—I already knew he'd been a shit. I kept seeing that young woman's eager, beady eyes and the calendar on the wall behind her desk. Something about all those color-coded lines marking when the doctors were out of the office. All those blue lines for Viktor. Why was it nagging at me? I couldn't stop hearing the assistant's whispered "a-ffair," or seeing Tedesco's feigned surprise as he said, "You didn't know about the prenuptial agreement?"

Suspicion is insidious; it grows like a weed, climbing and twisting and wrapping everything in its path. I couldn't stop thinking about it, but I couldn't talk to Julie, not with the police around her, and I couldn't risk confiding in Sarah given how much she'd been drinking. I was already worried about what she might accidentally let slip.

Heather wasn't home. I called her landline and heard Viktor's slightly accented English cheerily telling callers to leave a number. I called her cell phone multiple times, but always got her voice mail. I pictured the Nordstrom bag and Heather's smiling

face. Was she out shopping again? When she called back, I asked
if I could come over. Part of me wanted to talk over the phone
because I was embarrassed to ask her these questions, but I knew
that I needed to see her face in order to believe her.

"I've got to drive to my mother-in-law's to fetch Daniel," she
said. "She sets the schedule, of course. I don't know why he can't
just stay the night if she's that desperate to have his company."

"I guess she's concerned about him missing school."

"Would it hurt him to miss a day? This is elementary school,
not Harvard." She gave a bitter laugh. "I've got so many things
to do—meetings with the lawyers, trying to clear the house out."

"Can't the cleaners help with that?"

"I fired them—I never liked them. They were Viktor's choice,
not mine." She sighed. "That's just one more thing on my to-do
list—I have to find somebody, the house is a mess."

Couldn't she clean it herself? I heard a funny sound and realized she'd started to cry and I felt bad for even thinking that. "I
just want to be done with this," she said. "He kept all the money
so tightly locked up, I can't get to it without help from the lawyers,
and his mother is sniffing around for her share, believe me. Of
course she doesn't trust me and I don't think his lawyers do either."

I saw Tedesco's grin, heard him say "prenup." A sob slipped
from Heather and I tried to push away my suspicion. "I'll come
over and help you," I said on impulse.

"What about the police? What if they're watching my house?"
Heather said, but was that a little bit of hope in her voice?

"It's not against the law to help a grieving friend," I said, as
if that were my sole motivation. Of course I would help. But I
would also ask her the questions that wouldn't stop hammering
away inside me.

Heather's sigh held relief. "Okay, what about coming over tonight? About seven P.M.? I should be back by then."

Even as I drove to Heather's house, I told myself there was no
reason to go so early. It wasn't even five P.M. She wouldn't be

home. As I turned in to her drive, I worried about running into the police again, but there were no cars parked out front. What was I doing here? Even as I parked, I couldn't admit it to myself. Heather had said that Viktor disabled the security cameras so the police had no record of the comings and goings, but what if she'd hooked them back up? I rang the doorbell first, just to make sure no one was home, standing on the front steps through four rings before walking over to the keypad next to the first bay of the garage.

I'd kept the text with the four-digit code, but thought she might have changed it and was both startled and pleased when it whirred into action, lifting into the ceiling. Ducking under the door, I hastily pushed the button to lower it again. The door into the house was unlocked. I stepped quietly inside, feeling horribly nervous, afraid I might set off an alarm, but the only sound was that of my footsteps echoing on the marble tile.

It was obvious why Heather wanted to hire cleaners. The disarray had grown since the last time I was there, the pile of dishes higher in the kitchen sink and a faint but unappetizing smell of days-old fried food. A layer of dust was visible on the mahogany furniture in the living room, and the carpets were in need of vacuuming. I passed Viktor's study and peered inside. In all my visits to this house, I'd never been in that room before. It looked like a display in a furniture store, everything pristine and untouched. A large leather swivel chair sat behind an ornately carved dark wooden desk with a glossy sheen. There were floor-to-ceiling wooden bookshelves, complete with a library ladder. Each rung held a faint sprinkling of dust and there were deep grooves beneath the bottom legs as if the ladder had never been moved. Perhaps it hadn't. Most of the books were fakes, I realized as I studied them more closely, whole sets of cardboard covered in cheap leather and gilt. There were a few real books, mostly medical textbooks, but otherwise the room looked straight out of a Hollywood film. I could picture the script scene description: "The library of a wealthy man."

I scoured Viktor's desk in vain, searching for confirmation of what I'd noticed at the hospital, on the calendar. It had finally become clear to me the night before as I lay in bed, long after Michael had fallen asleep, pondering those blue lines that had marked Viktor's work schedule. I just needed to confirm what I'd realized, but for that I needed his own record keeping. He'd probably kept his schedule on his computer and that had been taken by the police, which made all of us extremely nervous. There was nothing in the desk drawers, just a stack of neatly arranged blank paper, pens and paper clips, a box of staples and a roll of breath mints. I found a single folder that had info relevant to utility bills—all of them in Viktor's name. The bottom drawer of the desk was locked. I tried to pick it with a paper clip without success.

I climbed the stairs to the second floor, passing the photos of the dead, Viktor and Janice Lysenko, both of them smiling. Some of Viktor's belongings had to be here; surely Heather hadn't cleared everything out, not when the police were actively investigating.

The master bedroom closet still held his clothes. I brushed my hand over a long row of expensive suits before pulling open a stack of drawers on his side. Sweaters that seemed to be arranged by color. Underwear and socks. There was a collection of cuff links in the top drawer, little black-and-gold footballs, burnished gold disks, miniature Ukrainian flags, and a set to honor his career—gold buttons embossed with a pair of snakes curving around a winged staff. Sitting next to them was a small, neat stack of receipts.

Time was passing; I heard a clock chiming the hour as I flipped through the receipts, one after the other, but they were all recent, the top one dated one night before his death. I searched the rest of the drawer. Some loose coins and—mixed in with them, so I almost missed it—a small brass key.

I ran back downstairs to Viktor's office, dropping to the floor next to his desk and trying the key in the locked drawer. It opened, the drawer sliding back soundlessly to reveal hanging files with financial and medical information. Of course they were well organized—I wondered if Viktor had ever been sloppy. I pulled out the file marked TAXES and found multiple manila envelopes inside, one marked DEDUCTIONS and another BUSINESS TRAVEL. I opened the latter over the desktop and several neatly clipped bundles of receipts plopped onto the leather blotter.

I sorted through each stack, searching for the time and date stamp on every receipt. It felt like it took forever, but it couldn't really have been more than five minutes before I finally found what I'd been looking for. There, at the bottom of one stack, were several receipts from Asheville, North Carolina, dated from October 22, 23, and 24. There was a Starbucks receipt from North Carolina dated October 23. I was shaking as I pulled out my phone to text Sarah and Julie.

They showed up together, both of them arriving in Julie's car, and I could tell why when I smelled the alcohol on Sarah's breath as she approached the front door where I stood waiting. She sounded surprisingly lucid, if peevish, as she demanded, "Where's Heather?"

"Come inside," I said, ignoring her question. "Hurry up." Julie seemed positively spooked, looking all around before she brushed past me to get inside. I locked the door behind them.

"What the hell are we doing here?" Sarah demanded. "The police could be watching, you know."

I led the way into the kitchen, where I'd laid out the receipts along the smooth white marble island. "What's wrong?" Julie asked, scanning the room. "Where's Heather?"

"She's picking up Daniel," I said. "I needed to show you these." I held out the receipts.

Julie peered at them before passing them to Sarah. "What is this? I don't understand."

"I went to the hospital the other day," I said, and recounted my conversation with the personal assistant and what I'd learned about Janice Lysenko's cause of death.

"Cancer?" Julie said. She looked confused. "I thought she fell down a flight of stairs—didn't Heather tell us that's how she died? Viktor pushed her—I mean, Heather might not have said that, but we all thought it, right?"

"Heather led us to believe that," I said. "She led us to believe a lot of things."

"I don't understand—what does that have to do with these?" Sarah said, waving the receipts.

"Look at the dates," I said.

She pulled them too close to her face and then back a bit as if she were having trouble focusing. "October twenty-second, twenty-third, twenty-fourth. So what?"

"Do you remember what happened on October twenty-third?"

"I don't know," Julie said, looking confused as she took the receipts back from Sarah and studied them again. "It was around the time of the fall play—but wasn't that on the twenty-seventh?"

"October twenty-third was the day Viktor trashed this kitchen," I said. "Remember? Only he couldn't have trashed it because he wasn't here. He was in Asheville, North Carolina, at a medical conference."

Sarah stared at me, then down at the receipts. "Wait, that's not—I mean, how can that be—" She struggled to form a coherent sentence.

"I don't think that was the same date," Julie said. "It must have been the week before."

"It wasn't. I checked against my own calendar. We had a play-date at Heather's house that afternoon, remember?"

"This has got to be some sort of mistake," Julie said, shaking her head. "Maybe the receipts are wrong, or maybe Viktor trashed the kitchen before he left on the trip?"

I shook my head. "There are other receipts—look at the dates, he was gone for days."

"I don't understand," Sarah said. "If he didn't do it, then who the hell did?"

Before I could say anything, we heard the garage door whirring open, and a minute later Heather appeared in the kitchen doorway. "What are you doing here?" she said, clearly surprised to see me, not to mention Julie and Sarah. She wore that same beautiful leather jacket over a loose blouse, with full makeup, and hair that looked professionally blown-out. Hardly the image of the tired, stressed-out, pregnant mom she'd sounded like on the phone.

Sarah spoke first, looking past Heather. "Where's Daniel?"

"He's at his grandmother's."

"I thought you were picking him up," I said. "Or was that a lie, too?"

"What are you talking about?" Heather said, looking from one to the other of us.

Julie's voice was hurt. "Why did you lie to us?"

"I didn't lie," Heather said. "He wanted to spend the night there so I let—"

"Viktor's first wife died from cancer?" Sarah interrupted her, speaking loudly.

Heather's gaze jumped to her, but she didn't otherwise react. "So?"

"So you told us that she died from a fall."

"Is that what this is about?" Heather sounded annoyed. "That I forgot to tell you that Janice had cancer?"

"You forgot?" Sarah scoffed. "How do you forget something like cancer?"

Before Heather could answer, if she was going to answer, Julie picked up the receipts and rushed to her side. "But Viktor trashed your kitchen that time, right? Look at these receipts—Alison says they prove that he wasn't here that day."

Heather made no move to take them, not reacting at all as she glanced at them. "I don't remember when it was," she said in a calm voice, "but you've obviously confused the date."

"No, I haven't," I said.

"I'm sure that's it," Julie said. "I'm sure you'll remember if you just check the dates." She pushed the receipts into Heather's hand, but her fingers wouldn't close around them and the slips of paper fluttered like snowflakes to the floor.

"How can you accuse me?" Heather said, tears welling in

those blue eyes, her lips trembling, "After everything I've been through, after everything we've been through together—"

"Oh stop it," I said. "Just stop lying." I hadn't even raised my voice, but my tone must have been enough. She stopped talking and froze, holding that wounded-deer expression that had moved me countless times, the doe-like vulnerable eyes, the flushed face, the hands nervously cradling her body. But I'd caught a tiny flicker in her eyes, a split-second calculation, and that was when I knew. Up until that moment I'd skirted along the edges of it, focusing on names and dates, specific lies, unable to face the big lie at the core. "Viktor never hit you, did he?" I said quietly.

She brought her hands up to shield her face, making a sound that might have been a sob, though everything she did was suspect to me now. Her muffled wail was clear enough: "How can you say that after everything he did to me?"

Julie shot me a nasty look. "Why are you treating her this way, Alison?"

"She's lying," I said to her, and then to Heather, "I knew it that day with the Nordstrom bag, but I didn't want to face it." She let her hands drop and looked at me, clearly confused. I walked closer and without warning I raised my hand as if I was going to strike her.

Julie cried "No!" but Heather didn't even step back—she stood there, still looking wounded, the paper evidence of her lies at her feet.

I gave her a hard smile. "You didn't flinch."

Sarah said to me, "What the hell are you playing at?"

"She didn't flinch. Not now, not the other day—not ever. If Viktor had been beating her, she'd flinch when someone came near her like that. That's how abused people react."

There was a moment of stunned silence, and then, to my surprise, Heather started to cry, not fake sobs this time, but real tears glistening like raindrops on her soft, rose-petal cheeks. "He hated it when I flinched," she spat, swiping at her eyes. "It took a lot of practice, but he trained me not to."

Julie gasped and said, "God, Heather, I'm so sorry," moving in to comfort her. She shot me a dirty look over her shoulder. Sarah also seemed concerned, and I felt a different sort of doubt rise within me. What if I was wrong about the dates? About the abuse? Maybe the only lies were the ones I'd invented? But I'd checked those dates. I'd double-checked.

The buzzing of my cell phone stopped me before I could say anything. It skittered across the marble island just as Julie's and then Heather and Sarah's phones all beeped or chirped. "What on earth?" Julie said.

It was a text from a number I didn't recognize, but the message was familiar: **$20,000 in 3 days or I go to police.**

chapter thirty-four

Immediately after the text came two photos. The first was the same grainy shot of the four of us by Viktor's car. The second was another photo from the same night, but this one included a clear shot of Julie's car, license plate visible.

"Oh my God," Julie said, dropping her phone on the island as if it were toxic. "How did he get our numbers?"

"We don't know it's a he. You couldn't tell, remember?" Alison said. "Maybe it's a she." She looked accusingly at Heather. "Did you send these?"

"What are you talking about? I got the same text," Heather said, holding out her phone so Alison could see. I believed her, but then I hadn't stopped believing her—it was Alison who suddenly doubted her story. Maybe Heather hadn't told us everything about Janice, but that didn't mean she was lying. As for the receipts, Julie was probably right and Alison had confused the dates. Although that didn't sound like Alison—I didn't know what to think about it.

"Then *who* is sending these?" Julie demanded. "We already gave him money—is he just going to keep asking for more and more?"

"Well, I don't have another five thousand dollars to give," I said.

"We don't have to," Alison said. "This can end today. Now. We can go to the police."

"Are you crazy?" Julie said. "We can't go to the police."

"Why not? She's the one who shot her husband," Alison said, pointing at Heather. "Let's see if the police believe her story." Grabbing her phone and purse from the island, she started out of the room, heading for the front door.

"You can't tell it's me in the photos with the body," Heather said in a shrill voice. "If you talk, I talk, and I'll tell them that you shot my husband."

Alison pivoted in the doorway. "What's our motive for killing him?" she scoffed. "They'd never believe you."

"Oh really? The gun wasn't even mine. It would be easy to convince the police that one of you shot him because you were trying to help me."

Julie looked like she was going to be sick. "Alison, they'll think I killed him."

"We could tell them the truth," Alison said. "You gave her the gun because Heather claimed she was being abused."

"How is that going to work?" I said. "They'll arrest all of us."

"It's three of us against Heather—she'll get arrested, but if we tell the police the truth, then it will be three statements against hers. They probably won't charge us at all."

"Do you really think they'd believe any of you?" Heather said. "They've been watching all of us, not just me. Julie stole the gun, Sarah isn't sober, and what do you think the police will make of your history, Alison?"

I opened my mouth to protest the smear, but stopped, distracted. What did she mean about Alison? I started to ask, but Julie spoke first. "She's right, Alison," she said in a pleading voice. "Even if they didn't charge us everyone would find out—I'd lose my business, you could lose your job, too."

"I'll take my chances," Alison said, but that was clearly just bravado speaking.

I sank into a kitchen chair, my head pounding. "What are we going to do?" I said. "I don't have any more money."

"Don't look at me," Heather said, and I saw that she was glaring at Alison. "The insurance company won't pay until the police investigation is over. I don't have the money either."

"Pawn some more of your jewelry," I said.

"I don't have that much to pawn—Viktor didn't give me that much."

"That bracelet has to be worth something," I said, looking her over. "And those earrings. I'm sure we could get something for those." I stood up again, filled with a sudden manic energy. "Let's go through the house—I'm sure we can come up with twenty thousand dollars' worth of things here."

Heather looked slightly panicked, but Julie started nodding, and I could see the fear wrestling with her usual Julie can-do positivity. "Yes, yes, we could sell the furniture for starters. That would raise the funds. People wouldn't notice—not if you said you were downsizing."

"And then what?" Alison said. "Say we come up with this twenty thousand dollars, who's to say that the blackmailer won't ask for another twenty-thousand-dollar installment and another after that?" She'd inched slowly back into the room, but she was still holding on to her purse.

"Surely he's got to realize that we're not made of money," Julie moaned, as if she were talking about a bill collector. I had a sudden memory of my mother complaining this way about her children when we were young and left lights on throughout the house. "We're not made of money," she'd say in a tone that carried exactly that same sense of futility.

"If we could just find out who this asshole is," I said.

Alison made a funny noise, like she'd just realized something, and, dropping her purse on the kitchen table, began typing away on her phone. "We can Google the number," she said, tapping two-thumbed with a speed I envied. "Cell numbers aren't listed, but it might show up somewhere." She paused, staring intently at the screen.

"What is it? What did you find?" Julie asked.

"Hold on, it's still loading." There was a brief silence in the room. "This is interesting—it shows up for some insurance salesman." She held up the phone to show us, and Julie and I clustered around her to look.

Heather approached more slowly, but self-interest overcame self-pity and she said, "Who is it? Do you have a name?"

Alison read it off the screen: "'Kevin Sullivan, Insurance Broker, 126 Whitcrest Road.'"

"Let's go get the bastard." I gathered my purse, ready to charge, but Julie stopped me.

"Don't be silly, we can't just show up at this Kevin Sullivan's door—wait a minute. Did you say *Whitcrest* Road?"

"Yes, number 126."

"I think I know that address. That's Terry Holloway's house. Her husband is Kevin Sullivan. Their daughter—Megan?—is in the third grade at the elementary school. Not Owen and Lucy's class—another one. Don't you know who I'm talking about, Alison? We served with her on that soccer fund-raising thing a few years ago, remember? I can't believe it."

"You're sure that's her address?" Alison asked. "Sullivan is a common name."

"I'm pretty sure. It makes sense—who else would have our phone numbers except someone we know through school? And she showed up at Heather's house after Viktor died—remember, Heather? I should have guessed it was her. That bitch!"

"But it's his phone," I said. "Maybe Kevin Sullivan is the one blackmailing us."

"Or he could have given her the phone if he has more than one," Alison said.

Heather shuddered and at my quizzical look said, "She could be out there, right now, watching us."

"Let's go and get her phone," I suggested.

"It's not just the phone," Alison said. "She probably saved the photos to a desktop or laptop."

"Then we have to get them off her computer, too," Julie said. "If we can somehow get you in her house, I'm sure you could erase the files."

Alison looked as if she was torn between being flattered that Julie thought so highly of her skills and skeptical that she could live up to the endorsement.

In the end, the rest of them reached the same conclusion I had
from the beginning—we would drive to the address on Whitcrest
Road, find Terry Holloway, and figure out a way to get her phone
and computer. We took Julie's car, reasoning that if the police or
anyone else spotted us, we could claim that she was showing us
houses.

Julie drove with Alison riding shotgun, while I rode in the back
with Heather. She hadn't wanted to come, trying to argue that
the police could be watching, but Alison had insisted.

"You're in this up to your eyeballs—you're going with us,"
she'd said, but she wouldn't sit next to Heather in the car. It was
like being with a divorced couple, neither of them speaking to
the other, while Julie and I tried to pretend we didn't notice.

Whitcrest Road was in a pretty, tree-lined residential area with
houses that Julie ticked off as ranch or two-story or Victorian or
gingerbread. Number 126 was toward the beginning of the block
and conveniently catty-corner to a Presbyterian church, a large
brick building with an austere white spire. We turned into the
church parking lot and pulled into a spot with a view of the
house. There were a few other cars in the lot, so we weren't too
noticeable, and Julie's car was partially obscured by saplings that
someone must have recently planted to brighten up the medians
serving as row dividers.

We'd tried to come up with a plan as we drove, deciding that
the first thing to do was to figure out if this was even Terry Holloway's house before we attempted to lure her out so Alison
could sneak inside.

It was sunset, long shadows creating a glare off the home's
windows, making it impossible to tell if anyone was inside. As
we sat there debating whether someone should knock on the
door, we got lucky. A car turned onto the block and then into
the driveway at 126, while we slunk down in our seats, trying to
hide our faces as it pulled past us. We could hear the car doors
slamming and the distant chatter of voices followed by a woman's
laughter.

Julie leaned forward as a couple came into view, the woman

trotting ahead of the man, who had a large briefcase swinging from his shoulder.

"That's her, that's Terry."

"You're sure?" Alison asked, trying to peer at the figures now cast in shadow on the porch.

"Yes, definitely. Call her! Call the number."

Alison hurriedly pressed the call button and we watched, breathless, waiting for Terry Holloway, or her husband, to pick up their phones. Terry dug in her purse and I thought, *Gotcha,* but she produced a key ring instead and unlocked the front door. Her husband was behind her, yawning and switching his bag to the other shoulder as if it were too heavy.

"Is it ringing?" I asked, looking from them to Alison and back again. "Maybe it hasn't rung yet."

"It's ringing," Alison said. "It's rung at least four times."

"It can't be," Julie said. "Neither of them is answering."

"Did you hit the right number?" Heather asked. "Maybe you hit another number."

"How could I have hit another number? I just pressed the number that shows up on my screen."

"Let me see it." Heather reached over the seat to try to grab the phone, but Alison fended her off. Terry and her husband went inside. We watched their large wooden door close.

"Maybe she won't answer the phone in front of her husband," I said. "Blackmailing is probably her dirty little secret. Maybe we're not the only targets—what was she doing out that late at night anyway?"

"We could blackmail *her,*" Heather said excitedly, but none of us responded.

After five interminable minutes, Alison finally called the number again. It rang and rang and rang. No voice mail, nothing. "Maybe she's got her phone on silent," Julie said, so desperate to believe this that it hurt to hear. "Let's give it another few minutes."

We waited five more, which felt like fifty. There was no answer again. "We can't just sit here all night," I said, pissed off. I undid my seat belt and started to open the car door.

"What are you doing?" Julie hissed, panicked. "You can't go out there!"

"You might be too afraid to do anything but sit here, but I'm not," I said.

"You're not sober enough to think straight," Alison said. "Close the damn door."

"Are you calling me a drunk?" I said. "How dare you."

"I call them as I see them," Alison said. "You need to get to an AA meeting."

"Take care of your own problems," I said. "You have plenty of them."

"Stop it!" Julie cried. "Just stop it."

Heather, the cause of all of this, remained silent, pushed up against her corner of the backseat, just waiting, as always, for things to be resolved. "We wouldn't be in this mess if it wasn't for you," I said to her. "*You* should go get that fucking phone."

"No one is going anywhere," Alison said, but then Julie surprised us all by unbuckling her seat belt.

"We have to get that phone," she said. "I'll pretend I was in the neighborhood looking for houses to list."

Before any of us could stop her, Julie got out of the car and crossed the street. We watched as she walked briskly up Terry Holloway's walk and onto the porch. We could see her at the front door. When the door swung open, Alison inhaled sharply. We didn't have a clear view and I couldn't tell who had come to the door and stood talking to Julie.

"Do you think she's scared to see Julie?" Heather said.

Neither Alison nor I answered her; we were too busy staring at the house. There was movement on the porch, and Terry came into view, walking to the top porch step and pointing up the street. Julie was right behind her and it was clear they were having an animated conversation.

"What the hell?" I said. "Terry looks totally relaxed."

"There could be a good reason for that," Alison said in a quiet voice. "It might not be her number."

"What are you talking about?" I said. "Didn't you just show us that it's Kevin Sullivan's number? And you found this address."

"It could be old information—numbers get reused. There's a way to find out." She pulled out her phone and started scrolling. "We need someone who's close with Terry. Do we know anyone from school?"

She was talking to me, but it was Heather who answered. "Jane. Jane Bartel." She pulled out her own phone and dialed. "Hi, Jane, it's Heather Lysenko." Silence for a moment. "Thank you, I appreciate that. Yes, Daniel's okay, thank you for asking. Listen, I have a quick question. Do you happen to have the phone number for Terry Holloway? I'm trying to reach her about the— oh, okay. That would be great, thanks so much." She covered the phone with her hand and whispered, "She's looking it up."

The number wasn't the one we had. Alison typed the number from Jane directly into her phone as Heather repeated it. Alison put it on speaker and we waited, intently watching Terry, who still stood there on her front porch talking with Julie.

It rang only three times before we saw Terry pull a phone from the pocket of her slacks, and then we heard a voice that sounded familiar. "Hello?"

Alison hung up. There was silence in the car. A sense of despair washed over me. It wasn't Terry Holloway; this whole thing had been a waste of time. If something seems too good to be true, it probably is—this was a phrase my father had loved to repeat, one of many maxims that had made up the majority of his conversational arsenal.

Less than a minute after we hung up, Julie said her good-byes and crossed back to the car. "It's not her," she and Alison said at the same time. The smile Julie had been wearing with Terry was gone; she looked pale and drawn. "What are we going to do?"

Nobody answered. Alison seemed particularly quiet, probably because she was the one who'd led us on this wild-goose chase.

She'd called me a drunk—and so had Heather—but it wasn't true. I'd had a glass of wine, maybe two, before leaving the house. Just to help take the edge off. I was perfectly lucid and I tried to examine all the different options, ticking them off in my head as we drove in silence back to Heather's.

Without telling anyone, I repeatedly dialed the number we'd gotten the text from. I'd hit redial, let it ring seven or eight times, hang up and then call again. If the blackmailer wanted to fuck with us, we would fuck with him. Still, I jumped when a new text bubble showed up on my screen as we pulled up in front of the house: **STOP CALLING! Three days. $20K same place or police.**

"He's texting again," Heather announced before I could say anything, just as Alison and Julie's phones also signaled new messages.

"Why does it say 'stop calling'? Maybe it *is* Terry," Julie said as we got out of the car. "Maybe she has another phone?"

I waited until we were inside the house to confess that I'd been making the calls, which earned me a look of disgust from Alison. "Are you *trying* to get whoever it is to go to the police?"

"I'm trying to drive them just as crazy as they're driving us," I said.

"We can't get another twenty thousand," Heather said. "Not in three days."

Nobody contradicted her. Julie dropped onto a chair the minute we entered the kitchen, sitting with her head in her hands, one foot nervously beating a tattoo against the marble tile. Alison picked up the receipts that had been left on the floor and stacked them neatly back on the island, while Heather ignored her, taking cups down from a cupboard.

Julie's repeated tapping annoyed me and I stalked over to the window to get away from it, staring out over that vast backyard. The tennis court looked forlorn, nets sagging, and clumps of left-over snow dotting the parched-looking surface.

The sudden whir of the coffee machine made me jump. Heather filled cups for each of us and brought them to the table, taking a seat across from Julie. I came over to sit down next to them, but

Alison stayed where she was, leaning against the island. Usually it was Julie who played peacemaker, but she was still staring down at the table. I cleared my throat. "Come have some coffee," I said to Alison, but she ignored me.

"What if we change the meeting place," she suggested in a musing voice. "We could pick another spot, someplace easier to stake out."

"Why would they agree to that?" I said.

"Because she—or he—is greedy. If they want the money they have to go along with our terms."

"We tried catching them last time—it didn't work."

"It didn't work because our view got blocked. We need to pick a place that's easier to stake out and harder for them to hide."

"A house," Julie said, lifting her head out of her hands. "What if we said we'll leave the cash at my listing in that new subdivision in Edgeworth? It's vacant—most of the houses there are vacant."

"They won't agree."

"We call this asshole's bluff," Alison said. "Either they meet us where we say or they don't get the cash—it's that simple."

"They'll go to the police," Heather said. "You're going to push them into it."

"No, they won't." Alison walked over to the table and picked up her mug of coffee. "Think about it. Sarah was right—if they go to the police they'll be charged with extortion. It doesn't help them."

"They probably wouldn't charge him," I said.

"Do you think he wants to bank on 'probably'?" Alison said before taking a sip of coffee. Nobody answered, but Julie looked more animated.

"Okay, yes, it might work," I conceded. "But what do we do when we catch him?"

"We take the phone," Heather said.

"And we get their address," Alison said. "We find out where he or she lives and get the computer and any other copies of the photos."

"You make it sound so easy," Julie said. "What makes you think this person will cooperate with that? How are you planning to make them give you anything?"

Alison was silent for a few seconds, and then said, "We're going to have to hit him or something."

"Too bad we don't have a gun." I looked pointedly at Julie.

"We can find something," Heather said. "What about a baseball bat?"

"That would work," I said. "We just need to knock them out so we can get the phone."

"We're going to crack someone over the head with a baseball bat?" Alison asked. "We could kill them."

"Maybe that's exactly what we should do," I said quietly.

Stunned silence greeted this remark. Then Alison said, "That's crazy."

"Is it?" I said. "What else are we going to do? Steal this guy's phone and computer and somehow he's just going to go away and not mention that to anyone? How exactly do you think that's going to work?"

"You're right," Alison said after a long moment, her voice so low I could barely hear it. "As long as he's alive he's a liability."

chapter thirty-five

O nce when I was talking about the past with my brother, he said that being a police officer had taught him that the line that separates the civil from the uncivil is very fine, and that anyone is capable of anything given the right set of circumstances. I hadn't believed him. There was a huge difference between the monsters and us, I'd argued. It wasn't a fine line at all, but a gulf separating the law-abiding from the lawless.

I hadn't understood that dozens of smaller choices lead to those big moral decisions, as if each step were a point along an invisible map leading to what only feels upon arrival like a surprise destination. As I stood in my garage, seriously contemplating killing another human being, I finally realized the truth of what my brother had been saying.

We no longer had a gun, a knife was too risky and messy, and there was no time for poison even if we'd had access to some, which we didn't. Who had we become, standing around discussing how to kill someone with such dispassion? I wasn't one of those people, I couldn't be, yet there I was standing in my garage, holding a baseball bat. It was Michael's—silver aluminum, graying sports tape wrapped around the grip, scratches and dents from years of play. An intramural team in college, if I remembered correctly. Is that when he'd gotten it? It wasn't from his Little League days, was it? I'd found the bat stuffed in a bin with other sports equipment. There had been an afternoon sometime last year when he'd hit balls around with Matthew and Lucy in the backyard. I swallowed hard, remembering George barking and chasing after the balls that Michael threw, while Matthew and Lucy laughed as they took turns hefting the bat. They hadn't pulled it out since. Would any of them notice it was missing?

We waited to reply to the blackmailer's text until Julie made sure that there were no showings scheduled for her listing at the vacant house in the new subdivision. Sarah composed a message that we thought struck the right balance between informing our blackmailer that this was where he or she could get the money and nowhere else, while managing not to push them into calling the police. To our surprise, they agreed to the house drop-off after we rejected a single threatening text demanding that we meet at the cemetery again.

Unlike the last time, we didn't spend the few days we had searching for money. We weren't planning to deliver anything remotely close to the $20,000 the blackmailer had pocketed before. We gathered together approximately $300 in twenties, tens, and ones, and wrapped it around bricks of paper money that we took from some kids' games. It looked real if you didn't examine it too closely. We were determined that whoever the blackmailer turned out to be, he or she wouldn't be pocketing any more of our money. Once we had the bills stuffed in another cheap duffel bag, we were ready to go.

The plan was simple. While we drove to the subdivision, Heather would head to the police station with her lawyer to ask for an update on the investigation. I was nervous about Heather going to the police, afraid that she might screw up and accidentally reveal something. I knew that if that happened she'd throw us under the bus to save herself, but we needed her to distract the detectives, so we had no choice but to trust her. At least she had a believable motive; the insurance company wouldn't pay out until the investigation was done and "favorably resolved."

"I think she should give us some of that settlement," Sarah suggested as we drove to the drop spot ahead of Julie. We'd stuck with the same basic plan, except this time Julie would carry the moncy to the house at the agreed-upon time, while Sarah and I would already be there, in position.

"If she ever gets that payout," I said, turning fast onto Backbone Road and keeping up my speed while watching out for police. The irony of the street name wasn't lost on me. It was a Tuesday, early afternoon. We'd wanted to meet earlier, but the blackmailer had balked at the time. We'd made that one concession; we hadn't really had a choice if we wanted them to show up at the house.

"Look, no drinking tomorrow, okay?" I'd told Sarah the night before. "We need to be alert."

"If you mention AA again I'm not going with you," Sarah said, obviously still offended. "I am not an alcoholic."

It was tempting to argue with that, but we needed to work together, so I didn't respond. My comments must have shamed her, because I didn't smell alcohol when she got in the car, although I couldn't tell if that gleam in her eyes was from excitement or the bottle. She seemed clear enough, talking about how she thought we deserved to be paid for being sucked in by Heather's "neediness."

"You seem more concerned about the money than whether or not Heather lied to us," I finally said. This was something I was still unsure about, the terrible certainty I'd felt when I'd found those receipts wavering in the face of her teary denials. I knew Julie didn't believe our friend had lied. She'd been cool to me since I'd pretended to hit Heather, but Sarah had never shared Julie's blind optimism.

"Look, she might have lied about Viktor's first wife, but those receipts don't prove anything," Sarah said. "Do you really think Heather trashed her own kitchen? Are you one hundred percent certain that you got the dates right?" Seeing my momentary hesitation, she quickly said, "I didn't think so."

I wondered if she was really dismissing the facts or dismissing me because of my comments about her drinking. "Well, I don't give a damn about being paid back, I just don't want to go to prison," I said, which essentially shut down the conversation. I'd found an extra-long yoga bag to hide the bat in, though it was narrow enough to look like a rifle case, which wasn't exactly less noticeable. Sliding the bat into the backseat felt surreal, as if I were playing some enforcer in a Mafia movie. We'd agreed that I would wield the weapon because it made the most sense. I was taller than both Julie and Sarah, so I could be more of a physical threat, but that didn't mean I wanted to do it. I'd taken a few practice swings in the garage, but when I imagined hitting somebody, all I could hear was that distinctive crack that a bat makes when it connects solidly with a ball.

The new subdivision was on the border of Edgeworth and Leetsdale, on a hilly piece of scrub property that no one had thought worth developing until recently. Low stone walls marked the entrance, and an overproduced brass sign announced in cursive that we'd arrived at Paradise Hills, a name that struck me as more appropriate for a cemetery.

"Paradise, huh?" Sarah said with a snicker as we drove up past barren lots with dead weeds poking through remnants of snow, and cookie-cutter houses sitting on small plots of land. The asphalt road through the development was slick in spots with gray slush. FOR SALE signs stood in front of some of the finished homes, but few of the yards were more than frozen mud pits, with barely any grass, even frozen winter yellow grass, visible.

As planned, we circled the subdivision several times, on the lookout for other people and cars, for anything odd. Just like the last time, we'd arrived over an hour ahead of schedule. If we saw anyone, we could masquerade as prospective home buyers, but as we drove up and down the streets it looked like we were the only people there.

"What if he's watching us right now?" Sarah said as she parked in front of a small cluster of semifinished homes. Their backyards abutted the yards of the houses on the next street, one of which was the house where Julie would arrive soon to drop off the money. She'd chosen that house because that street dead-ended, so the blackmailer would have to go back out the same way he came, and in some vehicle, we assumed, because unlike the cemetery, there was nothing right over the hill to reach on foot.

"He wouldn't be here this early," I said, trying to convince myself. I had that same creepy feeling of being watched, but there was nothing we could do about it. I hoisted the yoga bag from the backseat before handing Sarah the keys and reminding her to park as close as she could to the entrance of the subdivision. Then I ran from the car to the small strip of shadowed land separating two houses.

Hidden from view, I rested for a moment, turning back to watch Sarah drive off before looking ahead to assess how to get across the no-man's-land of open ground with the least exposure. The plan had been for me to enter the house from the back because the blackmailer, we assumed, would enter, like Julie, from the front. It made sense in theory, but now, confronted with the reality, it seemed like a foolish idea. I'd be totally exposed. There were no trees, no other vegetation or buildings to shield me from anyone who happened to look in the right direction. Julie didn't think anyone had actually moved into any of the houses yet, but we couldn't be sure and accessing the house by cutting through the backyards made it hard to pretend I was a prospective buyer. But it was too late to choose another option.

Shifting the bag on my shoulder, I started across the dirt yard, the bat bumping painfully against my back, my feet stumbling over the hard, uneven ground, my labored breathing loud in my ears. I ran straight to the house, up two steps and across the low wooden deck, yanking open the back door that Julie said she'd leave open, jerking to a stop only once I was inside.

I closed the door, leaning against it and breathing hard, looking out through the small glass panes to see if I could spot anybody, but there was no one. I turned around and examined the kitchen where I stood, hesitating to move because of the sudden thought that the blackmailer might have had the same idea and might already be hiding there, waiting until Julie came with the money. Flinging a hand over my mouth, I tried to stifle my breathing as I waited, listening. No sound other than my own thrumming pulse. I took the bag from my shoulder and clutched it in my hand, walking quickly and quietly through the house.

The house was pretty basic inside, too—pre-finished wood floors throughout with granite tile countertops and stock cabinets in the kitchen and baths. There were gaping holes where the kitchen stove and fridge should be, and some rooms still had naked lightbulbs instead of light fixtures. Julie was supposed to place the duffel bag in front of the empty living room hearth, and when the blackmailer bent to take it, my plan was to come out from hiding, whack him with the bat, and grab his phone.

"Hit him hard," Sarah had said. "We can't let him get away this time."

"Aim high," Julie added. "Hit him in the head or the chest."

"And then what?" I'd asked. "Are we going to dig a hole out there and bury him in the subdivision? Or will we make this murder look like a carjacking, too?"

Julie didn't answer, avoiding my gaze, but Heather said defensively, "It's him or us."

The awful truth was that I knew she was right. We had no more money to give this person, but we couldn't risk ignoring him either. The police were snooping around, suspicious of Heather and Julie; all they needed was proof. And they were suspicious of me, too. They'd already been to my house once. The photographs were more than enough to bring charges against all of us.

"Just bring him down and get the phone," Sarah said. "We'll worry about the rest of it later."

And I'd agreed to this plan because there seemed to be no other way.

Now was not the time to back out, not while standing in the house where the blackmailer would soon arrive to claim the money. I looked around, searching for a hiding space. There was a coat closet in the front hall, just off the room with the fireplace, and I stepped inside it, pulling the hollow door closed.

It was dark, so much darker than I thought it would be, and musty. I could hear hangers softly pinging against one another, but when I reached up to silence them there was only empty space. Memories assailed me. Another closet, another time. I always hid in the closet, crouching in the back, my hands covering my ears. It also had one of those hollow-core doors, because the house was *"cheaply built and not worth a shit!"* I can hear him complaining, proving his point by kicking through some drywall in the living room. He has knocked the door into the master bedroom completely off its hinges. This time because he's been locked out. *"Don't you fucking do that again!"* He's proud of the damage that I'm ashamed of, pointing to it with pride. *"There's proof."* "But he's not talking about his violence, he's talking about the house being poorly made, a *"crappy little Cracker Jack box."*

I pushed open the door, gasping for air and light. I couldn't hide in there, it was too much. Pressing a hand against my head as if to physically suppress the memories, I hurriedly looked for another spot. The builders hadn't finished the space behind the stairs. There was no door like the closet, but it was cloaked in shadows. I crept into it, crouching so I wouldn't smack my head against the rough wood, breathing in the scent of sawdust. I made sure my phone was on silent and unzipped the bag, lifting out the bat. The end of a nail scratched the back of my hand and I sucked at the wound, tasting blood. There was light streaming in through the windows in the living room—I could glimpse dust motes dancing in it—but it was cold in the house. Didn't they have to keep the heat on to stop pipes from bursting? I could see my own breath. Where was Julie? She'd said she'd text when she arrived, but there was nothing. I checked my phone once and then again. A minute lasted an hour.

Footsteps outside startled me. I sat up, banging my head against the stairs above me, and dropped back down into a crouch, suppressing a cry of pain as I checked my phone. She hadn't sent a text. I heard the squeak of a door opening and then footsteps inside. I moved forward, about to pop out to see her, when all at once I realized it wasn't Julie. The noise came from the back of the house and there was a strong, unfamiliar scent—an aftershave or cologne smell overlaid by cigarette smoke. When I heard the footsteps again I realized they were heavy. So the black-mailer *was* a man. Was it someone we knew? I heard the whine of another door and realized he'd opened the coat closet. Thank God I hadn't hidden in there. The footsteps continued on into the living room, and the light shifted as he stepped in front of a window. I stayed as still as I could, barely breathing, waiting until I heard him walk out of the room. Then the footsteps were right above me and I shielded my face from the sudden shower of dust as he climbed the stairs to the second floor.

The blackmailer had come early, too. How had he known the back door would be open? Had he seen us circling the subdivi-sion? Watched me running through the backyards? I gripped the bat more tightly and swallowed hard. Where the hell was Julie? Just as I was about to give up, her text appeared: Just pulled in.

It seemed like an eternity before I heard a new set of footsteps outside and a key turning in the lock. I heard Julie cough after she crossed the living room floor and I knew that she'd placed the money in the hearth. I held my breath, waiting, until her foot-steps came back across the polished hardwood and out the front door.

And then I was alone with the blackmailer. I could feel his presence in the house, but there was no noise, not a sound. What was he waiting for? Time passed, painfully slow. My back hurt from being so tensely coiled and my head ached. I strained to hear the slightest movement from upstairs, but there was noth-ing beyond the sound of my own nervous swallow. Had he heard that? Could he hear me breathing? I thought I'd go mad.

At last, finally, footsteps echoed above me before descending the stairs. My hands felt slick against the grip on the bat and I wiped them off on my coat. The heavy footsteps crossed the liv-ing room, heading for the hearth. Clutching the bat with one hand, I inched out from below the stairs, moving soundlessly for-ward until I could stand upright.

A tall man stood with his back to me, bending over the fire-place. This was it. *Hit him with the bat, hit him hard.* I took a silent step forward, raising the bat high just as he stood upright, duffel bag in hand, his back still to me. I had a perfect aim, either against his head or in that spot between his shoulders, but as I prepared to swing I flashed to a memory of other hands raised and more than ready to inflict a beating. Could I really do this? Could I bash him? It was a split-second hesitation, but the man turned and saw me and the opportunity was gone. He ran for the front door and I leapt forward to grab him, but his leather jacket slipped from my fingers. I chased after him as he went out the door and sprang down the front steps, running across the front yard with the duffel bag tucked under his arm. And then Sarah was there, chasing him with me as he ran across the neighboring yard and the one next to that, my lungs burning as we tried to catch him. He dashed between two houses, disappearing from view, and I pursued him, Sarah right behind me, both of us turning the corner in time to see him jump on a motorcycle he'd hidden down a driveway. We raced toward him, but the engine roared to life, and the bike leapt forward, wobbling dangerously as he swerved around us, the bag tucked against his lap. Sarah grabbed the bat from my hand, hurling it after him. It fell short, clanking harmlessly against the street as the motorcycle sped away.

chapter thirty-six

ALISON

How the hell did you let him go?" Sarah cried, grabbing the bat again only to hurl it at the ground in frustration. She paced the street, both hands on her head, while I stood there panting and defeated, feeling as shitty as it was possible to feel. I'd failed. I'd failed, and when he saw that we'd cheated him out of the money, this guy would take the photos to the cops and they would show up at my house to arrest me.

I remembered when my father was taken away, the sounds of the handcuffs snapping around his wrists, his bitter protests that *it wasn't my fault,* that he hadn't done anything wrong. I imagined saying this to Lucy and Matthew, calling out to them as I was ushered into the back of a squad car.

A car roared up the street toward us. Julie screeched to a halt and jumped out, hopeful and twitching with excitement. "Did you get it? Did you get the phone?"

"She let him get away—she didn't even hit him." Sarah was angry and scornful.

"What?" Julie looked at her then back at me. "What do you mean, you didn't hit him?" I didn't answer and I saw her take in the bat lying abandoned where Sarah had thrown it. "What happened, Alison? Why?"

"He saw me—there wasn't time." But there had been time, there'd been those few seconds that seemed to last forever when I could have cracked the bat across the back of his head. It had been long enough for me to see that his black hair was shiny and

damp, to notice the tattoo on the base of his neck, a detailed crucifix with a tiny hanging Christ. It had been long enough for me
to flash back to another arm raised, to the whoosh the shovel
made as it swung so fast through the air there was no time to
react. It had been long enough for me to remember the horror as
it connected, slicing through skin like a paring knife through a
peach, the blood oozing like juice, dripping down the face, rolling over the chin.

There was no point in explaining this to Julie or Sarah; it didn't
change anything. I started to weep then, sinking to the ground,
resting my head in my grimy hands and sobbing. Julie and Sarah
thought it was about my failure to stop the blackmailer—I could
hear them talking about what to do—but the tears were about
so much more.

"Look, it'll be okay," Julie said after a while, patting my shoulder. An ineffectual gesture, but I appreciated the effort. "Here,
take this." She shoved some tissues into my hands. I swiped at
my face, sniffling and struggling to regain some self-control.

"I got part of the license number," Sarah said. "And the make—
it's a Harley-Davidson." She scribbled it down on a piece of a
paper that Julie fetched from her purse. I felt ashamed. Here I'd
wondered if Sarah was fit to be there, and she'd done her job better than I had mine. Except where was my car?

"It's parked where I dropped you off," she said when I asked.
"I figured you might have trouble so I doubled back and crept
around the side of the neighboring house."

"Is there some way to look up who the bike's registered to?"
Julie asked as I slowly stood up, my body aching as if I'd run
for miles. "Do we know anyone at the DMV?"

"They wouldn't give us that information," Sarah said. "It's not
allowed. But maybe we could hack into their site?" She looked
at me.

I shrugged, wincing as my shoulders protested. "I could try, but
it's risky and would probably take a while."

Julie glanced at her watch. "We have to hurry—I'm sure he's figured out by now that he doesn't have twenty thousand dollars."

Another way to get the information suddenly occurred to me. "I'll ask my brother to look it up," I blurted, so eager to make up for my failure that I didn't add that I couldn't promise he'd help me.

"It's probably too late anyway," Julie said. "The guy could have driven straight from here to the police."

"I don't think so," I said. "He obviously wants more money and he's not going to get that from the police."

"But by now he knows we screwed him over," Julie said. "He's got to be pissed off about that."

"Maybe, but if we dangle the possibility of the money there's a chance he'll bite." I pulled out my phone and looked at the blackmailer's last message. "What if we send another text and offer him the cash?"

"Why would he believe that?" Sarah said. "He's got the fake bills—he knows we lied to him."

"Greed," I replied. "It's worth a shot—what do we have to lose?" I typed quickly and held it up for them to see before sending it: **Do you want what you asked for?**

We took wet wipes from Julie's glove compartment and wiped down the house's front and back doorknobs and brushed away any visible footprints. I retrieved the yoga bag from under the steps and loaded the bat back into it.

There was no response to the text, not in five minutes or in ten, taking away the last bit of hope that I was struggling to keep afloat. Julie drove Sarah home, ostensibly so I could make the call to my brother before the kids got off the school bus, but I imagined them spending the ride complaining about how I'd screwed us all over because I was too weak to take down the asshole who wanted to rob us blind.

As I waited for Sean to pick up, I berated myself for my failure to get the blackmailer's phone, even as part of me wanted to tell my brother that maybe he was wrong—that there was a line that some people wouldn't cross. That even the right circumstances didn't mean people always made the wrong choice.

"Hey, what's up?" My brother's cheerful greeting made me

well up again, but I blinked the tears back, careful to keep my voice equally light.

"Hi. I've got a quick favor. You have access to vehicle registrations, right? Could you look up a license number for me—I've got most of it—and see who owns this Harley-Davidson?"

"Look, Alison, we're not supposed to do that," he said, sounding uncomfortable. "That information isn't public."

"I know, it's a big favor, but what's the point of having an older brother who's a police officer if you can't ask him to help you out?" I forced a little laugh.

He didn't sound amused. "I can help you with a parking ticket, Ali, but this is different. Why do you want to know this anyway?"

I knew Sean would ask that and I'd played through several different scenarios before calling him. At first I'd thought of telling him that a guy on that particular motorcycle had cut me off in traffic, but Sean would ask the Sewickley police to give the guy a warning or, worse, he'd want to look into it himself, and neither of these would involve giving me the guy's name or address. I could tell him that the motorcycle owner was a Good Samaritan who'd helped me change a flat tire, and I'd forgotten to get his contact info so I could send him a thank-you. But he'd probably ask why I hadn't just called AAA or Michael.

"He had a FOR SALE sign on his motorcycle," I said, "but I didn't get the phone number and I didn't have the time to follow him in traffic until I could get it."

"*You're* going to buy a motorcycle?" It wasn't easy to shock Sean, but I'd achieved it.

I switched lanes, passing an old man crawling along, keeping an eye on the time. The school bus would be arriving in less than ten minutes. "I'm just thinking about it, for Michael, for his birthday. He's turning forty, you know—"

"And he wants a bike? Wow, I'm surprised you're okay with that."

"I'm not sure I am, it probably won't happen, but I'm looking."

"Have you looked on Craigslist? I bet he listed it there. And there are plenty of bikes for sale online."

"I checked online before calling you, but I couldn't find it," I lied easily, pulling onto the street where the bus arrived and taking my place at the back of the cars already queued up. One of the other mothers waved as I passed and I lifted my own hand in response. The bus would be there soon—I needed to get off the phone before the kids got in the car. "I really wanted to take a look at that bike. Please, Sean."

He sighed. "Okay, I'll do it, but you can't tell him—or anyone—how you got the information. Agreed?"

"Yes, definitely. Thank you so much, Sean, I really appreciate it," I said, just as the bus came chugging up the hill.

"Yeah, yeah," he muttered. "Just hold on a second." He put the phone down and I switched off the car and balanced my phone against my ear as I dug around in the glove compartment for a pen and something to write on. I found an old envelope as the bus wheezed to a stop and the door opened, the children clambering out, running to their mothers or the nannies sent to get them, chirping about their day like newly hatched chicks. I got out of the car, surprised to slip a little, weak-kneed with fatigue and relief. Lucy stepped off the bus, deeply engrossed in conversation with a friend. She nodded at me, holding up one finger in a perfect imitation of her mother staving off an interruption from her or her brother. Matthew came off a few kids after her, standing on the top step and looking around nervously before he spotted me and stepped down. My heart squeezed with the usual anxiety.

"Okay, I think I found it." Sean came back on the line. "The missing number makes it harder, a bunch of registrations popped up, but this one's tied to a motorcycle. You got a pen?"

"Yes, shoot." I held the envelope against the car, pen poised, while keeping an eye on the kids and the cars.

"That bike's registered to a Raymond Fortini." He rattled off the spelling of the name and then an address.

"Great. Thank you so much."

"Yeah, okay. Just remember—this is a one-time thing and you don't mention it to anybody."

"Got it. Thank you. Oh, and Sean, don't tell Michael, okay? I want it to be a surprise."

Matthew noticed the yoga bag in the back as the kids climbed into the car. When he asked what was in it, my tongue froze despite my having lied smoothly and successfully for weeks, and for a moment I couldn't think of anything to say.

He clambered over the seat before I could stop him and unzipped it. "Were you playing baseball with your friends?" he asked in the sweetest way.

That melted the irritation I felt, and I smiled as I helped him climb back over and into his booster seat. "No, Julie thought she needed to borrow a bat for Owen—"

"Owen?" Lucy said incredulously. "Owen doesn't play baseball."

"Maybe it was for Aubrey then."

"She doesn't play either. They don't like baseball—they only like soccer." Lucy spoke with her usual authority.

"I think their mother thought they might," I said. "But it turns out they had a bat, so they didn't need ours after all."

"Dad would be upset if you gave away the bat," Lucy said. "He *loves* baseball."

"Loves, loves, loves," Matthew repeated.

"Stop copying me, Matthew," Lucy said with more resignation than annoyance. "Mrs. Hammond says that people should try to be original."

Their bickering receded into background noise as I racked my brain, trying to remember if I'd heard Raymond Fortini's name before. Once we were home and I'd settled the kids in front of the TV with a snack, I grabbed my laptop and began searching for him.

Fortini didn't show up in the elementary school directory—no one with that last name did. While it was a relief, in one way, to realize that someone we knew wasn't blackmailing us, in another way it just made things harder. Who was this guy? He was surprisingly difficult to find; he didn't have a Facebook page or a Twitter account or any other social-media profile that I could locate, nor was he mentioned on anyone else's. There were plenty of other Raymond Fortini profiles, but I eliminated them one by one.

Odd to fly so under the radar in the digital age, which prompted another type of searching, although knowing my brother, if the man had a criminal record Sean would have shared that information with me. Eventually, I found an article from four years earlier about a bartending contest held at a Pittsburgh nightclub, and lo and behold if a Ray Fortini, bartender at The Crooked Halo in Bellevue, wasn't listed as one of the winners. They even had a picture of him—a white, thirtysomething man who was handsome in a scruffy sort of way, dark hair and eyes, a wicked grin, and one of those semi-beards that might not be a beard at all, but just a day or two without shaving. I'd only caught a quick glimpse of his face at the house and he certainly hadn't been smiling, but otherwise the man in the photo seemed to match my memory.

I was burying the bat back in the sports bin when my phone chimed. It was a shock, but a good one, to finally see a reply to my text: **10 a.m. tomorrow. Cemetery. Last chance.**

I hurried to call Julie and Sarah.

"A girls' night out on a Tuesday?" Michael said, surprised. "I thought you hated doing that on weekdays because you couldn't sleep in the next morning."

"It's a special case—Julie's celebrating a house sale."

"Oh, really? What house?" He was searching the fridge for a beer and didn't see my expression, which was fortunate because I was stumped.

"I don't know. Apparently it's some property that she's been trying to unload for months."

"That's nice." He had his beer, but now he was searching the kitchen, opening drawers.

"Here," I said, opening a drawer on the opposite side and finding the bottle opener. I passed it to him.

"Thanks," he said, popping off the cap. "I could have sworn we kept it in this drawer." We didn't—it had been in the same drawer for the entire eight years we'd lived in this house—but I just smiled. He took a swig of beer. "So, did you have any plans for dinner?" he said in the hesitant voice of a spouse who's really hoping no one's counting on him to cook something.

"There's some pasta," I said, opening the fridge. "There's chicken. You're great at improvising—I'm sure the kids will like whatever you feel like making."

"Sure, okay," he said with forced enthusiasm. "We'll be fine—you have a good time."

"Thanks." I gave him a quick kiss and headed out of the kitchen to get changed.

"Ali?" He called me back. His voice sounded funny—had he seen something? I walked back into the kitchen and froze for a moment when I saw that I'd left my laptop open on the kitchen table. Had he seen the search I had open on the screen?

"Yes?" Trying to sound as casual as I could. What would I say if he asked about it?

But he was busy unloading things from the fridge, not looking at the table at all, and he only said, "Where are you going to eat?"

"I don't know," I said, relieved and ridiculously pleased at not having to lie about at least one thing. "I think Julie's picking the place." I snapped my laptop closed and carried it out of the kitchen.

"If we steal his computer and phone he can report the theft, and while he's doing that he might decide to tell the police about the photos," I said to Julie and Sarah on the drive to Bellevue. "It would be better if I erase all his files. Just clear his electronics."

"He could still report that to the police, couldn't he?" Julie said.

She kept glancing at her phone, expecting to hear from Heather, whom none of us had been able to reach.

"Where the hell are you?" Sarah growled into Heather's voice mail. "This is so typical of you—leaving us to do all the dirty work."

It made me cringe. By that point, I was completely paranoid about any phone conversations and tried to keep things short and cryptic. I didn't know if the police were tapping our cell phones, but if they were, that blatant a message would be hard to explain away.

"Fortini might still go to the police," I told Julie, "but what evidence would he have? We're going to wear gloves and we can be in and out in about an hour."

"You do realize that's a felony, right?" Sarah had said when I proposed the plan. "Breaking and entering—you could get three to five before any other charges are added."

"And we could get twenty-five to life if we don't get those photos," I'd retorted. "Which sentence do you want to shoot for?"

She wasn't risking arrest anyway, or at least not for breaking and entering. We were dropping her off at The Crooked Halo, waiting outside long enough to get the thumbs-up text that meant Ray Fortini was working behind the bar, before Julie and I proceeded to his house.

We'd met at Julie's beforehand because Brian was out of town again. He was always out of town. Did she ever question what he was doing, I wondered as we headed into her garage. The latest temp nanny was feeding Julie's kids dinner just on the other side of the interior wall and we spoke in hushed whispers as we got ready to go. Off went my tapered slacks and kitten heels, the silky blouse and fine jewelry that I'd put on for our ostensible girls' night out. On went workout wear—black running tights and sneakers, a dark T-shirt and a thick gray jacket with a hood. Julie was dressed similarly; she'd told the babysitter that we were going to a yoga class and then maybe out for a meal after. Sarah wore skinny jeans and a trendy top, but I was still concerned she might look too mom-ish for The Crooked Halo.

"He'll recognize me," she protested when I suggested she be the one to sit in Fortini's bar.

"Not if you're wearing one of these." Julie pulled two wigs out of a bag, one a short brown pageboy, the other long, sleek, and jet-black.

"What the hell are those?"

"Brian and I went to a costume party last year—do you want Sonny or Cher?"

"Are you kidding me? I don't want either."

"If you wear one of these he'll never recognize you," I said.

"If you really don't want to be recognized, I've got Sonny's mustache as well," Julie said, giggling.

"No thank you," Sarah said, grabbing the Cher wig. It took a lot of tucking and a bunch of bobby pins to make sure her curls were completely hidden.

As we pulled up in front of The Crooked Halo, Sarah nervously adjusted the wig again.

"Don't touch it," Julie said. "You look good."

"Don't drink so much that you forget to text us if he leaves," I said, and she rewarded us by slamming the car door. "She doesn't exactly blend into the crowd," I commented as we watched her walk into the bar, that long black mane sashaying behind her.

chapter thirty-seven

The Crooked Halo had been around so long that its disco-era vibe was cool again. The bar was black onyx and over fifteen feet long, with a gold-framed, smoked mirror behind it that doubled the numbers of bottles and glasses. There were scattered round tables and curved booths with crushed velvet seating, and there was even a dance floor, one of those giant white plastic squares made up of smaller squares that lit up in different colors when someone stepped on them. Half the bulbs had burned out and no one had bothered replacing them, and the only reason I knew that was because of the odd couple swaying on the dance floor when I arrived.

I took a table in the corner nearby and waited for a waitress to come for my drink order so I could avoid getting too close to Ray Fortini. I was convinced he'd recognize me, even with that ridiculous wig. He hadn't looked in my direction yet, or if he had, it must have only been a passing glance. The bar was fairly crowded, a lot of people gathered to watch the Penguins game playing on various hanging flat-screen TVs. They were the only modern touch in the place.

An emaciated-looking man who might have been thirty or sixty and his equally emaciated-looking girlfriend shifted around the disco floor, moving their bodies in slow-motion calisthenics. Completely disconnected from each other and reality, dancing to the music in their heads, not the hard rock playing over the bar speaker system. When the woman extended a bony arm near me, I saw needle tracks and realized they were probably addicts.

No one else was dancing and no one bothered with them, although once, when the man bounced against another patron, Fortini yelled, "Hey, watch it, junkie!" Neither of them acknowledged this warning.

The waitstaff was small, just two women and a man wearing standard-issue black pants and T-shirts that had the name of the bar emblazoned across the front so that it rippled across the women's chests. Despite the short staff, my gin and tonic came quickly enough, slapped down on a little cocktail napkin, splashing slightly. "Get you anything else?" the waitress said, balancing a tray with three other drinks. The bright cherries in a whiskey sour bobbed in and out of view. I shook my head.

There were enough people between me and the bar that I was free to watch Fortini, sipping my gin and tonic and noticing that in between pouring drinks, he'd check a cell phone he pulled from beneath the bar. Was this the one with the photos? Only one way to find out. I took out my phone and called him.

The number rang and rang, but he calmly poured a draft for someone and made no move toward the phone. Remembering the previous time I'd tried this, I hung up and dialed again. I could hear it ringing, but could he? I couldn't tell over the din and he calmly mixed a drink for another patron. I tried a third time, but there was still no attempt to answer. Discouraged, I hung up after the tenth ring, but just then he wiped his hands on a towel and reached under the bar for the phone. I saw him frown at the screen, then furiously type something. Seconds later, my screen lit up: **Stop calling!**

Bingo. I smiled and took another sip of my drink, thinking about how I was going to get that phone.

"Hey, can I buy you a drink?" A man had materialized at my side without me noticing. My long "hair" obscured my peripheral vision—it was like wearing blinders. I tried to tuck it behind my ears and surveyed him. Medium height and build, receding hairline and a small paunch, holding a beer glass—your average, reasonably friendly-looking thirtysomething white guy whom I might possibly have accepted a drink from if I was single and not trying to spy on the bartender.

"Thanks, but I've got one," I said, raising my glass so he could see that I was still nursing my gin.

"You're not going to stop at one, are you?" he said in mock surprise, leaning a little on the vacant chair so that I knew he'd accept the seat if I offered it. I didn't.

"I'm the designated driver," I said, before taking a large sip.

"Oh, you're here with someone?" he said, swinging his head from side to side like a Labrador, searching the crowd for my companion. I didn't answer; it seemed safer to let him think so. He gave up and brought his gaze back to me, lurching a little against the chair. He was clearly on beer six or seven. "I've never seen you here before. You live nearby?"

"Oh, not too far away."

He smiled at this as if I'd given him my address. "You remind me of someone—can you guess who?"

I shook my head, cringing as I anticipated what was coming.

"Amy Winehouse."

Incorrectly interpreting the surprise on my face, he added, "Hey, that's a compliment. She was a good-looking chick, when she wasn't, you know—"

"Shit-faced?" I said dryly.

"Yeah, 'zactly." He swallowed the last of his beer, tilting the glass back to suck every bit of foam out. "Do you need another?"

I shook my head and he nodded again, raising his glass in a salute before letting go of the chair and listing in the direction of the bar.

Ray Fortini set the phone down as he refilled shots for a couple. Then he pulled a draft for a man, the phone still out on the counter. It was just sitting there and his back was turned. If I could just reach it in time. As I rose from my chair, a group of women stepped in front of me and I couldn't see the bar. I craned my neck, trying to see around them. Was it too late? A crowd clustered in front of the wall-mounted flat-screen in the opposite corner cheered as the Penguins scored. I pushed past the women and wiggled through the crowd to the bar. I looked up and down the long sleek surface, but it was too late. The phone was gone.

Ray Fortini turned at that moment to look at me. "Get you something?" My pulse jumped, but he only stared at me inquiringly, yet disinterested, no recognition in his dark eyes.

"Gin and tonic," I said, adding, "Hendrick's, please."

"You got it." He turned away and I checked the mirror behind the bar, hoping it would reflect what was under the counter, but it sat too high and there were too many liquor bottles in the way.

"Oh my God, I love it!" I heard someone say behind me, and then there was humming before someone started singing, "'If I could turn back time . . .'"

"Here you go." Ray Fortini slid my drink across the counter, plopping a stirrer in it.

"Thanks."

"My pleasure." A quick flash of a grin, easy charm, and he was already turning away to get someone else's order. Phone nowhere in sight.

Someone tapped me on the shoulder and I turned around, expecting to see the guy who'd hit on me earlier, but instead there were two twentysomething men grinning at me, one black, one white, both with shaved heads, wearing coordinated checked shirts, one blue, one green. A matched set. "Oh my God, you're so cute!" the white guy squealed.

"Ditto," I said, enjoying a sip of my drink.

"We love Cher," the black guy said. "Are these extensions?" He reached out a hand to touch the wig and I leaned back so he only brushed the ends.

"Yeah," I said, trying to smile.

"It's like you're Librarian Cher—I love it," the white guy said.

"Super fresh," the other guy added.

"Thanks." I forced another smile as I inched backward, before turning and bolting through the crowd for the corner, my drink held high.

My table had been taken over, so I leaned against the wall,

sweating a little and wishing I weren't here alone. Julie would
have known how to handle that conversation.

I pulled out my phone, but there were no updates from Julie
and Alison or messages from Heather. The bar was getting progressively more crowded. It was only Tuesday night, and not
that late, but the Pens game was a big draw. Lots of yinzers wearing team jerseys jostled in front of the wall-mounted screens,
bellowing happily every time we scored. I sipped my drink and
kept an eye on Ray Fortini, waiting and hoping he'd pull out his
phone again. I'd move faster next time, just swipe it off the bar.
I played through the scenario multiple times in my head, map-
ping various routes to the bar and out the door and onto the
street, but he was too busy serving drinks and the phone never
reappeared.

Just as I was starting to wonder if this was going to fail totally,
I saw a striking-looking woman walk behind the bar, tying a
small apron around her waist. She had magenta hair with black
tips and wore a black T-shirt cut to flatter her figure. She put a hand
on his arm and leaned in to say something to him, clearly struggling to be heard over the competing din of hockey game, rock
music, and loud conversation. He nodded at whatever she said
and then, gripping the back of her neck, pulled her in for a lingering kiss. Someone seated at the bar applauded and she pulled
away first, laughing. He grinned at her, swiping some things
from under the counter, and walked toward the back, slapping
her on the ass as he passed.

He was going out the back. Shit! Was he off work? I'd been so
engrossed in their encounter that I hadn't realized she was his
replacement. He disappeared through a service door and I quickly
swallowed the rest of my drink, shoved a twenty at a waitress,
and pushed out the front door. Trying to look nonchalant, I
walked around to the parking lot in the back, breaking into a
run only when I was out of sight of the front door.

I scoured the lot and there it was—his Harley. At that moment,
a back door banged open and I ducked behind the corner, peering around the side as Ray Fortini stepped outside, pulling on a

jacket. I pulled out my phone, starting to text Julie and Alison that he was leaving, but then I realized that he hadn't gotten on the bike. He took a seat at an old picnic table on a dingy concrete patio just to the left of the door, pulled out a pack of cigarettes, and lit up.

It was just a break—he wasn't leaving. I was so relieved that I sagged against the building. I glanced at my phone and saw that I'd missed several texts. Before I could read them, the back door opened again and I looked around the corner as the skinny male waiter, barely recognizable in a puffy parka, came outside carrying a plastic snack basket and what looked like a soft drink. He deposited his food on the table, hitching up his sagging chinos and taking a seat across from Fortini, who reached into the basket and helped himself to what looked like fries. The guy protested, turning sideways to try to shelter his food, but Fortini only laughed, half-standing to reach across the table and grab some more.

Looking back down at my phone, I saw that one of the texts was from Heather. "About time," I muttered, stopping short when I read the message: At hospital—miscarriage.

I stared in shock at the screen for a moment, wishing I hadn't sent that complaining voice mail. Just as I started to type a sympathetic—and apologetic—message, a new text came, this one from Eric: CALL ME.

Crap. I looked over at the table. Ray was talking and smoking, half his attention on the waiter, the other half on his phone. I ducked back around the corner and quickly called home. Eric sounded harried. "Do you know where Josh left his blanket?"

The fragments of a soft, once baby-blue blanket given to him as an infant and carried around so religiously that all that was left was a gray knotted string that he couldn't sleep without. "I don't know—did you check under his bed?"

"Yep. And under Sam's bed and in the sofa cushions and in our bedroom." He recited every place he'd looked while I half-listened, sticking my head back around the corner to see if anything had changed. Fortini was gesturing with his cigarette while

he spoke to the waiter, the phone sitting on the table. I ducked
back behind the wall. "I can't think of anyplace else to look."

He sighed. "I'll keep searching—it's got to be here somewhere.
What time do you think you'll be home?"

Not until I've stolen this iPhone. "Sorry, but I'm going to be
late." I latched on to the first excuse that popped in my mind.
"Heather's had a miscarriage."

"What? Heather was pregnant?"

Whoops. Distracted, I'd forgotten that she hadn't told anyone
else yet. "Um, yeah, it was kind of a surprise."

"But I thought Viktor had a vasectomy?"

Before I could reply, the door banged open a third time and a
female voice called, "Hey, Ray, your food's up." I looked around
the corner in time to see the waiter heading back inside as Ray
stubbed out his cigarette in a plastic ashtray and stood up, heading for the door. And miracle of miracles, he left the phone on
the picnic table.

"I've got to go, Eric—I'll call you back." I hung up without
waiting for his good-bye, stuffing my phone in my purse as I
walked toward the picnic table. It might have been the gin, but I
felt as if I were moving in slow motion, my hand closing over
Fortini's phone, the plastic case slipping in my sweating palm as
I pivoted, turning toward the street.

The slap of the door startled me. I didn't turn around, kept
moving forward, away from the bar, but when I heard him bellow "Hey, you!" I broke into a run, shoving his phone into my
purse as I dashed around the corner and fled up the street.

chapter thirty-eight

The address my brother had given me turned out to be an old Victorian in Bellevue that had been converted into three apartments, the "C" after the number the designation for the third-floor unit, which I learned was accessed on the side of the house via a long, rickety, and rusting set of metal stairs. A mailbox at the front confirmed that this was the right place: One of the slots read "Fortini" in slanting blue Sharpie.

Staring at Fortini's apartment, I wished I were the one sitting at the bar. I surveyed the house while Julie dug in her purse for the tiny set of screwdrivers that she'd brought along in case we had to pick a lock. That was looking likely, since it was going to be impossible to check a third-floor unit for any unlocked windows.

How were we going to get up to the apartment? At least the staircase was on the side of the house, but it was otherwise completely exposed. It was almost seven P.M. The sun had finally set, but there were streetlights, and a house with large windows right next door, not to mention that at the top of those long metal stairs, hanging above the door, was a porch light.

"We have to come up with a story," I said to Julie. "What do we say if someone sees us?"

We'd parked across the street, but hadn't moved from Julie's car, both of us scanning the building and the block. She took a long swallow from a bottle of water and rolled her shoulders as if limbering up for a run.

"How about this," she said. "We're considering buying property in the area and we wanted to talk to some renters."

"We're not exactly dressed for that, are we?"

"Maybe we were at the gym first? Believe me, if someone does question us it's not going to be about what we're wearing."

She had a point.

We got out of the car and closed the doors quietly, conscious of the noise. As we headed toward the side of the house, one of the doors in the front cracked open and a small, gray head poked out. "Hello?" a tremulous voice said.

"Good evening," I said, and Julie echoed me, both of us smiling.

"Do you have my dinner?"

"I'm sorry?" I said, confused.

The door opened wider and an old woman shuffled out onto the wooden porch, the ancient boards creaking underfoot. "Aren't you with Meals on Wheels?" She picked at the corner of a shapeless brown sweater.

"No, sorry, we're here to talk to your neighbor," I said, pointing in the general direction of the upstairs apartment.

She scowled, her round, wrinkled face like a wizened apple. "My meal is supposed to be here by now."

"I'm sure they'll show up soon," Julie said, both of us inching our way past the porch, desperate to go, but afraid to attract negative attention by hurrying away.

"Are you lying to me?" The voice suddenly suspicious and rising.

"No, of course not," I said in a soothing tone. "We wouldn't lie to you."

"Everyone is a liar," she declared, before abruptly shuffling back inside and slamming the door.

We saw no one else as we started up the metal steps, which vibrated like a rope ladder, slapping against the brick wall and squealing at spots, as if the screws were being tortured. The steps ended at a small metal landing with a potted geranium and a wooden door painted black. While Julie tried to shield me from view, I tried the doorknob—locked, as we'd expected—and ran

a gloved hand quickly over the jamb, searching for a key. There
was none.

We switched places, Julie fiddling with her small screwdrivers
in the lock while I tried to block her and scout the neighboring
house and the street for anyone watching. There were curtains
drawn over the upstairs windows in the opposite house, but had
one of them twitched? Was someone spying on us? "Hurry," I
muttered to Julie.

"I'm trying," she said in a stage whisper, "but it's hard with
the gloves."

My phone rang, the stairs swaying slightly as we both startled.
I pulled it out of my jacket. "It's Michael—I have to answer."

He sounded harried. "Hey, sorry to bother you, but is Lucy al-
lergic to mushrooms?"

"No, at least, not that I'm aware of—why? Is she okay?" I had
a sudden vision of my child red-faced and blown up like a puffer
fish, picturing a frantic trip to the emergency room for an EpiPen.

"She hasn't eaten any, so she's fine," he said. "She's just making a pretty convincing argument that this is why she can't eat
the pasta I made."

"Well, neither kid likes mushrooms so if it's got a lot of mushrooms in it they're probably not going to eat it."

"Matthew is eating it."

"Is he?" My people pleaser. Poor kid was going to need so
much therapy. "Have you tried picking out the mushrooms?"

"She insists the whole dish has been tainted."

"Well, there's always mac and cheese—we've got boxes in the
cupboard."

"I don't think we should coddle the kids like that—they should
eat what we serve for dinner."

"Hmm," I said, thinking that given how infrequently "we"
made dinner that "we" weren't really entitled to an opinion.
"Well, good luck."

"How's your dinner?" I caught an undertone of sulkiness that
made me long to tell him the truth about what I was actually
doing, risking my life on this stupid metal staircase, breaking the

law so I could avoid going to prison and leaving him to make dinner *every* night for our children.

"Delicious," I said. "They're serving the next course, so I need to go."

"Okay, well, you enjoy yourself, we'll just be here—"

I hung up the phone, my stomach growling because of course I'd had nothing to eat; I hadn't even thought of food, I'd been so intent on the task at hand. "Any luck?" I said to Julie.

"Stop asking," she hissed. "You'll know if I get lucky because the damn door will—" At that moment we both heard a distinct click. I turned around to look and she smiled. She stood up, placed a gloved hand tentatively on the knob, and slowly turned. The door opened.

The inside of Ray Fortini's apartment reminded me of Michael's bachelor pad: an emphasis on electronic equipment—a fifty-inch flat-screen, a PlayStation with multiple controllers, and a complicated-looking speaker system—at the expense of furniture and decoration. An exception was the bed, king-size wrought iron with ornate curlicues and expensive-looking sheets.

"Well, that's a surprise," Julie said, rubbing a corner between her gloved fingers as if she could actually tell the thread count through latex.

It took me a minute of glancing around before I spotted the computer, a large desktop set up on a table in an alcove. "Bingo," I said, powering it on and not surprised when a page with a password box popped up. "Let's see if we can find a birth certificate or any other personal documents. I need his birth date or his mother's maiden name or something like that to try."

Most people aren't that careful with their passwords; they think about something easy to remember for quick access, not realizing that this means quick access for other people, too.

Julie and I started opening drawers. The nightstand held a lifetime supply of condoms, ribbed and regular, thin and "stimulating," natural sheepskin, and some that were supposedly flavored. "Good to know he believes in safe sex," I said, slamming the drawer closed and moving on to the closet. A few boxes on a top shelf looked promising, but they turned out to hold child-hood mementos—an old Nerf football, a small Steelers jersey, some family photos that had dates but no names to identify the smiling faces.

"Check this out," Julie called from across the room. She was kneeling in front of an old-fashioned trunk, and before I reached her side I could see that it was full of sex toys. "Now we know how he spends his free time," she said, giggling, waggling a pair of leather-covered handcuffs at me.

"Fifty Shades of Cliché," I said, wondering if this was a seri-ous interest or just something he used to woo the people he man-aged to bring up here. I looked around again, frustrated. "He's got to keep papers somewhere."

"Maybe it's all online."

"Let's hope not." Heart sinking, I started at the front of the apartment and examined everything. The kitchen was small, but had a table next to a window that overlooked the backyard and some shared parking. I opened the refrigerator: several different types of craft beer, condiments like RedHot, a loaf of something labeled "Pepperoni Bread," and the only nods to healthy eating, a bag of moldering carrots and a perfectly round head of iceberg lettuce. The freezer held Hot Pockets and pizza snacks.

The cupboards were equally sparse: Pop-Tarts, a bag of Dori-tos, and a huge plastic jug of something called Fuel XXX, which looked like one of those protein powders you bought at muscle-bound health stores.

There were only DVDs and video games in the entertainment center and there was nothing hidden behind the couch. The small bathroom had a medicine cabinet stuffed full of prescription pill bottles—oxycodone, Zoloft, diazepam—all mixed in with the mundane toothpaste, razors, and shaving cream. I went back to the table with the computer, checked the single center drawer a second time, and slammed it shut in frustration.

"This is taking too long," Julie said. "Can't you figure out how to get in without a password?"

"Not easily." Finally, in desperation, I ran my hand under the bed and felt something hard. Using my iPhone flashlight, I spotted a gray box and pulled it out. A fire safe, but it was locked.

A third time through the apartment failed to reveal a key small enough to fit in the lock. Julie had a go with the screwdrivers, but this keyhole was too tiny even for them. Trying to pry it open with a knife was equally futile. "Aargh, this is so frustrating!" I said. "Maybe if we drop it out a window it'll break open."

"And maybe the neighbors would come running," Julie said. "Here, let me try again." She went at it with the knife, but only succeeded in snapping off the blade. "Shoot! Now what are we going to do?"

I tilted the safe and the broken metal tip dropped from the keyhole. "We'll just throw out the knife or put it back in the drawer. If we hide it in plain sight—" I stopped short.

"What is it?" Julie said.

Without stopping to answer, I ran back to the kitchen and opened the refrigerator again. The perfect head of lettuce. I reached into the vegetable drawer and knew the minute I touched its waxy leaves that I was right. Julie had followed me into the kitchen and she watched, perplexed, as I took the lettuce from the fridge.

"Isn't there anything else to eat?" she said as I set it on the counter.

"It's not edible," I said, tapping the plastic surface. On the bottom was a round rubber stopper like the kind in a piggy bank, but held on with a small knob. Julie's mouth dropped as I twisted it open and out spilled two tiny bags of white powder, a roll of bills bound with a rubber band, and a tiny key.

The fire safe opened easily with the key and I riffled quickly through the files inside, grabbing one that seemed to have personal documents and running with it to the computer. My hands shook a little as I typed in his birth date. No luck. His mother's maiden name. No luck. Maiden name and her birth year. No luck. His year and initials and her year and initials. The password screen slid aside, revealing his files, and I cried out in triumph.

"Shh," Julie cautioned, stepping past me to look out the window and then checking the ones on the other side of the apartment. "It's been over thirty minutes, we need to hurry."

Before I erased anything, I wanted to see what he'd been holding over our heads. I opened Photos and scrolled through them as fast as I could, a rapid blur of color, until I found the dark, grainy shot that he'd sent to us. There were other photos, over a dozen in all, of the three of us and the road and the cars, the headlights a smear of light illuminating first my face, then Sarah's. Julie stepping into the frame of another one. Heather on the side of several shots, head turned or looking as catatonic as I remembered. All four of us had been caught on camera, clearly visible. Viktor's leg dangled out of the car in one photo, and although someone else might not have realized what they were seeing, no one could miss that bottle-green Mercedes.

Something was odd. It took me a minute to realize that the close-ups were too close and too in-focus to have been taken with a smartphone. I clicked on one and opened the EXIF data, which revealed that the shot had been taken with a Canon. I quickly checked the others. All taken with the same camera, not a smartphone.

"This is really weird," I said to Julie, who was sitting on the bed sifting more carefully through the fire safe. "He took the photos of us with a regular camera."

"So?" She sounded distracted.

"So what was he doing out at two A.M. with a camera? He's a bartender, not a professional photographer."

"Maybe it's a hobby," she said. "People leave stuff in their cars all the time. Who cares? Just get rid of them."

But he didn't drive a car, so he didn't have a place to leave a camera. He drove a loud motorcycle. Could we really have failed to notice that revving sound in the silence that night? Except we had noticed—I suddenly remembered being startled by the noise of an engine somewhere in the distance. Could that have been Fortini?

Looking once again through all the photos, I was struck by

how deliberate the shots seemed, each one of us caught on camera either individually or in a group. The cursor jumped and I
accidentally clicked open a video. A naked man was having sex
on a familiar ornate iron bed, his back to the camera. Ray Fortini
seemed to realize that he didn't have the right shot, because he
pulled out, his face turning to the camera for a moment, a study
in concentration, before he reached up to wherever he had it
positioned—it appeared to be hidden on the tall chest of
drawers—and changed the angle slightly. As he stepped back, the
camera autofocused on a naked woman with her head covered in
a tight black hood that had an opening only for her mouth. She
was lying spread-eagled, handcuffed to long chains attached to
the bed frame and wearing ankle restraints that had a metal bar
between them, holding her legs apart. Fortini grabbed her by her
skinny hips, and unceremoniously hauled her in different directions so that he could capture more of her body and his on film.
He grinned at the camera as he reached for something out of view
and then stepped back in with what looked like a riding crop. He
started hitting her with it, flicking it over different parts of her
body while she twitched and turned but couldn't get out of range
because of the restraints. He flipped her onto her stomach and
whapped her across the butt over and over before he tossed the
crop aside and entered her again, slamming into her so violently
that she jerked forward on the bed, his hands on her hips forcing
her back into position, his grip and the restraints holding her in
place. I felt as if I could hear her body breaking apart; I winced at
every violent thrust, even though there was no sound. I couldn't
stop watching, as transfixed as I was repulsed, until he climaxed,
head back, mouth open in a long, silent scream. He fell forward
across the woman and grabbed the hood, yanking it off and jerking her head up by the long, light blond hair that tumbled down,
and then I was the one crying out, because as he forced her face
toward the camera I recognized her. It was Heather.

chapter thirty-nine

They'd been watching me. A video camera perched high in one corner of the room where Detective Kasper escorted me after I'd been summoned back to the local police station to discuss the "concerns" they had over the timeline for the night Viktor died. It was an innocuous-looking space. A laminate-topped table and three basic chairs and thin industrial carpeting on the floor. They'd probably been standing on the other side of the large mirror, waiting for me to crack and tell them everything. Sitting back in the chair, I'd resisted the urge to look directly at the camera or the mirror, or to tap my feet or do anything else that made me look as nervous as I felt.

Daniel was at his grandmother's again. He practically lives there now; Anna has seen to that. She stocks her house with his favorite foods and buys him lots of toys, claiming it's to comfort him because he lost his father. I think it's to help her because she lost her son. She wants to take him away from me, she's already taken away his affection, but she couldn't take the child that I carried. Not that she knew about the pregnancy. I was more than four months along, my bump still easily covered with loose-fitting tops. My daughter. I am sure it was a girl. I'd started thinking about names that I liked, Amelia or Isabel or maybe Elizabeth after my mother. Not Betty though, as her nickname. I'd let the names play on my tongue while lying in bed at night, or showering in the morning, jutting my stomach out and rubbing my hand across my belly in a way that I couldn't do in public.

That's when the bleeding started. A few drops splashing around my bare feet and the shower's stone floor like red rain. Nothing to worry about, at least according to the Internet. They swirled in the water and disappeared down the drain. Another drop or two meant nothing. I wouldn't worry. But then, sitting in the room at the police station, I felt a gush of blood, frighteningly warm, running down my leg. I stood up to get to the door, but doubled over with a terrible, cramping pain, and that's how I knew for sure they were watching me because the door opened and in rushed Detective Kasper and a female police officer and the next thing next thing I knew I was in an ambulance being taken to the hospital.

They couldn't stop the bleeding. The hospital staff talk to me in hushed and solemn tones. "Just rest, dear," a nurse says softly, helping me lie back on the bed as they whisk away the sheets carrying the rest of my baby. There is so much blood. Her blood. "This is very common in the first trimester," the doctor says in soothing tones, "it doesn't mean that you can't conceive again." But then someone whispers that I'm a widow, and I see the pity on her face. They feel bad that I just lost my husband and now I've lost his child, too. I don't correct them. No one must know that Ray is the father.

The first time he hit me I knew I liked him. His hand hard across my backside as I passed him in the dark hallway on my way to the restroom at his bar. I jumped, whirling around to give this guy a piece of my mind, and there Ray stood, grinning at me. "Sorry, I couldn't help myself," he said, and there was something in his smooth voice and dark eyes that stopped me from speaking. I could feel his handprint tingling for hours afterward.

I'd met him a week earlier. Viktor was away again at some conference, and Daniel was with his grandmother. My friends were all busy—it was a Saturday night and they were all occupied with their families. Sitting home alone, again, flipping aimlessly through the local paper while I waited for the microwave to cook my Lean Cuisine, I saw an ad for a band playing that night at The Crooked Halo. I hadn't been to a bar alone since I began dating Viktor, and we hadn't been to a bar together in several years, not since a hospital charity function. It had been at one of those overpriced jazz clubs with a multi-page cocktail menu and hipster waitstaff. The Crooked Halo was different. It looked like your average neighborhood bar hosting some barely known musical group, so nothing about it should have been appealing, but facing the prospect of another night alone in that house, I thought, why not?

It was fun getting ready. It reminded me of my modeling days, using clothes and makeup to transform into someone else. Skinny jeans, silver tank top, and heels. My hair in loose waves, hoops in my ears. I felt like a teenager with a fake ID, especially when I pulled up in front of the bar, which turned out to be in a blue-collar neighborhood similar to the town where I'd grown up, although it was only a twenty-minute drive from Sewickley Heights.

The band was just getting started—I could hear the thrumming of the bass outside. I paid the five-dollar cover and entered the crowd, feeling the energy from the music. It was pretty packed—maybe the group was better known than I'd thought. I jostled my way to the bar and waited to catch the eye of the bartender. He was a tall guy, well over six feet, and one of those men who fill out a T-shirt. Not a muscle-head, but muscular. Dark, curling hair, a bit of scruff. He was laughing at something a customer said as he slid a beer down the black bar. I saw him register my arrival, keeping an eye on the clientele. "What can I get you?" he said, strolling toward me, and then I saw him really look at me, and I saw his eyes react, while the rest of his face remained impassive.

"A Blue Moon," I said, leaning forward to be heard over the music.

"You got it."

He walked away and I got a better look at him. He was a hot guy, that was for sure, but I want to emphasize that I had no intention at that moment of doing anything with him. I hung around the bar, sipping my beer, enjoying the music. They sounded kind of like a Bruce Springsteen cover band. The lead singer had the same gravelly voice and ability to work the crowd.

Four young guys came over to talk to me. College students, they told me, celebrating their buddy's twenty-first birthday. They were well on their way to wasted, but not too bad at that point, just insisting on talking at me with their beery breath. It brought back the days of clubbing in New York and Miami with my girlfriends. I tried to back away from the guy doing the most talking, but he just pressed forward.

"Hey, why don't you give the lady some space," the bartender said. I hadn't noticed him, but he'd noticed the guys.

The talking one ignored him. His friends glanced at the bartender and away; they seemed too drunk to understand anything. "Do you date younger guys?" the Pitt student was saying. " 'Cause it would totally make my buddy's birthday if you'd be his date. Just for tonight."

"I'm married," I said, holding up my left hand and waving it at him with a smile. "Sorry."

"That's okay," the guy said. "You're a total MILF."

"Hey," the bartender said, smacking the bar with his fist to get their attention. "You heard her—she isn't interested. Why don't you go listen to the music?"

"Why don't you fuck off," the Pitt student said over his shoulder.

The next thing I knew, the bartender had come around the bar and grabbed that guy by his sweatshirt, hustling him toward the exit. His friends trailed him, protesting, but the big beefy doorman stood up to help and in another moment the students were all out the door. When the bartender came back, I thanked him. "My pleasure. I hate guys like that." He stuck out a hand. "I'm Ray, by the way."

I shook his hand. "Heather."

"Nice to meet you." He nodded at my almost empty beer. "Want another one? It's on the house."

I thought about him all week, replaying the moment he'd come around the bar, how he'd looked when he lifted that college kid practically off his feet. No one else knew that I'd been there, and that added to the attraction. He was my own secret crush. When Viktor had an overnight trip two weeks later, I went back. The second time felt more illicit, because I lied, telling both Viktor and the nanny that I was going to be out late with friends. That was the night Ray slapped my backside as I passed him in the hall. The hallway was in shadows, the music a distant hum. I'd been looking at my phone as I walked and hadn't realized who it was until I turned around.

No one intends to have an affair. It's not like I set out one day and said, let's see if I can betray my husband. At the same time, I can't deny that I knew what would happen if I accepted Ray's invitation to go back to his apartment with him that evening. There wasn't a single moment when I didn't think we'd end up in bed together. What I didn't anticipate was how often I'd return.

"I knew the moment I met you that we were the same," he said once as he tied my wrists to his bedpost. He liked to play rough, straddling my body, pinching and slapping, laughing as I wriggled underneath him. What is the intersection of pleasure and pain? That is what Ray explores. That is what I like. I'd never met a man like him before.

He didn't ask the first time he tied me up. We were on his bed, he'd been undressing me, interspersed with lots of touching and kissing, and then, without warning, he grabbed one of my wrists and tied it to his iron headboard with a thin scarf he'd pulled from somewhere. I said, "What the hell are you doing?," scrambling up and trying to undo the knot with my free hand. "Let me go!" He reached toward me, but he didn't undo it, he just grabbed my other wrist, tugging it to the other side of the headboard so I was forced flat on my back, before tying it, too.

When he climbed on top of me I started to scream and he placed one of his hands firmly over my mouth and pressed me back into the pillows. I was breathing through my nose, shallow and rapid, sure that he was about to kill me, but he leaned over, his breath hot in my ear, and said in a quiet voice, "Calm down. This is what you want." And then he released his hand and replaced it with his tongue and I loved it.

That's what made Ray different. He knew what I liked before

I knew, and he liked to play. That was his appeal: that he was different from Viktor, who believed in contracts and clear lines. The prenup he insisted on, for example. That was pure Viktor— orderly and calculated, summing up our relationship with sterile equations. With Viktor, the sex was infrequent and approached with his surgeon's precision, a scheduled and choreographed act, nothing spontaneous about it. Ray was the opposite. Lots of passion and completely free—no marriage for him, or children, or even a daytime job that impeded getting together. The fact that he worked nights was great. I could visit him during the day while Viktor was at work and Daniel was at school. It was perfect. Of course, I had to think fast to explain some of the bruises, but Viktor accepted my explanations that I'd bumped into things or injured myself while working out. "You've got to be more careful," he said once, frowning at a new mark on my arm. "Our friends are going to think I'm hurting you."

He was right about that. I tried to hide the bruises from them, too, but they noticed. I found out they were discussing me—it would have been hard not to notice, just as it was hard to hide anything from them. At one point, I considered telling them about Ray, just so they would stop thinking that Viktor was responsible. But they were so convinced that I was being abused that it was too difficult to confess that somebody else had made those marks and that I'd welcomed each and every one. Or at least I did at the beginning.

When I first saw Ray's box of toys I thought it was like his over-the-top bed, just for fun, nothing more. And it was fun at first. I liked it rough. I liked being restrained as he teased me. I liked the sting of leather followed by the caress of his palm. When I was away from him I thought about the feel of his hand knotted in my hair and the tickle of his breath hot in my ear. I craved the weight of his body pressing against mine.

An affair like this isn't sustainable long-term, not without everyone in your life turning a blind eye. Eventually, even distracted Viktor grew suspicious. Things came to a head at the Chens' party. I'd ducked down a hall into an empty room to respond to a text from Ray, but Viktor had seen me leave and came looking for me. "What's going on?" he asked, trying to see my phone. "Who are you texting?"

"Just a friend—her son's in Daniel's class," I said, slipping the phone in my clutch purse and heading toward the hall. "Let's get back to the party."

"Stop," he said, holding up his hand like a traffic cop. "Let me see your phone."

"What? Don't be ridiculous." I walked around him and he grabbed me from behind.

"You're not going anywhere."

"Let go of me!"

"You think I'm stupid? You think I don't realize what you're up to?"

We were tussling when we suddenly caught sight of Julie's reflection in the room's large windows. Viktor immediately released me. I could tell he was embarrassed and it was equally obvious that Julie thought he was mistreating me.

I couldn't tell her that it wasn't Viktor hurting me. It was Ray.

It started one afternoon when his large hand circled my throat and he whispered that he was going to choke me. I laughed and pushed him off. "No way."

"You don't trust me," he said. He'd been fitting a blindfold on me, but he yanked it off and stalked out of the bedroom. Surprised, I scrambled off the bed, running after him.

"That's not true," I said, grabbing his arm. "I love you."

"There's no love without trust."

"I do trust you, I swear."

He gave me a long, considering look and then he said, "Prove it."

It felt weird, but I said okay. I let him put the blindfold on me as I stood there naked and shivering, suddenly afraid to say anything that would make him think I doubted him. His hand on my throat was both warm and startling. He squeezed, tighter and tighter, until I couldn't talk even if I'd wanted to, and I did want to, I wanted to scream at him to let go. It came out as a gargle, the cry of a wounded bird, and I heard his voice deep in my ear. "Do you trust me?"

When I hesitated, his hand started to release me, it was like I could feel his disappointment, and I nodded, whispering a strangled "Yes." His hand tightened again and I struggled not to pull away even as he increased the pressure. How long did he keep me like that? I don't know. All I know is that when he finally let go, I fell forward, coughing and gagging. "You're wonderful," he said, undoing my blindfold, and when I started to cry, he thought my tears were from happiness that I'd pleased him. "These are like my collar," he said, touching the livid red marks that were already turning purple. "You belong to me."

I was angry, but at myself as well as Ray. I'd allowed this stupid game to happen and now I had bruises that I couldn't explain away. Luckily, the temperatures dipped that week, so I could hide the marks on my throat with turtlenecks and scarves. I told Viktor I had a cold and slept in the spare bedroom for a week and I didn't see Ray for a few days. He texted me repeatedly, telling me how much he missed me. I thought it was sweet. I didn't see it as controlling. As the bruises faded, so did my anger. It was just a one-off, I told myself. Ray hadn't meant to go that far.

So I went back to him. And he went further. The play got harder and more complicated. For a while it would be fun, but then he'd start talking about testing my pain threshold and how I was holding out on him. The bruises got bigger and lasted longer. I'd thought he didn't believe in rules and contracts and what he called the symbols of false relationships. That's what he'd said. It turned out that Ray just believed in his own rules.

He would text me throughout the day and night and he wanted me to text him back promptly. "I need to know that you're okay," he said. "I can't focus on my work if I'm worrying about you." I tried to explain that I couldn't do that, not if Viktor was around, but Ray got annoyed whenever I mentioned my husband. "Do you know how lucky you are?" he said as he watched me getting dressed one afternoon. "What other man would tolerate you going home to another guy?"

When I talked about ending our relationship, Ray slapped me across the face. I was so shocked that I didn't react, just stood there in his apartment, my hand to my cheek. Then he started to cry, big, sloppy tears rolling down his face, sniffling as he told me that he loved me so much that he couldn't live without me. That's when I knew it was over.

The irony was that my friends were begging me to leave *Viktor*. Believe me, I considered it. Leave Viktor and Ray. Except how would I support myself? Go back to modeling? At my age that meant catalog work if I was lucky. I had few other skills. In my case, what you see really is what you get. I didn't want to have to go crawling back to West Virginia with nothing to show for my time away but some nice clothes and a little bit of bling. If I left Viktor I'd come away virtually penniless; the prenup had seen to that. The trouble with being fortunate enough to live at a certain level of comfort is that it becomes so much harder to live without it.

Besides, Ray made it clear that he wasn't going to let me go. When I stopped replying to his texts, he came to my house, banging on the door until I finally let him in, terrified that some neighbor would hear and call the police. "Look, it's over," I said, trying to be friendly but firm. "It was fun, but we're done."

"We're done when I say we're done," he said in what he must have thought was a masterful voice, looking like an overgrown teenager in his black leather jacket and dirty jeans.

I laughed. I couldn't help it, he looked and sounded so pathetic, this wannabe dungeon master with his silly games and threats. The attraction I'd felt was completely gone.

He must have seen it in my face because he made a sound like a wounded animal, a loud bellow, as he reached into the dishwasher I'd been in the process of emptying and started hurling dishes. Then I really was scared, but I couldn't call the police. I couldn't do anything but wait until he'd gotten it out of his system. When he'd trashed the kitchen, his rage spent, he started sobbing again, repeating that he loved me and couldn't live without me.

When my friends saw the kitchen of course they assumed it was Viktor who'd done it. I was terrified that they'd end up confronting him and the lies I'd told would come out and Viktor would divorce me. He'd threatened to once, soon after the night at the Chens'. "If I find out you're cheating on me, I'll serve you papers," he said as I reheated dinner for him one evening after he'd come home late, as always, from work. He said the words so calmly, not bothering to make eye contact as he picked at the lasagna on his plate, sniffing as if he could tell that it was Stouffer's even though I'd hidden the box in the trash.

A few weeks later, his words came back to me when I found out I was pregnant and I knew it couldn't be Viktor's. I didn't want to believe it at first, even though my cycle had always been like clockwork. I waited to buy the test and then waited to take it, and then I couldn't bear to look, circling the bathroom as the timer went off, hands clenched into fists as I chanted "Please no, please no, please no" like a mantra. When I finally dared to look I didn't believe the results. I bought a second test. And a third. Only when I saw those two matching lines for the third time did I finally accept the truth.

I was trapped, well and truly trapped. The smart thing to do would have been to have an abortion, but I couldn't do it. Maybe it was just the hormones, but I realized that this was the first thing I'd have in my life that belonged solely to me. I wanted it. I wanted her. I knew it was a girl, even though they said it was too early to tell. I just knew. I'd started thinking of the two of us together. Little Emma or Charlotte or Ava.

But how could I keep this baby without losing the way to support her? If Viktor found out, it was over. Going back to West Virginia was bad enough, but going back with a baby in tow? I couldn't let that happen. And when I realized that, I also realized that my friends' fundamental misunderstanding, their insistence that Viktor was abusing me, might provide the perfect way out.

And it could have worked. It almost worked. But now none of it matters. The only thing that mattered was my little girl and now she's gone. A miscarriage. Such a strange word. How do you mis-carry something? As if my baby were a football that I fumbled. It's not an emotional word, it doesn't mention what I've lost, but it's a judgment against me nonetheless. As if it could all have been prevented if I'd just carried my baby correctly. If I'd just been able to stop the bleeding.

chapter forty

JULIE

Have you ever been betrayed by someone? Someone you continued to trust even when everyone and everything told you not to, but you loved them so much that you couldn't stop believing until the truth came smacking you full across the face? That was how I felt as I watched Heather allow Ray Fortini to chain her, hit her, and debase her in multiple ways as if she were a kind of personal blow-up doll.

I hadn't wanted to believe that Heather had lied about her relationship with Viktor, even after Alison found the evidence. I'd excused her behavior the way we all do with our friends— brushing away the inconsistencies in character, finding plausibility in the implausible because we want to believe that the people we love are incapable of ugliness. She had to have truly feared Viktor in order to shoot him, that's what I'd told myself. He'd brutalized her for so long that these particular dates and times that Alison was so hung up about were just that—particulars that didn't matter.

Except they weren't, not when they were attached to these videos. Alison clicked open video after video, going back in time, proving from the dates affixed to each that Heather had been in the relationship for months. Alison was furious, but eager to make a connection between the lies she'd already uncovered and this new information, determinedly checking the dates on each clip.

I could only stare, fascinated, at the footage of Heather with her lover. Who was so ordinary, so uninteresting, with his over-the-top bed and cheap box of toys. It was like watching a low-budget porno, and after seeing a lot of clips, I thought that was probably exactly what they were. If we searched long enough I was sure we'd probably find some PayPal site set up to commoditize Ray Fortini's home movies.

And any attempt to paint Heather as a victim of this second man didn't work. It was clear that she was a willing and eager participant in this relationship, and I was surprised to realize that I was as much disappointed by the tawdriness of the whole thing as I was by the deceit itself.

"Look, this one is from September," Alison said, pausing another video. "See what he's doing?"

She'd paused on a frame of Fortini holding Heather's arms above her head, zooming in on his hands gripping her wrists.

"I've seen more than enough," I said, turning away. "Just delete them."

"This is just before I saw that bruise on her wrist," Alison said in a low voice. "Jesus, I was so wrong."

What was the point in rehashing it? We'd been duped. The whole thing was sickening. "Delete them," I repeated, going back to finish searching his fire safe for anything else incriminating. "We need to get out of here."

"I will in a minute," Alison said, distracted.

In the back of the fire safe, in a manila envelope, I found print versions of the photos that Fortini had taken of us, as well as a USB drive. "Look, you were right, the bastard had backups," I said, taking them to the alcove to show Alison. She had her own phone plugged into the side of his computer. "What are you doing?"

"Taking some insurance," Alison said. "If we delete all of this she could just deny knowing him."

"You're copying her sex tapes?"

"And some of his others," she said, nodding at the screen, and that's when I realized that the woman in this one was different.

Alison said, "Do you suppose Heather knows that he's done this with a lot of other women?"

I shouldn't have been surprised; of course there were others. Men like Fortini never have just one lover if they can manage two or three. Other women, but the same sex acts, the same bad camera angles and centerfold close-ups.

My phone suddenly rang, startling both of us. "Hello?"

"Get out now!" Sarah screamed, so loudly that Alison heard her. "He's chasing me—I need help."

Alison yanked the cord from her phone and began hitting keys, windows closing, one after the other, on Fortini's computer screen, while I said to Sarah, "What happened? Where are you?"

"I've got the phone, but he saw me. I'm hiding in an alley, but he's looking for me—he's on his motorcycle."

"Oh, shit," I said, panicking as I watched Alison typing as fast as she could, windows disappearing and new ones reappearing. "Just stay hidden. We'll be there soon."

"Are you kidding me? I need you now!" Sarah cried. I heard a noise in the background, the revving of a motorcycle, and then the line went dead.

"Sarah?" I tried to call her back, but it went straight to voice mail. I grabbed the file with Fortini's personal information and stuffed it back in the safe, then locked it and shoved it back under the bed. "We have to go," I said to Alison, "just delete those files."

"It's better if his whole system crashes." She sounded distracted. I ran the key back to the kitchen, stuffing the drugs and the money back inside the fake head of lettuce and ramming the plastic ball back in the fridge.

"Are you done?" I called, quickly surveying the apartment. "We need to leave." I thought I heard an engine in the distance and ran to the window that overlooked the street to check, but I couldn't see anything.

"Done!" Alison called from the other room. I ran back to see her powering off the machine.

"Everything's erased?"

"Yes, let's go."

We set the door to lock behind us, clattering down the metal steps as fast as we could, no longer caring if anyone heard us, so anxious to get away that I tripped as we came down the last step, twisting my ankle and falling hard on my right side.

Alison was trying to help me up when we heard the rumbling noise of a motorcycle and saw a single headlight racing toward us down the street. We couldn't get across the street to our car without being noticed.

"This way, quick." Alison hauled me to my feet, and with her arm under my shoulders she pulled me into a row of scraggly trees and overgrown bushes that ran along the back of the property.

The engine noise got louder and then the light was coming down the opposite side of the house. I'd forgotten about the parking out back. We pushed farther into the scrub, Alison yelping as she brushed against a prickly bush, both of us trying to hide from the blinding light of Ray Fortini's Harley.

The light switched off as the engine stopped, and there was nothing but the silent dark and both of us breathing a little easier. Until we heard the low growl a few feet away. There was a dog chained in the backyard next door. We hadn't noticed him when we'd gone inside the apartment; maybe he hadn't noticed us. He saw us now or smelled us, pulling hard against the chain that tethered him; we could hear it slither and clank against the ground. The growl got louder, a sound that made the back of my legs tighten in anticipation of his jaws.

We couldn't see Ray Fortini, but we could hear his feet crunching on the gravel driveway. "Shut up, King," he said, crossing close to the place we were hidden on his way around the side of the house to his apartment. The dog barked, a small yip to start with, as if King were warming up, and then louder and progressively more aggressive. There was a light on the edge of the building and we could see the silhouette of Ray Fortini, shielding his eyes and trying to peer into the trees. We were crouched behind an overgrown evergreen shrub, holding as still as we could, although my ankle was throbbing so much that I rolled forward onto my knees, feeling the ground, hard and icy, beneath my fingers.

The dog kept barking, we could hear it whipping itself into a frenzy, and we saw Ray Fortini dig in his pocket for something, and we both tensed. I felt Alison's hand on my arm and thought she was trying to steady me, but then I realized she was scared.

He stepped forward, out of the light, and we had no idea what he was doing until we spotted a tiny red glow. A cigarette. I could smell it as he stepped closer, and Alison's hand tightened on my arm. I tried to breathe shallowly and silently, hoping that the dog's incessant barking would cover any noise we were making.

"What are you barking at, dumbass?" Fortini's voice was so close that we could hear his own, heavier breathing as he walked around. Then he drew closer to the dog and said in a softer voice, "Hey, there, buddy, what's got into you tonight?"

There was an ominous silence for a moment, but then the crunch of his footsteps again and the tiny red light disappeared around the side of his building. A few seconds later we heard the sound of the metal steps clanging against the brick.

"C'mon," Alison said, pulling me by the arm she'd been clutching. "Now's our chance."

We crept out of the bushes and I hobbled after her as fast as I could around the other side of the house and over to our car across the street. I didn't know if Ray Fortini had gone inside his apartment or whether he was still outside, standing on the landing. I was afraid to look back.

We found Sarah six blocks away, lingering in the back of an all-night Laundromat. She'd taken the wig off and was carrying it like a long, hairy purse. Her real hair looked matted and her makeup smeared. She'd taken her heels off, too, and was massaging one bruised foot as we pulled up. "Why did you come here?" I asked as she hobbled into the car.

"Having other people around seemed safer." She handed over

the phone she'd taken from Fortini and we pulled over so Alison
could clear all the data from it.

"Maybe we should drop it back off at the bar?" Sarah said.
"What if he reports it stolen?"

"We can let Heather return it to him," Alison said darkly.

"What does that mean?"

"He's her lover," Alison told her, and Sarah responded to the
details first with shock and then with fury.

"We should go to her house and confront her," she began an-
grily, but stopped short, digging in her purse for her phone. "I
forgot—she's not at her house, she's at the hospital."

She told us about the miscarriage and I couldn't help it, I felt
the anger over Heather's betrayal tempered by sadness.

"Where is she?" Alison said. "Text her and say we're coming."

We drove to Sewickley Valley Hospital, and I don't know
about the others, but I felt shaky. I had been in the ER only once
before, when Owen broke his arm in first grade, and I hadn't
remembered it as so busy and chaotic, but maybe that was
because I'd been there on a weekday morning and now it was
after nine at night. As we came through the sliding doors we
could hear a child screaming. It was jarring, an old woman groaning in pain as her middle-aged daughter fussed over her, a man
wearing a dazed expression and holding an ice pack against his
head, and a teenage mother, heavy black eyeliner smeared, trying to hush a screaming, red-faced toddler. Sarah led the way to
the front desk, where a harried-looking woman sat wearing a
lab coat over a Penguins jersey. She had a phone against her ear
as she typed away on a computer keyboard, eyes fixed on the
monitor. We stood there, the child howling behind us, as the
woman said, "Yes, they've been moved upstairs." She hung up
and shifted one hand from her keyboard to tap a clipboard on
top of the desk without making eye contact. "Just sign in and
we'll call you back in a few minutes."

"We need to see—" Sarah began.

"Just sign in," the woman repeated in a louder voice, whapping the clipboard harder. I would have just done it at that point, but I wasn't Sarah.

"We're not patients," she said. "We're here to see Heather Lysenko."

The woman looked up then, clearly annoyed, but all she said was, "Spell the last name."

Sarah rattled it off and the woman typed it in, frowning at the screen and moving the mouse for a moment with beringed fingers, before jerking a thumb toward the doors. "She's still here. Through those doors and down on the left."

The child's howling seemed to intensify as we passed through the heavy doors, but when they closed behind us the noise faded, replaced by beeps of various machines and the rapid footsteps of doctors and nurses hustling past us on the shiny linoleum floors. I've never liked hospitals, with their strong disinfectant and rubbing-alcohol scents that can never fully cover the smell of blood and disease. I tried to avoid touching anything as we walked past empty or curtained beds. A nurse in a purple smock stopped us. "Who are you looking for?"

"Heather Lysenko?" Alison said, and the woman led us down the row to the one bed whose curtains were completely closed. She pulled it back just enough to poke her head around and said, "There are some people here for you, Mrs. Lysenko."

We heard Heather say, "Okay," in a low voice, and I felt a tug at my heartstrings. She sounded sad and exhausted. The nurse stepped aside to let us through, briskly pulling the curtain closed again around us. Heather lay on the bed wearing one of those horrible hospital gowns, tightly clutching the thin sheets and blanket covering her lower half. Her face relaxed when she saw us. "Thank God," she whispered. "I thought you were the police. They're the ones who brought me here."

"Sarah told us," I said. "We're so sorry about the, well, the baby." I felt awkward, and Alison and Sarah sounded equally awkward as they echoed me.

"She's gone," Heather said, tears filling her eyes. "I thought the bleeding would stop, but she's gone." A sob escaped and she pressed a shaking hand to her mouth, but the tears spilled over. I turned to Alison to whisper that this could wait, surely a day wouldn't matter, but Sarah spoke before I got the chance. "Viktor wasn't the father, right?"

Typical Sarah—abrasive and straight to the point. Heather looked as stunned as I felt. Through her tears she said, "What are you talking about?"

"He couldn't be because he had a vasectomy, didn't he?"

"Really?" I said as Alison said, "What?"

Heather's already pale skin blanched and she tried to hide her reaction, bringing her hands up to cover her impossibly beautiful face. Perhaps she thought we'd stop Sarah, but nobody did.

"So who's the father? Ray Fortini?" she said.

Heather's gasp was muffled, but we heard it. She tried to cover it with a cough, before saying, "Who?"

Sarah snorted. "Nice try, but it's too late to lie to us."

The sudden churn of a motor made three of us jump, but it was only Heather raising the bed. She repeatedly jabbed the button on the bed's remote control, struggling upright with it, swiping at her face.

"I don't know who you're talking about," she said.

"Cut the crap. We know he's your lover," Alison said. "What we don't know is when the two of you came up with the blackmail plan."

"What are you talking about?" Heather frowned and I was surprised as a look of confusion overtook that Little Miss Innocent expression she'd been giving us. She was a skilled liar, but I searched her face and the confusion seemed real.

"The decision to blackmail us—was it yours or his?" Alison said.

Heather just stared at her.

"Ray Fortini," Alison said. "He is your lover, isn't he?"

Now there was a flash of something else—anger? "That's none of your business."

"Oh, it's very much our business," Alison countered. "Especially since you've both been terrorizing us for the last eight weeks."

"Terrorizing you? What the hell are you talking about?" Heather grabbed a tissue from the box on the rolling stand next to her bed and blew her nose.

"*You* are the blackmailer, you and your asshole of a boyfriend," Sarah said.

"Don't bother denying it," Alison added. "We've been to his apartment, we know *everything*." She pulled out her iPhone and opened one of Ray's videos that she'd copied, wordlessly turning the screen to Heather.

Heather flushed, looking more embarrassed than I'd ever seen her, but she pushed the phone away, sounding defensive. "Fine, I've been having an affair with him, but that has nothing to do with the blackmail."

"We also found the photos on his computer," Alison said. "Stop lying."

"What are you talking about? What photos?"

"The photos of us that Ray Fortini took that night. They're gone now, by the way. I've seen to that."

Heather stared at her for a moment and then she shook her head. "That's crazy. There's no way that Ray is the one who took those photos. No way."

"I should have figured it out," Alison said. "It had to be someone who recognized us or knew that we were going to be there. Someone who could get our names and addresses. Our phone numbers. You must have been on the phone to him before we got to your house that night, right? You called him after you shot Viktor? What I want to know is when you thought up the whole plan."

"Jesus Christ, I didn't think any of it up!" Heather exclaimed. "I paid my five thousand dollars just like you did." She looked from one to another of us wildly, twitching like a nervous Thoroughbred. "You've got to believe me." She seemed sincere, but she'd lied so often and for so long that I couldn't tell. "Look," she said, leaning over the side of the bed and stretching to reach a plastic hospital bag stuffed with her belongings. She jerked it up onto her lap and rooted around in it. "I got the same texts you did." She found her phone and offered it to Alison, who wouldn't take it.

"That proves nothing," Sarah said. "Of course you'd make sure that he sent the same letter and texts to you, so we wouldn't suspect."

"No," Heather insisted, shaking her head. "I didn't do that, I swear." She looked from one to another of us and her face was stricken. "I don't believe it. He's the one who sent the letter? The photos? It can't be."

"Well, it is," I said. "It's him."

At that moment a nurse poked her head around the curtain. "Ladies, I'm going to have to ask you to step out for a minute so I can get her vitals." We moved out of her way, waiting on the other side of the curtain. An orderly came down the hall pushing a folded wheelchair and stopped by us.

"Knock, knock," he said before pulling back the curtain. "Ready for your ultrasound?" he said to Heather, in an obscenely cheery voice, as if he were talking about going to a spa. The nurse helped Heather out of bed and I felt another pang of sympathy as I watched her skinny, pale legs wobble as she stood up. They helped her into the chair while we stood around and the nurse placed Heather's bag of belongings in her lap.

"You ladies will have to go back to the waiting room," she said. "Your friend will be back soon."

"Can't we go with her?" Sarah said as the orderly lifted Heather's listless feet onto the metal footrests and released the brakes.

The nurse shook her head. "No, I'm sorry, you'll have to wait out there." She steered us away while the orderly popped a wheelie to turn back the way he'd come. Heather didn't look back or say good-bye.

The waiting room was blessedly quiet, the screaming child gone, and I wondered where, since we hadn't passed him or his mother in the ER. We plopped down in chairs in a corner and I considered asking for an ice pack for my throbbing ankle, but decided against it since that would involve talking to the grumpy Penguins fan at the front desk. "At least I don't have to lie about where we are," Alison said in a low voice, as she pulled out her phone to text her husband. I dug in my own purse for mine, wondering if Brian had tried to call, but there was only a message from the temp nanny asking when I'd be home. I texted her, explaining the situation, and then there was nothing to do but wait. I stared numbly at the TV where *Dateline* was playing, covering the case of a man who'd shot his wife so he could be with his lover. A little too close to home. I shifted in my seat, wishing they'd change the channel. Sarah was flipping rapidly through a cooking magazine, pausing on glossy photos of elaborate desserts. Alison was reading something on her phone. I started going through my email.

Ten minutes passed. Then twenty. And forty. "She's got to be done by now," Sarah said, tossing her fifth magazine aside. "Let's go back."

"That nurse said she'd come and get us."

"Look, I don't want to sit here all night." She got up without waiting for us and headed back toward the doors into the ER.

"We're just going to be told to wait again," Alison said, but she got up and followed after her and I did, too. As we passed through the doors, we saw Sarah in conversation with the nurse we'd spoken to before. Sarah looked agitated and I wondered if she was arguing with the woman.

"She's gone," Sarah said as we approached, sounding shocked.

"What? How?" For a horrified moment, I thought she meant that Heather had died.

The nurse patted my arm. "I'm sorry, but your friend checked herself out. We wanted to keep her overnight for observation, but she declined."

"She just left?" Alison said, looking around. "How did she get out of here without us seeing her?"

"She must have gone out another exit," the nurse said. "I guess she just wanted to be alone. I'm sorry." She gave us a sympathetic smile before continuing on her way.

We hustled out to the parking lot, looking for Heather as we walked toward Alison's car. "Where did she go?" I said. "You don't think the police came back and got her, do you?"

"No," Alison said. "But how did she leave? She doesn't have her car."

"Maybe she called Ray," Sarah suggested in a dark voice.

We thought about driving back to his apartment to look for her, but I was afraid to go there, not least because we still had his phone. With nowhere else to look, we decided to drive to Heather's.

It was almost ten by the time we turned in through the stone pillars and made the steep climb toward the dark house at the top. The headlights caught tiny buds forming on the forsythia bushes. I thought of that drive barely two months earlier when I'd raced up this hill in the night, unsure of what I'd find at the top, but knowing it would be bad.

We pulled into the circular driveway, the house still and silent. The light was on over the front door, but no one answered even as Sarah rang the bell again and again. Had Heather gone off with Fortini? Where the hell was she? We decided to wait, Alison moving the car to the side of the farthest bay in the garage, the darkest corner of the drive. It was freezing, gusts of frigid wind shaking the trees, but adrenaline fueled us and we waited next to the car. I kept obsessively checking my phone for the time. Three minutes passed. Five. The sweep of headlights climbing the hill startled us and it occurred to me that it might be Fortini. "What if it's him? We should get in the car," I said, reaching for the door handle.

"Just wait," Alison said, stopping me. We shrank back and watched as an unfamiliar sedan pulled up out front and Heather stepped out of the backseat.

"Thank you," she said to the driver, the slam of the car door echoing in the night.

We waited until the unseen driver had pulled away and Heather had her key in the lock before we stepped out of the shadows. "Was that an Uber driver or another lover of yours?"

Alison said, and Heather leapt, dropping her purse as she whipped around.

"What are you doing here?" she said in a nasty voice, but she looked pale and shaken. She'd changed out of the hospital gown, but in her haste she'd put her sweater on inside out and backward. I could see the seams running along her arms and the tag tickling her neck, but she didn't seem to notice. There was a large dark stain on her jeans and I realized it was blood and remembered how she'd met us outside wearing bloodstained clothes on that other, awful night.

Sarah snorted. "Where have you been? You left the hospital before we did."

Heather didn't respond, but the nervous look on her face answered for her. Alison said, "You went to see him, didn't you?"

Heather swayed on the steps, and despite everything that had happened, my sympathy kicked in and I ran to catch her before she fell. "You shouldn't have checked out of the hospital," I said. "Are you still bleeding?"

Alison supported her on the other side, as Sarah grabbed her purse and opened the door and we half-walked, half-carried Heather into the house. "She needs water," Alison said, and we took her into the kitchen and sat her down in a chair. I hurriedly filled a glass at the sink as Alison asked, "When was the last time you ate?"

"I don't know." Heather's voice was barely audible, and when I carried the water to her I saw that she'd dropped her head onto her arms. Sarah rummaged through the pantry and passed a box of crackers to Alison.

"Here, eat something," she said, breaking off a saltine and pressing it, none too gently, to Heather's lips. She tried to turn her head away, but Alison wouldn't let her, taking hold of Heather's neck and attempting to force the food into her mouth. They struggled for a moment, and then Heather gave up, accepting the single cracker, chewing and swallowing as if it were something twice as large that had stuck in her throat. She took the glass with shaking hands and gulped, water splashing down her chin and onto her inside-out sweater. When Alison offered a second cracker, she didn't protest, just put it in her mouth.

Sarah ate one, too, crunching loudly, and then she walked across to the wine fridge and I wasn't surprised when she pulled out a bottle. A dark red merlot that seemed too reminiscent of blood as she poured it into glasses for us. My stomach felt uneasy, but I sipped it anyway, tasting that strange mixture of earth and oak and fruit left long on the vine. For a moment it was like it had been before, all of us drinking together in this kitchen where we'd hung out so many times, although Heather didn't touch her glass. The illusion was shattered when Sarah set the bottle down hard on the island and said, "Did you get the money from Fortini? I want my money back."

"He wasn't there," Heather said in a low voice. "I couldn't find him."

"All your bruises were from him, right?" Alison said. "There's no point in lying anymore, Heather—we all know the truth. Just admit it—Viktor never abused you."

For a long moment Heather said nothing, but then something changed, and I felt queasy as I watched her wide-eyed expression morph into a look both hard and jaded. "There are different types of abuse," she said coldly. "Emotional and psychological, not just physical."

"You shot an innocent man," Sarah said. The stark truth of that was too much, and I bolted for the sink and retched, my stomach heaving and heaving as if I were expelling every terrible lie that I'd believed. I reached with a shaking hand for the faucet, cupping handfuls of water into my mouth and splashing it over my face.

"Innocent?" Heather spat the word, her voice rising, carrying over the running water. "Viktor wasn't innocent. Do you have any idea what it's like to live with someone like him—someone who makes you account for every nickel and dime? Someone who expects you to just be there all the time, to cook and clean and be a perfect, uncomplaining hausfrau for him to fuck the few times of year he feels like it? Nothing here was mine—his house, his son, his possessions, of which I was one. It was like being trapped in a golden prison."

"And you got us to help you break out," Alison said.

"Well, it was *your* idea." Heather gave a bitter laugh. "I didn't think this up on my own—it's all down to you and your assumptions. But of course *you* would make assumptions, wouldn't you?"

"Shut up," Alison said, her voice a warning.

Heather laughed again, a horrible sound. "What, you don't want them to know that poor little Alison sees abuse everywhere because her daddy killed her mommy?"

chapter forty-one

Julie and I looked from Heather to Alison. "Your father killed your mother?" I asked. Alison's face flushed and her gaze flitted to ours. She opened her mouth as if to refute this crazy statement, but nothing came out. Grabbing her wineglass instead, she took a long swallow. My mind reeled. It would explain a lot of things, like why Alison almost never talked about her parents or her childhood. I just thought she wasn't close with them, although I knew she was close with her brother. I remembered the topic coming up in conversations over the years, usually around the holidays, when we'd talk about what everyone was doing for Thanksgiving, for instance, but I never stopped to question the fact that she only mentioned her brother or Michael's family.

I felt a stab of guilt. She was my close friend and yet I'd never asked anything about her past, at least nothing beyond what she'd wanted to tell us. If it was true, if her father had killed her mother, then no wonder she didn't want to talk about it. Was her father still alive? Was he in prison? I suddenly recalled being at her house one afternoon and seeing an envelope poking out of a pile of mail tossed on her kitchen counter, a dark line of text stamped across the bottom proclaiming PENNSYLVANIA DEPART-MENT OF CORRECTIONS. And I'd said with a laugh, "What's this? Do you have a prison pen pal?"

"No, never," she'd said with a shudder, quickly scooping up the mail and sticking it in a drawer while asking what I'd like to drink. Out of sight and out of mind. And I'd let it go. I hadn't

asked any more questions because it was clear that she didn't
want to talk about it. Sometimes we're too polite.

A phone rang, a sharp trill breaking the tense silence. "Whose
phone is that?" I asked. The ringtone wasn't familiar, but we did
that thing you do automatically when you hear ringing, everybody pulling out their phones to check. Or at least three of us
did. Heather just sat frozen in her seat. Alison pulled out Ray
Fortini's phone, but it wasn't his either. The ringing continued. I
followed the sound to Heather's purse, which I'd dropped in the
kitchen doorway as we came inside. I pulled out her iPhone, but
I knew her ringtone and hers wasn't the one ringing. The sound
continued and I dug in her bag, pushing past a hairbrush and
makeup, breath mints and an unopened pack of cigarettes.

"You have a second phone?" I said, pulling out another iPhone
just as it stopped ringing. It looked virtually identical to the first
one. I dropped it next to hers on the kitchen table. The look on
Heather's face said it all. We knew who the caller had been.

"He gave it to me—I didn't want it," Heather said, pleading.
"Viktor was getting suspicious and then the police were snooping around—I couldn't talk to Ray on my phone."

"Do you still expect us to believe that you had nothing to do
with the blackmail?" Alison said.

"I didn't know about the blackmail, I didn't. Look, check it if
you don't believe me. There's nothing on it about the blackmail,
I swear!" She picked up the phone, but as she glanced at the
screen something seemed to occur to her, her face lightening as
she thrust the phone at Alison, just like she had at the hospital.
"He can't be the blackmailer—look, this proves it! Ray called me
from *his* phone. That's *his* number. So that phone you have can't
be his!"

And just like at the hospital, Alison made no move to take it.
"All that proves is that your lover also had a second phone."

Heather opened her mouth to argue with that, but I stopped
her before she could begin. "He had this phone," I said, picking
it off the island and waving it at her. "I stole this phone from him
at The Crooked Halo tonight."

Heather seemed to deflate at that, both her face and her arm falling, the phone dropping from her hand to clatter against the table.

Julie said, "So you've had this phone since before you killed your husband?"

"You don't understand."

"You're right—we don't," Alison said, "but we're starting to get the full picture. You called Ray Fortini the night you shot Viktor, right?"

Heather's perfect chin jutted out defensively. "What difference does that make?"

"That's how he knew where to find us," Alison said, looking at me and Julie. "She told him where we were going to leave Viktor's car."

"I didn't! I had nothing to do with it. Okay, I called him, but I was panicking. I didn't tell him anything except that I'd shot Viktor."

"Which he needed to know, right, because that was all a part of your plan."

"I've already told you—there was no plan." Heather stood up, clearly agitated.

It was Alison's turn to laugh. "You're not seriously going to try and tell us that you didn't plan to kill Viktor, are you?"

"I didn't. At least, not like that. I thought I could use the bruises to force his hand. Like, I'd tell his job that he was beating his wife unless he tore up the prenup. But that probably wouldn't have worked—he would have made it look like I was lying."

"You *were* lying," Alison said with another bitter laugh.

Heather looked sulky. "I didn't even think about killing him until you guys did. You're the ones who said I should defend myself, and Julie gave me the gun, and Sarah said I wouldn't be charged if it was self-defense."

"Yeah, well, maybe if you hadn't shot him in the back of the head, dummy," I said, tossing back the rest of my wine and heading to the island to refill my glass. Julie beat me to it, but instead of pouring another glass, she gave me a dirty look and deliberately stuffed the cork back in the bottle.

"Why *did* you do it like that?" Alison said to Heather. "Why that night? Why in his car?"

"Because he found out about the baby! He was going to leave me." Heather sank back down in the chair, looking exhausted.

"So it was true about the vasectomy?" Julie said.

Heather nodded. "He had one before Janice got sick. She couldn't risk having any more kids, she almost lost Daniel."

"And he didn't think about reversing it after you got married?"

She shook her head. "I didn't want kids. Or at least I didn't think I did."

"Vasectomies fail," I said. "Why not try to claim it was his child?"

"He's a doctor, dummy!" Heather snapped, glaring at me. "They have tests to prove those things. Besides, it didn't matter, somehow he found out about the affair and then he found my pregnancy vitamins, and the camera you guys gave me. He said he was going to divorce me. He was leaving me that night."

"It was his suitcase in the doorway," I said, putting it together. "Not yours."

"So you shot him," Alison said in a flat voice.

"What else was I supposed to do?" Heather cried. "Let him leave me with nothing? Leave us with nothing?" She cradled her stomach for a moment as if the baby were still there and then she remembered, her hand falling along with her face, and she started to weep.

No one moved to comfort her. I thought of all the times we'd done that. Opening our arms and our homes and our hearts for poor, fragile, abused Heather. I looked at her face contorted with tears and couldn't believe that I'd ever found her beautiful.

"You are a greedy, selfish bitch," I said, spitting each word at her, and she flinched as if they were blows.

And then the doorbell rang. That ridiculous, overproduced, twinkly peal echoing through the house.

chapter forty-two

ALISON

For a moment, nobody moved, and then Julie whispered, "What if it's the police?"

"We can say we came because of the miscarriage," I said. "We're just helping a friend."

"It's not the police, it's Ray." Heather was looking at one of her phones. "He sent a text."

"Don't answer," Julie said, clearly panicked.

"That's not going to work—he won't go away." Heather sounded resigned.

"Good, let's get our money back." Sarah started walking toward the front hall.

Julie grabbed her by the arm. "Are you crazy? He could hurt you!"

"We don't want to provoke him," I said. "The last thing we need *is* the police showing up."

"Just wait here," Heather said. "I'll try to get rid of him."

We held very still, listening to Heather open the front door. We heard her say that she was tired and she'd get in touch tomorrow, and then a male voice, demanding to know "where the hell" she'd been.

More muffled conversation, and then Heather's voice rose and she cried, "You can't just barge in here!"

"Quick, we've got to hide," Julie hissed, and we grabbed our things and ducked in the laundry room, leaving the door ajar, just before Ray Fortini stepped into the kitchen with Heather at his heels.

"What the fuck are you acting so nervous about?" he demanded, looking around. "You two-timing me? Got someone hiding in here?"

"Of course not."

"Yeah? Then what are all these from?" He flicked a finger against one of our wineglasses.

"My friends were over earlier," she said, hurriedly grabbing the glasses and taking them to the sink. "Do you want something to drink?"

"Sure, I'll have some of your chichi wine," he said, tilting the bottle back to read the label. "What is this? Like, a fifty-dollar bottle?"

"I don't know," she said, over the sound of glasses clattering in the sink. "Viktor bought the wine."

"What the fuck?" he exclaimed, and for a moment I thought he was angry that she'd mentioned her husband, but as I edged my face closer to the door I spotted, too late, what we'd left behind on the island.

"Where did you get that phone?" Ray demanded.

"Where do you think I got it?"

Silence for a long moment. I pressed my face even closer to the door, trying to see if Heather was secretly communicating with Fortini, but they were just standing there, staring at each other.

"So it's true," Heather said, when it became clear that Fortini wouldn't answer. "I can't believe you've been blackmailing me. How could you?"

"That's my insurance," he said. "You think you're going to leave me? I told you—it's over when I say it's over."

"I don't understand—how did you know where to find us that night? I didn't tell you what we were going to do with Viktor's body. I didn't *know* what I was going to do when I called you."

"I tracked you. I've been tracking you for months on that phone I gave you and on the one your dead husband gave you, too." He laughed.

"You are such a *loser*," Heather spat. "I don't know what I ever saw in you."

He just laughed again. "What you saw in me? What did I see in you? Just look at you—you're a mess! You don't even have your sweater on right. Is that 'cause you were out fucking someone else tonight?" He sniffed the air. "Is it a doctor? I can smell him on you."

"You can keep my money, but you've got to give theirs back," Heather said, her voice trembling as she started speaking, but steadying as she went on.

He kept laughing, too brazen and too stupid to take her seriously. "I'm not giving back anything."

"You have to—they know all about us, about you. They'll go to the police."

"They're not going to talk to anybody," he said with a laugh. "I've got copies of the photos and I'll show them to the cops."

I watched through the crack in the door as Heather shook her head. "No you won't," she said, and gave him a tight little smile. "They've been erased. All your files have been erased."

Fortini's easy grin vanished. He struggled to speak, looking and sounding like someone who'd been hit across the head by a two-by-four. "What the hell does that mean? Did you fuck with my computer?" He moved toward her and Heather backed away, around the island.

He followed, grabbing her by the arms and pushing her up against the counter. "Answer me, bitch!" He slapped her hard across the face.

The smack was loud, echoing off all the marble and glass. I slammed open the door, reacting on impulse, forgetting my fear, forgetting what Heather had done, forgetting everything except the child I'd been, hiding in that closet as my father had grabbed my mother just like that, had her hit her just like that.

"She didn't touch your computer, you asshole. I did."

He whipped around, still holding Heather pressed up against the counter, that same stupid stunned look crossing his face. "Where the fuck did you come from?" And then his eyebrows rose as I heard Julie and Sarah step into the room behind me. He looked from us to Heather. "You let them into my apartment? You stupid bitch!" He slapped her again, a casual backhand that knocked her sideways.

It was just like my father had lashed out years ago, that same animalistic anger, fueled in his case by alcohol and the sense that the world owed him. I didn't know the demons driving Ray, but Heather cowered from him just like my mother had done, trying to shield herself, helpless in the face of that rage.

"Let go of her!" I screamed, my own rage, the rage of the scared child I'd been finally bursting free. I grabbed the wine bottle from the island and this time there was no hesitation as I swung.

Fortini moved and the blow only clipped him, but it was enough for him to drop Heather and clutch his head, yowling in pain. He stumbled back, scrambling to get away from us, trapping himself in a corner of the countertops.

"Get away from me, you crazy bitch," he said as I advanced on him with the bottle raised for a second blow.

"You're going to give us our money," I said. "Pass me your wallet and your bank card."

"I'm not giving you anything." He tried to laugh, but he looked nervous.

"You'll give it to me or I'll tell the police you shot Viktor Lysenko."

He snorted at that. "You think they'd believe that I shot him? She's the one who stood to gain from killing him."

"You have no proof that you didn't," I said. "We'd tell them that you were the one. You did it."

"They're not going to believe that, because it's a crock of shit. She killed him because he found out about the affair. Cut and dried. Your average domestic homicide. They'll know the truth because I'll tell them the real story. I'll tell them how I told Viktor."

Heather cried out, and I saw that she'd gone pale.

"Told him what?"

"I told him his wife was cheating on him, that's what." He

laughed. "She wasn't ever going to leave him so I helped speed up the process."

There was a strange sound, a snick as Heather pulled a knife from the block on the counter, and before we could stop her she ran toward Ray with the blade raised.

"You bastard! You killed my baby, you asshole!"

He stopped her, grabbing her wrist and trying to turn it, and Julie was screaming, a tinny, high-pitched hysterical sound, and I tried to stop them, pulling Heather back, but she was immovable. Then, all at once, she gave a strange "Oh!" and her weight fell against me and I stumbled back with her in my arms. And that's when I saw that the knife was stuck in her chest, and blood was pouring from it, a stream of crimson across the blush pink sweater.

"Call 911!" I cried, folding onto the kitchen floor still cradling Heather. Sarah hurried to phone the police as Julie grabbed dish towels and we pressed them against Heather's chest, trying to stop the bleeding that was now a bright red river gushing from the wound.

"No," Ray Fortini moaned. "No, Heather, no, baby, no." He pushed past Sarah, who tried to block him, dropping to his knees by Heather and trying to take her from me.

"Get away from her!" Julie screamed, hysterically shoving and kicking him. "Don't you touch her! Don't you touch her again!"

He backed away, hands raised, trying to block her onslaught.

None of us heard him leave. All I know is that he was gone before the ambulance came screaming up the hill, before the paramedics raced into the kitchen, equipment clanking and radios squawking, before they transferred Heather from my arms onto the stretcher, careful not to dislodge the knife. But it was too late. I think we all knew that, watching her face turn gray as each dish towel we pressed against her soaked through with blood. It traveled down her body, mingling with the baby's blood that stained her jeans. Heather was gripping my hand and staring, unseeing, up at us when the paramedics reached her side.

chapter forty-three

F unerals for murder victims are distinguished from other services by the curiosity seekers. Those who come even though
they have no real relationship with the victim, but have been
fooled by the publicity surrounding the death into thinking that
they had a personal connection.

We watched them, these sobbing and wild-eyed men and
women, and endured the long service in stiff pews, part of the
much smaller crowd of the truly bereaved. We were very aware,
in the way the others weren't, of two guests who didn't pass by
Heather's casket, the men standing at the back of the chapel in
forgettable suits, watching us with gimlet eyes.

They waited until we rose, stiff-legged, and followed after the
coffin, which rose and fell on the shoulders of the pallbearers like
a small ship at sea. They waited until we'd stepped into the cold
chill of that winter morning, all of us blinking in the hard light,
wind whipping the corners of our coats as we grabbed the hands
of our children. They waited until we'd loaded into our cars
behind the hearse, queuing up to follow Heather's body to its final resting place, high on a hill on the outskirts of town. And
then they got into their nondescript sedan and joined our procession slowly wending its way through slush-covered streets
toward the gravesite.

The estate paid for Heather's funeral and she was buried next
to Viktor, which surprised me given her mother-in-law's hostility. Julie assumed it had been done for the sake of appearances,

but Sarah had a different theory. "Every time Anna looks at her son's grave she has the satisfaction of knowing that his wife didn't outlive him, at least not by much."

Perhaps that's too harsh—it might have been a simple act of charity given that Heather's parents probably couldn't afford a funeral for their daughter. They were there, at the front of the church, looking both devastated and confused, and just as out of place in Sewickley as they'd ever been. I remember seeing Heather's mother reaching for her grandson's hand, but he wouldn't take it and took Anna's instead. She didn't even pretend to mourn, but that was no surprise and who could blame her. I saw her smile as she walked away from Heather's grave, firmly holding on to Daniel. She no longer had her beloved Vitya, but she got all of his money and her grandson.

We worried about Daniel, of course. Heather had been the only mother he'd ever known, but our attempts to arrange playdates were rebuffed by Anna, and I have no doubt that she's doing her best to rewrite history as if Daniel were actually her son.

Sarah was the one who gave the cops a description of Ray Fortini and his motorcycle. I don't remember that, but she told me later. We were asked to explain the scene to the police many times; it all blurs together.

Later that long night, we heard that Ray Fortini died. He raced away from the house on his Harley, trying to run from the murder or his guilt, going well beyond the speed limit, making it all the way to Route 65 before he heard the first siren pursuing him. It was the sort of death he might have appreciated, high-intensity and cinematic, crashing through a guardrail and plunging thirty feet into the river. A swift end to a short life, but people like that seem destined to die young.

I remember Detectives Tedesco and Kasper arriving in Heather's kitchen, their narrow-eyed appraisal of the three of us standing there, bloodstained and shaken, but it wasn't our first murder scene. We'd had time, before the paramedics arrived, to figure out what we were going to say and what we weren't.

"Keep it short and simple," I'd said as Julie and I kept pressing dish towels to Heather's chest even though by that point we both knew it was futile. "We tell them we didn't know about Ray Fortini before tonight. We came here to comfort Heather because of the miscarriage and he showed up."

I remember Julie weeping, leaving traces of Heather's blood on her face every time she swiped at her eyes. Sarah stuffed the phone she'd stolen from Ray—the one he'd used to blackmail us—into her purse to be disposed of later, before clearing all of the texting related to the blackmail off Heather's phones.

"What do we do with her second phone?" Sarah picked it off the table.

"Put it back in the hospital bag for the police to find," I said. "It shows her relationship with Fortini."

The story we told was mostly the truth. We hadn't known about Ray Fortini, she'd kept him a secret from us. He stabbed her in a fight because she was trying to leave him. We had Heather's second phone as proof of their affair, which provided a motive for Viktor's murder.

It was a neat and tidy explanation, although I'm certain that Tedesco and Kasper knew there was more to the story. Lying by omission—isn't that what they call it? I'm sure they would love to have charged us with that at least, but ultimately there was no concrete evidence to support any charge at all.

In the end, we were just the friends, bystanders to what had happened to Viktor and Heather. As I said to Detective Tedesco that night, "You never really know what happens in someone else's marriage."

As for our own marriages, our husbands asked a lot of questions, too, but were more easily satisfied than the police by the explanation we offered. I remember the warmth of Michael's arms as he pulled me to him that night despite the blood coating my clothing. "It'll be okay," he murmured, but I felt his fear in how tight he held me. It was only when he brushed a gentle hand against my face that I realized I was crying.

Apparently Brian and Eric reacted this way, too, each of our husbands, like the best of spouses, moving quickly from questions to providing comfort and support. And don't we all want to believe that everything is going to be okay?

Almost four years have passed since I first noticed that bruise on Heather's wrist, and everything that happened after has started to fade a bit in my memory, the events less sharp, their exact sequence less clear. My family moved five months after her funeral, the job transfer for Michael back to Philadelphia that I'd once dreaded. He waited to tell me, afraid of my reaction, only to be surprised when I didn't protest leaving Sewickley.

The children are settled in a new school with new friends and we've lived in this new house long enough that I've stopped opening the wrong drawer in the kitchen or hesitating before making the turn onto our street. It's been long enough that Lucy and Matthew don't talk as often about their old neighborhood or their Pittsburgh friends. They're so young that it's something they'll barely remember; that past won't haunt them the way it does me.

I miss Sewickley's charm and walkability, Pittsburgh's rolling hills and its rivers and bridges. Most of all, I miss my closest friends and the bond we once shared, which I know we'll never have again. For the first few months after the move, I kept in touch with Julie and Sarah, but then it stretched out longer and longer, and the other day I realized that it had been over six months since I'd spoken to either of them. It's been said that a shared trauma can bring people together, but just as often it pulls them apart.

Sarah did end up joining AA, and soon after that she went back to practicing law full-time. She and her husband are selling their house in Sewickley and moving back to the city. Perhaps they already have. Ostensibly, it's to be closer to her law practice, but I wonder if she needed to get away as much as I did. Apparently she spends all her free time doing pro bono work, so much so that the *Tribune-Review* wrote a nice article about her, highlighting her "selfless fight for the rights of the underprivileged and underrepresented." I think I know what fuels this obsession with justice.

Julie is still selling houses. There was a slight dip in her home sales after the murder, but she rebounded from that and has gone on to enjoy an even greater level of success than before, a fact that she apparently credits to a religious experience in some way connected to Heather's death. She told me about it once, how she'd been afraid that Ray would turn the knife on her after Heather and how she'd held on to her belief that this wasn't the plan. It's an interesting spin on that story, I told her, unable to keep the bitterness out of my voice, but I don't know why I was surprised. Wasn't she always afraid to look at the dark side of anything? Maybe she holds on to her beliefs because she thinks they will save her. And perhaps they will. All I can say is that I don't share that certainty.

Here is what I know: We helped to kill a man. We might not have pulled the trigger, but we set the events in motion and placed the weapon in Heather's hand. Will we be judged for what we did and didn't do? Certainly I have judged myself for it. Sometimes I still have nightmares about it, seeing his body slumped over the passenger seat or lying in his casket. Once I had a dream in which I was back in Braddock, wandering through the house where I'd lived as a child, the same thin walls and hollow doors, but it was Viktor bleeding on that old linoleum floor, and as I ran to help him I caught my reflection in a window, but the face staring back at me was my father's.

The letters still make their way to my mailbox, my father's handwriting shakier now and his observations less acute. "I saw a movie last week that reminded me of you," he wrote a month ago. "There were two little kids in it and I thought of you and Sean. Do you remember running through that sprinkler I set up for you?"

He isn't the monster I remember. There are no monsters, just deeply flawed people, all of us given that power to choose, some of us making choices so damaging that they ruin the lives of those we claim to love.

I believed once in those clear lines, the good and the evil, the perpetrator and the victim, and now I see that all of us end up playing both roles at some point in our lives. We hurt those that we love, we make choices that we can't undo, we throw ourselves headlong into battles in the name of rescuing people who never asked to be saved. Not everyone is as guilty as my father, or Heather, or Ray. But none of us are wholly innocent. We are all the damned and we are all the saved.

Could we have saved Heather? In my grief over her death, I've asked myself this question many times. If she'd only left Viktor instead of having an affair. If she hadn't been attracted to such a damaged man or put so much value on money. If we'd only realized how lonely she was and taken her away from that stone house on the hill, just as we'd thought of doing so many times. But you can't save those who don't want to be saved.

This was true of my mother, and for all those caught like her, who keep going back for the embrace that is a stranglehold, like the fragile and frantic moths that find their way to my back porch on summer evenings, doomed to turn their bodies again and again toward the light that will destroy them.

I walk my kids to the bus stop in our new neighborhood, bringing something to read just like I used to all those years ago when Lucy started preschool. This morning, after the bus pulled away, another mother called after me as I started for home. "We were thinking of going for coffee," she said with a lovely smile. "Why don't you join us?"

I hesitated, memories of those mornings at the coffee shop in Sewickley filling me with a longing so great that tears sprang to my eyes. But I could feel the weight of the latest letter in my pocket, and the email Sean sent was fresh in my mind. He's offered to meet me at the prison hospital, but when it's time, I'll walk into that room alone to face my father.

"I can't today." I smiled at the welcoming faces of the woman and her friend. "Maybe another time," I said, and kept walking.

Acknowledgments

A special thank-you to the Village of Sewickley and its many charming businesses, especially the Crazy Mocha Coffee Company and the Penguin Bookshop. And thank you to my dear friends Heather Terrell, Mark Garvey, and Kathryn Jackson, residents who've shared their love and knowledge of Sewickley with me.

Local readers will notice that I've created names and places that don't exist in the region, and amalgams of places that do, including Sewickley Elementary School, which is a composite of the two public elementary schools in the area. I hope readers will still recognize the Village, the Heights, and the 'Burgh in these pages.

To try to convey the complexity of abusive relationships, I relied on many sources, including the National Domestic Violence Hotline (thehotline.org) and the U.S. Department of Health and Human Services' Office on Women's Health (womenshealth.gov), which offer excellent resources for identifying and ending the cycle of abuse.

Many thanks to my lovely and talented agent, Rachel Ekstrom, and all the wonderful people at the Irene Goodman Literary Agency. And thank you to my two great editors, Melanie Fried and Holly Ingraham, and to the fantastic team at St. Martin's Press; I'm honored to be one of your authors.

This is a story about female friendship, and I'm privileged to be friends with many incredible women. Thank you to all of my many writing pals, including Meredith Mileti, Lila Shaara, Nancy Martin, Nicole Peeler, Kathryn Miller Haines, Heather Terrell, Kathleen George, Annette Dashofy, Gwyn Cready, Meryl Neiman, and Shelly Culbertson.

And thank you to my walking and book club pals, including Lisa Lundy, Mary Lou Linton-Morningstar, Sharon Wolpert, Marilyn Fitzgerald, Becky Mator, Ann Paulini, Eun-Joung Lee, Shabnam Mirchandani, and Susan Moore.

A special thank-you to Donna Wallace and Lisa Bartunek for being early readers and champions of this book.

And finally, heartfelt thanks to my lovely and talented daughter, Maggie, for being such a great sounding board and editor for this book. Thank you also and always to my two Joes, for your amazing love and support. I'm so lucky to have you all.